NOTHING PROVED

JANET WERTMAN

First printing 2025 in the United States of America; Palm Desert, California

ISBN 978-1-7354911-6-5 (Kindle edition)
ISBN 978-1-7354911-7-2 (EPUB edition)
ISBN 978-1-7354911-8-9 (Paperback edition)
ISBN 978-1-7354911-9-6 (Hardcover edition)

Library of Congress Control Number: 2025900210

Cover design by James T. Egan of Bookfly Design
Formatting by Sweet 'N Spicy Designs

CONTENTS

PART ONE: SWEET SISTER TEMPERANCE

PART TWO: MUCH SUSPECTED

PART THREE: THE LORD'S DOING

PROLOGUE

December 2, 1544

*E*leven-year-old Elizabeth Tudor twirled her quill to mark the final period of the assignment John Cheke had given them, translating a Pythagorean teaching. Of course Cheke chose a Greek text: he was the foremost Greek scholar in England. This was why Henry VIII had appointed him chief tutor to Elizabeth's seven-year-old half-brother, Edward – nothing less would do for the heir to the English throne.

Elizabeth looked past the other students lucky enough to share the young Prince's lessons, the sons and daughters of courtiers lofty or favored enough to have their children with them at court. She was happy to be back here after her yearlong exile, and she silently thanked her latest stepmother, Queen Katherine Parr, for persuading the King to forgive.

The south-facing windows drew Elizabeth's gaze to the sun bouncing off the red bricks of Hampton Court Palace, Henry's favorite of his many royal residences – and therefore a frequent base for the Court. The sight lent warmth to the royal classroom and a glow that felt almost like love. Elizabeth cherished that feeling as much as the rosy radiance it brought to her cheeks. Of course, her governess would tell her to hide such vanity.

Tearing herself from guilt, Elizabeth exchanged quill for needle, keen to finish the elaborately embroidered cover for her translation of Marguerite de Navarre's *Mirror of the Sinful Soul*. Gold and silver braid joined the initials *K* and *P* in the center, surrounded by heartsease in purple, green, and yellow silk. It would not be the most valuable present Katherine Parr would receive for the New Year, but it would be the most personal.

Robert Dudley laid down his own quill with a lazy smile. "I am done as well," he said.

Robert – Robin to his friends – was a year older than Elizabeth, a fourth son constantly testing his limits and often in trouble, though his good nature and glib tongue kept the worst consequences away. Robin was one of three similarly aged Dudleys crowding the classroom, the other two being Ambrose and Mimi. All had athletic temperaments like Elizabeth's own, all shared the shame of treason in their blood. That gave them a secret bond.

"Stop lying. There is no way you have finished," William Cecil said, looking up from his own paper. At twenty-four, he was in service to the Earl of Hertford but sometimes visited the royal classroom to lend assistance to his former brother-in-law. An intellectual not an athlete, Cecil loved the lessons. Too, he deserved some help counteracting the lingering grief over his dead wife, a grief that had turned him serious much earlier than most men.

Robin's eyes flashed but he quickly donned a smile and laughed politely. "I did not say I was finished. I said I was done."

Cecil pointed a bony finger at Robin's paper. "Get back to it."

"Why should the lady Elizabeth be the only one to relax?"

She bristled. "How can you accuse me so? My fingers are not idle." Elizabeth's fingers were rarely idle: she felt uncomfortable when she was not accomplishing something, as if people would find her irresponsible – or worse.

Robin turned to his sister, laughing. "Mimi, help me here. You always say needlework is relaxing."

Mimi shifted in her chair, unwilling to cross either of them. "It can be."

Robin whirled to Elizabeth, his black curls bouncing. "Do you enjoy it?"

She grinned. "Ecclesiastes tells us to find satisfaction in our toil."

He grinned back. "Once again, you awe me with your piety." He turned to Cecil. "And as I learned from my translation, our capacity for awe is our defining strength, 'the engine of creativity, discovery, purpose, and health.' Virtue comes from putting teachings into practice, so—"

Interrupting his justification, Robin leaped to his feet and faced the door. "Oh, hey, Ned," he called as sixteen-year-old Edward Seymour passed by their classroom. Ned, too, had outgrown the group lessons; he, too, was in Hertford's service. But because Hertford was his father, Ned felt free to belittle lesser mortals, a category in which Elizabeth featured far too prominently.

Elizabeth worked to arrest the curl that threatened her lip: Hertford was brother to Jane Seymour, the woman who had supplanted Elizabeth's mother in Henry VIII's affections. Jane was long dead but the Seymour influence persisted: she had given Henry the son that Anne Boleyn had not.

Ned loped in but froze at Cheke's scowl. "I apologize for intruding – it seemed lessons were over."

"They are not. I merely allowed an exchange to go on long enough for Robert Dudley to forget himself."

Robin's face filled with the contrition that always worked well for him. "I also apologize. But they said the King would soon assign the rule of Boulogne, and I thought Ned might have news."

"Oh, please allow this," Edward called out, reaching a hand towards the teacher. "We have been eager to hear. We have worked well and patiently until now, and we will resume our work right afterwards."

Cheke harrumphed. "Your argument was well constructed and persuasive. It deserves reward more than Robert's actions deserve punishment." The students chuckled with relief at the scolding averted. Many things were excused when the heir to the throne intervened. "And, therefore," Cheke continued, "I agree that Ned may share his news."

Ned furrowed his brow. "I must beg your further indulgence. I do not yet have news. I have merely been pacing the halls to make sure I catch my father the second he leaves the King's apartments."

Cheke's eyes narrowed. "Why such eagerness?" He looked around the room. "Why are all of you so eager? There is something more here than just the future of Boulogne."

"If my father is sent to govern," Ned replied, "I hope to go with him." He puffed out his chest. "It is the logical next step now that I have proven myself in battle."

Ned had been part of the "Rough Wooing," a series of devastating military attacks to force the Scots to marry their infant queen to Edward and so unite the island, though Elizabeth doubted that Hertford had let Ned see danger.

"I wish I could prove myself," Edward said. "I am not allowed any job of importance."

"Your most important job is here, Cousin," Ned said, as if a seven-year-old's desire for dominance was reasonable. "Preparing for your future."

"Kings must know the art of war," Edward said, his nose in the air.

"We would miss you terribly," said little Jane Grey. Another cousin, this one the same age as Edward. Some whispered Edward adored her, hoped to marry her instead of the Scottish queen. Of course, gossip was often wrong, but it made sense that the two priggish souls would get along.

"We must all make sacrifices to pursue our highest calling," Ned said, more pompous than ever in his flattery of the young Prince.

Yes, Edward would be King one day. Because Elizabeth had been a girl.

Unable to hold back, she finally allowed herself to comment. "Our highest calling is reason, not destruction."

"We need both, as the Ancients' examples continue to shout," Cheke said. "Life requires balance."

"And there are many reasons to justify war in this case," Cecil said. "More than for peace."

Even Cecil was against Elizabeth on this point. Logical, reasonable Cecil with his endless weighing of pros and cons. She bowed her head, chastened.

"You decry the cost, we crave the reward," Robin added, his face earnest. "For men, war is a path to greatness, the ultimate proving ground. We claim bravery and power on the tiltyard, in all our competitions. But we all hope to live up to the test of the field."

"Put that way, it sounds noble," she said. "But it still seems a waste."

"We could have avoided the war if the Scots had just sent us the girl," Ned said.

"Is that all it takes?" Elizabeth asked, biting back a more caustic assessment of the incongruity of pursuing marriage through aggression.

"Women cement alliances. It is why you were restored to the succession, though it did us little good. Even a claim was not enough for Charles V to choose you over Maria of Portugal for his son."

Elizabeth kept her face a careful blank. Most people pretended to forget her illegitimacy, but the Seymours took every opportunity to remind her.

"Philip is seventeen, as is Maria, so they could marry immediately," Ambrose said. "It would have been folly to wait the three years for Elizabeth to turn fourteen."

"Also," said Robin, another defender, "I cannot imagine Spain interested in anyone but Mary." Elizabeth and Edward's older half-sister, whose mother had been a Spanish princess, would have indeed been much more acceptable to Spain than the daughter of the woman who had exposed Catherine of Aragon's marriage for the fraud it was.

"How?" Ned asked. "She is twenty-eight, far too old for Philip of Spain. And once betrothed to Charles himself. Imagine Philip's reaction at finding himself tied to such a one."

Elizabeth raised her chin higher, imagining her own reaction to a stranger. There were too many men who inspired her with revulsion – what if her intended repelled her? Her father had put aside his fourth wife, Anne of Cleves, rather than bed her. Elizabeth would not have such a choice.

"I do not want to marry," Elizabeth said. Her mind's eye conjured her childhood friend Liza Fitzgerald, the morning after she wedded a man almost thirty years her senior, whimpering about the smell of decay that assaulted her even more piercingly than his manhood. By the afternoon the sixteen-year-old bride had a resigned smile plastered on her face, but Elizabeth could tell how hard Liza was working to maintain that equanimity.

Elizabeth's breath caught as her memory dissolved Liza's face, reforming it into that of another teenaged woman married to a much older man: Henry's fifth wife, Catherine Howard, the most graceful woman Elizabeth had ever met. The Howard cousin, whose affection had led Henry to smile again at Anne Boleyn's daughter, if for too short a time.

"I do not want to marry," Elizabeth repeated, then froze as

she saw her father's sixth and – please, God, last! – wife in the doorway, shock on her face.

"What is this I hear?" Katherine Parr asked. Without waiting for an answer, she entered the room followed by her ladies, Liza among them.

Elizabeth felt heat flood her face, mortified at offending the stepmother she adored, another woman forced to wed a man who surely must disgust her.

"She does not want to marry," Ned said.

Katherine drew back, more sympathetic than bothered. "Why ever not?"

Robin put a protective hand on Elizabeth's shoulder. "She has always said she would never marry." Elizabeth had first confessed to Robin this longstanding resolve three days after Catherine Howard's arrest for adultery. The young Queen had escaped confinement in an attempt to reach her husband and beg for her life. Elizabeth could still hear Catherine's piteous screams as the guards dragged her back to her rooms.

"It is not as bad as you think," Liza said, in her gentle Irish brogue.

That only worsened things. As dejected as Liza had been that first morning after her wedding, at least her husband was Master of the Horse, a post only granted to athletic men – making the age difference less gruesome than most.

"Womanhood will change your mind," Katherine said.

Katherine was as close to a mother as Elizabeth had known. And just like a mother, she was sometimes forced to offer advice that rang hollow. "I cannot imagine that," Elizabeth said.

"Unfortunately, you will have to," Katherine said. "You are the King's daughter and your duty requires it."

Elizabeth bit her lip, half expecting Ned to make a snide comment. There had been a time when people claimed she had been sired by one of her mother's alleged lovers, usually Mark Smeaton. But while Elizabeth had inherited Anne Boleyn's oval face and natural grace, everything else came from the Tudor side: Elizabeth had her grandmother's thin lips and slightly hooked nose, her father's red hair and pale skin, his athletic build and genial nature, even his wit and gestures. The uncanny resemblance had led Henry to restore her to the succession so that she might be useful to him; though it had not helped him to love her: he had left her illegitimate, one of those souls that Deuteronomy declared unfit for the congregation of the Lord.

Still, Katherine was right that Elizabeth had no choice in the matter. And maybe Katherine was also right that a heart could change. If that was true, maybe marriage would also finally remove the stain from Elizabeth's name, give her a real place in the world. She wanted that more than anything, a world where she might be admired for her accomplishments, not disdained for her very existence. But that would be a long road to trod.

"I will, of course, obey," Elizabeth said. Under her breath, she added, "Though I fear it will kill me."

Robin leaned his head close. "*Superabo*," he whispered. "Just keep repeating that to yourself until you believe. I swear it works."

I will survive.

PART ONE: SWEET SISTER TEMPERANCE

CHAPTER 1

June 9, 1548

arved wooden panels lined the Queen's Chamber at Chelsea Place. Henry VIII had not bequeathed the manor to Elizabeth, even though it had been her domain for years; instead, the late King had willed it to his final wife, to make it easy for Katherine Parr to preside over his young son's court. Of course, Henry had not expected his widow to elope with the boy's uncle Thomas Seymour and create a whole new life for herself there.

The paneling that had always felt protective to Elizabeth now felt hard, and her cheeks burned in her drawn face. She did not trust herself to speak. To avoid even meeting her stepmother's eyes, the fourteen-year-old examined her long, thin fingers clasped in her lap.

Across from her, Katherine leaned forward. "My dear daughter, you are far too vulnerable to this kind of scandal." Her voice was soft but steely. "People already see lightness in your blood."

Black ice suffused through Elizabeth at the injustice of life. Her mother, Anne Boleyn, had been convicted of adultery with five men, one of them her own brother, the false charges instituted to untangle the King from a marriage he had come to regret. No one could defend Anne during Henry's lifetime, and no one could defend her now that the throne was occupied by the son of the woman who had supplanted her. But at least they could keep their insults to themselves.

"You must always show yourself as a king's daughter," Katherine continued.

Elizabeth's throat tightened until she could barely breathe. All her life, her claim to that rank had come with a modifier. "A king's illegitimate daughter," she muttered.

Katherine leaned further forward. "Illegitimate or not, your father and Parliament restored you to the succession. And while your claim will recede with every child born to your brother, you will always be among the highest ladies in the land."

Elizabeth pressed her lips together.

Katherine sighed and leaned back in her chair. "The Lord has a purpose for everyone. You are now a king's sister, not just a king's daughter. That is an even greater responsibility. You have a chance to make a good marriage, live a good life. But you will forfeit that with bad behavior."

Elizabeth stared at the ground, unable to respond.

Katherine pushed herself to standing. With one hand cradling her pregnant belly, she lumbered to the window and looked out upon the fields shrouded by grey raindrops. "You know, the harm also goes the other way," she said, before turning back to Elizabeth. "Your actions resurrect the charges brought against your poor mother."

Elizabeth's head jerked up in horror over this new consequence. As she had feared, Katherine's eyes held as many conflicting emotions as her voice: anger, love, hurt, compassion. But maybe contempt.

Resentment and fear forced Elizabeth's gaze down. "I did nothing wrong."

But Katherine's husband had. For the last few months, Thomas Seymour had come regularly into Elizabeth's bedchamber in the mornings. Early on, she was still abed, in only her linen nightshift, and he had opened the curtains as if to come after her. Sometimes he actually had, tickling her mercilessly until screams pierced her squirming giggles. Locking the door hadn't helped: the man had keys to every room in the house. Her governess had complained, but Katherine had defended him, even joined him several times. Elizabeth could only take to rising earlier and earlier to limit him to leering at her and giving her a familiar strike on the back or buttocks.

"Your behavior was incautious."

My behavior? What about that time in the garden? Elizabeth wanted to shriek. *When you chased me and held my arms while your husband slashed my gown and exposed my legs?* Instead, she clenched her teeth and only said, "Nothing happened."

Katherine sighed. "I know." She turned to Elizabeth and sighed again. "But now I see how something could."

Katherine's hurt pierced Elizabeth's heart, and shame filled the wound. Katherine had caught them, walked into a room where Thomas Seymour was on his knees kissing Elizabeth's hands. Elizabeth would have stopped him before he went much further, but her inner resolve was invisible. Her shining eyes were not.

"I would not have let it," Elizabeth said, her voice breaking. She did not know how to explain that the ardor had been too potent a retort to the voice in her head that constantly reminded her how little she mattered. Especially in a world dominated by Edward Seymour, who had risen from Earl of Hertford to Duke of Somerset and now commanded all as Lord Protector for the underaged King.

Katherine sighed again and walked to her desk. A small volume lay at its center, a gift of love that had returned to Elizabeth true gratitude from Katherine and grudging admiration from

Henry. Its title was painfully prescient: *The Mirror of the Sinful Soul*. Katherine caressed its ornately embroidered cover before whirling around to Elizabeth. "Your good name hangs by a cobweb. You must leave here."

Panic gripped Elizabeth. "Where will I go? That will spread scandal faster than anything." She flushed as her brain flooded with the full extent of her shame.

"Anthony Denny has agreed to bring you to live with his wife at Cheshunt while you meditate on the life ahead of you. You shall leave within the next few days, before my husband returns from court."

The worst of the terror loosened its hold: Sir Anthony's wife Joan was niece to Elizabeth's governess, Kat Ashley. The Dennys would provide discretion, as well as comfort and safety, after this dark episode. And Elizabeth would be spared a further meeting with Thomas Seymour.

Katherine reached out and touched Elizabeth's arm. "I will speak of this with no one. Ever."

Her beloved stepmother might not despise her. There was hope for reconciliation. Closing her eyes to better inhale the comfort, Elizabeth placed her hand over Katherine's.

"And I will warn you if I hear any evilness spoken of you," Katherine said.

Comfort was joined by gratitude that this episode would be kept buried. Her father's death had awakened people's sympathy for her. Now they cheered for her when her carriage or barge passed by, happy as they had been for her father, and their goodwill warmed her heart. She would lose that with scandal. They would hiss at her, as they once hissed at her mother.

She breathed a "Thank you," but Katherine pulled away and turned toward the window. Elizabeth bowed out.

Katherine's ladies, sewing in the small antechamber, looked up at Elizabeth as she entered the room. Their faces were blank but their eyes suggested a range of reactions: skepticism from

Lady Tyrwhitt, indifference from Jane Grey, sympathy from Liza Fitzgerald. Elizabeth gave a small, tight-lipped curtsy and continued silently to her room, whirling to shut the door with the same energy that had opened it.

She took in the room she would soon leave, its ghosts crowding the corners. She broke away from them and lurched to her cabinet to put some order to her books and papers, to her life, for the journey.

Her index finger pulled the spine of the first book. Hall's *Chronicles of England*, published just last year since it ended with her father's reign. Elizabeth had gloried in the book that had dedicated so little attention to her mother's arrest and execution, so much more to the Church she inspired. Henry himself had defined his legacy by that Church: in his final speech to Parliament, he had exhorted his people to unite in its congregation, one that was large enough to serve anyone with goodwill.

Now see what she'd done.

She lowered the book to the table and quickly covered it with others.

Better to assemble her papers.

June 12, 1548

The country road took a sharp turn, and the small group paused. Elizabeth found herself looking down a long *allée* of trees that led to a two-storey brick manor.

Anthony Denny reined his horse and turned around slowly in his saddle to smile at Elizabeth, who had kept pace with him the whole way. She had chosen to enjoy the open air rather than hide herself away. She was a skillful rider – why should she not show herself to best advantage? Besides, the fresh air helped counteract her lingering regret over the life she was leaving behind.

Denny had been her father's most trusted servant, his Groom of the Stool, the only man brave enough to warn the King of his impending death. Denny had likely also counseled the great Henry to be kinder to his daughters. Other than Katherine, few would have dared.

"This is Cheshunt." Denny doffed his feathered cap and bowed his head. "I bid you welcome."

Enormous windows dominated the façade, promising light and charm and suggesting redemption. "How beautiful," Elizabeth said.

"I thank your father every day for such a gift." Denny straightened and trotted down the gravel path.

Saying a quick prayer that this residence might bring the peace she sought, Elizabeth followed him after a glance at the carriages that contained her ladies, the ones who would shepherd her through this season of change. In the first, Kat Ashley and Blanche Parry, maternal figures who had been with her forever. Blanche had rocked Elizabeth's cradle and served her ever since with fierce Welsh loyalty. Kat had arrived when Elizabeth was three, serving as a gentlewoman before graduating to governess and inspiring Elizabeth's love of learning.

The second carriage held two other dear women. Twenty-four-year-old Catherine Carey Knollys, available between pregnancies while her husband Francis helped the King press for religious reform. And sixteen-year-old Missi Cheke, whose husband John was preoccupied with the rare opportunity to shape the education of a royal mind.

All craned their heads out the windows, eager to glimpse their destination.

Joan Denny came to meet them in the courtyard. Like Kat, the almost-forty-year-old Joan was beautiful, though Joan's frame had thickened from the twelve children she had borne. More important, her mien was soft and kind.

Joan came right to Elizabeth's horse and grabbed its bridle. "Welcome, my Lady," she said gently, giving no indication she knew of anything amiss. "And you, dear aunt," she called to Kat before going to kiss her and the others.

Chatting while the rest of the convoy dismounted and Elizabeth's gentlemen arrived with the carts, the ladies made their way to the house, whose main entrance opened directly into a large great hall. Elizabeth paused to admire the ceiling's carved corbels that featured human heads or angels holding shields.

"Your father built the house for Cardinal Thomas Wolsey," Joan said. "I suspect the angels were for him."

Elizabeth nodded and continued to look around. The floor was paved with square slabs of black and white marble. Directly opposite the front door, a large portrait of Edward VI hung over the fireplace, his look severe. Elizabeth grinned. "My brother does not look happy about the angels."

Edward was as ardent a reformist as their sister Mary was Catholic. He was said to be doing everything in his limited power to purify the Church he nominally headed, narrowing their father's broad religious net. It felt a sad thing, to lose holy music and images.

And yet, Edward's Church did not include confession as a sacrament; instead, it required sinners to seal their forgiveness through self-imposed correction. Elizabeth found that more comforting, happy to impose a harsher penance than any priest ever would. She had resolved to become the most austere woman at court. Eliminate every emotion but piety. Wear simple clothes, eschew flashy jewelry, and spend all her time in study. The visible emblems of her chastity and wisdom would help Katherine forgive her, and surely stop anyone else from believing more ill of her than they already did.

Please, God.

September 8, 1548

Elizabeth dipped her quill into the ink, intent on the double translation her tutor had assigned. Roger Ascham was considered one of the finest Latin writers of his generation and one of the most pleasant teachers. She owed Anthony Denny a great debt for recommending him. Along with everything else.

The sound of hooves distracted Elizabeth, and she looked up from her work to check the view from the window. Ascham did the same, and together they watched the stableboys and the Dennys' chamberlain hurry to the courtyard to greet the new arrival.

"Things are lively when Sir Anthony is in residence at Cheshunt," Ascham said.

From her post near the fire, Kat craned her neck to see. "It cannot be that important – the messenger does not wear royal livery."

Catherine Knollys stood to check. "And yet he moves as quickly as if he did."

"That means nothing," Blanche said.

They all shrugged and Elizabeth and Ascham returned to Cicero, losing themselves in the work. Ascham believed that the best way to master a language was to translate it to another, then translate it back and compare the result to the original. The approach certainly made the rules of grammar come alive.

Moments later, Joan Denny appeared at the door, lower lip wobbling and tears staining her face. The grim sight brought Elizabeth immediately to her feet, with Ascham and the others only seconds behind.

"What is wrong?" Kat asked.

Joan came to Elizabeth and took her hands. "The Queen Dowager has died."

The words hanging in the air did not belong there.

"That is impossible. She just wrote me last week," Elizabeth said. The letter had been warm, sparking Elizabeth's confidence in forgiveness.

"Childbed fever took her after the birth of a daughter," Joan said.

Elizabeth's body tensed from her core to her extremities, and she squeezed her eyes shut as visions of a smiling Katherine filled her mind – but then a laughing Tom joined her, and Katherine's face returned to the tired reproach she had worn when Elizabeth left Chelsea. Elizabeth would never truly discharge the debt she owed her stepmother. She hid her face in her hands to sob.

Joan Denny put an arm around her, and the gesture lent Elizabeth strength. Slowly she stopped shaking and Joan stepped away, wiping her own tears.

"What of the child?" Kat asked.

Childbed fever usually killed only the mothers; somehow the babies usually survived. Elizabeth had never more resented that reality.

"Lady Seymour has joined her son at Sudeley to care for the babe," Joan replied. "Poor motherless thing."

Kat looked sharply at Elizabeth, bit her lip and looked away.

October 3, 1548

Elizabeth surveyed the garden while she and Kat digested the crisp air of a morning walk. The trees blazed orange in the soft light above shriveling plants, ready to be tied down so their decaying leaves could feed the sleeping roots.

The sight inspired vague melancholy. Elizabeth, glad to indulge it with silence, glanced at Kat. Unfortunately, the connection loosed Kat's tongue to her favorite subject of late. A topic that was still unwelcome, though less offensive than when Kat first raised it.

"You should write to the Admiral to express your grief."

Kat's voice held a strange tone. "He must be the heaviest man in the world right now."

Elizabeth blushed at the thought of Tom Seymour's sardonic smile, the one he had worn when he came bare legged to catch her still abed. But the memory of Katherine Parr's pain quickly slowed Elizabeth's racing heart. "No."

"Will you abandon a friend when he needs comfort?"

Elizabeth stopped short and looked squarely at her governess, who was trying to hide the small smile that played around her lips. "If I write to him, I might be thought to woo him."

"Would that be so terrible?" Kat said. Her forty-five-year-old face was as eager as a young girl's.

"Yes. It would make people think I encouraged him during my stepmother's lifetime."

"No one knows about any of that," Kat's voice wheedled. "His daughter needs a mother, and he needs a wife. Why should that not be you?"

Elizabeth shook her head. Who was the reasonable adult in the situation? Age should have made Kat far more circumspect than her newly fifteen-year-old charge. "I must be more careful in my relations with him."

"He was almost your husband once, and now he is free again," Kat said.

Elizabeth bit her lip. Thomas Seymour had sought the Council's permission to marry Elizabeth before he wed Katherine Parr. Not for the first time, Elizabeth prayed Katherine had not heard about that. Though it might have led her to put an earlier stop to the advances she originally dismissed as innocent.

Oh, God, but they were. Nothing actually happened. It was only a game, and anyway, Elizabeth had thwarted him. So why did she feel so guilty?

"My stepmother is not yet cold in her grave. How can you think of this now?"

Kat snorted. "I would be shocked if the Admiral has not thought of this already."

Elizabeth waved a hand, swatting away the idea like the flies that pestered them. "Though he himself may want me, I do not think the Council will consent to it. Somerset was furious when Thomas married the Queen Dowager, took it as a challenge to his power."

"The fury meant nothing because the Admiral had your brother's blessing." Kat lifted her chin in triumph. "The King loves him better than Somerset and will refuse him nothing."

"You think too highly of his abilities." Elizabeth infused a chiding note into her voice. "It is one thing to marry an old king's widow, quite another to wed a young king's sister."

"A young king's illegitimate sister." Kat raised her palms. "I mean no insult to you. But others have – and marriage to the King's uncle will stop that dead."

Elizabeth's lower lip pouted and they walked on past wilted blooms, the silence weighing until Kat broke it. "And it would save you from being sold to an old foreigner as part of an alliance."

Elizabeth had long feared such a fate, yet regret over Katherine Parr and her own missteps lingered. She had resolved to be ruled by logic, not lust; she would not abandon her penance now. "This is not the time to speak of such things."

"It is never the time to speak of such things," Kat said. "But the two of you are compatible. So many women have to work hard to alter their natural impulses through force of will and prayer – to have it from the start is a blessing from God. Oh, my Lady, it would be a good life for you here, at the English court instead of far away in some strange place. I think the two of you are destined for each other."

"The choice is not mine to make but my brother's," Elizabeth said.

"It will not be your brother's choice but the Lord Protector's. And he has the malice to stick you with an old man."

The thought made her shudder. "I do not know that I ever want to marry."

"Marriage would be good for you. Thomas Seymour would be good for you," Kat said, kicking aside a branch on the path. "And I've seen the way you look at him."

Elizabeth closed her eyes. Desperate as she was to deny it, she did find Thomas Seymour exciting, and marriage to him would allow her to finally throw off the stain of bastardy and live a good life. But this was an indecently short time after Katherine Parr's death – especially given the cloud under which Elizabeth left her stepmother's household.

Kat hooked her arm through Elizabeth's, interrupting her thoughts. "You don't have to write today," Kat said. "But I wish you his wife of all men living. At least frame your mind to write soon."

Elizabeth crossed her arms against the sudden chill that tickled her shoulders. She could not be the one to act – she was sworn to piety. "No."

"I will write if you will not," Kat said.

"Not on my behalf," Elizabeth said.

She was determined to prove her innocence, to herself and the world. Anne Boleyn had refused to cede her honor without the church's blessing; it was for her that England had thrown off the yoke of Rome. It was time for Elizabeth to be her mother's daughter.

If Tom Seymour really wanted her beyond the games he once played, he would have to prove that his affection was not mere impetuosity. He would have to woo and win her, honestly. He would have to earn her love.

When the time was right, of course.

December 7, 1548

The River Lea's churning waters appeared gunmetal grey through the soaring windows of Cheshunt's library. Elizabeth stared out as she often did, seeking inspiration from the sweeping view. Somehow, staring out the window allowed her to stare into her own soul.

"Is it so hard to respond to a simple letter?" Kat asked, making Elizabeth jump.

Elizabeth laughed. "It is when there is no response to make. It is little more than a list of the latest inside snipings along the path to reform."

The King, the Council, and Parliament were still negotiating the terms for the Act of Uniformity that would introduce the new *Book of Common Prayer*. The fight was flanked by the conservative wing, who wanted to keep a slow pace, and anarchists who wanted nothing Romish to survive in the religion, even vestments. Funny how Thomas Cranmer, the Archbishop of Canterbury, who had represented sweeping change since leading Henry VIII's break with Rome, now stood as the ultimate centrist.

"Matthew Parker is merely keeping the connection to you," Kat said. "Just honor that."

Now Master of Cambridge's Corpus Christi College, Matthew Parker had been Anne Boleyn's chaplain, entrusted with Elizabeth's spiritual well-being four days before Anne's arrest, a responsibility he fulfilled with occasional letters.

"It is hard not to chide him for his hypocrisy, racing to marry when it was allowed the clergy but now siding with the conservatives on all other points."

Kat shook her finger at Elizabeth. "No one should be denied the joys of marriage. No one."

Elizabeth ignored the pointed hint. "I need to reply quickly so I can turn to my present for the King."

Elizabeth was translating Ochino's *Sermon on the Nature of*

Christ for her brother. The choice had been a delicate one, since Ochino was far more radical in his views than Elizabeth herself. In the end, she settled on a text focused on faith and the loving Christ. Much as she was following Edward's lead in reform, she needed to remain true to herself.

From behind her, a voice made her jump for a second time. "My Lady, may I have a word?"

It was Tom Parry, Elizabeth's Comptroller, and she smiled. She had been waiting for him. "Of course." She indicated the chair opposite.

He placed his hat on the table as he sat. "I spoke to the Admiral, as you asked."

Kat Ashley's eyes lit up and she put down her embroidery, excited that she might be overcoming Elizabeth's resistance. The woman sang Tom Seymour's praises every day, especially as more time passed since…especially as the mourning period lengthened.

"As she asked, did you say?"

Elizabeth shot Kat a warning glance: this was legitimate business, or at least justifiable as such. "Somerset promised to make Durham House available to me as a London residence, but turned it into a mint," Elizabeth explained to Kat. "I hoped the Admiral would intercede with his brother for me so that I might visit court for Christmastide."

Kat's smirk made Elizabeth blush: they both knew the two brothers did not get along. Too much jealousy between them.

"He gave me a wonderful welcome," Parry said. "Clearly, he respects your position, and mine as your servant."

Kat simpered but said nothing.

"Can he help me?"

"He said he doubted his brother would change any policies. Apparently, he rarely does," Parry said. "But he assured me that if you needed somewhere to stay in London, he would lend you his own house for as long as you needed. Said he would be honored and pleased."

Elizabeth felt the heat in her cheeks and hoped Kat hadn't noticed. The teasing would be terrible if she had. "That was kind of him," Elizabeth said noncommittally, wondering whether she could survive the gossip that would flow from such accommodation.

"He also said he would be honored and pleased to help you assemble your new household."

Elizabeth was preparing to leave Cheshunt and head her own independent household. This step, open only to the highest-ranking women, would require her to take on full responsibility for the manor's operations – two manors, actually, Ashridge and Hatfield – plus smaller properties to be upkept.

This would involve far more than merely supervising the traditionally female areas like brewing, baking, cooking, and cleaning; she would also oversee the traditionally male concerns. She would review books of account, make sure her stewards were collecting rent, and so much more. She was more excited than nervous over the challenge and the opportunity to prove herself.

"How did that offer arise?" she asked.

"He asked me about your lands," Parry said. "He also had a great deal of advice about them and ways to economize on household expenses. Most helpful."

"You asked for this advice?" Elizabeth was surprised: Tom Parry had no idea how much help he needed in his job. He had gotten his position as Comptroller through family and friends more than skill, and he kept it through deep resourcefulness and utter loyalty. Although he could barely add two and two, he could persuade any other man in the household to any other task that was needed.

"Nay, he offered it," Parry said. "Gave more with every detail I mentioned about your holdings and financial situation.

He has excellent ideas about how much more you might earn if you traded for lands adjoining his."

Elizabeth felt her eyes narrow. "Why such curiosity about me?"

Parry exchanged a smile with Kat Ashley before answering. "I could not tell why, unless he means to have you."

In spite of herself, Elizabeth smiled. She waved her hand as a distraction. "He can do nothing without the Council."

"Unless he has the King," Kat said.

"Would you marry him," Parry asked, "if you had permission?"

The conversation had gone on long enough. Elizabeth's station did not permit her to discuss her marriage with a cofferer. Worse, it sounded like there was something behind his impertinent questions. "I have no intention of telling you my mind," she said. "And who put you up to this in the first place?"

Tom Parry waved a hand. "It was just my own hope. And a desire to be prepared."

Elizabeth's relief was tinged with vague disappointment. She reminded herself to be patient, that anticipation was always more agreeable than the event itself. And that this was not real wooing.

She raised her chin. "If anything comes to pass, I will do as God shall put in my mind."

"May I tell him that if he asks?" Parry said.

Elizabeth cringed. "Stop it. You should not be having any conversations about such a topic. It is unseemly and reflects badly on me."

Parry's face changed. "I would never do anything to harm you, my Lady. You know that. I thought this would help you given the…the…occurrences during the Queen Dowager's lifetime."

More heat flooded Elizabeth's cheeks. Before she could

respond, Kat was on her feet wagging a finger at Parry. "I told you in strict confidence, and you promised to never speak of it."

Elizabeth was appalled at the idea of people gossiping about her, revealing her shameful secrets. Even people she loved. Especially people she loved.

Parry looked insulted. "I did not think this counted as not speaking of it. Wild horses could not drag the stories from me to anyone else."

With that, Kat Ashley made a big show of picking up her embroidery and reclining in her chair.

Elizabeth turned on her heels and left the room without another word, resolved to stay away from London – and Thomas Seymour – at Christmas.

CHAPTER 2

January 18, 1549

lizabeth lowered her chin against the chill as she paced the length of the grounds, mentally reviewing the books of account again: she had been forced to reduce her household from the unmanageable one hundred forty people that bloated the initial payroll, people who had flocked to her, begging to serve her before she had learned how to separate the lazy opportunists from honest, hardworking friends.

Now she knew how. Now she understood that it was a privilege to serve her, and she acted that way. She had even learned how to turn men's greed around and extract love and promises of future support from men she sent away. One or two had tried to shame her into keeping them, arguing that dukes might have more than a thousand in their train. They did not expect her to know that those men paid for the privilege or sweetly offer similar terms.

Again, she reveled in the feeling of being mistress of her own household. Two households really, though one a skeleton. She was grateful her rank allowed her this privilege, so rare among unmarried ladies. Another thing that made her loath to consider relinquishing this honor. Not that she'd been asked to.

She felt hopeful here, even though January was one of the few months that the Hatfield gardens lacked life. Oh, the carefully laid out paths and beds were beautifully structured, but this was not enough reason to look up on a frigid day.

She touched her muff to the crowned column that presided over the end of the aisle. Six *allées*, six *retours*, a little under an hour. "We can return to the house now," she said to Kat, who puffed along next to her, as always. "I've had my exercise, enough that sleep should find me tonight."

Kat's quick smile evaporated into a shiver. "Gladly. Besides, there will likely be gossip when we return – I heard horses."

A sudden gust of wind swirled their skirts around them. Kat hooked her arm through Elizabeth's and dragged her toward the house.

Ignoring the commotion at the front, they entered through the side door and went straight upstairs to Elizabeth's rooms. Two green-liveried guards flanked the door, impervious to everything around them.

Elizabeth pressed her lips together, annoyed that whatever visitor this was had not waited for her permission to make himself at home.

Kat patted Elizabeth's shoulder soothingly. "I'll wager Sir Anthony persuaded the Council to check that you have everything you need in your new household," Kat said. "How kind."

Elizabeth grumbled. "I still would have preferred they wait in the Hall."

Inside, a man with wavy grey hair was rummaging through her cabinet. "Sir?" Elizabeth said.

The stranger did not close the cabinet doors when he turned to the new arrivals. Elizabeth recognized Robert Tyrwhitt, formerly one of Katherine Parr's officers, now working for the

Council. He bowed to her, but it was more nod than bow. A shiver crept up Elizabeth's spine.

"Good day, Sir Robert, I trust you are well," she said with a nod of her own. "To what do I owe this pleasure?"

Tyrwhitt sighed. "No pleasure, my Lady. Trouble."

"How does trouble bring you here?"

He motioned to have her take one of the chairs at the desk and took the other, across from her. He steepled his hands pompously before beginning. "The Admiral had foul plans to supplant the Duke of Somerset as Lord Protector. In furtherance of those plans, he minted coins from church plate and took bribes from pirates he should have brought to trial. All to pay mercenaries, who would be armed from the stock of weapons he amassed at Sudeley."

The enormity of the scheme shook her. *Had Tom Seymour really done such things?*

Tyrwhitt leaned towards her. "And four nights ago, he almost kidnapped the King."

Tom Seymour's face loomed before her eyes, wearing the same look as the day he slashed her dress to shreds. She brought herself back: she needed all her wits and more. "You say 'almost kidnapped,' so clearly he failed. Is my brother all right?"

"Yes, praise God." Tyrwhitt rubbed his forehead. "But angry over being assaulted in his bedchamber."

In his bedchamber. "How could such an assault occur?" she asked.

"The Admiral had keys to every room in the castle."

She shut her mind to the echoes of the past. "What did he say to explain such an act?"

"He claimed he was testing the King's security," Tyrwhitt said. "But the Council knows him for a liar."

She closed her eyes and shook her head. "God help him. God help us all."

Her bewilderment grew when Tyrwhitt did not continue. "What has this to do with me?"

"I am sent by the Council to take your confession."

Elizabeth jolted backwards. "Confession?"

"You are part of the plot." Tyrwhitt slapped the desk. "He planned to marry you."

For a moment, Elizabeth's entire world dimmed. Everything around Tyrwhitt's face went black, and dizziness tingled all the way to her fingers. She breathed deeply to return herself. "No," she whispered.

"The Admiral first tried to marry you right after your father's death and was refused permission. The Council knows that after the Queen Dowager's death he approached you directly."

"The Council is wrong. I have not seen the Admiral since my time at Chelsea."

"Ah, yes. Chelsea. You left the Queen Dowager's household quite suddenly. Why?"

Panic blurred her concentration. All the incidents flooded her mind. But they all looked sinister now, distorted by this terrible lens. She prayed for strength. "The Queen Dowager encouraged me to accept an invitation from a great lady who is sister to my governess. I left with her blessing, not her curse."

"My sister had long wished for my Lady's presence," Kat said, stepping forward. "The visit was overdue."

Kat's support shifted the energy in the room and Elizabeth breathed a little deeper. At least until she saw the guile in Tyrwhitt's smile.

"We already know the fault lays with the Admiral." Tyrwhitt's voice was unctuous. "He took advantage of your youth."

Elizabeth bit her lip, wanting to believe she could so easily escape this trap.

"He took advantage of your nature."

She froze, wounded by the reference to her mother. How dare he?

The answer stung: He dared because any involvement was guilt. No matter what they said.

Tyrwhitt leaned forward. "Your own part in this plot was small. Confess and you will be shown mercy."

Mercy? Like Mark Smeaton was offered mercy to bear false witness against Anne Boleyn? His mercy had been to be spared the full traitors' death. They still killed him in the end.

Elizabeth raised defiant eyes to Tyrwhitt. "I did nothing for which I need mercy."

Tyrwhitt's own eyes narrowed. "It is treason to reach so close to the Crown without permission."

Elizabeth's mind filled with the image of a dancing Catherine Howard, innocent of adultery but still sent to the block for having been deflowered before Henry married her. Francis Dereham had been executed as well, for seducing a woman no one could have expected to wear a crown.

"No," Elizabeth repeated.

"Your denial confirms your guilt. It tells us you agreed."

The harder he pressed, the more she resisted. She had done nothing wrong, and for all she knew neither had Tom Seymour. They were wrong about her; they could be lying about him. Somerset hated him, after all. "I am well aware of my duty to the Council and my dearest brother, and I would never entertain a match they had not blessed."

"Resistance is futile," he said. "It will only make the punishment worse in the end."

Righteous anger banished Elizabeth's fear and shame. Her fists balled hard enough that her shoulders shook. "If I am punished, it is for crimes I did not commit. I never agreed to wed the Admiral. I have nothing to do with his actions."

"We'll see." Tyrwhitt stretched elaborately. "The truth will out when your servants are questioned."

"Kat will tell you; she'll tell you right now." Elizabeth turned to her governess, who had turned the color of dried moss.

"Not right now," Tyrwhitt said to Elizabeth. He raised a hand and the guards came racing in. "You may take her," he said to the men.

They crowded Kat, grabbing her arms and almost lifting her off her feet. "Unhand me," Kat said, but the men ignored her struggles.

"What are you doing?" Elizabeth's voice was almost a screech, and she turned to Tyrwhitt. "What is this?"

"It is not I who will question her, but the Constable of the Tower," Tyrwhitt said. "Mistress Ashley and Thomas Parry will soon be on their way to their new lodgings."

Kat Ashley screamed and slumped into the guards' arms. They dragged her away anyway, the toes of her shoes scuffing the polished stone floor.

Elizabeth tensed her legs to keep them from buckling. She could not let herself seem that fearful, but she could not stop from bursting into tears. "I have done nothing wrong," she repeated. No one had.

"The Tower has a way of eliciting truth," Tyrwhitt said.

She shut her eyes and shook her head. *I have done nothing wrong*, she repeated to herself.

February 5, 1549

Normally, Elizabeth found the library at Hatfield to be the most inspiring room in the manor, filled with ancient texts that elevated the soul. But today, a messenger from the Council had delivered copies of the confessions her servants had made from their Tower lodgings. Now, the walls seemed to scowl at Elizabeth as fiercely as she scowled at herself.

"You see?" Tyrwhitt lifted his chin triumphantly. "Every line speaks of treason."

Elizabeth looked down at the pages before her. Kat's writing was much wilder than her usual careful script. Parry's was spidery, as if he could barely grip the quill. But the content was worse.

Elizabeth cringed at the shameful stories she thought would remain buried. The jailers had elicited all the sordid details, like the Admiral's bare legs when he came to wake her, and her own nakedness when she was still abed.

"Young girls your age are of a nature to entertain and nourish voluptuousness and idleness. These letters prove it." Tyrwhitt was practically drooling.

Her face blazed with shame. The whole world would hear of it and laugh at her behind their hands. They would judge her as they had judged her mother. They would condemn her as they had condemned her mother.

Elizabeth shook off the spiraling thoughts and continued reading. Bad as it was, she needed to face the beast. Still, horror quickly stopped her: Kat and Parry had not only revealed all the scandalous goings-on, they had also disclosed their own crazy urgings: *The first time I did hear talk of the marriage of the Lord High Admiral with the Lady Elizabeth...*

When she finished the accounts, she was consumed with the agony of betrayal and the fear of how to answer. She had to react. And yet she could not. She needed more time, to absorb, to think. To accept the fact that two of the people she most trusted had revealed such shameful secrets.

"May I have some wine?" she asked, flipping the pages to read them again, looking from one to the other to compare their disclosures.

Finally, Tyrwhitt could bear it no longer. "You see how you are shown to be a liar? Confess now, throw yourself on the Council's mercy." He leaned in. "You were young, your servants misled you."

It sounded so innocuous, but she did not trust him.

She looked down at the pages again, and the answer became clearer: the stories might embarrass her, but Kat and Parry had said nothing that damned her, nothing that involved her own wrongdoing. Thank God, she had honored her resolve. Contrition and circumspection had saved her. If she had yielded, even an inch, she would have been lost, as the law would have presumed her guilty.

"Well?" Tyrwhitt asked, bringing her back to the room.

"You asked me about treason," she said. "This is naught but gossip."

Tyrwhitt threw up his hands. "How can you maintain your innocence despite all that is in these pages? Tell me that."

"These pages show that innocence." Elizabeth raised her chin, the better to swallow her shame. "Not once did they say, even in the worst of their prattle, that I intended to take any action not approved by the Council."

"Then why did you deny any talk of marriage?"

"I still do. My servants may have speculated about his possible interest, but he never broached the topic. And if he had, I would have invoked the Council."

"That is a pretty twist."

"That is the truth." Elizabeth was breathing more easily now, grateful for the latitude provided by her early denials.

"I doubt that," Tyrwhitt said. "Thomas Seymour is an ambitious man who wanted to be Lord Protector instead of Somerset. He used the poor Queen Dowager to further his power and tried to play the same game with you."

She swayed at the reassembled facts. She had only ever seen Tom as rash, never as a danger – to Edward or herself. Had she merely been blind? No, she needed to remember they were wrong about his proposing to her, they might be lying about all of it. As they had lied about her mother.

Tyrwhitt twisted his face into what he likely thought was a

smile. "No one seeks your death. We seek only the truth so that a traitor may be condemned."

Even in the heat of the moment, she recognized the lie: they would use any confession against the both of them. Well, she had nothing to confess. "I have told you the truth. You will have to look elsewhere for proof of his intentions."

Tyrwhitt sniffled. "The full extent of facts must be known, to stop the Lord Protector from pardoning such folly."

The argument confused her. Was Somerset not the one driving this? If not him, who? Regardless, it was clear Tyrwhitt wanted Tom Seymour dead, and her too most likely. She pushed the papers away. "Did the Lord Protector waver when his brother was brought before him?"

"The Council refused to allow such a meeting. Sympathy should not interfere with justice."

She kept her gaze steady. "Sympathy is the very center of justice."

Tyrwhitt checked his notes and his grimace turned mean. "You all sing the same song. You must have set the note before."

"We speak the truth," she said.

Tyrwhitt drummed his fingers on the table. "Write your confession anyway. I will send it to the Council."

She saw from his sneer that he resented her highhandedness. Probably because he did not believe her. No one believed her. And she had brought this on herself. "I will write my account, not my confession," she said. "Confessions are for the guilty."

"Just write."

This was the time to push. That was the only way to shift the outcome. And return the favor she owed Kat and Parry. "As long as I am writing, I will ask them to release my servants."

Tyrwhitt guffawed. "What makes you think the Council would consider such a request?"

Elizabeth drew herself to her full height and held up her thumb.

"First, because they have been with me a long time. Kat Ashley has taken great labor and pain in bringing me up in learning and honesty. Saint Gregory says we are more bound to them that bring us up well than to our own parents." She added her index finger. "Second, because I think that whatsoever she hath done in the Lord Admiral's matter as concerning the marrying of me, she did it because, knowing him to be of the Council, she expected he would not go about any such thing unless he had the Council's consent."

Tyrwhitt looked a little dazed and Elizabeth added another finger. "Third, because it shall make men think I am not clear of the deed myself, but that it is pardoned to me because of my youth, because she that I loved so well is punished for it. She and Parry are innocent as I am innocent, and the Tower is a fearsome place. They are kinsmen of mine; I would have them with me."

"Ah, that is an answer I can give you now," Tyrwhitt said. "Whatever they decide as to her liberty, the Council deems Mistress Ashley unmeet to serve as your governess. My wife will take her place."

Lady Tyrwhitt. A thin, colorless bitch. Elizabeth burst into tears. "Mistress Ashley has been my loyal servant all my life."

"It is not her loyalty in question but her judgment," Tyrwhitt said. "My wife will see you act more appropriately."

What would life be like? No merriment, nothing. Elizabeth bowed her head, and the confessions came into sharp view, their sordid details mocking her again.

That's exactly what life will be like, she decided. She had once resolved to be chaste, austere, but God's test had almost proved her wanting. Now she would truly quash everything within her that was sensuous, raging, unruly. Prayer and study would be enough. It would have to be.

March 20, 1549

Elizabeth glanced out the library windows, half to stare into the distance and summon a word for her translation – and half to check whether anything had changed since the messenger's arrival about a half hour before. His green livery meant he was sent by the Council.

Thank God they had left her Ascham. Elizabeth prayed this message was not taking him away to serve the King. She needed the mental exercise of her lessons for calm as much as she needed physical exercise to dissipate her nervous energy. It terrified her to contemplate her future after all the damage done to her inherently shaky reputation.

From her chair in the corner, Lady Tyrwhitt sniffed and wiped her nose with the back of her hand. The gentlewoman had served three queens without learning decent manners. At least it didn't distract her: the woman focused on her needlework all day, every day. Someone had once told her she had talent at it, and ever since she had clung to what was likely the only compliment she ever inspired.

Everything that woman did or said irritated Elizabeth. Some women could not put a foot wrong; Lady Tyrwhitt could not put one right.

Elizabeth forced herself to calm down. At least the needlework kept Tyrwhitt occupied enough that she did not try to talk to Elizabeth. Not that Elizabeth would be stupid enough to choose work that lent itself to that. She did translations, wrote poetry, or played her virginals to forestall a conversation that would only annoy them both.

Finally, Elizabeth heard the sound of boots in the hallway, and Robert Tyrwhitt was at her door. "Yes, my lord?" she asked.

"I have news from the Council," he said.

His voice twanged with mockery. Or was she just imagining

it? She said a quick prayer anyway as she steeled herself to receive the message.

"Thomas Seymour met his just end on Tower Hill this morning."

She kept her face impassive as the day dimmed to grey. In her mind's eye, she saw the man she would have married, watched him kneel and touch the sides of the block before laying down his head. She saw the executioner, wearing a black leather mask, raise the axe.

Elizabeth forced her attention away from the horror and back to the room, back to her own danger. A danger she had brought upon herself. She should have known better. *I will never marry,* she had said so many years ago. Where had that wisdom gone?

"They say he was angry and unrepentant," Tyrwhitt said.

Lady Tyrwhitt stabbed her needle into her cloth. "He was a wicked man who gave his wife many shrewd taunts. The realm is well rid of him."

Such savagery merited an answer; the news merited a response. Elizabeth could not defend him, but she would not condemn him. "This day died a man of much wit and little judgment," she said.

Lady Tyrwhitt resumed her sewing. Her husband nodded pensively.

"Is that all?" Elizabeth asked, hoping he would leave. She wanted to hide her face in her translation so her grief would not betray her.

"Your servants are to be released," Tyrwhitt said. "And my wife and I will be leaving soon. The Council is eager to put this incident in the past, where it belongs."

Lady Tyrwhitt harumphed, but for once Elizabeth cared nothing for her coarse noises. Thomas Seymour's execution had ended the bloodlust. They were recalling her gaoler and releasing her servants. Everything would return to what it was before the nightmare began. So why did she still feel sick?

"May they rejoin my household?" Elizabeth's voice was little more than a croak.

"Kat Ashley should not serve as your governess," Lady Tyrwhitt said.

Elizabeth's temper snapped at the woman inserting herself where she did not belong. "It is for the Council to decide, not you," she said.

"She is not fit to protect you. Because of her, there is a rumor abroad that you are with child by the Admiral. She—"

"With child?" Elizabeth's words came out as a scream. "That is a vile slander."

She reined in her outrage: hysteria was not helpful. Summoning all her inherent authority, she kept her voice calm. "How did it come about? How could you, who have been with me, who know the truth, allow it? How—"

"You see how she should not be your governess?" Lady Tyrwhitt said.

"In fact, I am too old for a governess," Elizabeth said, reminding herself she would soon bear no more of Lady Tyrwhitt's venom. It was the truth: Kat would be a much better lady-in-waiting than a governess, a better friend than advisor.

"The Council has not yet said they may return," Tyrwhitt said.

Elizabeth drummed her fingers on the table. She needed to address this. They had acknowledged her innocence; they owed her its full measure. "I shall write again to ask," she said. "And for a proclamation to clear my name."

"You can't stop people from talking."

"I cannot stop them, but they will stop themselves if they know their gossip to be shameful slander."

Tyrwhitt waved his hand. "It is for the Council to decide, not me. I will not stop you from writing your foolish requests."

Elizabeth fell silent as despair flooded her.

She just wanted to crawl into bed and pray that time would

heal this wound, allow her to rebuild her life. Thomas Seymour had paid the penance for the pain he caused Katherine. Elizabeth could only hope she had as well.

July 20, 1549

The roses at Hatfield were at the height of their lasciviousness, calling out to random passersby with their shocking colors, enticing them closer with scents as heavy as incense. They were rich and gaudy and showy. Everything that Elizabeth had not been – for the past six months, anyway.

Elizabeth smoothed the front of her skirt. It was plain white, like her gown and sleeves. Even her jewelry was functional, just a simple silver girdle from which hung a prayer book. She had become a pure, Protestant princess, of whom no ill could be thought. A deliberate contrast to her sister Mary, who piled on jewelry and finery along with her superstition.

Surely Mary would not resent Elizabeth too much for this? Though in truth there was no harm if she did: Mary had no influence. Like Elizabeth, Mary had been sidelined, living the life of a private person to escape scrutiny – though Mary guarded her religious practices, not her reputation.

A man rode up, and Elizabeth recognized James Croft, a former servant of hers who had found favor with the Duke of Somerset. Elizabeth's first instinct was to run inside to avoid Croft, but she forced herself to stand her ground: courage was second only to honor as a quality of the mind. And this was but one man.

She picked one last spent bloom off a stem and walked to the courtyard to greet him.

"Greetings, Your Grace," he said from atop his horse. "I had not expected to find you, but I am glad I did. Your illness has worried the court."

Melancholy had attacked Elizabeth's stomach, but until now

she had not realized how widely this was known. Unsettled, she looked into his eyes but saw only concern. None of the leering accusation that filled her imagination. She relaxed and started the standard exchange of pleasantries, but he broke in. "Pardon my haste, but I was on my way to see your Steward to exchange some horses. I need thirty, so I will take all you have."

"Thirty?" Elizabeth was shocked. That kind of urgency certainly excused the rudeness. "Why so many?"

"I am on my way to help put down more uprisings."

Custom required every man with a title to be ready to lead troops for the Crown; even high-ranking women like Elizabeth would be expected to provide men and arms. Croft was not even a knight; this must be on Somerset's behalf.

"I thought those had been subdued," she said piously. "It is a shame that men's eyes are closed to God's true glory."

In January, Parliament had managed to pass the Act of Uniformity; within five months, rebellion had broken out in the West Country, calling for a rejection of the *Book of Common Prayer* and restoration of the Mass.

"No, these are over the enclosures. A man named Kett has raised Norfolk to protest them."

Elizabeth heard the words, but they made no sense. "I don't understand. Somerset is on the peasants' side of this issue. Why do they rebel?" Somerset had publicly supported the centuries-old right of the people to plant common land and use the food to feed their families. It infuriated the rest of the nobility, who wanted to convert their holdings into pastures for sheep, whose wool fetched premium prices.

"The Protector pardoned the prayer-book rebels instead of crushing them. His weakness encouraged more complaints."

"Lord, save us," Elizabeth said. "I wish you Godspeed in calming the country."

Croft shook his head. "I will need the Lord with me, because the Protector is not. He still discourages bloodshed, and I do not know how long the Council will tolerate this."

Not for the first time, Elizabeth marveled how gossip was like the kitchen maid's cat, coming to sit on her lap when she least expected or cared. "The Council disagrees?"

Croft rolled his eyes as if he were speaking to an idiot. "The Councilors are the biggest landowners in the realm. Of course they disagree."

Trying a different tack, she infused archness in her tone. "I should have asked, the Council disagrees *publicly*?"

That loosened his tongue. "Warwick had fences on his property torn down by vandals; he wants to see Somerset curbed. Permanently."

The Earl of Warwick. John Dudley. Elizabeth had grown up with his sons. Less haughty than Somerset, more personable. And for that reason, more dangerous.

"There is little a single man can do," she said as mildly as she could.

"Warwick has enormous influence. Did you not know? Southampton and Arundel are with him."

The Earls of Southampton and Arundel were traditionalists. Was Warwick one as well?

"Well, that's still only three," she said.

Croft laughed. "Always trust a woman not to appreciate strategy."

Elizabeth smiled through the insult. It was, after all, safer to be misunderstood. The last thing she wanted was to appear to be supporting dissent. Still, that didn't solve the mystery…

"So you think there may be others?" she asked.

Croft shrugged. "There are always others."

Elizabeth nodded while she turned over the facts in her head. Croft clearly did not have the judgment to really understand what was going on at court, so his conclusions were questionable. But what of his facts? Could Somerset's control really be precarious? And what would that mean for government policies?

"Will they succeed?" she asked.

"Aye," Croft said. "Warwick will win," Croft said. "He's the better man: he would never send his brother to the block."

Elizabeth was not sure she understood. "But if Warwick has such influence, why did he not save the Admiral?"

"Save him? Ah, lass, a rabid dog must be put down. Seymour was a danger to the Protector. And to you, my Lady. He got his just due."

Elizabeth let the words settle around her, their weight reminding her that no one defended a traitor. "Well, I wish you well," she said. "My brother needs you. We all do."

She was safest here, in the country, where only the Hatfield roses displayed passion.

CHAPTER 3

November 20, 1549

William Cecil absentmindedly bit the tough skin next to his thumbnail as he contemplated this latest mutation of fortune. His career had long been blessed, most recently with an appointment as private secretary to the highest man in the land, next to the King. Cecil's talent had been noticed, and he had gained quiet – and increasing - influence. But now he had fallen further than he'd risen, and through no fault of his own.

He raked a hand through his thinning hair as he again measured the bare stone walls of his cell, cold and dank already. They said the Tower would be truly nasty in the winter, that its walls provided little protection against the frigid wind. They said even Thomas More had complained – a man who had gloried in the pain of a hairshirt.

A roar from one of the beasts in the Lion Tower menagerie shook the sky. Cecil flinched and wondered again whether he would ever get used to the sound. Something told him he never would, that his hackles stemmed from his earliest ancestors: dogs shared this primeval trait, where threat invariably raised the fur on one's back.

He had been in this nightmare for almost a month now, along with just about everyone surrounding the Lord Protector. *Former* Lord Protector, Cecil corrected himself. The Duke of Somerset had responded to the Council's threat by seizing the King and fleeing to Windsor. Had Tom Seymour's treason – and his fate – taught his older brother nothing?

A low growl told Cecil the Tower's resident lion was feeding, and the symbolism made him hide his eyes. He was only thirty, young to die, though he had already buried a wife who had been only twenty. At least he would leave behind a son, a legacy. God had given him that. Cecil's parents would take care of little Thomas and Cecil's second wife forever, or at least until she found another husband, which she likely would: Mildred was a handsome, learned woman. Cecil had been lucky that way.

He jumped up and paced the cell, trying to banish such maudlin thoughts. He hadn't gone along on Somerset's ill-fated escape attempt; he had been left behind. He was only an administrator, not a soldier. Surely that did not deserve the ultimate penalty.

Heavy boots stopped outside his door, and keys clanked in the lock. It wasn't time for supper, so this visit would bring either very good tidings or very bad ones. Cecil's knees weakened. He stumbled over to his chair and tried to steady his nerves.

John Gage, Constable of the Tower, swept in with a smile. Cecil relaxed: Gage would not rejoice at delivering bad news. He and Somerset may have had a stormy relationship, but Gage had never blamed Cecil for any of it. That was all the friendship needed in the Tudor court.

"Three of the afternoon and I find you lazing in your chair," Gage said. "Well, at least you are not abed."

The gaoler's bantering tone was further balm, fueling Cecil's courage. "You should be more charitable," Cecil said. "It is difficult to kill time when my only weapons are sleeping, sitting, and pacing." He smiled to blunt the dig.

"I already asked the Council about that," Gage said. "And Warwick holds you in enough esteem to allow you to walk the grounds."

"Warwick?"

"The Council is looking more and more to him as their leader. His opinion means enough that, starting tomorrow, I will have guards accompany you on the eastern battlements."

Savoring the imagined warmth of the sun on his face, Cecil smiled. "That is indeed good news, and I bless you for bringing it."

"Actually, I bring even more. The Dowager Duchess of Suffolk has written, and I come with her letter." Gage held out the folded page.

Cecil turned it over, noticing the broken seal. Not that he expected any privacy, but he felt like they should at least pretend.

Gage laughed, clearly unashamed by his intrusion. "You have a good friend there, working hard for your release."

Release? The very word was promising. "May I harbor such a hope?"

"Those who want to see Somerset dead are fewer every day, and there is even talk of releasing him. His wife has already been freed; perhaps you are next."

The prospect made Cecil smile. "May more and more men find their hearts softened."

"Have faith. We are entering a holy season." Gage clapped Cecil on the shoulder and strode to the door. Before closing it behind him, he looked back. "I forgot, Warwick also said you should have paper and ink. Books too. I'll have the guards bring it all tomorrow."

The specter of death retreated further.

Warwick holds you in enough esteem to allow it.

It was actually reassuring. Warwick heading the Council would produce better policies for England than Somerset's mistakes. And releasing Somerset would send a powerful signal of governmental strength and unity. Warwick was a smart man, risen on his judgment and talent. Surely Cecil could trust the process right now.

He resumed pacing to dampen some of the hope pulsing through his limbs. And to pass the time that now weighed less heavily.

December 15, 1549

Elizabeth fixed her gaze on the oriel windows of the Holbein Gate, praying for strength. Somerset's fall had diverted attention from her transgressions. She needed to face the world again, or she never would, and Christmastide was the season to begin.

She clucked her tongue to urge her horse into Whitehall's imposing courtyard but reined him in when she saw the long row of servants waiting there for her. This was how important guests were received, a welcome from the men and women tasked with seeing to their needs. Much as she appreciated the honor, she dreaded the prospect of looking into so many pairs of eyes. She forced herself to thank the Lord for more chances to practice equanimity.

"Surely they are not all for you alone," Kat Ashley whispered, her horse just a length behind. "That is more than ever accorded you."

The half-smile in Elizabeth's glance was enough to hush her new attendant. Kat had been freed and allowed to return to Elizabeth's household, though not as governess. The change in relationship was welcome for them both: Elizabeth was an adult now, entitled to authority.

Together, the servants bowed and curtsied, their faces bearing none of the judgment Elizabeth had feared. It had been the same with the honor guard of more than a hundred men who met her at the London gates to accompany her through the city, and the droves of people who came out to smile and wave to her — though they had been too far for Elizabeth to trust their reactions.

Her lingering fear dissipated. *Lord be praised.*

A man stepped forward, a hand shading his eyes and obscuring his face. He wore a furred black coat over a jeweled doublet, but the black leather knee-high boots of a highwayman. He lowered his hand. It was John Dudley, Earl of Warwick.

"Welcome, my Lady," he said as he bowed, ignoring everyone but her. "Your brother is excited to see you. Indeed, the whole court welcomes the land's greatest example of piety."

Elizabeth bowed her head in modest thanks: it helped to hide her astonishment over such flattery from the man who had overthrown Somerset.

As they walked to the palace entrance, Warwick continued to court her friendship. "I shall bring you to your apartments so you can change out of your riding clothes. The King hopes you will join him in his Privy Chamber in an hour from now."

"I would be delighted."

"He will be happy to hear that. And I am sure he will also want to know whether you were pleased with the welcome."

"It was far more than I expected," she said in all honesty. "I was greatly touched by this show of my brother's love."

Warwick stopped to look into her eyes. A small smile played around his lips.

She kept her face calm as her mind exploded in thought. Was he taking credit? What was his game?

"I cannot imagine how you will outdo such a display for my sister's arrival," she said.

"Your sister was not invited."

Croft's account had suggested that Warwick was a traditionalist, which should have made him prefer Mary to Elizabeth. Had he abandoned the Catholics now that he had what he wanted?

Before she could respond, he resumed walking, still wearing the half-smile. "The King and I talked about the importance of giving you the honor of which the Seymour family deprived you. In more ways than one."

Elizabeth kept her eyes on the path, steeling herself. The barb he aimed at the Seymours also grazed her.

"You should never have been put in a position where your dignity could be questioned," he continued. "You never will again."

Elizabeth sniffed and nodded, mollified.

Several paces before the entry stairs, Warwick stopped in his place and snapped a finger. "Ah," he said, "before I forget, the Council spent a great deal of time recently reexamining your father's will. We realized you never received all the properties due to you – another way in which your father's last wishes were subverted. I intend to see you get everything no later than this spring."

The promise was a surprise, and words failed her.

"One of the properties was to be Durham House, so you could have a townhouse when you visit your brother. But now Somerset House has come available."

Somerset's forfeited property. She kept her gaze level as his pause continued, but he was clearly awaiting a response. "Ah?" Elizabeth said.

"It would look spiteful for me to take Somerset House. But you could take it instead of Durham, so that the King could gift us both rich townhouses. I would take your cooperation as a personal favor."

Whatever her preference, there was only one possible answer. "I could not deny you this service," she said.

He held out his arm for her. "Shall we continue on?" Elizabeth looked up. She would ponder Warwick's motives later. For now, she allowed him to lead her into the palace, where someone was running towards them. A dark-haired man in a shirt and jerkin. A young man, smiling. Robert Dudley.

She had not seen him since her father's death. He was seventeen now, much grown in the last two years. A man.

He stopped short with a double take and bowed briefly to her. "Greetings, Your Grace," he said before turning to his father. "The King is asking for you."

"Would he like me immediately?" Warwick asked. "I was showing his sister to her apartments."

"Perhaps I could do that?" Robin turned to her, tucking a mesh behind his ear. "With your permission. It would give me great pleasure."

Now Warwick turned to Elizabeth. "My Lady, I hope you will allow one of the King's gentlemen to do you this favor on his behalf."

"Of course," she said, glad of the respite. She loved the Dudley children, especially Robin. Older than her by only fifteen months, they had often been paired together over the years because of their similar skills in dance or at hunt, spurring each other on to new heights. Plus, she enjoyed his claims of devotion.

She thanked Warwick for his kindness, and he strode off quickly. Robin turned to Elizabeth's ladies. "Greetings to you all as well. And special congratulations to you, Mistress Knollys. What is that, seven children?"

"Eight," Catherine said proudly. "Five of them boys. Only the Duchess of Somerset has proven herself more fertile."

"Actually, my own mother exceeds her," Robin said.

"Especially now," Catherine said with a catty tone to her voice.

Robin hooted at the sly reference to his father's coup. "What can I say, I have never thought as much of the Seymours as they do of themselves."

He turned back to Elizabeth. "I suspect you feel the same."

He took her arm and hooked it around his, the muscles in his arms firm as he guided her down the hallway.

As they walked, Elizabeth pondered the new world order she found, one which seemed to benefit her. She would see.

And keep an open mind.

January 25, 1550

Dust danced across the slit of light slanting through the narrow window of the Tower cell as William Cecil honed the end of the plume with his penknife. He felt as much peace as possible under the circumstances: Gage's good-natured reassurances and Cecil's new privileges made patience much easier. Gage had not even hesitated to give Cecil a potential weapon, accepting his word of honor that he would not misuse such trust. Again, Cecil apologized to the Lord that he had ever resented the scrawny awkwardness that made him seem so harmless – though even the burliest man would make little headway with the tiny blade against the heavily guarded stone walls of the Tower complex.

The clinking of keys echoed in the hall, louder and closer, until it stopped outside his cell door. Cecil turned in his chair and waited.

Warwick entered, Gage just behind. Cecil jumped to his feet and bowed.

Warwick looked around the room, finally letting his gaze rest on the desk and the papers that covered it. And perhaps the penknife. "You are well here?"

Cecil could not help but smile. "I would prefer to be elsewhere, but I appreciate the kindnesses shown me. I understand you are behind many of them, and I thank you."

"You're a good man. Always have been," Warwick said. "Capable, too. That's important. Somerset always did know how to hire smart men."

The compliment sounded sincere, but Cecil still worried

about the price Warwick might exact for it. "Thank you," was all Cecil said.

"We don't seek his death, you know."

Cecil was unsure whether Warwick was speaking for the Council or invoking the royal "we". For now, it didn't matter. "I am sure he would have been executed long ago if you did."

Warwick laughed. "We don't seek yours, either. You are to be released."

Cecil's heart lifted tears to his eyes. "That is the best news I have heard in some time."

"It is a new beginning," Warwick said. "For you *and* England. Do not sully it." With those cryptic words, he turned and left.

June 3, 1550

The massive tent that stretched across the Richmond Palace green had been borrowed from a royal progress and contained a suite of comfortable rooms. The giant main chamber housed four large rectangular tables; smaller squares around the edges were furnished with cushioned seats for more intimate conversations.

Great majesty had been summoned to celebrate the wedding of Warwick's heir to Somerset's eldest daughter. As soon as Warwick had been elected President of the Council, with all the power the former Lord Protector had once exercised, he released Somerset from the Tower and even allowed him to return to a small role on the Council. Now, in true royal tradition, the two men cemented the peace between their houses through their children, in an agreement sanctified by the King himself as host of the celebrations. With a nod to tact, the location was referred to by all for the occasion as Sheen Palace.

Such had been its name before Elizabeth's grandfather had rebuilt it. Warwick's father had been the debt collector who bled the country to provide Henry VII the funds to pay for the transformation, then found himself executed by Henry VIII as a scapegoat for the avarice that would otherwise have been imputed to the Tudors. Not wanting to conjure such history with the name, they had reverted it. Though in truth it only made things worse.

The bedding of the new couple done, the guests settled in to enjoy the festivities. Elizabeth chose to remain in the main chamber, where her brother was. Mary was not present – she had claimed illness, though some said she was planning her escape to Spain. Again, Elizabeth thanked the Lord for returning her to favor.

A shout from the next table turned her around to smile at her brother. To minimize issues of precedence, protocol had been bent to create a "family-style" atmosphere: Edward and Elizabeth, as heads of tables, were close together in the center of the tent. Warwick and Somerset headed the two others, though both had retired to their own chambers; other guests had rearranged the carefully considered seating, allowing couples like John and Missi Cheke to trade seats lower down at Edward's and Elizabeth's tables to be together and closer to the center.

Elizabeth had made sure to leave room at her table for her Boleyn relatives, so many of whom she had welcomed to her household. Most prominent were Mary Boleyn's children and their spouses: Henry Carey and his wife Anne, and Catherine and her husband Francis Knollys. But there were so many more – even Kat was a Boleyn relation, having married John Ashley, one of Anne Boleyn's cousins.

"We were toasting the many members of Parliament at the table," Edward said. "Younger and younger now, as is fitting." The defensive tone in the thirteen-year-old's voice revealed his eagerness to be old enough to rule.

"We are blessed as well," Elizabeth said. "My cousin Henry represents Buckingham at only twenty-one. Though since he has already left to prepare for the lists, we must raise our glass to his wife."

Another round of toasts and the tables returned to their own pursuits.

"Did your husband tell you when the tilting is to begin?" Elizabeth asked Anne.

"Alas, Your Grace."

"The hall is still full," Blanche said, "and there would be more commotion at the doors if the time were close." She craned her neck for a better look and startled. "Oh, Cousin!" She rose to greet William Cecil and his wife, Mildred, both wearing silk damask in blacks and greens, a fitting choice: rich and festive but not showy.

Cecil was more distantly related to Blanche than the term "Cousin" implied, but family was family. Now, a month shy of thirty, he had finally gained the gravitas to be taken seriously, and remarriage had brought him the comfort he needed to shed his gloom. Mildred Cooke Cecil was a learned woman – another one-time student of Ascham's – with a wide forehead and intelligent brown eyes.

"It is good to see you, Master Cecil, back from the brink after Somerset's fall and looking no worse for the wear," Elizabeth said.

"We are all entitled to mistakes, especially when the mistakes were committed by others," Mildred answered. "I am relieved to see your own good name fully restored."

"As am I," Cecil said.

Elizabeth could see the muscles in Blanche's jaw clench, though her own stayed relaxed. Mildred and Cecil had always been honest and opinionated, and their support blunted the sting of her former scandal. Still, Elizabeth had no intention of dwelling on the topic, especially not when surrounded by so many people so close to the former Queen. "I had not seen you earlier. Where have you been keeping yourselves?"

"Somerset's chamber," Cecil said. "We wanted to offer our particular congratulations." That made sense: Cecil had been Somerset's personal secretary, the perfect post from which to develop the reputation that served him so well. Cecil had become famous for habitually proffering whatever paper the Duke needed even before it was requested, often completing a task before Somerset assigned it. Cecil even owed his marriage to Somerset, since Mildred had been one of the Duchess's ladies. The intellectual conversations of Anne Somerset's salons showed them both to good advantage.

"And now we are on our way to visit Warwick in his own parts," Mildred said.

"They say he has retired already," Elizabeth said. "That his stomach is bothering him, as it often does."

"Well, we will bow to his wife," Cecil said. "After all the kindness he has shown me, I certainly intend to express my thanks."

"Not just kindness past," Mildred said. "He is apparently dropping broad hints about a possible post with the Council. Perhaps as a secretary. It would be nice to have revenues coming in."

Cecil waved his arm. "Hush. There has been nothing definite said. We cannot count on such a thing."

"He has been kind to me as well," Elizabeth said. "He arranged for me to receive all the properties my father bequeathed to me, even exchanging distant properties in Lincolnshire for ones closer."

"I heard about your shrewd trades," Cecil said. "Well done."

"Well, he exacted a fee – he had me trade Durham for Somerset House—

"How did I not hear this part of the story?" Cecil interjected.

"I believe you were in the Tower at the time," Elizabeth said. "I am amazed you heard as much as you did."

"Ah yes." Cecil nodded ruefully. "Well, he could not keep Somerset House himself."

"Exactly. I was happy to do him the favor."

Cecil and Mildred both chuckled.

A thought burst into Elizabeth's brain, a way to save herself by helping a friend: although she had stepped into her role as landowner naturally, although she had shown she could run her household as a *femme sole*, she needed help: certain roles were not permitted her – and beyond the capabilities of the people around her. There was no shame in knowing her limitations – and others' value.

"But now I need someone to administer all these properties," Elizabeth said. "And I can think of no one better than you. Would you consider it? Especially since you are between positions."

William Cecil had helped Elizabeth in some minor suits in the past; she knew what an asset he would be. No one worked harder, and few could boast of such a combination of administrative skills and a shrewd business mind.

"I would be honored," Cecil said. "Though with your excellent grasp of mathematics, and your natural presence, you could do this yourself."

Elizabeth laughed. She loved compliments, especially from smart men. "I intend to be watchful and involved. But I need a man to act as a steward of courts, bailiff of liberties, lieutenant of forests, auditor…" She knew there were more, but they were not coming to mind.

Cecil chuckled. "I can see how a woman would go unheeded in these areas. Yes, you will need those men and more. A high warden—"

The added post jogged her memory. "High warden, keeper and master of game and parks and woods…to say nothing of the waters and warrens." She looked up for inspiration. "I know I am still missing some."

"Not many," Cecil said. "Just keeping the manors and their farmers and mills." He cocked his head to one side. "Does Parry have people you trust for the physical work or shall I hire my own?"

"Parry is begging me to let this cup pass entirely from his lips. Hire whoever you need to be able to focus on making sure all the endeavors are inuring to my greatest profit and benefit. I have read the grants, and know their assets, but there is much more to be done to see them work together properly." She thought again of the daunting pile of parchment rolls, their red legal ribbons fluttering like the banners atop the wedding tent: every page had bared the need for an expert's touch.

Cecil nodded slowly. "That would be the most valuable part of my work – making sure you don't own forests without a mill, or sheep without looms." He looked over at Parry and laughed. "And then supervising all the pieces."

"That sounds like you accept," she said. "How quickly can you begin?" She wanted to secure his commitment before some new office opened up at court. He was too talented not to be tapped.

"As my wife said, we could use the money now. More important, I have the time now, and it would be good to get the bulk of the work done before a new opportunity comes along."

"I expect you will be offered many other commissions," Elizabeth said. "So, yes, I would have you begin tomorrow."

Cecil stuck out his hand for her to shake. "It will be a sincere pleasure to work for you."

"The pleasure will be mine," she said, relieved that she had a capable administrator, proud to have thought of it and brought it about so easily.

His eyes narrowed again, but she knew from experience that it meant concentration. "I will start a list of what I will need," he said, clearly already contemplating the work.

Mildred rolled her eyes at him. "Thank you, dear," she said to Elizabeth. "And now will you join us in Warwick's tent?"

"I spent too long there with Mimi and Ambrose – I had to leave them to entertain other guests. Especially with Robin's wedding tomorrow," Elizabeth said. Robin's nuptials, while also at Sheen, would be a much more private affair than the alliance between the nation's top nobility, and would leave most of the tent's private chambers unused. The bride, a Norfolk lass named Amy Robsart, had neither title nor prospects. Just a large bosom and an even larger dowry.

"We have been invited as well," Mildred said. "And we will attend despite our disapproval."

"Disapproval?" Elizabeth asked. That seemed harsh. The girl's blood was not gentle, but neither was theirs.

"He is giving in to lust. That is no reason to wed," Cecil said. "Respect lasts. Wits last. Looks do not. A mature man would realize that." Cecil had always charged Robin with immaturity. Robin always countered that Cecil was too serious, that life was meant to be enjoyed.

Blanche waggled her finger. "You left money off the list. He found himself an heiress."

"An important factor for a spendthrift," Elizabeth said. "It would rightfully be far more valuable to him than political help, given that he is one of the King's gentlemen."

"I cannot fault his strategy," Mildred said. "But…did you meet her?"

Elizabeth tried to stop the smile from playing around her mouth: Amy Robsart had struck her as simple, even stupid. Not the woman she would have picked for Robin.

"They say the sacrament of marriage overcomes many obstacles," Elizabeth said primly.

"God is merciful," Mildred said. "May He be so here."

Conversation flagged, and Elizabeth allowed herself to wonder how Robin would act after his marriage. He had introduced Elizabeth as the woman who had long held his heart; this suggested he intended to continue their game of courtly love, which made her inexplicably happy.

"I see a commotion at the door," Catherine said excitedly. "The tilting must be starting."

Elizabeth put all thoughts and questions behind her. As she made her way to the entrance, she almost collided with Bess of Hardwick, Lady Cavendish. Like Amy Robsart, Bess had vaulted from local gentry to court. But Bess had worked hard to do it, even if she had been helped by lucky circumstances: hired in Derbyshire as maid to Anne Gainsford, Lady Zouche, Bess accompanied her new mistress to court, where her beautiful face and enticing figure caught the eye of a rich older courtier, William Cavendish. Her wit and determination held it, and they wed quickly.

"Your Grace," Bess said with a quick curtsy followed by a hug.

Elizabeth felt the jutting stomach, and when the hug ended she saw that Bess's face had lost its angled cheekbones, "I see congratulations are in order," Elizabeth said to her old friend.

Bess started to cross herself, stopped, then shrugged and resumed. "No congratulations yet. Not until it lives past its christening."

Elizabeth bit her lip, remembering the miscarriages and still-births poor Bess had endured. "I am so sorry."

"Our lives are in God's hands," Bess said. "You said nothing amiss – but if this one lives, you must be his godmother. Especially if it is a son: my husband had ten children with his first two wives, but only three daughters survive. A son would inherit everything, and I would be safe for life. Even more so with your own august blessing."

Elizabeth laughed. Trust Bess to find the opportunity in any incident. And fold in a compliment at the same time. "August? Me?"

"You are the greatest lady in the land and will only be greater still."

The prediction made Elizabeth shiver. Cavendish was Treasurer of the King's Household, friend to both Somerset and Warwick and in a position to hear many things. "I worry about your 'greater still' – does this mean there is a plan to marry me off?"

"I know of no current plans," Bess said carefully, "but the day will surely come."

"I pray that day is a long time in the future. I also pray they choose someone I can stomach, for I swear I do not relish the thought."

"At least you know it will be someone rich, who can provide you with a good life," Bess said. "For the rest of it, you close your eyes and imagine someone else."

"Surely it is not as easy as that." Tickled as always by Bess's bluntness, Elizabeth was unable to stop herself from responding in kind. "Is that what you do?"

Bess's eyes darted before answering. "Just bits and pieces here and there. I have been lucky with my husband. William is a good man." She dimpled and leaned closer. "It helps that he has settled Chatsworth on me with free rein to make all the renovations I choose. My mind is so consumed with the work, with my legacy growing brick by brick, that I always receive him with excitement."

Ah, Bess. Elizabeth had to envy her friend's satisfaction with her lot. Not that Elizabeth could ever bear that life, or William Cavendish. To Bess, marriage was salvation; to Elizabeth, it meant subjugation, even death – for a list of reasons that somehow kept lengthening. Bess wanted to rely on a husband, Elizabeth wanted to rely on herself alone. And yet their differences only improved their friendship, pushing Elizabeth to chuckle. "Unfortunately, I did not inherit my parents' love of building."

Bess shrugged. "You have no need, since your royal blood assures your legacy."

Elizabeth's mind filled with the face Ned Seymour wore when they greeted each other earlier. "There are indeed fewer who question my royal blood," she said, knowing Bess would understand the reference. Elizabeth did not mention the resentment she had seen under Ned's newfound deference, a vestige of his old contempt.

"Their time has passed," Bess said. "Warwick will treat you better."

"I would like to believe so," Elizabeth said, knowing that political pragmatism often vanquished even the best intentions. "Still, I pray you, pass on my worries to your husband, urge him to take my side if he ever hears the topic raised."

"Done," Bess said emphatically. "You will have an ally to speak for you. And in exchange you shall be godmother to my son."

"Done," Elizabeth echoed, happy with the bargain.

Bess smiled and linked arms. "Wonderful. Now let us go watch athletic men flex their muscles."

December 28, 1550

Greenwich Palace always upset Elizabeth around her mind's edges, because it was here that her mother had been arrested. And yet it was also here that Elizabeth had entered the world, the palace where her mother had made her first appearance as Queen. And regardless of such conflicting personal significance, it offered the perfect setting for Christmas, the ultimate canvas for the season's transformation. Edward had determined the court would pay homage to the legend that Martin Luther had been returning home one winter night and found himself awed by the brilliance of stars twinkling among the evergreens. Luther had shared that inspiration with his family by bringing in a tree to their main room and attaching lit candles to shine in its branches. A whole forest had sprung up in the Great Hall, encircled by a backdrop of evergreen boughs hung on the walls. More than a thousand courtiers gathered in small, glittering circles, their jewels refracting the candlelight and torch flames into thousands of tiny prisms.

A special glen had been formed for the King's dais, which Edward had invited Elizabeth to share. Her chair was only a touch below his, another mark of special favor. Together they waited for Mary, who had reluctantly agreed to celebrate Christmastide at court this year after the Council insisted.

A hand raised and waved to Elizabeth. It was William Cecil, standing with the Dowager Duchess of Suffolk, Catherine Willoughby, who gave a little curtsy. Mildred's speculation had proven correct: Cecil had been named a secretary to the Council.

Elizabeth waved back, prompting waves from another group, this one composed of Nicholas Throckmorton and Robin, both recently knighted as spontaneous favors from the boy King, and Mimi Dudley and her fiancé Henry Sidney. Elizabeth responded to all of them, her happiness increasing with every added show of friendship.

Warwick entered from the side door and approached quickly, ignoring everyone but the King. He bowed before the throne before leaning in for discretion. "The Lady Mary is proceeding from her apartments and will be here soon to bow to you."

Elizabeth looked at Warwick, a patient smile on her face. "Greetings, my Lady," Warwick said, for the second time that day. The first was at church, where Elizabeth had fulfilled her promise to Bess Cavendish and stood godmother to her son. If illustrious godparents presaged good fortune, then little Henry Cavendish was truly blessed, as only Mary ranked higher than Elizabeth, and only Somerset ranked higher than Warwick and Henry Grey.

"Ah, my Lord, it was a pleasure to see you earlier, but my joy is even greater now that I am by the side of my dearest brother," Elizabeth said.

"As is mine," Warwick replied. "Remember, if you require anything, anything at all, you have only to ask and I will see to it."

"As you have proved, thank you," Elizabeth said.

Edward gave an approving nod but stiffened when Somerset slipped into the room by the same side door to join the group on the dais. He gave a deep bow to Edward, a quick bow to Elizabeth, and barely a nod to Warwick. "Lady Mary approaches," he said.

"Thank you," Edward said, giving no sign he already knew.

"The Spanish Ambassador is not with her, but I would still counsel you not to rebuke her."

"The Spanish Ambassador was not invited," Warwick said laconically.

Somerset's eyes widened and he surveyed the room. His eyes stopped at the French Ambassador, who bowed to him with a smile that lifted only one side of his mouth.

Embarrassed for Somerset, Elizabeth looked down at her hands, as if fascinated by something in her lap: Warwick was doing everything he could to show Somerset how unimportant he was. Three months earlier, when Somerset's mother had died, Warwick even refused to institute formal court mourning, arguing that the King's grandmother was sufficiently outside the 'immediate family circle' to warrant such treatment. Now, with Somerset favoring Spain, Warwick had decided to befriend France.

"You want me to pretend all is well?" Edward said. "Would it not be best to first resolve the issue that is destroying our amity?"

Somerset squinted and continued despite Edward's clear displeasure. "A public shaming would provoke Spain needlessly."

"You fear their power far too much," Edward said.

"I do not advise concession, only to treat your sister well in public. At least until the French alliance is certain."

The French alliance was to be cemented by Edward marrying the French King's daughter, but Edward's excommunication— the excommunication of the entire Church of England – complicated matters. France was working to soften the Bishop of Rome, to ensure his dispensation would not require a concession that England could not make. But there was no guarantee of success.

"I will try," Edward said. "But if she raises the matter, my temper may well get away from me."

Elizabeth squirmed, praying that her sister and brother would not quarrel in public. Not in her presence. "Perhaps I should retire," she said.

"Not unless you disagree with His Majesty," Warwick said.

Edward turned to look at her, his eyes flat. She had no choice but to stay.

Before the discussion could continue, Mary appeared at the door. A yellow underskirt peeked out from her rich gown of burgundy velvet furred with sable, as if she were flying the Spanish royal standard. Still, a purse, not a rosary, hung from her belt, suggesting she might be reasonable.

After a pause that drew all eyes in the room, Mary curtsied deeply. She rose and approached, eyes locked on Edward. She stopped just before the dais and curtsied again. Her eyes flickered to Elizabeth, and her lip curled. Elizabeth shivered but shook off her dread: Mary's anger could not hurt her.

"Dear Sister," Edward said. "It does me good to see you."

"I am glad to see Your Majesty looking so well, and I thank God for the grace of being together." Mary crossed herself, and the gesture brought a flush to Edward's cheeks.

"Unfortunately, you thank God contrary to the laws of the land. I understand you still hear Mass in your chapel."

All expression disappeared from Mary's face. "My soul is God's. My faith will not change."

"This is a matter of obedience," Edward said.

"I follow our father's ways, Your Majesty. I have been permitted to do so by your Council."

Out of the corner of her eyes, Elizabeth could see Somerset redden. Edward stood to tower over Mary, in a scene that reminded Elizabeth of their father. "You were permitted to do so when our laws were first promulgated; now you should do out of love for us what the rest of the country does out of duty."

"I was promised I could worship in accordance with my faith for as long as Your Majesty was still a child."

The word *child* landed like a slap that stung even Elizabeth, and the thirteen-year-old's face twisted. "Scripture abounds in instances proving that the best-ordered church of the people of Israel was instituted and upheld by kings younger in years than we." His voice was still too high to thunder, but his anger was clear.

Mary's eyes flickered. "You are too young in years as yet to weigh the arguments."

"In truth, Sister, our youth is an advantage, for perhaps the evil has endured in you so long that it is more strongly rooted than we supposed."

Mary cringed, holding herself like a drawn bow. "Your Majesty, praise God, is indeed gifted with understanding far beyond that possessed by others at your age." She spread her arms. "But consider that both sides of the question are not brought before you. The people advising you all think the same way; there is no one but me to argue the other side." She clasped her hands as if in prayer; they trembled violently enough that she seemed to be shaking them at him. "I beseech Your Majesty to suspend your judgment on spiritual matters until you reach riper and fuller years. Then, with better knowledge and understanding,

Your Majesty will exercise your freedom to decide according to your pleasure."

In truth, Mary was right. Naïve, perhaps, but right. Still, a public argument was never a good idea. Indeed, Edward's response dripped with icy self-righteousness. "We do not wish to presume beyond what our age concedes. That is to say, in matters yet doubtful we place no reliance in our own wisdom – but in things which are plain we believe there is no difference between us and older men. This is plain."

Mary peered out of the lower left corners of her eyes, as if trying to gauge the crowd behind her. The huge group was frozen and silent, more like a painting than real people. "My faith and my religion," she said loudly, "are those held by the whole of Christendom, formerly confessed by this kingdom under the late King, my father, until your Council altered them with new laws."

Elizabeth cringed over Mary saying "my father," not "our father." She was no longer appealing to family; she was claiming a right. Elizabeth wished harder for this terrible scene to end.

Mary bowed her head briefly. "I hope God and nature will so work in Your Majesty that when you reach years of greater understanding, you will not be wroth against this poor supplicant. I pray you consent to no changes in religion until you have reached the age to judge for yourself."

"If our father was building a ship and died before it could be finished, would you suggest I leave it until I was grown? How is it different with religion, where he brought us only so far down the path? If I give you leave to follow your conscience, I have to allow others to violate my laws. You ask too much."

Mary's face twisted. "It is just my household. More specifically, me and my chaplain, who has been taken away from me for questioning. It seems to me not suitable that he should be robbed of freedom by laws and statutes on spiritual matters passed during your minority. No such thing has ever been seen in any Christian kingdom; and God knows whether Your Majesty may not take it amiss in time to come."

"If you intend to govern your faith according to the practices of what you refer to as Christendom, and not according to the Anglican Church of which you are a member, you err on several points. Our father would never have tolerated this."

Mary's eyes opened wide, but instead of apologizing and surrendering, she began to weep. Not loudly, not angrily, but sadly, as if she had lost something precious.

Elizabeth's heart went out to her, and Edward's must have as well because his own eyes watered and he descended the steps to put a hand on her shoulder. "Dry your tears, Sister," he said with a catch in his throat. "I think no harm of you."

Mary sniffled and raised a knuckle to her nose. "Praise God," she said. "With your leave, I will retire now, gladdened by the news."

Edward waved a hand, clearly emotional. Mary curtsied and backed away. Elizabeth tried to signal to Mary greetings, commiseration, love, anything that spoke of connection, but Mary kept her eyes fixed on Edward.

It was hard not to pity the sister who had once again been brought low. After a lifetime of being their brother's favorite, Mary had found herself excluded from everything. Still, it was by her own choice. A minor religious concession was all that was needed.

Not that Mary would ever make it.

"This would be a good time to begin the dancing," Warwick said. "Now that the unpleasantness is over."

"Thank you, yes," Edward said.

Somerset opened his mouth but closed it without a word.

CHAPTER 4

October 11, 1551

s the procession entered the Presence Chamber, the trumpeters raised their instruments to their mouths. William Cecil's entire body vibrated with the jubilant sound, and he took a deep breath to drink in all the levels of magnificence surrounding him. The massive room had been lined with tapestries featuring brave knights triumphing in battle, and small laurel wreaths encircled the plaster medallions on the walls. More evidence that today's ceremony was second only to a coronation in pageantry.

Two dukes were being created: Henry Grey was being granted his father-in-law's dukedom of Suffolk, and John Dudley – for whom the earldom of Warwick had already been a massive rise – was adding the newly created dukedom of Northumberland to his estates. Also, William Paulet was being named Marquess of Winchester, and William Herbert would henceforth be Earl of Pembroke.

And sharing somehow in this glory were four young men becoming knights: John Cheke, Henry Sidney, Henry Neville…

and William Cecil. Four young men rewarded for promise rather than blood – though Neville had always been a Dudley ally and Sidney had married Warwick's daughter.

As the higher investitures drew to a close, the four new members of the nobility retired together to the King's Closet to don velvet robes of estate edged with fur, before proceeding on a snaking path through the Great Chamber. Cecil had caught glimpses of his parents beaming with pride and Mildred pointing to make sure his son missed nothing.

Now the four made reverent obeisance to the King and knelt as one before him. To the side, William Petre read aloud the Latin text of their new patents, a job that would have fallen to Cecil had he not been on this side of the ceremony, elated at the wonder of it all.

The time passed quickly in a glowing blur, until the trumpets blared and the crowd filed out. Cecil followed the line blindly as it returned to the King's Closet, where the men could remove their formal robes before repairing to the Great Hall for the celebratory banquet.

The exultant trumpets continued with their every move, such was the formality of the day. Fanfare even celebrated the moment they took their seats. Granted, the pomp primarily honored the higher stations, but it benefitted all of them.

From his seat on the dais, Cecil had an excellent view of the room and quickly found his family at their assigned table near the rear. He raised a glass of the free-flowing wine, and Mildred and his mother returned the salute with giggles and kisses.

The aroma of roasted meat filled the room as servers arrived bearing a civet of hare, a quarter of stag that had been salted overnight, a stuffed chicken, and a loin of veal. The last two dishes were covered with a German sauce, gilt sugarplums, and pomegranate seeds. The dishes went first to the King's table then to the guests in decreasing order of importance. As expected, the expanding Dudley family dominated the seats closest to the choice morsels, with greedy Robert taking more than his share.

Cecil bit his lip. He needed to tamp down his natural antipathy for his patron's son, overcome his frustration that physical prowess too often counted for more than mental ability. The lad was maturing; he would eventually grow into responsibility.

After the second course, which included chickens and rabbits and even a wild boar, Somerset stood. "A toast," he said, raising his glass. "To good friends – the new peers who will guard this realm." But his tone was a strange one, and his smile was crooked. He wagged a finger at the new Duke of Northumberland. "Ah, my Lord, do you realize you are the first duke in history without even a trace of blood connection to the royal family?"

Northumberland's eyes narrowed. "The King knows how to reward loyalty."

"Or the semblance, it seems."

Northumberland's eyes had a hard glint as he brought his cup to his lips.

Cecil looked away. He loved Somerset, owed much of his life to the man, but the court and its politics had changed. Warwick's – no, Northumberland's – leadership was better for the country. England needed a firm hand, one driven by reason over passion. Not that Cecil's opinions dictated policy. Though someday they might.

He was a knight now, after all.

December 28, 1551

Somerset House was a magnificent example of Renaissance architecture. Facing onto the Strand, the two-storey building, built around a quadrangle, had a gateway that soared to a third storey, giving it a majesty greater than many royal palaces. Elizabeth had come to be grateful that Northumberland had initiated the trade for Durham.

Tonight the court celebrated the Feast of the Holy Innocents. The masques would be starting soon, the dancing afterwards.

Robert Dudley awaited Elizabeth at the bottom of the stairs, his jeweled black doublet highlighting strong, broad shoulders. The King had named him Keeper of Somerset House, one of many wedding presents, another factor that made Elizabeth's time in the lavish residence so pleasant. Though his wife made things less pleasant.

Robin had married Amy Robsart before his father's impossible rise, when an heiress with no family pedigree was considered a fine match for a fourth son. Once his father became a duke, Robert had lamented his rashness, pretending his rising star and father's preeminence might have permitted him to court Elizabeth. A fitting regret for the valiant knight pining after his unattainable lady, a game Elizabeth enjoyed more than she let on.

"Henry Carey came down but wandered off," Robin called up to her. "Anne went after him."

"You should send a page to find them both," Elizabeth said. "And hope he does not get lost as well."

Pinching her silver gown high, she took her time descending the steps so as to allow the heavily pregnant Catherine Carey Knollys, lumbering just behind Elizabeth, a chance to breathe between steps. Catherine was leaning heavily on the arm of her husband on one side; on the other, she pretended her eight-year-old-daughter was also helpful.

Catherine's looks were all Boleyn. For twenty years, people had secretly wondered whether the King might have sired her, since Mary Boleyn had been his mistress during that time of her marriage to William Carey. Many thought the mystery solved some eight years ago, when Catherine's daughter Lettice was born, a miniature version of Elizabeth.

Robin released a low whistle as Elizabeth reached the final step. "What a gift, to glimpse such ankles."

Elizabeth waved her skirt at him in response, clacking its pearls against each other. While ostentatious jewels were incongruous with the reputation she had created, pearls were somehow excused from the scale. And Elizabeth did adore pearls.

A serving woman in a brown kirtle stepped out from the shadows. Upon realizing it was Amy Dudley, Elizabeth jumped but then caught herself quickly. "Oh dear," she said, "you did not leave yourself much time to dress."

Amy's tinkling laugh contained a false note. "Thank you, Your Grace, but I am not coming tonight."

Young Lettice looked horrified. "Why would you forego the splendor of the court at Christmastide? I would give anything to be there."

"Just last week you were willing to give everything just to be here," Catherine chided. They all laughed when Lettice did not respond, and Catherine patted her daughter's head. "Have patience."

Elizabeth smiled at Lettice's pout. She was an imperious thing, a little overly so. Right now, Lettice needed a gentle reminder to be seen and not heard, so Elizabeth turned to Amy, drawing the room's attention back where it belonged. "Why would you not join us? There is plenty of room in the barge."

Amy lifted her gown to show her feet, looking ungainly in *sabots*. "I cannot dance."

"That does not matter," Catherine said, a hand on her stomach. "Neither can I."

"You have an excuse," Amy said, "being so close to giving birth."

Catherine flinched but kept a smile on her face. "I am not that far along despite my size. This is my tenth child and my stomach reverts quickly to habit."

Amy flushed, embarrassed. "Still, I wager no one would challenge you."

"My father made wagering illegal," Elizabeth said. "Otherwise you would win that bet." Amy froze, as if unsure whether to trust the jest.

Catherine rolled her eyes. "Amy, you can just come and sit on the side with me."

"Or I can teach you to dance while you dress," Lettice said.

"Please no," Amy said. "I will be happiest staying home to help with the children. They are all so wonderful."

Catherine and her family were not the only Boleyn relatives who had brought their children to share the joys of the season: Henry and Anne Carey, too, had helped fill the nursey. Their youngest, Cathy, was one of the few toddlers Elizabeth really liked – she did much better when children were old enough to reason. Cathy's presence was inspected with curiosity by the other guests, in particular Mimi and Ambrose Dudley and their spouses, both couples still waiting for their own tiny blessings. Admittedly, the Dudley siblings were enjoying more the chance to witness their hapless brother fulfilling household responsibilities.

"Are you sure? Elizabeth asked Amy.

"Quite," Amy replied.

The ensuing silence stretched on awkwardly until Amy broke it. "Where are the others, anyway?"

"They are still tarrying upstairs," Catherine said.

"As long as Mimi is not alone with Henry," Elizabeth said. "Or we will never leave."

Mimi Dudley had married Henry Sidney in March, another lust match in the Dudley household. Though, unlike Amy, Henry was blessed with both fortune and family. He also had a promising political future, having been raised as a close companion to the boy who had become King.

"I should go get them," Catherine said, not moving.

"No, no," Amy said. "Save yourself the stairs. I would be happy to. And I will bring Lettice with me."

"Thank you," Catherine said, a smile playing around her mouth.

When Amy had run off, Elizabeth turned to Robin. "Teach your wife to dance," she said. "Practice in the morning, not just for the balls, but also for exercise. I myself dance at least three galliards each morning, and I have for years. I get ill-tempered without movement."

He shrugged. "I danced galliards – four or five – each morning during Advent. But she refused to join me."

"You should have tried harder," Elizabeth said.

"It is not just the dancing," Robert said. "She also is not confident in her conversational skills or her clothes. Trust me that she is more comfortable here."

His eyes showed flat resignation, and Elizabeth decided to return to jest. "Well at least resume your galliards," she said. "Laziness is not becoming."

He raised his hands in defeat. "You must not think of me as lazy. I live only for your approval. Do I get no credit for my other exercise? The hunting, the jousting, the tennis?"

Her inspection could find no fault with his physique. Not that she expected to. "I suppose," she said. "I apologize, Sir Robert."

"Sir Robert? Call me Robin," he said. "Why would you change the habit of a lifetime?"

"You are married now. I would not want your father to think ill of me," Elizabeth said, trying to create an opening to express her dismay over a disquieting rumor – and solicit more help than William Cavendish could provide alone.

"That would never happen." Robin scratched at the scrawny beard he was growing. "I daresay my father thinks more of you than he does of me."

"And yet I hear he is considering a French duke for me, an

older man they say resembles a toad. I beg you to discourage him if you get the chance. My brother as well."

"You have not changed," he said. "I daresay—"

"If we are not leaving," Catherine interrupted, "I need to sit."

"Please do," Elizabeth said, happy to avoid a philosophical conversation about marriage. "Even once the others arrive, I still want to tarry. I want to arrive after anything controversial." The other night, the dancing had been interrupted by a group of men dressed as Catholic bishops in their red-and-gold copes and miters, gathered together under a cloth tabernacle carried by black-cassocked priests. One of the bishops had turned, lifted his robe, and farted loudly at the crowd. Another bishop had lasciviously licked a representation of the holy sacrament in its monstrance.

Robin laughed again. "No controversy. Just a reformist court."

"The French and Venetian Ambassadors looked completely disgusted at such mockery," Elizabeth said.

"They were the exceptions," Robin said. "The Englishmen were happy to ridicule the ecclesiastical estate."

Not wanting to show her own discomfort with this extreme, especially to the son of the man who had commissioned it, she again shifted the conversation. "I am surprised Cawarden took things so far," she said, as casually as she could. "Perhaps it is a blessing that my sister was not there."

Thomas Cawarden had served as Master of Revels for almost eight years, a reward from Henry VIII for the diversions that brightened the time spent sieging Boulogne.

"It was not Cawarden who arranged this; it was George Ferrers."

Elizabeth stopped in her tracks, shocked. "Cawarden has been replaced?" Would such artistry really have been sacrificed just to make room for reformist views?

"No, no. My father just wanted to make things particularly

gay this year in light of the…to comfort the King. So he resurrected the role of Lord of Misrule."

"Well, this is indeed misrule," Elizabeth said. "And of a type to particularly enchant my brother."

Robin's blush confused her. What part of this distressed him? It must have something to do with Somerset's downfall. Northumberland had uncovered a plot to overthrow the government, and his investigations had led to Somerset as its source. Somerset was in the Tower now, soon to become the second of the King's uncles executed for treason. Were the rumors true that the alleged plot was an invention, a way to remove a dangerous rival? It seemed poetic justice if that were so, after Somerset killed his brother for the same reason. Or had Northumberland been behind that as well?

"The misrule intensifies with the lateness," he said. "If you want to avoid mischief, we would be better off going now."

"And leaving early," Catherine said. "To retire all the sooner to bed."

"To bed?" came Ambrose's voice from the landing above. "Are you already speaking of bed before we have even left?"

"Is bed a choice?" Henry Sidney said, skipping down the stairs with Mimi's hand in his.

"You spend enough time there," Elizabeth said.

"Never enough," Mimi said.

Elizabeth laughed, but noticed Robin was not joining in. Indeed, he seemed melancholy, as if being in bed with his wife was the last place he wanted to be.

Even love marriages could fail. What hope was there for her with the toad-faced duke?

April 15, 1552

William Cecil quickened his step as he turned onto Canon Row, the street of choice for courtiers who wished to live close to court. He whistled as he walked past the row of townhouses to his own. Well, it actually belonged to his father, but Cecil enjoyed it as well, like the country home in Stamford Baron where the copses, ponds, and birdsong restored his soul. Well-placed residences were certainly a wonderful benefit of well-placed parents.

He found Mildred in the Great Room with his mother, Jane, sitting near the mullioned windows. The women stopped chatting when he entered. "You look quite happy, husband," Mildred said.

His mother nodded. "You do indeed, son."

"With good reason," he agreed.

"Oh?" said both women. They put down their needlework, clearly ready for the story he was bursting to tell.

"The King has risen from his sickbed," Cecil said with a broad smile. "He was well enough to insist on a round of archery today." The entire court had huddled in terror when the lad had fallen ill with measles and smallpox. Today had answered widespread prayers.

"The Lord be praised," Mildred said.

"What a blessing he is young and strong," Jane said.

Mildred cocked her head. "Was this a trick of Northumberland's, or did the King truly seem recovered?"

"He was thin and pale, but his eyes were bright."

"Bright eyes could still be feverish." Mildred looked unconvinced, and Cecil smiled at her inevitable cynicism.

"I was right there on the field," Cecil said. "As close as we are on Sundays when the men shoot behind the church. Though I admit the crowd made it hard to see sometimes."

"Were there so many people?" Jane asked.

"The whole court was curious as to how he fared. Even the Council adjourned its business to attend the King's first outing."

"I will certainly say prayers of thanks for the Lord's mercy,"

Mildred said. "The King recovered where so many do not, and his salvation rescues us all."

It had indeed been a terrifying few weeks: Edward's death would have hurt so many important causes. To say nothing of reformist careers, especially Cecil's own.

As if she could hear his thoughts, Mildred pressed on. "How do you think a Queen Mary would have viewed you?"

Cecil shrugged. "She was friendly when I was in service to Somerset. Now that I work for Northumberland, she is far less so. Now, *there* is a man who would lose much from Mary's accession."

Not that Cecil had taken any part in Somerset's arrest or condemnation. No, Cecil never betrayed that friendship, though he could see how his honest name might be tarnished by his ties to Northumberland. Except what choice did Cecil have? Despite the pretense that the King ruled all, Northumberland wielded more power than Somerset ever had – and was far more vindictive.

"Northumberland would be smart to try to persuade her he had nothing to do with Somerset's downfall," Cecil's mother said.

Cecil smiled ruefully. "Even those who love Northumberland blame him for Somerset's downfall. Including the King."

"Surely not," Mildred said.

"Judging from what he said today, I would bet this house I am right."

"Oh?" Mildred arched an eyebrow.

"During one of the rounds, Northumberland's arrow landed in the white, far from the center. The King turned to look at him —" Cecil shuddered.

"What?" His mother leaned forward.

"Sorry. It's just the look the King wore. His eyes were flat, like a soldier aiming a gun at an enemy. He told him, 'You aimed better when you cut off the head of my uncle Somerset.'"

Cecil's mother paled; his wife swallowed.

"The King believed his uncle was innocent but still let him die?" his mother said. "Why would he do that?"

"Because Northumberland allows him to pursue more reformist policies," Mildred said. "Now, *there's* a bargain with the devil."

Cecil scratched his beard. "I thought on that a great deal and decided the King must have decided so afterward. Too late to do anything about it. It helps to tell myself that."

"It does help," his mother said. "I can't bear to think of a young boy being so twisted."

Mildred harrumphed. "As twisted as his father, you mean."

"It is power that does it," Cecil's mother said. "Great Harry came to the throne as a generous, loving lad."

Cecil nodded. "The promise of power also corrupts. Edward was always a little twisted. Elizabeth was spared that, living so much of her life as a bastard."

Mildred knotted her brows. "Mary was also named a bastard."

"Ah, but Mary always had Spain calling her Princess," Cecil said. "Elizabeth had nothing – so now she has judgment."

His mother sniffed. "Blanche credits her with that, too. And yet, that same judgment got her tangled up with Thomas Seymour."

Cecil wagged a finger. "He had no business meddling with her. And she has changed since then, matured. She is a brilliant young woman, and I am glad to work for her."

"Well, she'll be fine in the end," Mildred said. "Much better than Mary, who'll never know the love of a husband."

"Of course she will," said his mother. "Mary is too important a bargaining chip to waste."

"But one too dangerous to use until the King marries and sires an heir himself," Mildred said. "With him only fifteen, she'll be well over forty before that happens – too old to birth a babe of her own. How jealous must she be of Elizabeth, who's not even twenty?"

"Now, *there's* a woman who is even luckier than we are that the King recovered," his mother said. "Can you imagine her life if Mary became Queen?"

March 26, 1553

Elizabeth's procession snaked along the road to London. Fifty attendants rode with her, including drummers and pipers to create a festive atmosphere. Since she was paying their salaries, she intended to use them. Yes, her brother would send his own people to welcome her, but this would show her status well before that.

As always, the commoners ran out as she passed, to wave and cheer and throw flowers. She always smiled and waved back, looking right in the eyes of as many people as possible as she thanked them – which spurred the crowds to even greater demonstrations of support. They said her father had done the same in his day, and it always surprised Elizabeth that neither of her siblings copied him like she did. As if the people's love was a right, not a wonderful privilege.

Just before Camden, she saw a small group of green-liveried riders coming toward her. Only ten or so, instead of the hundred her brother had sent the last time.

As the riders approached, she recognized her cousin-in-law Henry Grey, now in high favor as Duke of Suffolk.

She signaled to stop her convoy. When Suffolk was close enough, she called out to him. "My Lord, it does my heart good to see you."

"And mine, you," he answered loudly as he continued his approach.

"Does this mean your dear wife is at court?" Elizabeth's

smile was wide, even though she had never really liked Frances. "I would love to see her."

He waited to reply until his horse was alongside hers, and kept his voice low. "What are you doing here?"

"I have come to see my brother. I heard he was feeling better after a bout with a rheum cough, and wanted to celebrate his return to good health."

Suffolk took an embroidered linen handkerchief out of his sleeve and wiped his forehead. "His Majesty is indeed much recovered, but this is not a good time for a visit. We are limiting the number of people at court, to lessen the chance of further infection."

Elizabeth narrowed her eyes. Something about Suffolk's behavior gave her pause. "I did not consider that," she said. "I would not have brought so many attendants, even knowing them to all be healthy."

Suffolk sniffed. "Of course."

"I am happy to leave them all behind and just come myself if my presence might comfort the King."

He looked up to a corner as if considering the matter, but the empty look in his eyes betrayed that he was just biding time. "That is kind of you, but your visit might tax his strength."

"I could wait at Somerset House for his summons."

Suffolk shook his head, another in an exaggerated series of gestures meant to show sincerity. "That would place unnecessary pressure on him. Surely you understand."

She didn't, but recognized the futility of further argument. "I have no desire to be a burden. I only thought to express my love."

Suffolk's face twisted. "Feel free to write to him."

Elizabeth ignored the chill that gripped her shoulders. Why did they not want her visiting? Her brother must be sicker than they had let on. But even that did not explain why Elizabeth's presence would be unwelcome. Now would be the time for siblings to draw closer – unless there was some reason to keep them apart. Was someone trying to drive a wedge between them? To what end?

"I shall," she said. "Thank you."

She looked over her shoulder, and Blanche, also on horse-back, approached immediately for instructions, which Elizabeth had not yet formulated. All she could think was that she was being publicly snubbed. What would people think when she just turned around?

"Perhaps I might stop a bit," she said to Blanche.

Blanche nodded and pointed. "That manor house right there, do you see it? It belongs to Jerome Palmer – husband to my Lord Paget's daughter. You could rest there."

Suffolk's face reddened. "That might be true."

Perfect. William Paget had been well trusted by Elizabeth's father. And while his reputation had suffered from his connection with Somerset, his name still carried great weight.

"Perhaps you would join me in a visit," Elizabeth said. "Surely you could use a rest before you ride back, and this would allow you to carry back my letter."

"I will gladly accompany you," Suffolk said, tuning his horse so he could lead the now-wilted convoy.

For the first time, Elizabeth ignored the people on the side of the road. Their presence embarrassed her now, knowing she would be turning right back around. Perhaps she could choose a slightly different route home, so fewer people would know of the incident.

She also had to be careful about her note. She did not know who had issued the directive to return or what secret it hid. She almost regretted the decision to write, except that quick responses were always better than slower ones. Approaches tumbled in her mind as she sought one that would not sound accusing. Finally, it came to her: her brother had been fascinated by ships since visiting England's coastal defenses during last summer's Progress; she would bend his favorite topic to her own purposes.

Like as a shipman in stormy weather plucks down the sails turning for better winds, so did I, most noble King, pluck down the high sails of my joy and comfort. I do trust one day that as troublesome waves have repulsed me backward, so a gentle wind will bring me forward to my haven.

That would do the trick.

May 24, 1553

The minister raised his arms for the concluding prayers. "Take us and use us to love and serve you, and all people, in the power of Your Spirit and in the name of Your Son, Jesus Christ our Lord. Amen."

Elizabeth barely remembered the shock she had experienced when she first returned to worship at St. Ethelreda's after Edward's reforms stripped the nave of decoration. She was now accustomed to the whitewashed walls, though she did still miss the music.

With the service ended, she stood with her ladies to leave, smiling to the other congregants and exchanging wishes of peace as she did every week, conscious of the example she set.

Just outside the church, a burly, somewhat familiar, fellow came to address her. His canvas doublet was not expensive enough to make him a merchant, but he might be a craftsman or journeyman. His reluctant posture suggested he had been prodded to approach her. "Might you attend the archery competition, Your Grace? We are shooting against the village of Stanborough, up the road." His voice held a nervous tremor. "We will set a special place for you."

"How kind," Elizabeth said. "But are these the champions who bested us last year?"

"We have all been practicing for months," the man said.

"Much as a Sunday afternoon begs for a well-earned nap, we have used our days of rest to work hard." A sudden wide smile revealed a lacking front tooth, and she recognized the glover's assistant. "At least until the pub opens."

Elizabeth infused warmth into her voice, to show she was teasing. "What? On the Lord's Day?"

"When you have only one day to yourself, you have to make the most of it," he said. "And the extra pastimes help me praise God all the more for His grace."

Elizabeth smiled at his good nature. "Your name is Harry, as I recall?" She had a fantastic memory for faces and used it whenever possible for the effect it had on people.

Sure enough, his chest puffed with pride. "Yes, Your Grace. Harry, after your father." He grabbed the woman just behind him and pulled her forward. "And this is my wife Lissa, after your grandmother."

Despite the woman's grey hair, her nimble step suggested she was not much past twenty, like Harry.

"We have that in common," Elizabeth said.

Lissa curtsied low. "Thank you, Your Grace, and may I say it is good to see you recovered. We were worried about you."

"Worried?"

"When you did not attend the weddings. We feared you were ill."

Elizabeth felt her eyes narrow. "Weddings?"

"Three of them at the Duke of Northumberland's estate. His son to Jane Grey, his daughter to the son of the Earl of Huntingdon. And Katherine Grey to the son of the Earl of Pembroke."

A huge celebration from which Elizabeth had been excluded. Powerful alliances cemented in the face of the King's purported relapse. Her mind turned over the facts like a locksmith picking at a tumbler. "Ah, yes," Elizabeth lied. "I was sorry to miss them. But how do you know about them?"

"One of the sellers on market day had just come from

London, from the market near Durham House, with no asparagus left because it was all taken for the feast. The Duchess was so grateful for his spears that she let him onto the grounds to watch. Lots of others too. She must not have planned well."

"That must have been quite exciting." Elizabeth kept her voice light. "Was he close enough to see the bride and groom? Or, rather, brides and grooms."

"He saw them all arrive, and said it was as many dukes and duchesses and earls and countesses as Christmas at court. Even Ambassadors – they say the French one came with a horse as a gift. No one was missing but the King." She broke off and curtsied, embarrassed. "And of course you, Your Grace. And the Lady Mary. I pray she is healthy as well."

All the highest people, even ambassadors. A rushed state occasion without the King or the next heirs. Why had Northumberland not waited? And why had he snubbed her after courting her friendship so diligently? Most important, how sick was Edward that he did not attend?

As always when fearful things happened, Elizabeth felt ill. She added one or two questions, silly ones about jousts and dances, as if that was all that mattered. "When does the archery tournament begin?" she asked.

"In about an hour, once Stanborough has arrived."

"Alas, I cannot tarry. But I will pray for your victory now and plan to attend next year," she said, taking off for home as soon as she could. Walking calmed her and she needed calming right now.

As soon as Elizabeth and her entourage were far enough away not to be overheard, bedlam broke out. "What the devil is Northumberland doing?" Catherine asked.

"He's up to no good, marrying a son into the line of succession," Blanche said.

Elizabeth snorted. "And two more matches besides."

Only Parliament could change the succession, and they had

not been called. This was likely Northumberland seeking to protect himself in case Edward worsened. But why exclude Elizabeth? Something felt off.

June 11, 1553

William Cecil coughed loudly into his fist, the sound echoing across the linenfold paneling and off the gold stars that studded the azure ceiling of Greenwich's Council Chamber. This was his first day back at court after a monthlong illness. Rumors were everywhere that the King was close to death, that crazy plans were brewing. Cecil had stayed away as long as he could, but Northumberland's summons left him no choice.

"Are you ready?" asked William Petre, who had stepped in for Cecil as the Council's principal secretary.

"Ready for what?" Cecil asked.

Petre shook his head. "It is not for me to say. Just prepare yourself."

The Councilors filed in and took their places at the table, staring pointedly at the row of chairs that had been added to the room. Cecil, too, questioned the significance of the additional seats.

Footsteps in the hallway signaled a group. Edward Montague entered, followed by Thomas Bromley; was it coincidence that both were justices of the King's Bench? Next followed the Attorney General and the Solicitor General.

The four men looked as nervous as Cecil felt, and took their chairs tentatively. They clearly knew as little – and feared as much – as Cecil did.

The side door, the one that connected the Council Chamber to the King's apartments, swung open. Northumberland swept in as they all leaped to their feet. Without acknowledging anyone, he went straight to the King's chair of estate and angled it closer to the table before nodding to a waiting page, who whirled around and disappeared back through the door. Northumberland went to stand at his own chair, staring silently at the door with the rest of the men in the room.

After several minutes, the King shuffled in, watching his feet as if it took great concentration to place them one in front of the other. He was emaciated, grey, and the smell of decay suffused the air around him. His hat covered most of his head, but sores were visible under the brim, amid bristles that suggested his hair had been shaved.

After sitting, he coughed into his handkerchief. When he lowered the cloth, Cecil saw flashes of black and red before Edward crumpled it in his hand.

Cecil broke out into a cold sweat. Despite all the official announcements of the King's happy recovery, the boy was dying. Cecil could not doubt it. Nor could he doubt that he was about to get drawn into something nefarious.

"Good day, gentlemen," Northumberland finally said. "The King has asked you here to discuss a matter of vital importance for the realm."

Northumberland nodded, and William Petre jumped up. He handed out copies of a document, first to the lawyers in the chairs, then to the Councilors, and finally to Cecil. The page was titled "My Devise for the Succession." Cecil's stomach fell even further.

That explained the lawyers. The King's Bench was the land's highest court, with jurisdiction over all cases involving the Crown. It could legitimize Edward's plan – and quickly. While its records might be subject to review by Parliament, that wouldn't happen until it was too late for anything to be done about it.

Northumberland had figured that out.

Cecil scanned the document, seeing quickly that Edward wanted to bequeath the Crown to Jane Grey. Surprisingly, the first person to speak against the idea was not the Catholic Henry

FitzAlan, Earl of Arundel, but rather Thomas Cranmer, Archbishop of Canterbury. As others joined in expressing their reluctance, Northumberland's scowl. Finally, he slammed his fist on the table. "The King wants this done."

The judges exchanged glances.

"The succession needs to be settled," Edward said.

The Lord Chief Justice, Edward Montague, coughed. Not an indication of illness, but an expression of discomfort. He sat back and stroked his long white beard. "The succession *is* settled, Your Majesty. Settled by your father and Parliament."

"This King wishes to change that," Northumberland said. "This is the framework he wants you to turn into a legal document."

Montague coughed again. "We will need some time to consult on this. My own opinion is that it would be treason to overturn the existing plan."

Edward glared at him. "Shall nothing ever change, then? Must we continue decisions that time has proven to be mistakes?" He leaned forward. "I cannot allow Mary to inherit my throne; she will overturn all the progress we have made in matters of religion."

"Perhaps she could be required to promise to maintain the prescribed services," Montague offered.

Edward's lip curled. "Do you really believe she would honor such a promise? Or that she would even make it?"

"Well, we could ask and—"

"You are here to fulfill my command," Edward said, his voice rising so high on the last word that a fit of coughing gripped him.

The boy's display was feeble despite his passion; he clearly had no idea where the real power lay. Tears rose to Cecil's eyes and he prayed no one would notice.

Again Northumberland slammed his fist on the table. A purple vein throbbed in his forehead, an unmistakable sign of one of his rages. "I will fight in my shirt with any man living before I permit this insult. The King must be obeyed."

Montague, shoulders cowed, tried to respond. "But the treason…"

"My sister Mary would provoke great disturbances and leave no stone unturned in her efforts to gain full control of the throne and its policies," Edward said. "I tell you again, it would end the religion whose fair foundation we have laid together."

Eyes darting, Montague tried a different tack. "By what argument do you set her aside?"

"Mary was the daughter of Catherine the Spaniard, who before she was married to my worthy father had been espoused to my father's elder brother. For this reason, she was divorced by my father."

"Why do you bypass Elizabeth?"

Cecil pricked up his ears, curious as to what argument had persuaded Edward to reject this perfect Protestant princess, albeit one who would never let Northumberland retain the control he craved.

"It was her fate to have Anne Boleyn for a mother, a woman cast off because she was more inclined to couple with a number of courtiers rather than reverencing her husband. Thus, in our judgment, neither she nor Mary deserves to be considered among the heirs of the King, our beloved father."

Cecil sniffed. Of course the son of Jane Seymour would believe the accusations against the King's second wife. Another display of Northumberland's evil genius.

The judges exchanged glances again.

"I demand Jane Grey be made my heir, demand that you draw up the letters patent of my will." Edward leaned forward and banged his own fist on the table. "You worry it might be treason to change the will of my late father; well, I tell you it is treason to refuse me now."

Northumberland nodded his approval, his mouth set. "What say you, gentlemen?"

Montague and the others leaned in and spoke with low voices. Try as Cecil might, he could not make out the words. Finally, Montague turned to the King. "I beg your pardon, Sire, we never intended to displease you. If you order us in writing – under the Great Seal of England – to take this action, it will not be treason. Though to be sure, you must issue us a pardon, also under the Great Seal, for having obeyed."

Cecil swallowed. That sounded like they were prepared to agree to this nonsense, the crazy notion of an underage boy. And the opportunism of an ambitious man loath to cede power.

Northumberland pointed at William Petre. "Do you have all that?"

"Aye, Sir," Petre said.

"Good," Northumberland said. "You and Cecil shall sit with Lord Montague after the meeting to draw up the documents with all the language he requires."

Cecil's mouth was dry as wool. How could he refuse? Northumberland was vindictive, as they had all seen.

If only Cecil hadn't returned to court.

CHAPTER 5

July 4, 1553

Elizabeth Tudor gazed out the window at the green-liveried messenger galloping towards Hatfield. She smoothed the front of her simple damask gown, a trick she had learned long ago to surreptitiously calm her nerves.

"He must be dead," Kat Ashley said, looking over Elizabeth's shoulder.

The flippant words plucked at Elizabeth's heart. "Hush, you mustn't say things like that," she said, with caution rather than rancor. Kat had embraced the loss of authority that came with her new role and was more reckless than ever.

"It's only treason if he is still alive," Kat said, keeping her eyes on the messenger who had just entered the courtyard. "And from what we hear of his sickness, he cannot be."

Reports spoke of giant tumors covering the youth's emaciated body, and black and bloody sputum projecting from his mouth. Kat was right, he was certainly dead. Elizabeth closed her eyes and said a prayer for her poor brother.

The messenger leaped from his horse, and Elizabeth sighed

before making her way to the center of the manor's Great Hall for the news that her sister Mary was Queen of England. A sobering thought, given Mary's rigid adherence to the Catholic faith. A scary thought, given Mary's obvious resentment of her younger sister. Things would certainly be different from now on.

The messenger entered, bowing only briefly. Kat bristled at the insult, but Elizabeth patted her arm to keep her silent. This was not the time to insist on full protocol.

"My Lady," he said, his nose in the air. "I bring a message from our good King."

Elizabeth felt Kat's quick glance but managed to keep her own eyes fixed on the newcomer. "My dear brother is recovering?" A soft smile graced her face. "The Lord be praised."

"Amen," the messenger said. "The Duke of Northumberland sent me to express the King's desire for your presence, as a comforting balm to help him heal still further."

The Duke of Northumberland. The man who had sent away her cortege and left her off the guest list for her cousin's wedding. "How kind of him," Elizabeth said, her mind casting frantically to understand the abrupt change.

"I have been given the honor of escorting you immediately to the royal presence."

The hair on her arms stood at the urgency but her smile did not waver. "Immediately?"

"Aye, my Lady. That was the word he used."

Elizabeth's mouth went dry as the clues united, and she placed a hand on her stomach. "That will not be possible, good sir. I have been ill lately. I would be in bed now but for your presence. I cannot travel – but more important, I could not risk approaching His Majesty right now. The danger would be too great."

The messenger's eyes widened. Elizabeth kept her silence while his mouth opened and closed as he tried to respond to this unexpected twist. She had given the one excuse that would override his orders.

Elizabeth swayed on her feet. "Kat, help me."

Kat put a reassuring arm around her and helped her to the chair in the corner.

Once Elizabeth was seated, she brought her hand to her mouth and coughed loudly before closing her eyes and sighing.

"My Lady?" Kat said, her voice quavering.

Elizabeth fluttered open her eyes and focused them on the messenger. "Good sir," she said to him, "please convey to my brother my great joy over his recovery. I have prayed every day to hear this news, and I thank the Lord you brought it. I shall count the seconds until I may come into his blessed presence again."

The messenger still looked bewildered. Kat grabbed him by the elbow and walked him to the door.

After she had closed it firmly behind him, she whirled around.

Elizabeth placed a finger over her lips to caution silence, beckoning Kat with the other hand. "I don't trust the message," Elizabeth said in a whisper.

"Why not?"

"Northumberland worked hard to keep me away. This sudden change of heart sits poorly with me."

Kat pursed her lips. "And he snubbed you with the wedding last month…" Her voice trailed off.

"It was more than a snub. Jane Grey is next in line to the throne, after me. Now she's married to his son – with both of them but sixteen, they still need a regent. Him."

"And the other two weddings added Pembroke and Huntingdon to the plot."

"Exactly."

"But Parliament has not been in session," Kat said. "He cannot subvert the Succession Act without a new vote.

"He controls the Council and the country. And he will make this travesty legal somehow," Elizabeth said. "It has happened before." She closed her eyes and saw her mother's face, the one from Holbein's sketch, staring off to the side with her lips pinched as if contemplating a dangerous future.

"But why bring you to London?" Kat asked.

"Somerset did the same when my father died: assembled all possible claimants before announcing the new reign. If you hold a person, they must bow to your plans," Elizabeth said.

"Which may include killing you," Kat said. "Like the princes in the Tower, suffocated to make way for a usurper."

Elizabeth started to pace to shake off her dread, but Kat jumped up to stop her. "We should get you to bed before they think to force you."

Elizabeth moaned loudly and allowed Kat to escort her to her rooms. Not that she thought that any in her household would betray her, but this way they could all truthfully swear to her pain.

If it came to that.

July 12, 1553

A slight thrumming suggested feet urgently running. Elizabeth opened her eyes and darted them around her bedchamber. Nerves stretched taut had turned her feigned illness into a real one, and only lying on her side with her eyes closed gave her stomach any relief.

The feet were getting closer; she could hear them in the hallway. They were light steps, women's steps. Elizabeth raised her head as Kat and Blanche burst into the room and rushed to Elizabeth's bed.

"We have just come from town," Blanche said. "And—"

"Jane Grey has been proclaimed Queen," Kat interrupted.

While the news was expected, the words snatched all hope

from Elizabeth. Much as she had guessed the truth, the hurt was real in a way it had not been earlier, the loss heavier than when she was merely trying it on.

"Of course," was all she said at first. Northumberland controlled every measure of power in England: the Council, the judges, the treasury, the Tower, the ships, and the artillery. Few men ceded that kind of control. "At least I didn't obey their summons," she added. "I would be a prisoner now."

"And they're letting you be," Kat said. "I pray that will continue." She looked around and dropped her voice. "There is a rumor that Northumberland intends to put away his wife and marry you. Could this be another reason he has left you in peace?"

"God help me," Elizabeth said, then thought a moment. Crazy rumors always surfaced in circumstances like these. Sometimes the craziest ones turned out to be true. She sighed, thinking of the last man accused of proposing to her, but shook off the melancholy to focus on the situation at hand. "I don't think that brings him much: he already has his puppet, and my claim means nothing while Mary lives," Elizabeth said hesitantly, praying she was right.

Then a thought bolted her upright. "Mary! Do they hold Mary?"

Blanche slapped her palm on the coverlet. "That's what I started to say. Mary has fled to Kenninghall Castle. She means to fight."

Kenninghall was in Norfolk, the most Catholic part of the country, the safest place for her.

"Well, she'll find supporters there," Elizabeth said. "Though I can't imagine she could win; they've had two rebellions fail."

"Fortune might well shine upon the third," Blanche said.

Elizabeth slumped. "There aren't enough Catholics to overcome Northumberland's advantage. He controls London and the South; that's all the strength he needs."

"Forty thousand men joined the Pilgrimage of Grace," Kat said.

"Almost twenty years ago, and much good it did them," Elizabeth said. "Four years ago, only sixteen thousand rebelled with Kett – and they were fighting the enclosures as well the prayer books."

"I'll still pray for Mary to win," Blanche said. "It's the right order. But more important, her victory is your only hope for the succession."

The stomachache that Elizabeth had forgotten about during the excitement came rushing back like a wave to the shore, and she pulled the covers around her chin. "I just thank God I am safely here, away from it all."

Blanche winced. "I worry you will come to regret not standing with your sister to preserve your rights."

"Supporting Mary is supporting an insurrection against the sovereign," Elizabeth said. "That way leads only to death."

"Jane is not the rightful sovereign," Blanche leaned earnestly towards her. "Supporting her leads to death as well."

Elizabeth gave a small shake of her head. "I am not supporting Jane; I am not supporting anyone. Yet."

She patted her chest and a small burp offered relief. She picked at a pull in the light wool blanket as she sought to explain the lesson that kept repeating itself in her life. "The safest solution is always to delay until the situation shows the path."

"That is not always possible," Blanche said.

"No, but waiting until the last possible minute is. Look how well it has served me already," Elizabeth said. "Time offers the ultimate strategy. I pray I am always given the chance to use its gifts."

July 18, 1553

William Cecil stood to acknowledge the entry of the Lord Mayor of London and deputation of aldermen invited to join the meeting of Queen Jane's Council. William Herbert, Earl of Pembroke and one of Northumberland's closest allies, had summoned every man of import in London to his magnificent stronghold, Baynard Castle. Cecil initially found it curious that Pembroke had chosen this venue rather than the Tower where the court was stationed, but then decided it was meant to show the strength of Northumberland's coalition. And keep it together.

Cecil tucked an errant strand of hair behind his ear as he sat. He picked up his quill to be ready, and shifted the inkpot closer to the still-blank page. He and William Petre had been named Secretaries to Queen Jane's Council: all Edward's officers had been kept in their posts to obscure the change to a new reign. It also made them all complicit in the coup. Cecil pressed his lips together.

"Gentlemen," Pembroke began. Cecil dipped his nib.

"I believe you know that the Duke of Northumberland rode out yesterday with fifteen hundred men and a small artillery train to subdue the rebels," Pembroke said.

The Duke of Suffolk, Queen Jane's father, leaned forward. "He should have gone right away, before Mary was able to rally any supporters, but Godspeed him now."

In fact, Northumberland had tried for several days to send Suffolk on this very errand, but Queen Jane had insisted her father remain with her. No one had been able to dissuade her from this mistake.

"That may not be enough," the Lord Mayor said. "They say three thousand have flocked to Mary's banner."

"Farmers with pikes cannot stand up to soldiers with guns." Suffolk waved a dismissive hand. "Especially with England's greatest general at the helm."

"And surely more men to send him if he needs," said Archbishop Thomas Cranmer. Cranmer's objections to King Edward's Devise had ceased once it was sanctioned by law: after the sanctioning, objections were treason. It was the boat they were all in, oaring as hard as they could toward the banner that promised them safety.

Pembroke raised a hand. "Gentlemen, stop. This is why I asked you here: Northumberland has already written to request more troops. He wants five thousand men."

"Well then, we must authorize them," Suffolk said. "Arundel, Pembroke, the three of us alone can supply all he needs."

The Earl of Arundel, sighed. "Perhaps not. Men are turning to Mary's banner by the thousands – including sailors on the ships that Northumberland sent to guard the Norfolk coast. My Lord Mayor, you said three thousand stood with Mary – the figure I have heard is closer to twenty."

Twenty thousand? Was such a number possible? Even half that would be a dangerous movement. Cecil worked to calm himself, still shocked at Northumberland's carelessness. Cecil remembered Somerset's caution, six years ago, in the transfer of power to a new King Edward. Somerset had taken no chances that someone would step in to disrupt the legal machinery, even though the succession was unquestioned. Northumberland should have made sure he held Mary long before Edward died. Instead, he had waited until the boy's last breath, then sent his self-indulgent son Robert with only three hundred men, barely an honor escort.

"Surely twenty thousand is a great exaggeration," Suffolk said. "Or Northumberland would have asked for a larger force. The five thousand should be enough."

"I have none to send," Arundel said.

"Nor do I," Pembroke added.

Suffolk blanched but recovered quickly. "Well, reinforcements will arrive soon from France."

"Just because we asked? Don't be naïve," Arundel said. "Why would France back Northumberland's ambition? That Catholic country might well rejoice to see Mary on the throne."

The smirk in his voice reminded Cecil that Arundel's nominal allegiance to Northumberland obscured his long friendship with Mary. Cecil's stomach turned over as he heard Northumberland's coalition begin to collapse like dough left too long to rise. This was undoubtedly why Northumberland had tried to avoid leaving to take the field in the first place, knowing he needed to be here to keep the Council in line.

Cranmer stood. Spreading his arms as if inviting them into one of his sermons, he tried to herd the room into obedience. "All the more reason to stand firm. Remember the holy oaths we swore to uphold the last wishes of our beloved King Edward."

Cecil bowed his head. King Edward had indeed been beloved, but his wishes had been manipulated throughout his reign.

"And our holy oaths to my daughter," Suffolk said.

Arundel slapped his hand on the desk. "Enough! We were all worried about the legality of King Edward's Devise for the Succession. More and more, these fears appear well founded. If the country supports Mary, it seems to me that we must too." He looked around the table. "Or accept death for our treason."

The Councilors paled. All of them.

"Our decisions are protected by the law," said John Cheke.

Arundel's eyes gleamed. "The law is fluid. The victor will decide whether we are traitors."

Shock silenced the room. Cecil held his breath, watching the men exchange glances.

Pembroke shook his head as if making a sudden decision. "Well, gentlemen, our choice is clear." He stood and drew his sword. "If the arguments of my Lord of Arundel do not persuade you, this sword shall make Mary Queen, or I will die in her quarrel."

Northumberland's ardent supporter, father-in-law to Katherine Grey, had just been the first to place himself firmly in Mary's camp. The rest of the room hurried to join him with their own shouts of approbation.

Pembroke's choice to meet at Baynard took on a different meaning: he had been open to defection from the start, to save his neck, The shock of such a quick and complete reversal reverberated through Cecil's brain and made the quill in his hand tremble. He threw down the symbol of his position with what was now a traitorous body.

Thomas Goodrich, the Lord Chancellor, stood. "Gentlemen, I can no longer perform my office properly." He picked up his purse to take out the Great Seal of England and placed it before Arundel. "I beg you, my Lord, please carry this to Queen Mary, to be disposed of as Her Majesty shall deem proper."

Cecil raised his head: he needed to be another early swell in this wave. "The Council must formally declare for Mary. We have not yet done so."

Arundel pointed at him. "Write it up now, so we can ride through the streets to proclaim her at Paul's Cross and all the principal stations of the city. After that, Paget and I will go to her and beg forgiveness on behalf of us all."

Paget. Another man who had long supported Mary, another man who had been close to Somerset. That boded well for Cecil. Better than Arundel, anyway: Paget was more likely to remember that Cecil had suggested proclaiming Mary. Friendship always influenced memory; Cecil would help it along. "What shall we do with Northumberland?" he asked.

"That is simple," Arundel sniffed. "Inform him that we consider Mary our true Queen, and order him to desist his efforts on behalf of Jane Grey."

"I will order the horses," Suffolk said.

Cecil picked his quill back up. As he dipped it into the inkpot, he noticed his hands were no longer trembling.

July 30, 1553

Elizabeth's black jennet swung its head from side to side; she leaned forward in her leather and velvet saddle and patted its neck reassuringly. Beaulieu's red brick chimneys had been visible for quite some time above the trees, but the woods had finally begun to thin. "Almost there, she whispered.

She was on her way to kneel to Mary and offer her loyalty, here, before the new Queen left for London to formally claim her throne. Elizabeth had managed to assemble an escort of two thousand horses to London, all in her own version of the Tudor green and white, a show of force from Northumberland's other intended victim. Now she rode to Beaulieu with a small personal retinue: Parry, Blanche, and Kat joined her on horseback; fifty more followed behind in coaches and carts. She had chosen this number carefully, to seem substantial yet neither inconvenient nor threatening to the sister who had defied the odds.

The smell of roasting meat caught her attention. Just ahead of her on the trail, Parry turned around in his saddle. "It should be no more than a mile or so now."

The aroma grew with each step closer to Mary's palace, as did sounds of celebration. Laughter and splutters of well-wishes, clinking of goblets and jugs and whatever people had in hand. When the woods finally fell away, the vista revealed people thronging Beaulieu's massive fields amid small piles of unused stakes and swords that dotted the landscape.

Elizabeth slowed her horse to a walk, smiling at the people she passed, the men and women who had come to wait upon Mary and loudly proclaim their loyalty to the rightful heir. England's people, England's voice, refusing to be silenced by an opportunistic politician.

"The world is here," Blanche said. "Even those who originally supported Jane Grey."

Kat laughed. "Especially those who originally supported Jane

Grey. They came before Her Majesty could change her mind about pardoning them."

Mary had shocked the world by accepting all the defectors from Queen Jane's banner. Their grandfather Henry VII had shown similar mercy on his accession in order not to squander the resources he had only just come into. Their father had taken the opposite tack, condemning men after only a single mistake.

"Hush," Elizabeth said. She was not in the mood for jests. She wanted to revel in this demonstration of the English spirit. The people had never shown much love to Mary, and most of them likely did not approve of popery, but still they had fought to vanquish her challenger.

Elizabeth pressed her lips together, to make sure her thoughts could not somehow escape her lips. At almost thirty-seven years old, Mary was old to have a first child – if she could have one at all. Elizabeth could actually see her own hazy path ahead to the throne of England.

She swallowed hard to shove down the surge of emotion. Covetousness was the root of all sins. She had seen how hope could vanish in a flash. This might be taken from her, as it almost was before, as it once was from her mother.

The crowd continued to thicken as Elizabeth's retinue approached the bottleneck that was the Beaulieu gatehouse, but her group was waved through with smiles and good wishes. "God bless you, Princess," people called out as she passed.

She smiled at the title, even though it was premature. Mary had argued during their brother's reign that the heir apparent should be referred to as Princess of England; by her same logic, Elizabeth should have that title now. But monarchs were often capricious. And Mary and Elizabeth had not been close in recent years.

Regardless, it was nice to hear how the people loved her. Mary had just proved how great a protection that was. "God bless you," Elizabeth called back.

Inside the courtyard it was a little easier to move. Tom Parry stopped his horse and pointed to a short, wiry fellow standing by the chapel gate, brown hair flecked with grey over a thin face with pink cheeks. "I see your cousin," he said to Blanche. "Will! Hey, Will!"

William Cecil whirled around and waved and immediately made his way towards them.

Elizabeth shaded her eyes to see better. He seemed older. Perhaps it was just worry she read on his face.

Cecil grabbed her bridle with one hand and signaled a stableboy with the other. When he could not get anyone's attention, he started to walk Elizabeth's horse toward the side. "Follow me," he said to the others.

Elizabeth relaxed, happy for the opportunity to observe her surroundings.

"Your timing was good," Cecil said over his shoulder. "Any later and you'd be racing after Mary to London."

"I wanted to make sure to kneel to her here," Elizabeth said. "Filled with God's grace at the news of her victory."

Cecil shot her a heavy-lidded glance before pointing at the doorway to the East wing, where the crowd was thickest. "That is where you will find the Queen."

Cecil hailed a groom and handed him Elizabeth's reins before helping her dismount. When she was balanced on the ground, he leaned in, his face serious. "I will think no less of you for avoiding me after this, as some others have done. The Queen never liked me, and while she has been blessedly merciful, she is unlikely to show me favor for the foreseeable future. I do not want my friends tarred with my brush."

"My loyalty will not be in doubt," she said, patting his hand. "And I cannot really believe yours will be either. You are welcomed here now; keep faith."

"'Those who seek the Lord understand justice,'" Cecil said, turning to help Blanche and Kat. Cecil had always been able to build his cases upon verses from Scripture. It would serve him well with this new reign.

Elizabeth turned to walk towards the East wing, smiling and greeting people as the crowd opened to let her pass. She considered waiting for Kat and Blanche but decided that Mary would appreciate excitement more than formality. They would catch up soon enough.

The crowd thinned from the other side, and Elizabeth was surprised to see a small purple orb of a woman speeding towards her. The crowd parted, cheering and kneeling hurriedly. It was Mary. "Sister, Sister," she cried as she ran, arms outstretched.

"Your Majesty," Elizabeth said, falling to her knees. "I praise God for this blessed sight and the opportunity to proclaim your rightful title."

Mary was quickly upon her, reaching down to touch her shoulders. "Rise, child, and embrace me."

Thrilled by such warmth, Elizabeth swept to her feet, gracefully leaning down to hug her heavyset sister.

The people cheered and Mary looked around to address them. Already she exuded the confidence of established authority. Reaching her arms to the sky, she declared, "See here, my people, the two daughters of that noble King, Henry VIII, whom foul traitors ignored at their peril. The Lord has brought us here, and you, for which we shall give Him proper thanks, this day and always."

Despite the effusive welcome, Elizabeth felt a small chill at the thought of what her sister Mary would consider "proper" thanks. Mary's identity was steeped in Catholicism, in loyalty to the Church that still held her mother's marriage valid.

Elizabeth put aside her trepidation: surely Mary would be tolerant after suffering under their brother's Protestant reign.

Once the cheers had died down, Mary turned back for a more private conversation. "You have arrived just in time, Sister. We leave tomorrow for London."

"The news makes my heart sing," Elizabeth said. She bowed low. "I thank God for preserving you in this fight. And for confounding the Duke of Northumberland."

"'It is the Lord's doing, and it is marvelous in our eyes,'" Mary said.

The Psalm was well chosen, an effective way of framing the narrative. And highly appropriate, given that the Lord must have had something to do with Mary's impossible victory. Elizabeth would have chosen the line directly preceding it: *The stone which the builders refused is become the head stone of the corner.* But that triumph stemmed from bitterness; Mary's was better. "Amen," Elizabeth said.

"Have you heard he hopes for mercy?" Mary asked, her voice a catty whine.

"'The Lord hates a heart that devises wicked plans,'" Elizabeth said. Cecil and Mary were not the only ones who could quote Scripture.

Mary sniffed. "When he received the Council's notice that they had declared for me, he himself proclaimed me Queen on the spot, throwing up his cap as though he were thrilled." Her lip curled. "And laughed so hard that the tears ran down his cheeks for grief."

Appeased as Elizabeth was by the justice, she still felt a chill. It was hard not to be sobered by someone's recognition that they would soon die a traitor's death. "Was he arrested then?"

"Arundel arrived the next day to escort him to the Tower."

The next day. Northumberland would have known the country was against him, would have known the ports were closed and that he had nowhere to go even if he could board a ship. Elizabeth's mind watched him waiting, still free but knowing his sentence was even then imposed. She stifled a shiver – she did not want her own distress to look like pity. Traitors never deserved pity, and those who gave it were themselves suspect. "To very different lodgings than when he left, I hope."

"The entire Dudley family has been moved to the Beauchamp Tower. There will be ample room there soon – I intend to free everyone but them."

The laughing faces of her childhood friends appeared before Elizabeth's eyes and she worked hard to hide her sadness. "That is merciful." The words sounded inane to Elizabeth's ears, but she could think of nothing else to say.

"You shall ride with me tomorrow, by my side," Mary said. "Sisters both, lion cubs both, to make the people rejoice."

Elizabeth bowed her head. "I am honored."

PART TWO: MUCH SUSPECTED

CHAPTER 6

August 3, 1553

Mary made good on her promise, keeping Elizabeth at her side during the entire joyous march to London. Elizabeth exulted over being allowed to share in the powerful narrative of Great Harry's two daughters avenging his throne from the usurpers.

Thousands of people thronged the streets, singing and clapping as they watched the sisters ride by. Elizabeth raised an arm to wave, and hundreds threw their caps into the air. Elation filled her heart at their support, and she had to remind herself that this was Mary's triumph, not hers. She had to be grateful for this moment alone, without wishing or hoping for what might ensue…

As they approached the Aldgate entrance to the City, Elizabeth was struck by the vision of the Mayor of London and his aldermen seated on magnificent grey destriers and surrounded by guards with bows and javelins, waiting to formally welcome their rightful ruler. Gaily colored streamers – hundreds of them –

fluttered around the gate. Past its open doors beckoned a white road, specially laid with gravel for a legendary occasion.

"Good day, my lords," Mary called as she approached in a gown of purple velvet, its kirtle thick with goldsmiths' work. But it was her baldrick set with great pearls that Elizabeth most admired.

The officials bowed deeply and the crowds copied them, cries of "God Save the Queen" bursting from loyal breasts. All the breasts were loyal now, all the world pretending they had never bowed to Queen Jane. Mary had continued to accept excuses from people abandoning Northumberland late in the game – even Suffolk had been pardoned – and she had promised religious tolerance. No one could fail to rejoice on this day.

"And God save the Princess Elizabeth," yelled a voice. Elizabeth smiled broadly and waved again, causing the cheer to echo even more loudly. Mary turned, eyes narrowed, but cheers resumed for her and the moment passed.

The Earl of Arundel began the formal welcome, his role a clear reward for his longstanding loyalty. He reared his horse loudly, and his cape billowed with the grace his own squat form usually lacked. With all attention on him, Arundel stepped his horse to the front, where the Mayor awaited him.

The Mayor waved two of his guards forward. The first brought the sword of state, laid sideways on a purple cushion; he lifted it carefully to present it to Arundel. The second brought the mace, similarly ensconced, and presented it to the Mayor. When the two officials had the symbols of royalty and legitimacy properly displayed, they nodded to the trumpeters, whose tantara would accompany the procession all the way to the Tower.

As Arundel and the Mayor passed through the gate, artillery thundered a welcome from the ramparts, and church bells pealed in celebration. The clamor continued well after Mary's entrance and accompanied the aldermen, the guards, and all the rest who followed. More than three thousand on their horses – eight hundred of them nobles and other gentlemen wearing the green and white of the Tudors, the red and white of dress uniforms, or even the blue and green of Mary's personal standard – turned the road into a sea of color.

The retinue proceeded through the crowd, Mary making an uncharacteristic show of returning every wave and accepting every bouquet held out to her. That slowed their pace, and the trek that should have taken no more than fifteen minutes extended to over an hour. Elizabeth, right on Mary's heels, maintained a delighted smile even as the air grew thicker with cloying floral notes.

Elizabeth's smile was further challenged by a growing sense of unease as they neared the Tower. She had never been this close to the fortress that had claimed the lives of so many people she loved, and she had to stifle a shudder when the greying bricks of the White Tower came into view.

Elizabeth shook off the distress: this was a time for gratitude. This was the time to let the compound's ghosts rest – nay, more than rest: exult. She was next in line to the throne, and while experience had shown her that anything could happen, only a child born to unmarried, thirty-seven-year-old sister could dislodge Elizabeth's place in the succession.

Elizabeth widened the smile on her face and banished the terror from her eyes as they passed under the sharp metal spikes of the gate's portcullis. She kept telling herself that the day was no less bright inside the battlements, but still a chill invaded her bones. She widened her smile again despite the ache in her cheeks.

A crowd awaited in the yard to greet the cortege: servants and yeomen to one side, Councilors and courtiers to the other. Anne of Cleves at the forefront, a place of honor for their father's fourth wife. She knelt deeply. "I am blessed to see this day."

Mary dismounted and went to kiss her stepmother, inviting

Elizabeth to join this family moment. "You must ride together at my coronation," Mary said. The crowd applauded.

Next came the ancient ritual: the forgiving of prisoners. In the middle of the yard, four carefully chosen inmates knelt in a row, waiting patiently. This was their moment of redemption, and their smiles betrayed their confidence.

First to be raised was the eighty-year-old Thomas Howard, former Duke of Norfolk, who had escaped death in the final hours of Henry VIII's reign. He was a small man, about Mary's height, and she embraced him warmly, promising the return of his former leadership of the traditionalists. As Mary moved on to the next humble supplicant, Norfolk gave Elizabeth a twisted smile of support. For all her disgrace, Anne Boleyn had been a Howard.

Next came twenty-six-year-old Edward Courtenay, another prisoner who had escaped death. In 1539, he was imprisoned with his father, the late Marquis of Exeter, for little more than having royal blood. Exeter was executed but Courtenay, then a child, was allowed to mature in surroundings that offered little chance to cultivate his mind: Courtenay was good-looking, but vapid. Mary kissed him on both cheeks and told him that he would have an earldom. He simpered at the news, and, when Mary moved on, his face settled into a haughty grimace at Elizabeth, rather than a kind smile. Perhaps he had heard how people were already suggesting him as a good husband for Mary. Either way, Elizabeth did not like him.

The third prisoner scrambled to his feet. Stephen Gardiner, the former Bishop of Winchester, was a spry seventy-year-old who towered over most men. A Catholic who had tried to bring down Katherine Parr, the orthodoxy that had lost him his post under Edward VI was now transformed into virtue. Triumph shone from Gardiner's face, and Elizabeth had to look away from the man who would have killed her beloved stepmother.

"You shall have far more than your former bishopric, my Lord," Mary said. "You shall be my Lord Chancellor."

Gardiner made the sign of the cross and bowed his head as she moved on. He didn't acknowledge Elizabeth, didn't even glance at her.

The final prisoner to be raised was Anne Seymour, Duchess of Somerset until her husband's attainder. Promised her old honors, she, too, snubbed Elizabeth, adding another shadow to the already dimmed day.

Mary turned to the crowd. "These people are prisoners no longer. I order their immediate discharge and command their utter loyalty to my reign."

People surged forward to congratulate the group, and Elizabeth found herself ignored. Out of the corner of her eye, the Beauchamp Tower loomed. That would be where the Dudleys were lodged. As angry as she was at Northumberland's treachery, her heart went out to her friends, caught in the web spun by their father.

For that very reason, she avoided looking in their direction. Contempt could be displayed, but not pity.

Even if it was unlikely to be noticed.

August 8, 1553

William Cecil looked up from his prayers to the somber sights surrounding him. The walls and aisles of the Lady Chapel in Westminster Abbey had been completely covered in black cloth to mourn the dead King. At the altar, Archbishop Thomas Cranmer presided in his purple cassock, the carved pendants of the fan-vaulted ceiling framing his head like a halo.

Cecil faced the chapel entrance, where the pallbearers had paused to allow Edward's choristers to begin chanting the psalm that would accompany his final journey. The progress down the aisle was slow and careful, to avoid jolting the life-sized effigy atop the casket. Carved by the Italian sculptor Niccolo Bellini, the figure was arrayed in silver and gold, holding a jeweled scepter and wearing a crown. It offered the only splash of color in the somber nave.

As the wood statue passed by, its face as earnest and tender as the boy himself had been, people moaned and lamented loudly – but Cecil held his silence. So recently under suspicion, he could not chance such a public display. He merely stood, his blinks restraining grief over the future being entombed with this dead monarch.

Not just England's future, but Cecil's own. The new Queen had accepted William Petre as a secretary of the Council, but not Cecil. Today, Cecil was seated with the congregation rather than the honored guests. He sighed. He was alive and free; he would make it back. Eventually. Happily he had not overspent while he was still in favor.

As the procession reached Elizabeth's row, she swayed slightly, offering her own example of appropriate public grief, one that would call minimal attention to her presence at a service that was already straining Mary's promise of religious tolerance.

When the casket reached the magnificent altar, the one Henry VII had commissioned from the great Pietro Torrigiano, it was placed on a bier draped in seventy-two yards of black velvet, surrounded by tapers on thirteen branched stone pillars. Like the music, candles were a Catholic encroachment on the ceremony, but at least the staunchly Protestant King was not being buried with a Mass.

Cecil had been shocked at how contentious that compromise had been. William Paget, happy to gossip with his old friend, had shared how Mary had wanted to bury her brother with Catholic rites, so that his soul might be welcomed into the Heaven she believed in. But her advisors, to a man, had warned of a backlash against such highhanded treatment. Even Charles V had urged her to allow Edward to be buried in the faith in which he'd lived.

Unfortunately, no one could dissuade her from having a Catholic service of the dead performed for him in her own chapel. At this very moment, in the Tower, Stephen Gardiner was saying a Requiem for the boy King, and Gardiner would say more Masses over the next few days to save the lad from the Purgatory that scared Mary.

Cecil composed himself as Cranmer stepped forward to deliver the service from the *Book of Common Prayer* that young Edward had so proudly pressed on the realm. Tears fell from Cranmer's eyes as he read the words he himself had written and with which he was burying his beloved godson. Cecil's heart went out to him, to all of them in this chapel, defying the future that Mary was sure to impose on them.

Too quickly, Cranmer finished. Edward's body was lowered into the white marble vault that awaited him. The attendants who followed broke their staves of office and threw them into the chasm. The hollow sound was followed by a sigh that seemed to come from the entire church.

It was truly ended now.

September 7, 1553

"Wait for me," Elizabeth said to her ladies before walking into the octagonal Council Chamber. Like the other royal apartments at Richmond Palace, the sunlit room overlooked a large internal courtyard. But this was not the time to admire the view. She had been summoned to meet with a group of Councilors and she needed all her wits to withstand the pressure they would undoubtedly place on her.

She scanned the faces crowded around the table – Gardiner, Arundel, Derby, Sussex, the Bishop of Duresme. All Catholics.

Mary's initial gratitude to her supporters had led her to promise that people would be allowed to worship as they chose. But every day she spent on the throne added to her conviction that the Lord had given her victory to return His flock to the fold of Rome. She was now moving quickly to impose papism throughout the land, hastening the departure of thousands of French, Flemish, and German Protestants that had flooded to England during Edward's reign. Many of her early supporters were seeing their jubilation turn to fear and anger.

Elizabeth forced a smile onto her face. "Gentlemen," she said with a small curtsy.

The group deferred to Gardiner to reply, the man to whom Mary had entrusted supreme religious and secular power. "My Lady," he said, with a nod.

"How may I help you?" Elizabeth asked. Realizing how hard her voice sounded, she adopted a friendlier tone. "Is this a way of celebrating my birthday?"

A mean smile flitted across Gardiner's face. "Why would we do that?" He shook his head. "No, we ordered you here because we have reason to be concerned about your religious practices."

Even though she had expected this accusation, she had to stifle a gag. "What have I done that might concern you?"

"It is what you have *not* done," Gardiner said. "You have not attended Mass."

"I pray every day for the belief that will allow me to do that. Until then, it would dishonor my soul to dissemble."

No need to mention that she did not intend that day would ever come. Elizabeth recoiled at the idea of embracing a religion that bastardized her. She also worried what the people would say if she capitulated to the Catholics. Now that she could see a path to the throne before her, she wanted to keep it clear. Reform had dug deep during the past twenty years, deeper than Mary recognized, and the people looked to Elizabeth to stand firm for them, as Mary had stood for the Catholic voice during

Edward's reign. Elizabeth needed to avoid the Mass as best she could.

Gardiner sneered. "Dissemble?"

"I was raised in a different faith," she said.

"You were raised in exactly this faith," Gardiner said. "The Mass you are expected to attend is no more than the one your father mandated. You have no excuse."

Like a horse being dragged too hard by its bridle, Elizabeth reared. "When I was the tender age of eight, my father married a woman who taught me to question traditional doctrine," she said. "And my father himself told me he expected his son to push reforms still further, which indeed my brother did. I have been a long time in the new learning, and it will take some time for my heart to embrace popery."

"It is not popery," Gardiner said.

Elizabeth raised her chin. "I have heard talk of a return to Rome."

Gardiner scowled at her down the length of the table. "Gossip about a potential future does not affect your obligations in the present."

"I cannot without belief," she said. Surely that would be enough for a churchman.

"Your belief is irrelevant. This concerns your attendance."

Elizabeth ignored the burning eyes. Gardiner was a bully. "Surely my sister will show me the same courtesy that our brother showed to her during his reign. She was never required to attend Reform services."

"Your brother made no secret of his intention to deprive his subjects of the Mass," Gardiner said. "I spent most of his reign in the Tower for failing to comply with his government's heresies. And the Queen almost suffered my same fate."

"But she did not," Elizabeth said. "She continued to hear Mass."

"The courtesy stemmed not from her position but from the

King's age. Our Queen is an adult and entitled to compliance." Gardiner leaned in, threatening. "You will attend Mass tomorrow."

He spoke the last sentence in a normal tone of voice, but it hit her like a shout. She stood there, open-mouthed, remembering how Edward had softened at Mary's tears. Only now did Elizabeth realize that Mary would be harsher.

"The people will see you bend your knee, or they will see you punished for it," Gardiner continued. "The choice is yours."

The calm with which he spoke, and the line he had drawn, shook Elizabeth to the core. With stakes such as these, she had no choice. She would find ways to let her followers know her heart was not in it.

"I will attend Mass tomorrow," she said.

The triumphant smile on Gardiner's face was twisted by his sneer. "Fine. We will see you then."

She curtsied and left quickly, her ladies quickly falling in behind her. When they were halfway down the hallway, Catherine Knollys whispered loudly. "What happened?"

Elizabeth shook her head and held her tongue until they were back in her apartments and the door was closed. Only then did Elizabeth close her eyes and allow the tears to well. "I had to agree to attend Mass."

"How will you do this?"

"I can sit in a pew without engaging my soul," Elizabeth said. Observance did not require belief, it only rendered to Caesar the things that were his. Elizabeth's martyrdom would serve no one, least of all the Lord.

"What of the rest of us?" Catherine asked. "What of me?"

Elizabeth bit her lip. "Mary will insist you join me." Elizabeth believed that with all her heart. Catherine was probably their half-sister, however strongly the secret was denied, however deep it was buried.

A tear slid down Catherine's cheek. "What if I refuse?"

"You will be punished. We are to be examples to the world."

"Francis said it would come to this," Catherine said, shivering. "He leaves for Geneva next week to see about creating a haven for English reformists."

"You would rather leave England than submit?" Elizabeth asked.

"It is different for us," Catherine said. "You have too much here to lose."

Elizabeth recalled her brother's reign, the rumors that Mary had considered escaping to Spain. Had she done so, Jane Grey would still be Queen of England, permanently ensconced on the throne she had stolen. If Elizabeth left, she would forfeit all rights.

"What about your children?" Blanche asked Catherine. "What will you do with them?"

"Francis is taking Henry with him now," Catherine replied. "If we do flee, the children will come with us – they run as great a risk as we do."

They all fell quiet as they contemplated the fear that had spurred such a solution. Finally, Elizabeth spoke. "Neither distance of place nor length of time can separate the love of friends. Whatever happens, I wish you all godspeed."

"I hope it does not come to this," Catherine said. "I would hate to leave you."

Elizabeth patted her friend's arm. "My heart may break over your absence, but you will never be far from its pieces. And if you need anything, I will make sure you get it."

"Thank you," Catherine said. "So many have promised the same."

"Let others promise, and I will do," Elizabeth said. "My power may be small, but I believe in deeds over words. And I would never forget or abandon you."

November 29, 1553

Cold anger settled on Elizabeth as she stared at her hands folded on the pew cap rail. Nauseous, she wanted to breathe deeply to calm her roiling stomach, but the cloying incense fueled her revulsion and forced her to breathe shallowly. It was an impossible predicament, and it was all Mary's fault.

Elizabeth leaned her head to her shoulder and cracked her neck. Usually she avoided such common gestures, at least in public, but she needed the release. The priest was approaching the part of the Mass that never failed to drive Elizabeth's resentment: its apogee, the moment when the bread and wine were said to become the body and blood of their savior. Not a sanctified representation, but the actual body and blood of the Son of Man crucified more than fifteen hundred years before.

Elizabeth squirmed in her pew. She hated that her supporters would think she had lost faith. It was not fair.

And it was not legal. Parliament – bless their souls – had resisted Mary's worst urgings. Although they had returned the Church service to the form Henry VIII had given it, they had refused to compel attendance. Not that it stopped Mary from insisting on the submission of those around her.

For the hundredth time, Elizabeth questioned whether she should or could leave court. In restoring the Mass, Parliament had also overturned the Great Divorce, making Elizabeth even more of a bastard than her father had made her. Though they had left her heir apparent.

Religious zeal mixed with the anger in her breast and pushed Elizabeth to act. She groaned loudly, and several people turned around. "What is it?" Kat asked.

"My stomach aches."

The Latin droning continued, and the people returned to their worship. Someone in the back giggled, and the sound fueled Elizabeth's sense of theater. "I feel I will faint from the pain."

"Don't agitate yourself." Kat rubbed Elizabeth's stomach. "Is this better?"

"*Hoc est corpus meum*," said the priest, raising the Host high above his head.

Elizabeth groaned again and let her ladies fuss over her in full sight of the worshippers approaching the altar to receive communion.

Finally, the Mass was ended. As soon as she could, Elizabeth made her way down the aisle. A figure in the last row stood: the French Ambassador, Antoine, Comte de Noailles.

"May I offer my hand?" he asked. "I fear you may need some assistance after such pains."

Elizabeth smiled. With Mary favoring Spain, the French had befriended Elizabeth.

Her first allies were definitely a better-looking lot than the Spaniards, though Noailles himself was not handsome. His Gallic nose was too large and his forehead had receded so far on both sides of his temples as to give him a small skullcap of hair on his forehead. But his confident intelligence and his calculated gallantry could have overcome much worse looks.

Elizabeth nodded and allowed him to lead her out of the chapel.

"Perhaps some air might do you good?" he said.

In truth, the ending of the Mass had dissipated all her frustration and anger, and she was feeling better already. "I believe it would," she said.

Noailles said nothing, just started walking towards the gardens. When they had passed the shrub with vibrant red berries that signaled the entrance to the quiet back *allée*, he turned to her but his eyes turned further, looking behind her at Kat and Blanche who followed a few steps behind. "I know you trust them," he said in a low voice. "But have them give us some room."

Elizabeth turned to her ladies. "Perhaps the two of you would like to sit while we walk?" The two curtsied and walked to a nearby bench.

Noailles put out his hand again and they began to stroll. "So, what is it you have to tell me that cannot be overheard?" Elizabeth asked playfully. Coquetry was always an effective tone, especially with a Frenchman.

"Just advice," the Ambassador said.

"Advice?"

"You should leave court."

Despite the menace, or perhaps because of it, Elizabeth maintained a teasing tone. "Would you not miss me?"

He fiddled with his earring. "The court will soon become a dangerous place. You should be far from it."

"More treacherous than now?" Her tone no longer teased.

"You know, yes, that the Queen intends to marry Philip of Spain?"

Elizabeth did know that. As Ned Seymour had said all those years ago, Mary was too old for Philip. But this sounded more like gossip than warning.

"Why is that dangerous for me?"

"It has dislodged discontent. A great deal of discontent." Noailles glanced behind him. "The English people resent the religious changes the Queen has imposed, they despise her choice of husband, they refuse to allow England to become a vassal of Spain. I have it from excellent sources that they intend to replace her."

Shock, fear, and awe exploded in Elizabeth's brain and muddled her thinking. The French Ambassador had just shared treasonous plans. Perhaps she had misunderstood? That would be her defense…

She swallowed to loosen the muscles in her throat, which had closed protectively to stop her from saying something stupid. But she needed to respond. "I cannot imagine such a thing," she said.

"Perhaps you cannot, but others have," he said.

"I cannot listen to this," she said.

"I do nothing but pass on rumors. Surely this cannot implicate you."

They walked in silence for several paces under the interlaced linden trees. Fallen leaves crunched beneath their feet, but a few golden stragglers still clung resolutely to their branches.

"Why would men pass on such rumors?" she finally asked.

He gave a little bow. "I am the ideal accomplice. I can promise an army to help, yet I cannot be tortured into betraying secrets. The worst punishment for me is exile."

More silent walking as Elizabeth's mind raced over the revelations, all colored by the fact that the French Dauphin was betrothed to Mary Stuart, the Scottish Queen – who had an excellent claim to the English throne. It was in France's interest to encourage revolt; there might be nothing behind this.

"I find it hard to believe that anyone in England would prefer the prospect of French control to Spanish rule," she said.

Noailles paused to laugh. He exaggerated his mirth, grasping his stomach and bending over. Finally, he straightened and wiped a fake tear from his eye. "Ah, Princess, not at all. England wants to see you as its Queen, married to Edward Courtenay instead of a foreigner."

Marry Courtenay? The thought was repugnant. "His face is pretty, but his mind is empty," she said. "Is he a part of this?"

"I would be a poor ally if I named the conspirators. My main purpose is to keep you safe. You need to be far from court, far from the royal clutches when the rising occurs. They could too easily accuse you of being involved and execute you quickly to dishearten the opposition."

The same wisdom had kept her out of Northumberland's clutches during the attempted coup. But this situation was different. "I would appear involved if I left and rebellion broke out right afterwards," Elizabeth said.

"Nothing will happen until March," Noailles said. "No one is foolish enough to war in the winter – or to rise without making careful plans. No, the rising is planned for Palm Sunday, perhaps Easter."

"Such symbolism," Elizabeth said. "And here I was planning to leave before then anyway." It was a lie, but there was no reason to let him know. "Now you will think I have taken your advice."

"I need no credit; I care only for your safety." He bowed, then winked. "Besides, no one will know we ever spoke, let alone guess the topic."

November 30, 1553

The Privy Chamber at Whitehall had unsettled Elizabeth since the day her brother had acceded to the throne, when Somerset had brought the two siblings to their dead father's apartments. Then, the Privy Chamber had been clouded from the stench of Henry's diseased leg and decomposing corpse; six years later, Elizabeth still imagined a pungent haze shrouding Mary and the courtiers assembled around her.

The thought of her father made Elizabeth all the angrier. Yes, she was conspicuously at her sister's side while Mary sewed and accepted the adulation of sycophants – but it was the left side. Their cousin, Margaret Douglas, sat on Mary's right.

Margaret, the Countess of Lennox, was the daughter of Henry VIII's older sister, Margaret Tudor. Her absent husband, a Scottish Lord, was not liked or trusted in England, and in truth neither was she. Henry had set aside that entire line in the succession, but both women acted as if this would soon be changed. Again, Elizabeth blessed Parliament for standing firm so far.

Elizabeth bit her lip. She was tired of sewing, tired of pretending that all was glorious in the new Catholic order. But she had to be here to attend the Queen until Mary, too, grew tired of pretending sisterly love. Luckily, Mary had less natural patience than Elizabeth.

The deep breath Elizabeth took to calm herself emerged as a loud sigh, shocking her and everyone around her. She looked at Mary apologetically. "I beg your pardon, Your Majesty. I had a sudden pain."

Mary rolled her eyes and waved a hand. "You should retire."

Elizabeth hastened to curtsy deeply, glad for the reprieve and relieved it had not been dearly bought. But before she could rise to bow out of the room, Margaret turned to Mary. "Vespers are starting soon, dearest cousin. Perhaps prayer might do the Lady good."

Margaret's wheedling tone intensified her taunting, and Elizabeth balled her fists behind her skirts.

Mary's eyebrows rose in her face. "Yes," she said, and turned to Elizabeth. "Sister, you shall join us."

It took all of Elizabeth's self-control to restrain a *You can't make me*. Because, of course, Mary could: regardless of Parliament, no one could ignore a direct royal order.

Stephen Gardiner stepped forward from the shadows behind the throne. "What an excellent idea."

Elizabeth drew back like a trapped deer but composed herself and allowed dismay to show on her face. "I thank you for your kind thoughts, but my stomach aches and I beg to be allowed to retire to my room."

"Your health is certainly changeable," Gardiner said with a sniff.

"I was in pain yesterday as well," she said.

Mary looked uncertain, but Margaret wore the same deadly eyes as Gardiner. "Yes, I hear you required your ladies to rub your stomach," Margaret said. "At the very moment of the elevation of the Host."

Elizabeth winced at how exposed she felt. "I was in pain," she repeated.

"Your pain ended quickly enough," Margaret said in a cruel drawl. "You were able to laugh with the French Ambassador after the Mass."

Mary's face hardened. "What is this plotting?"

Plotting. The word shattered Elizabeth's calm and she struggled to avoid stammering. "No plotting, Your Majesty. My pains ebb and flow."

"There are murmurs from the countryside, talk of traitors grumbling over the Queen's religious policies," Gardiner said. "Does this stem from you?"

Elizabeth felt the color drain from her face. "I am Her Majesty's most loyal subject."

He squinted like a hunter readying his shot. "So loyal that you insult the holy moment of Communion?"

"I did not realize where we were in the service," Elizabeth said, knowing her words rang hollow but having no others.

Mary grunted.

The hint of a smile played on Gardiner's lips. It made Elizabeth realize just how much of an enemy he was, and how much damage he had already done. Gardiner, Margaret, the Spanish Ambassador – the people Mary most trusted were united against Elizabeth.

"It is why I ask to be excused from Vespers," Elizabeth said, hoping to reassure her sister. "I do not want to fall ill in front of you."

"Because Her Majesty would recognize your deceit?" Gardiner said, the smile twisted now.

"Because it would distract Her Majesty from the comfort she receives from the Mass," Elizabeth said, trying to sound indignant rather than terrified.

"A comfort you do not share?" Gardiner's tone was arch.

The trap was springing; bolting was the deer's only choice. Elizabeth turned to Mary. "Your Majesty, we discussed this; you know my reservations. You yourself assured me that belief would come with action." She spread her arms. "I am taking action, going to Mass. It is hard to find comfort when I am in pain."

Mary's mouth slackened. "You mock me."

Elizabeth stretched her arms forward. "I love you, Sister. I beg you extend me the same patience as our brother should have shown to you."

Mary pulled back, and her eyes went as flat as Gardiner's, as Margaret's. Elizabeth's appeal to Mary's sense of justice had hit the wrong note.

"You were there that Christmas when our brother tried to refuse me," Mary said. "You know the line I drew. I told him I would gladly die for my faith, for the true faith." She leaned forward and narrowed her eyes. "Would you die for the Lutheran heresies?"

Elizabeth felt as if she had been punched.

"As I thought." Mary straightened in her chair. "You shall accompany us to Vespers."

Elizabeth nodded and looked down.

Mary stood. "Come, Margaret," she said. "Come ladies."

As the group filed off, Elizabeth glanced at Gardiner. He was smiling fully now, an evil smile that did not reach his eyes. He motioned her to precede him and Elizabeth did so, hands clasped in front of her.

They walked through the crowds of courtiers, many of whom hastened to join the procession. Elizabeth kept her eyes lowered to hide her anguish. It was indeed time to leave this snake pit, and her mind raced with prayers and plans to persuade Mary to allow it.

The sound of scrambling caught her attention, and a loud voice cried out the dreaded word: "Traitor." Elizabeth froze as pandemonium erupted all around. Courtiers scattered in all directions to escape the expected assassin, but the armed guards at the doors barred the exits.

Only Elizabeth and Mary remained where they were. Mary seemed almost bored, as though she found it impossible to believe the Lord would permit her to be killed after all the favor He had shown her. Elizabeth was terrified, unable to stir. All she could do was tremble violently.

Silence reigned as the seconds stretched on. One at a time, courtiers began to creep back with sheepish looks to take their places around their Queen. But the calm was shattered again by guards dragging in a struggling commoner and shoving him before Mary. "This is the man who yelled."

Mary looked him up and down. Everyone did. The malcontent had matted hair and dirty clothes – and the wide blue eyes of a youth.

"He does not look armed," Mary said.

"I meant you no harm, Your Majesty," the lad said. "My quarrel is with Bishop Gardiner. He is a traitor, and you should beware of him."

"I serve Her Majesty in God's truth," Gardiner said. "You know not of which you speak."

"I know you want to force the Mass on us," the lad said.

"I want to save souls," Gardiner said. "Even yours."

"Take him away," Mary said.

When she turned back, her wilting gaze weakened Elizabeth's knees. "Why are you so fearful?" Mary asked. "Or did you know of this plot?"

Gardiner sniffed. "Perhaps this is why she did not want to come to Vespers. Perhaps she should be questioned along with the malcontent?"

Elizabeth's stomach joined in the revolt, but she had to respond. "Nay, Your Majesty. I simply thought there was danger to you. I am ashamed of the weakness that left me unable to protect you." She allowed herself to retch and dropped to her knees. "My apologies, Your Majesty. Remember, I am ill."

One of Mary's ladies, Jane Dormer, rolled her eyes, but a

kinder one, Susan Clarencieux, came to sit on the floor next to Elizabeth. "There, there," she said, rubbing Elizabeth's stomach.

The kindness was a balm and prompted mercy from Mary as well. "I wish you comfort, Sister. You may join me another time."

Elizabeth felt the color start to return to her face. She needed to be far from court, and the sooner the better. Whatever it took, she had to persuade her sister to let her go.

CHAPTER 7

December 6, 1553

Arriving at the door to Mary's Privy Chamber, Elizabeth carefully stifled the joy that threatened to make her whole body buzz with excitement: Mary had finally agreed to let Elizabeth retire to Ashridge. This audience was the only thing standing in the way of freedom.

The page disappeared to announce her, but it took some time for him to return. Elizabeth pretended indifference at being kept waiting, but the insult strengthened her grim determination.

When she was finally admitted, she understood the delay: Simon Renard, the Spanish Ambassador, stood next to her sister's throne, the two of them nodding like old crones.

Elizabeth knelt before Mary, trying to stop her eyes from flashing to the life-sized portrait of Philip of Spain that dominated the room even from its position in the corner. Titian had painted him in ceremonial armor, one hand on his sword to show a confident man of action, the other resting on his desk to suggest thought and reflection. Mary was in the habit of glancing over, as if seeking Philip's approval of everything she said.

Not surprisingly, Mary's ladies whispered that she was obsessed with the painting, and every day grew more determined to marry the young man who had inspired it, undeterred by the eleven-year age gap and the mounting grumblings of her people.

Elizabeth could not understand such an attitude. Yes, the face was handsome, more so than when he had been proposed as a match for Elizabeth. Yes, the calves were strong and fine. But to risk discord in the realm over someone she'd never met? Elizabeth thought back to the way her father had fallen in love with an image then rejected the real-life Anne of Cleves. Had Mary learned nothing from that experience?

Mary held out her hand, and Elizabeth kissed it with as much reverence as she could, to heighten the show of loyalty.

The formalities handled, Elizabeth stood and squared her shoulders. "I came to take my leave, dearest Sister. I shall count the days until I see you again."

Mary's only answer was a piercing gaze. Elizabeth smoothed the front of her skirt, reminding herself that it could as easily be nearsightedness as malice.

Finally, Mary spoke. "Be faithful."

Next to Mary, Renard snorted. "Does she know what that means?"

"I am Her Majesty's most loyal subject," Elizabeth said to him, which prompted another snort. The Ambassador's hatred had never been so obvious.

"We shall see," he said. The gleam in his eye unnerved Elizabeth, enough that she questioned the wisdom of seeking safety through distance. What lies might Renard tell about her when she was not there to counteract them?

She turned to Mary. "Sister, I beg you, people can easily accuse me of anything. Don't ever believe what anyone might tell you about me without first giving me leave to defend myself."

Mary smiled gently. "I will always allow you to explain."

The statement was vague enough that it could easily be forgotten or discarded. Elizabeth wanted more, *needed* more. "Promise me?"

Mary's eyes hardened but she nodded.

Still not the assurance Elizabeth craved, but she dared not persist. She made the sign of the cross in thanks and rose. She backed away, bowing again with each step until she was out of the door. Then she quickly turned and raced towards the court-yard where her household awaited her.

She mounted quickly, desperate to leave her fear behind, eager to breathe freely. Instead, her worries gnawed harder as she rode, and the ache in her head intensified. In seeking safety, she had not considered the extent of Renard's enmity towards her, and now she had abandoned her direct access to Mary, her chance to diffuse the accusations that were certain to fly. Accusations more likely to be believed of a heretic.

Barely ten miles from London, the terror grew so over-whelming she thought she might faint. She needed to reassure Mary somehow, keep her from believing the worst lies.

Elizabeth stopped the procession and had her ladies spread a blanket on the ground for her. When she had calmed her ragged breathing and could concentrate, she sent for a messenger. "I have two important requests for the Queen," she said. "I beg you to render them both with equal urgency."

The lad's eyes widened and he sucked in his breath. "I promise."

"First, ask her to send me one of her litters, for I can no longer ride."

"Certainly."

"But also tell her I need similar succor for my soul." Eliza-beth glanced at Kat Ashley. "I suddenly realized I do not have the proper chapel ornaments at Ashridge, and I beg her to send me what I need. Copes for the priests to celebrate Mass, crosses to be borne before them in procession, chalices…she knows best."

"I shall tell her, Princess," said the man and ran off.

Kat came to sit next to Elizabeth. "Nice touch, my Lady," she said in a low whisper.

Elizabeth merely nodded. The tableau of belief she had just painted would protect her for a time.

Hopefully for as long as she needed.

December 20, 1553

The cold, damp day drained light and hope from a person's heart. The fire roared in the Library hearth, but still Elizabeth's chill reached to her bones.

A quiet knock as William Saintlow, the head of her security detail, peeked in his head. "Do you have a moment?"

"Come in," Elizabeth said, putting down her quill.

Saintlow's step was heavy, his face grim. On arriving before her, he hesitated, shifting from foot to foot. "James Croft came to see you," he finally said.

Since Elizabeth had seen him, Croft had traded his position with Somerset for a better one with Northumberland, but had been thrown in the Tower for supporting Jane Grey.

"Croft? Released?" she said.

"Released and up to mischief," Saintlow said. "Which is why I would not let him in. Indeed, from now on I do not plan to allow anyone to see you. I ask for your cooperation in enforcing this ban."

"This sounds serious."

Saintlow glanced at Blanche and Kat in the far corner, hunched over their sewing and seemingly ignoring the conversation. They were not the ones to worry about.

"Croft wants you to move away from the City," he finally said.

Elizabeth was already out of Mary's easy grasp. What was this new necessity? "Is it some sort of plague?" she asked, offering a safe metaphor.

He shook his head. "Rebellion."

She froze. It was happening.

Saintlow leaned forward. "People around the country are saying they did not put Mary on the throne to see England sold to the Spaniards. Or the Pope. Their efforts have coalesced now. They have leaders…and plans."

Elizabeth raised a hand to silence him. "I do not want to hear anything about plans or—"

"The rebels will pass quite close on their way to London, and there may be fighting nearby."

The words swayed in the air like a dead man from a noose. "I cannot leave here," she said, though she already knew she would – just not in a way that looked like she was heeding Croft's warning. "I have only just arrived; a quick departure will arouse suspicions. It would be more dangerous to appear to have some involvement than to take my chances with the…"—she paused to search for the right benign word—"deputation."

"What is to stop you from visiting one of your other properties?" asked Saintlow. "Like Donnington Castle, in Berkshire. Far off and a heavily fortified stronghold to keep you safe."

Elizabeth silently blessed Noailles for the forewarning that the uprising was planned for March. "I cannot believe how you happened to guess the very house I planned to use when it was time to air out Ashridge. I will be there in February."

"February will be too late," he said.

Too late? Noailles was wrong? Now it was Elizabeth's turn to look over her shoulder. "When will this deputation look to… *influence* my sister?"

"They hoped to wait until after the winter, but they had to accelerate their plans. Simon Renard has gotten whiff of something."

Elizabeth's blood iced.

"Which is why I would settle you in strength," Saintlow continued. "We have guns at Donnington; we can raise thousands there if need be."

"To support the rebellion? Are you mad?"

"Not at all. I only want to wait out events. Suffolk is with the rebels – he might look to crown his daughter again. You should be ready to assert your rights if need be. Can I at least send supplies? And the strongbox, to keep it safe."

Elizabeth's careful management of her properties and income – even selling the produce from her gardens rather than sending it as gifts – resulted in annual surpluses. She was rightfully proud of her cash reserves, nervous about parting with them.

Saintlow pressed. "We can still say it is in preparation for February."

Slightly nauseated, Elizabeth nodded. "As long as there is no danger to me."

"I turned Croft away and told him I would neither let him see you nor pass on a message. Especially a written one."

"Written?"

"From Thomas Wyatt, one of the leaders."

Elizabeth balled her fists to keep from fainting. She knew the name. Wyatt's father, also Thomas, had courted her mother. That connection made things even worse.

"I thank you for knowing my loyalty," she said. "But I fear others do not. Do I stand in any danger from the fact that Croft came here?"

Saintlow shook his head. "They are unlikely to find him – he is on his way to raise Wales. But even if they do, no ill can be imputed to you: he was discreet and saw only me."

She rubbed the twinge in her temple. "Why, oh why, did he come here?"

"To see you safe," he said. "No one will ever know."

No one will ever know. Noailles had said the same thing. "I pray you are right. And I thank you for keeping him from me. Take whatever steps you need to make sure no one else can reach me."

She reached for her quill, thinking to put this behind her, but Saintlow did not move. "One more thing," he said. "Croft thought you should reply to Wyatt."

She drew back, appalled. "Never. That would be an overt act of treason."

Saintlow gave a grim nod. "I said as much, that he was a fool for asking you to put your head on the block."

"Thank you."

"But he said that if Wyatt was not sure his warning was delivered, he might try again to give it."

Her knees weakened. She could not let that happen, not now. "Can you get him a discreet message? Nothing in writing."

Saintlow's eyes lidded, but not enough to hide his sidelong glance at Kat and Blanche. "Aye."

"Thank him for his goodwill. And tell him I will do as I have cause." A disavowal, though not condemnation. Still safer than risking a second warning.

Saintlow nodded. "I will pass that on. Thank you, Your Grace."

She shook off the sudden chill. She had no choice.

The moment he was gone, Kat Ashley stood and heaved a loud sigh. "Good Lord."

Elizabeth rubbed her temple again. "You heard?"

Blanche widened her eyes. "Heard what? Was there something to hear?"

Kat looked confused for a moment, then nodded. "I heard nothing."

"Thank you," Elizabeth said, comforted by their care. "Actually, I have been thinking it has been too long since I have visited my properties. Perhaps we should consider removing to someplace new?"

"If it's newness you want, Donnington Castle would be ideal," Blanche said. "It has been years since we've been there."

"I shall consider it," Elizabeth said. "Meanwhile, I could use some prayer. Leave me and shut the door after you."

Charges of treason had come to slither around her ankles like a snake, and she breathed deeply to calm herself. Saintlow had shielded her from Croft's visit and its dire implications, thank God. She was still safe.

So why did she still feel chilled?

January 27, 1554

Elizabeth opened her eyes. Fire overhead faded to red damask as the tester came into focus and she sighed over the dread that accompanied each new day.

Rumors flew that rebellion had broken out or was at least imminent. But even if she had wanted, Elizabeth could not move to safety: she was still abed after weeks of misery. Fear had not been satisfied with her stomach; it had attacked her entire body. She was swollen and distended and altogether miserable. This was what poor Edward had gone through. Swelling, then death. Was this a sign?

A banging at the door startled her. She had barely sat up when soldiers crashed it open and their leader barged into her bedchamber. Five more burly men filed in after him. "I am sent by the Queen," he said. "She requests your immediate return to court and has sent me to escort you."

Fear gripped Elizabeth. She could not put herself in her sister's hands. Not now. Not at the height of the danger. She had left court to avoid exactly this.

Part of her wished she had fled to Donnington, though the other part knew that such a move would have magnified her perceived guilt. "Good sir," she said. "I am in no condition to leave my bed, let alone my house."

A shadow flashed across his face – maybe pity? – before he answered. "Travel you must, as the Queen commands it. Here is the order."

Elizabeth took the letter gingerly and kissed the seal before opening it slowly. Her heart resumed beating when she saw that it was a letter from her sister and not a writ from the Council. *Right dearly and entirely beloved Sister, we greet you well.*

The rest of the letter was equally cordial, as if Elizabeth would be an honored guest rather than an implicit prisoner. Elizabeth was indeed ordered back to court, though reassured that she would be "heartily welcome".

She clutched the letter to her breast and sighed. "Good sir, I would love to comply but I am too sick to travel."

The guard narrowed his eyes. Elizabeth flung off the blanket to reveal her swollen limbs, mottled with red streaks. "Look at me."

He winced. "Lord, have mercy," he said, almost under his breath.

She pressed her advantage. "Please, just a few days. Only a short time. Surely Her Majesty will forebear."

"But…but I have my orders."

"Good God, man," she said. "Look at me."

The guard's face twisted, and Elizabeth pushed tears to her eyes. "Have you worked at the palace long?" she asked. "Did you serve my brother? He, too, had an illness marked by swelling of his arms, legs, and head. I do not know what disease this is, but I beg you to take pity on me. Have my sister send her physicians; they will agree that I cannot be moved."

The captain swallowed. "I did serve your brother, our good king." He shook his head as if convincing himself of something. "But he also had pustules and bleeding."

"That was at the end," Elizabeth said. "It began with just swelling."

More twisting of the guard's face suggested the arguments

were swaying him. Elizabeth pressed her luck. "At least let the Queen's doctors decide. I will do as they say. But for the love of God, let them decide so I do not die on the road."

February 10, 1554

The clatter outside told Elizabeth someone had arrived, many someones. Either another royal deputation or rebels, and Elizabeth was not sure which she dreaded more.

She considered stirring from her sickbed but rejected the idea. She would find out soon enough. Instead, she rubbed her eyes – gingerly, because disease swelled her face and limbs and gave her sharp pains everywhere. Even worse was the terror that twisted every thought and banished all possibility of rest. She had never felt this hopeless. Never.

She heard her door open and a swish of skirts, then Kat Ashley beside her, clucking and stuffing pillows behind her to prop her up. "The Queen," Kat explained as she worked. "This time she sent a kinsman."

Moments later, Thomas Parry appeared in the open doorway. "They sent William Howard to see you, along with Edward Hastings and Thomas Cornwallis. They are with the physicians now and will all come in together."

Elizabeth stared at Parry for a long moment. He shook his head sadly. "I told him you were in no condition to receive anyone, but they have orders."

Elizabeth grunted and closed her eyes until Parry returned. "Your Grace, the lords for you."

Even before she had finished beckoning with her index finger, Howard entered, a man whose allegiance had been turned as many times as the fur collar on his court coat, the latest time to hold Calais for Mary against Jane Grey.

Behind him crowded Hastings and Cornwallis and the three royal physicians, whose efforts over the past week had done nothing for Elizabeth's symptoms. Doctors Owen and Wendy, good men who had served Elizabeth's father, and Cesar Adelmare, an evil man Elizabeth hated.

Howard stepped to the front of the group and bowed. "I am sorry to see you still ailing, Cousin." He was half-brother to Elizabeth's great-uncle; "cousin" was not the correct term, but Elizabeth was not about to criticize a claim of closeness. It might be all that would save her.

"I am sorry that my sad state does not match the pleasure I have in seeing you, Uncle," she said. "You look well." She turned to the others. "As do you, gentlemen. Greetings."

Howard ignored her answer. "Her Majesty will wait no longer for your return."

Elizabeth flung away the blanket to show how the streaks on her swollen legs had darkened to purple. "You see how this illness has ravaged my body. I cannot travel, or I will surely die."

Howard let his eyes travel again over Elizabeth's tortured form, squinting as if evaluating a horse. A flash of pity crossed his face, and he bit his lip.

Kat Ashley took a step towards Howard. "My Lord, you see how it is with my mistress, you see for yourself how sick she is. Does the Queen really mean for her to travel down dangerous roads? We do not hear much here, but we do know there are rebels about."

Howard snorted. "The treason has been put down. The only rebels about now are hanging from trees."

Elizabeth had to work hard to keep her face calm. "Praise God."

"Aye," Hastings said. "The realm is safe again."

"It sounds as if the royal forces had an easy time of it," Elizabeth replied, trying to draw out more details. "We had heard there were too many insurgents to hope for such an outcome."

"The royal forces had the support of all London after the Queen went among them. Clad in armor, she spoke to the crowds at Guildhall and turned everything around," Hastings said.

"Oh?" Elizabeth overcame her shock to add another "Praise God."

"It was like seeing your father himself, in all his glory." Howard's eyes shone with admiration. "She invoked his name and inspired every man's loyalty and devotion."

Was that all it took? Elizabeth pressed on, hoping her doubt would not show on her face. "But what of the people's misgivings over her marriage? Did she address their fears?"

Howard nodded. "Her Majesty swore she would do nothing without the advice of her Council and even Parliament. That this alliance was for England, for she was married to her people. She even pointed to the ring put on her finger at her coronation, told them that relationship was the most important one in her life."

The coronation ring transmuted into wedding band was a powerful image and brilliant strategy. This was the side of Mary that deserved the great station to which she had been called.

"Our father would have been proud," Elizabeth said. "To so move men with words alone."

"It was not just words," Howard said. "Monarchs are meant to lead their men, to show the courage and the spirit their men need. The Queen visited the troops stationed around the City to rally them all, from the Three Cranes in the Vintry to London Bridge. Then, while her Councilors cowered and begged her to take shelter in the Tower, she went to Westminster, where the fighting was heaviest."

Admiration tinged with bitterness in Elizabeth's breast. She wondered whether she would have been as brave as the granddaughter of the warrior Queen of Castille, or whether fear would have conquered her as it had these past weeks.

Howard leaned his head forward as if waiting for Elizabeth's reply.

"Formidable," she said. "I praise God she is safe."

"Amen," Howard said. The others echoed him.

"And I look forward to congratulating her once I can travel again," Elizabeth said.

"That will be quite soon," Howard said.

Elizabeth rolled her eyes. "You see me, don't you? I am telling you I could die. Will you really take that chance?"

Owen and Wendy exchanged worried glances, but Adelmare stepped forward. "We can tend to you on the trip to keep you out of danger."

"How can you tend to me when any movement is agony?"

"Surely we can travel slowly, to minimize the jarring," Adelmare said.

"We will travel as slowly as we need," Howard said. "As long as we move."

"There is no speed that will not have me screaming in pain," Elizabeth said.

Adelmare shook his head. "All your swelling speaks to a phlegmatic disease, my Lady. And as we know, water ebbs and flows."

"So?" Elizabeth said sharply.

"So, we will travel during those times when your strength flows, and rest when it ebbs."

"If we travel little enough to keep me alive, the thirty miles will take weeks," Elizabeth said, though in truth she appreciated the delay such an approach would represent.

"The important thing is that you will be obeying the Queen's command," Howard said. "That must happen."

Tears of frustration stung Elizabeth's eyes. "Why does she insist?"

Howard sighed. "We are kinsmen, and I will tell you frankly: the Queen is increasingly resentful that you put your own comfort above her needs."

"This is not my comfort but my life," Elizabeth said.

"And yet your doctors say otherwise."

Elizabeth narrowed her eyes, as much from anger as from pain. "Only one of them."

"Your absence made you suspect, and your continued refusal screams guilt. It is time to demonstrate your loyalty."

The words landed like a slap. She raised her chin to respond. "I am Her Majesty's true subject."

"And I will tell you again: skulking here makes you look otherwise."

The words whipped and she lashed out. "How can you say such a thing?"

"You are a Howard, and it is time you act like one. My father, your great-grandfather, escaped from the treason of fighting for Richard III, and clawed his way back to the family dukedom. Be his scion now." He leaned over her, until his eyes were close. "You need to address what you have done – or not done." He straightened, his smile gentle. "Mind you, it helps to be righteous in the first place."

"I have been," was all she could say.

"Hopefully Her Majesty will see that," he said. "The sooner the better."

Elizabeth felt the noose contract around her neck. "I must rest," she said, hoping for any reprieve at all.

"Your ladies can pack while you do. We leave tomorrow morning." He spun on his heels and marched out the door, making the group scramble to follow.

Elizabeth pulled the covers over her head.

CHAPTER 8

February 22, 1554

*E*lizabeth steeled herself, determined to seem oblivious to the frigid cold. She had ordered the curtains of the litter to be drawn back so that the world might bear witness to her hollow eyes, deathly pallor, and grotesquely bloated body.

Despite all that Howard had done to hurry things along, it had taken more than a week to cover the thirty miles. A week of passing corpses dangling from hastily erected gallows, victims of the failed uprising. The closer the retinue got to London, the more death they saw; this close to their destination, the stench was inescapable.

The Whitehall gates were closed even though the rebellion was defeated and Jane Grey was dead, executed because her father had raised her banner again. Edward Courtenay, Elizabeth's putative suitor, was back in the Tower. No wonder Elizabeth doubted the assurance that she would be an "honored guest".

The gates opened and twenty guards came out to flank the sides of the stone arch. The captain of the guards went straight to confer with Howard; Elizabeth closed her eyes to wait, needing the rest and happy to display her weakness.

When the crunching of shoes on the gravel told her he had arrived at her litter, she opened her eyes to find him peering in. She gave him a hard look and he waved her cortege through with no words of welcome, no fanfare.

They had barely gone two horse lengths when he called, "That's enough."

She turned to see Parry arguing with the captain, his voice rising. Howard was looking away. She closed her eyes again until more crunching told her someone approached. "You are only allowed a dozen attendants," the captain said. "The rest of your party will have to return to Ashridge or find lodgings in the City."

"Surely, you can find room in—"

Elizabeth's words were cut off by the swing of the gate closing off the crowd behind her. Howard still had not spoken. Even his expression had not changed. She swallowed.

Panic rose when her litter was waved to the right rather than toward the main grounds. She raised her hand and the guard was immediately beside her. "Where are you taking me?"

"Your lodgings are in this wing of the palace," he said.

"I beg you, good sir, this area is too close to the river and will worsen my illness," she explained.

The captain shook his head. "These are my orders."

"Her Majesty's own doctors pronounced my troubles phlegmatic – surely they would have advised to keep me far from the water."

"All I know is what I am told."

Tears rose to Elizabeth's eyes at this sign of Mary's hatred. Elizabeth fought to restrain the desperate sobs that threatened to follow.

"I will pass on your request, but for now you will cooperate," the captain said. He waved the cortege on.

"Thank you," she said, and her voice sounded small and breathless even to her own ears.

She looked around at this new part of the grounds, far removed from the center of the court. She would be isolated, that much was certain.

She had regained some control when they arrived at the entrance – until she saw John Gage, who was not only Lord Chamberlain but also Constable of the Tower, awaiting her with still more guards.

Howard rode to Elizabeth's side. "I will be leaving you now. Remember who you are."

He turned and made his way to Gage, exchanging pleasantries with him before riding off. The sky darkened, or maybe it was just her thoughts.

She turned to Gage. He had been kind enough to her in the past. "Greetings, Sir John," she said. "I thank you for welcoming me and apologize for the state in which you find me."

"I shall show you to your rooms," was all Gage said.

"Is there a chair to roll me, like my father used to have?"

He shook his head. "You must walk."

"I cannot."

"There is no other way." His eyes were flat, merciless.

She summoned strength and courage as Kat and Blanche helped her out of the litter. Her knees buckled slightly from her weight, but Gage was right there with his arm for her to lean on. And lean she did.

The walk was not as painful as she had feared, as if her illness realized she had worse things plaguing her. And needed her wits.

"When will I be brought to my dear sister, the Queen?" she asked after a few paces. "The sight of her will do my poor soul good."

"You will await Her Majesty's pleasure in your rooms."

Elizabeth ignored the menacing furrow of his bushy black

brows. "May I also ask that I be moved further from the water? Surely—"

"This was discussed," he said. "You will remain in a quiet wing until you are cleared of all suspicion."

The tiny hope remaining in her breast dissolved, and she sank to the floor under the weight of her justified fears. "I need to rest," she said.

Gage lifted an arm and the guards surrounded her. "Help me carry her," he said. "She cannot stay here."

March 8, 1554

Elizabeth tossed and turned in the bed, tired of being miserable. Every part of her body was painfully swollen. Her doctors warned she was in a delicate state, but no one cared.

It had been a month since they'd taken her from her home, forced her on a march that might have killed her, and put her in this room by the water that was sure to weaken her lungs. A month of lying around, neither worsening nor improving.

Kat stroked her forehead. "You need to prepare yourself, lass. They have no mercy for your illness."

"Not you too," Elizabeth said. "I can do nothing about it, especially not when I am so scared."

"Aye, that's why you are sick. Your stomach always bothers you when things go wrong. But Mary and her minions don't care about your pain. And now that her proxy marriage has been sworn, attention will recenter on you."

"What would you have me do?" Elizabeth asked, ready to explain why any solution would fail.

Instead of answering immediately, Kat took a place next to her on the bed and held her as she would a small child. "When your blessed mother was brought to the Tower, her fear was used against her. You must not allow your weakness to be used against you. You must steel yourself for the coming ordeal. And trust in God's mercy."

The words dislodged something, but not all the way. Anne Boleyn had died in the end, after all. "It is hard to trust in His mercy when He is the one who brought me here."

"He brought you here and not the Tower. Trust in Him."

"As did Jane Grey?"

Kat's face darkened. "Jane Grey claimed the Crown. You did no such thing. Now pull yourself together so they believe you when you say it. Remember what Howard said, cruel as he was. Remember who you are."

"I am the daughter of a woman executed for treason."

"An innocent woman who patiently suffered what the Lord decreed for her. As should we all."

The comfort of Kat's embrace allowed the wisdom to penetrate the shell of Elizabeth's misery. Kat was right. Resistance would not help Elizabeth escape this Gethsemane. It was just making Mary mad and Elizabeth miserable. And depleting the mental and emotional resources she needed during this time, resources already weakened by the morbid excesses of a phlegmatic illness. She had brought this suffering on herself, and it would remain as long as she wallowed in it. Better to let it go, to accept that no one would come to save her. Indeed, they would soon come to attack her, and she needed to be strong when they did.

If Elizabeth were to have any chance of getting out of this, she had to get well. She had to. *The Lord helps those who help themselves.* It was time to rise. To build her strength, or die trying.

She studied her swollen limbs. They were not so bad as yesterday. Leaving Kat's embrace, Elizabeth swung her legs over the side of the bed, and in a single motion rose to sitting with her feet flat on the floor. She rested there a while, to let the dizziness pass. She needed to stand today and walk around her room, so that she might resume real activity before the week was out. That would do a great deal for her strength and sanity.

March 16, 1554

Rising from her sickbed and resuming her walks had brought Elizabeth's body back to normal in only a week. Well, as normal as it could be given the silence of her isolation. They had erected barriers to the area, so even her walks were lonely. Only smells, not noise, permeated her apartments – which made the clanking in the hallway all the more startling.

Elizabeth held her breath as the noise approached, until the sound arrived at her door and a guard entered. A guard, not a page.

"The Lord Chancellor and members of the Council are on their way to wait upon you. Prepare to receive them."

She swallowed, summoning strength. On the one hand, they were finally dealing with her. On the other hand, they were finally dealing with her. Until this moment, she had been both at risk and safe. Now only one of those statements would be true.

Moving to the center of the room, she motioned to Kat and Blanche to take their places beside her. She could hear the quieter sound of leather boots now; that would be them. Not a lot of warning, but happily she needed no more.

Stephen Gardiner entered first, followed by William Paulet, the Marquess of Winchester, and Henry Radclyffe, the Earl of Sussex. More career courtiers with shifting values: Winchester was as fervent a Catholic under Mary as he had been a passionate Protestant under Edward. Sussex was a Howard; at least his Catholicism was more plausible.

"Greetings, gentlemen," she said with what she hoped was quiet confidence.

"We have come to discuss certain accusations that have been made against you," Gardiner said.

"I am happy to finally refute these claims," she said. "I am a true woman, and it has been a sorry thing for me to have my loyalty questioned."

"Your loyalty is questioned because we have proof against you," Gardiner said.

Her heart thudded, filling her ears and head. "Proof? That is not possible. There can be no proof of something that does not exist."

Winchester and Sussex exchanged glances. Gardiner crossed his arms. "Thomas Wyatt wrote you a letter, asking for your blessing."

She put as much force behind her words as she could. "I would never condone treason."

"We also found one of your letters to the Queen in the French Ambassador's pouch," Gardiner said.

Again, Noailles's dangerous confidence proved disastrous to her. "How did he get one of my letters?"

"How do you explain it?" Gardiner asked.

"I cannot," Elizabeth said. "Any more than I could explain how the daffodils outside my window know to bloom each year."

"I say you sent it to him as a signal."

Elizabeth furrowed her brows. "My letters to my sister express love and loyalty. I cannot imagine what signal they could offer France."

"Your words are not matched by your deeds. I advise you to beg the Queen's pardon, pray that her gentle heart might bend to mercy," Gardiner said.

"Only the guilty need pardoning."

"My Lady, my Lady," Gardiner said. "We know you are guilty. Confess and the Queen will be merciful."

The words hardened her heart. Robert Tyrwhitt had said the same thing. It was a trap then, and a bigger one now.

"I cannot confess to a crime I would never think on, let alone commit," Elizabeth said, her voice rising. "And it pains me to think that Her Majesty might think I did."

"Her Majesty knows you did. It is her will and pleasure that you be taken to the Tower."

The Tower. The name took away Elizabeth's words, and she swayed, grasping at Kat for balance. "Why would Her Majesty send me now? What new lies have been told of me?"

"No lies, just truths," Gardiner said. "The only way to escape this fate is by confessing your sins."

"So the truth would condemn me but a lie might set me free?"

Sussex stepped forward. "The Queen is removing to St. James Palace, and the royal army must go with her. Your unprotected presence here might be too much of a temptation for any remaining rebels."

"Silence!" Gardiner said it so loudly his skullcap shifted. "Traitors deserve no explanations." He turned back to Elizabeth. "You have the night to prepare yourself."

"I do not deserve this," Elizabeth said.

"The Queen is adamant; prepare yourself." With that, Gardiner turned on his heels and stalked out. The startled Council members hurried after him without further comment.

Gage raised a hand and guards poured into the hall. Four ringed the room, and more kept coming, spreading out throughout Elizabeth's apartments and the gardens beyond. There must have been a dozen in all. Elizabeth tried not to visibly cringe, but it was hard not to react to such a dreadful show of force.

When Gage was satisfied his men were where they should be, he pointed at Elizabeth's attendants. "Three of you may remain with your lady. Another three will join you, having been appointed by the Queen."

Three friends and three spies. All Elizabeth wanted to do was weep and curse.

March 17, 1554

The guards had refused to leave their posts, insisting on keeping Elizabeth constantly in view. They gave her privacy in her close stool only after checking that the window was sealed shut and the drain too small for escape.

She was like a mouse trapped in a corner by a hungry cat, waiting for the attack to begin.

Her headache made reading impossible, sewing too. Walking was prohibited – she was not allowed to leave her rooms. Nothing could fend off the barrage of apocalyptic thoughts as she sat in her chair, staring with blind eyes at nothing, praying for strength.

A page stepped into the room. "The Marquess of Winchester and the Earl of Sussex," he announced.

Squaring her shoulders, she rose to receive them, happy that at least Gardiner was not with them.

"We have come to accompany you to the Tower," Winchester said.

Much as she expected it, the news made her want to howl. Instead, she screwed up her courage to fight. "You must take me to the Queen first."

The two men inhaled sharply. "The barge is waiting," Winchester said. "The Lord Chancellor himself chose the timing."

"That is exactly why I need to see my sister. Her Majesty cannot know of this cruel and unjust order being undertaken in her name. She cannot know how I have been treated and degraded. My sweet sister would never see me treated thusly; she knows I would never betray her. This is all a travesty – you must take me to the Queen."

Winchester's mouth had fallen open during her speech; now he closed it and shook his head. "We cannot. You have been accused of treason and there is evidence to support the claims."

"But she promised me," Elizabeth said, trying not to wail.

"A traitor is not worthy to come into a monarch's presence," Winchester said. "This has always been the rule."

"Well then, let me write to her," Elizabeth said.

Winchester shook his head again.

His intransigence was infuriating. "This does not violate your rule," she said. "And it will allow her to fulfill her promise to me."

Sussex put a hand on Winchester's arm. "That does not seem so unreasonable."

Elizabeth's lower lip wobbled her thanks for the advice that made Winchester throw up his hands. "Fine. You may write to Her Majesty."

Triumph quickly ceded to panic in Elizabeth's heart. She was about to pen the most important letter of her life. "May I pray until the instruments arrive?"

Winchester nodded and Elizabeth flew to the *prie-dieu* in the corner, bowing her head over her rosary in a scene that would stir Mary's pity. But she was not wasting time reciting prayers; all her thoughts were centered on this letter, her one hope for creating an argument that might persuade her sister. Phrases swirled in her mind, images to conjure, references that would hit home. She would make the most of this God-given chance. As He would have her do.

She ignored the commotion behind her as the table was prepared. But when silence told her the time had come and she prepared to stand, she faltered, and this spurred real prayer. Prayer for inspiration, for forgiveness, for grace, for her life. She had never prayed so hard before, and she was lost in her entreaties until she felt a gentle hand on her shoulder. "My Lady, you must begin. The tide will not wait."

Dazed, Elizabeth patted Winchester's hand and rose. She licked her lips and let herself be led to the table. Before her, a short stack of paper and a white quill. *White for purity*, she told herself. *White for luck.*

Everything about this letter mattered. Everything she said, everything she did not say. Everything had to ring with innocence. The document alone would never be able to persuade Mary to trust her fully, there had been too much between them and their mothers before that. But if Elizabeth could keep Mary unsure of her guilt, she might keep her life.

She would start with Mary's promise. Remind her that she had committed to keep an open mind, to not believe the stories people might spin. Stories that would only inflame once Elizabeth was in the Tower, whose grim stones sullied the innocence of its inmates. Only guilty people were sent there, stripped of rights and dignity before forfeiting their lives...

She swallowed and calmed herself. Writing needed a clear head.

She dipped the nib into the ink and breathed away the worries, the what-ifs. Only the words mattered, only the arguments.

If any ever did try this old saying that a king's word was more than another man's oath, I most humbly beseech Your Majesty to verify it in me, and to remember your last promise that I be not condemned without answer, which it seems that I now am. Without cause proved, I am commanded to go unto the Tower, a place more wonted for a false traitor than a true subject. And though I know I deserve it not, yet in the face of all this realm appears that it is proved.

She paused and massaged her palm. Again, she said a quick prayer that her handwriting was clean and distinctive. That took effort to maintain, but this was more important than ever. The first reading would be by the messenger, but if Mary reread passages to herself, she would see the writing she knew so well. It would be almost like Elizabeth was talking to her, and would hopefully spark some remaining ember of intimacy.

Elizabeth reread her words. The appeal had turned into indignation; she had to pull it back across that line. Righteousness was proper, vanity was not. She dipped the nib again.

I pray God I may the shamefullest death that ever any died, if I mean any harm to you. I protest before God (Who shall judge my truth) that I never practiced, counseled, nor consented to anything that might be prejudicial to your person in any way, or dangerous to the state by any means.

Elizabeth prayed Mary would recognize the truth of her words. The people around Mary hated Elizabeth for the threat she represented, but the threat stemmed from her identity, not her actions.

The law could still condemn her. The law would always arrange itself around the monarch's wishes, else her mother would still be alive today. But Mary had a conscience. Mary could be swayed, God willing. If only Elizabeth had the chance.

And therefore I humbly beseech your Majesty to let me answer before you, and not suffer me to trust to your Councillors. Yea, I pray you allow me that before I go to the Tower – but if that be not possible, then at least before I am further condemned. Let conscience move your Highness to take some better way than to let me be condemned in men's sight afore my desert is known. Also I most humbly beseech Your Highness to pardon this my boldness – but my innocence requires it, together with hope of your natural kindness, which I trust will not see me cast away without desert. I would desire no more of God but that you truly knew my innocence, but I fear you shall never know it unless you hear it for yourself and not through reports.

Thomas Seymour's face loomed before her. He was another whose intentions and actions had been twisted by ambitious men who sought his death.

I have heard in my time of many cast away for want of coming to the presence of their prince; and in late days I heard my Lord of Somerset say that if his brother had been suffered to speak with him he had never suffered; but the persuasions were made to him so great that he was brought in belief that he could not live safely if the Admiral lived, and that made him give his consent to his death. Though these persons are not to be compared to your Majesty, yet I pray God that evil persuasions persuade not one sister against the other, and all for that they have heard false report, and not harkened to the truth. Now therefore, once again, with humbleness of my heart, because I am not suffered to bow the knees of my body, I humbly crave to speak with your Highness, which I would not be so bold as to desire if I knew not myself most clear, as I know myself most true.

Tom's face receded into a cloud of wistfulness and fear. She had to stop this. She could not rely solely on emotion, not when they thought they had proof.

And as for the traitor Wyatt, he might peradventure write me a letter, but on my faith I never received any from him. And as for the copy of the letter sent to the French King, I pray God confound me eternally if I ever sent him word, message, token, or letter, by any means, and to this my truth I will stand to my death.

The word *death* dominated the page, standing out as if there were nothing else around it. She couldn't end there, but she was done. Her argument was complete. Anything further would deflate her declaration, and that was the last thing she wanted to do. And yet, more than half the page was still blank. Enough room for someone to add something, a fake postscript with a false confession to whatever came into their minds.

She inked the quill again, and drew lines across the space to leave no doubt that nothing written there was from her. Just under the lines, she signed the letter:

Your Highness's most faithful subject, that hath been from the beginning, and will be to my end,
Elizabeth

She took another look and realized she had left space to the left. She dipped her nib again to fill it.

I humbly crave but only one word of answer from yourself.

Now she was well and truly done. All she could do now was pray that, like an arrow, her words might find their mark. "Very well, gentlemen, you may take this to the Queen."

Winchester looked at the letter as if he would spit on it. "This missive has already allowed you to escape this tide," he said. "Was that your intent?"

In truth, instinct had urged Elizabeth to delay for that very reason. But she was not about to admit it. "My intent was to defend myself. Am I glad to not be in a worse place? Naturally. But it is my name and my innocence that matters most."

Winchester shrugged, and his indifference cut like a knife. She curtsied to hide her hurt, and he and Sussex bowed out.

With them gone, Elizabeth thought again of her letter, prayed again that it would earn her freedom. She turned to her ladies, and much as she needed their succor, forced herself to appear calm. Her own mother had shown her the folly of speculating which of her actions might have been misconstrued. Spies would report only the actions, not the justifications, so Elizabeth would display only innocence. She would be confident and pure in every breath she took, every sound she made.

"Pray help me dress properly in case Her Majesty calls for me."

"You should wear white, the color of innocence," Kat Ashley said.

Kat was right, but the advice vaguely suggested trickery. Elizabeth had to say something to return its honesty, lest anyone twist its meaning. "As I am, so should I look."

Confidence had started to return. She had, after all, escaped the Tower for today. "Guards!" she called imperiously. "Please retire to the other side of the door. You see there is no way for me to escape, and I need to be ready to meet the Queen."

The guards sheepishly filed out, though they did check the corners again before they did.

Elizabeth maintained her silence while her ladies dressed her. Expressing any plan of what she might say would make her sound dishonest. Discussing the politics and trying to gauge who hated her and who would support her was inappropriate. Silence was the only safe option.

John Gage entered as her sleeves were being attached. His bushy black brows were knit even tighter than usual.

"Do you bring an invitation from Her Majesty?" Elizabeth asked. She closed her eyes while awaiting his reply, offering the deepest prayer she could muster.

"Nay, my Lady. And I wouldn't expect one would be forthcoming." He shifted his weight from foot to foot. "The Queen was furious that her orders were disobeyed."

Elizabeth clasped her hands. "And what of my letter?" she asked in a small voice. "Did she give any reaction to my letter?"

"She didn't read it. She was too busy chastising Winchester and Sussex. Said they would never have dared to do what they did if King Henry were still alive and warned them that she could be even meaner when crossed."

"So, it is the Tower for me," Elizabeth said, her voice cracking. "When do we leave?"

"We're not chancing the midnight tide, if that's what you're asking. Tomorrow morning will be more than enough time."

The morrow would be Palm Sunday. Mary had resurrected the practice of carrying palms, so all Englishmen would be at church. No one would witness Elizabeth being taken to that dread place from which so few prisoners ever emerged.

It made her feel alone. She should have let them take her today: it would have made no difference and Mary would not have been so angry.

Of course, Elizabeth did not know how she would sleep between now and then.

Truth be told, she didn't know how she would sleep in that fearful place, either.

But she couldn't think of that now.

It would surely drive her mad.

March 18, 1554

Elizabeth had closed her bedcurtains to shut out the spies who would witness her terror. She didn't want anyone to know that only sitting up abated the burning in her throat, only praying curtailed the whimpering. She had to appear righteous or she would be destroyed.

Faint bells tolled for Lauds, and the sound gleamed in her mind. She could rise now; it would be easier to pass the crawling time that crushed her tighter with every passing second.

She drew back the curtain to reveal a dawn both grey and cheerless, heralding the second day of a cold rain blanketing the City. Kat was immediately beside her.

"Yes, my Lady?"

Elizabeth looked into her mournful eyes. "How will I do this?" she asked, as if Kat might have some unexpected trick to share.

Kat climbed in next to her and held her tightly, as if trying to infuse courage through touch.

"How will I do this?" Elizabeth asked again, hoping a new response would result in as much comfort as the first.

"You have no choice," Kat said.

Elizabeth sat with that truth, marshalling sheaves of courage until a new wisp of fear mingled in. "How frightening was it, really?" Kat had been brought roughly to that terrible place, thrown in a cell so cold she could not sleep, so dark she could not see by day. And yet, she had survived. Kat was proof it was possible to withstand the land's most fearful prison.

"My own experience does not matter," Kat said. "Nothing matters, for you have no choice."

"I know that. I know that as well as anyone, but I cannot help but remember the malice in its bricks even when we celebrated Mary's victory. It will be worse now."

"You did not approve the rebellion," Kat said.

"They know about the letter," Elizabeth said.

"You never received it."

"They accuse me of things that have nothing to do with me – like Noailles getting one of my messages."

"They still need proof."

Elizabeth knew all of this. She told herself all of this again and again, but no matter how many times she repeated it, she could not fully convince herself. Because of the final argument in the chain. "As they had with my mother?"

Kat enfolded Elizabeth in her arms and the two women wept.

Finally, Kat spoke. "You have no choice but to submit to God's will. Oh, I wish your cousin Catherine were here; she would be able to convey your mother's courage during those terrible last days."

Last days. Kat's mind had skipped ahead as many stages of the judicial process as Elizabeth's own. For some reason, that consoled Elizabeth, proved she was not crazy. "She did share the stories. She made sure I knew my mother was determined to follow Christ's example, how it gave her strength to do so and communicated her innocence to the world."

Elizabeth's ears filled with Katherine Parr's words of long ago. *You know, the harm also goes the other way. Your actions resurrect the charges brought against your poor mother.*

"I would get dressed now," Elizabeth said.

She allowed her mind to empty as she accepted the ministrations of her ladies, though gradually she became aware that they, too, were distracted. "Take care to dress me as carefully as you ever have," she said. "If the Queen changes her mind, I must be ready."

They had only just finished when Winchester and Sussex arrived, their faces even more stern than the day before. They were clearly in no mood to brook any delay or to indulge in common courtesy. "There will be no more of your tricks, my Lady," Winchester said as he hurried her along.

Elizabeth sighed. "'And if I say the truth, why do ye not believe me?'" Neither man gave any sign of having recognized the quote from the Gospels. They just marched her in silence to the barge, walking ahead of her as if she were a commoner. Kat and Blanche remained behind her, as if to counteract the insult, but nothing could change the fact that Elizabeth was a prisoner.

The Thames was eerily empty, the solitude intensified by the faint sound of singing from the churches near the river.

She sat in the fore, oblivious to the drizzle that was hard to distinguish from the thick mist rising from the water's surface. Her back straight and her chin high, she gazed defiantly ahead.

As they approached London Bridge, Elizabeth surveyed the merchants' homes stacked atop each other, quiet and empty now. Spikes rose here and there above them, culminating in liver-colored blobs. Realization mounted in her throat that these were rebel heads, that all of them had taken this ride to the place she was going now. She leaned over the side of the boat to vomit into the frothing waters.

A jolt in this precarious position almost sent her overboard. The stern of the barge had struck the ground around one of the bridge's piers, and now the craft titled dangerously. Behind her, Blanche screamed.

Several of the bargemen jumped out to move the boat by hand; others crowded around Elizabeth. She thought it was to help her, but when no one reached out a hand she realized it was to prevent her escape or rescue.

If she had considered the possibility earlier, perhaps she

might have tried to run. But with no plan and no supporters, she could never succeed. Indeed, the attempt would ruin any chance she still had.

She sighed, knowing how stupid she sounded even to herself. But she had to believe she might survive. No matter how outlandish the possibility, she had to pretend that her wits might see her through this latest test. While she would submit to the Lord's will, she would not strain His generosity.

The men quickly righted the barge and pushed back into the current. Elizabeth had not moved a muscle; and while Winchester kept his jaw clenched, she read approval in Sussex's eyes. That was a good sign. Or so she told herself.

The calm lasted until the White Tower loomed into view and her heart thudded with fear. She had tried to bury the ghosts of the greying bricks when Mary seized the Tudor throne, but now they were resurrected.

The barge veered to land at Tower Wharf instead of Traitor's Gate. Elizabeth said a small prayer of thanks, though her comfort was short-lived: her mother, too, had entered the Tower by the Privy Stairs. They might even have used the same barge.

Just beyond the drawbridge, Gage awaited them with his Lieutenant, John Bridges. Off to the side, a dozen bedraggled servants had gathered to watch Elizabeth's entrance, despite the foul weather. A very different welcome than the last time she'd arrived, in preparation for Mary's coronation.

Elizabeth raised her chin. "Here landeth as true a subject, despite being prisoner, as ever landed at these stairs."

Two of the guards dropped to one knee, and several of the waiting women wept. Their concern warmed Elizabeth's soul. She was not forgotten, as she feared, and the knowledge strengthened her.

The sudden boom of cannon fire shook the ground around her, the jolt rattling her innards. And then she remembered: tradition required the City be alerted when a prisoner of note entered the Tower. She stopped and turned and sat on the small staircase, oblivious to the puddles around her.

"My Lady, rise, so that we may bring you to shelter," Gage said.

"I am better here than in a worse place," Elizabeth replied. "For God knoweth, not I, whither you intend to lead me."

A mighty roar punctuated her reply, and this second shock broke Kat Ashley, who sank to her knees and wailed loudly. Instead of annoyance over Kat's hysterics, Elizabeth appreciated the expression of emotion she herself could not show – and the chance to demonstrate the serenity of a quiet conscience. "Calm yourself, Kat," she said. "My innocence will be seen; my truth is such that no man will have cause to weep for me."

She turned to Gage and Bridges but changed her mind and instead spread her arms and raised her face to the sky. "I speak this before Thee, O God, having no friend but Thee in whom to put my confidence." She lowered her arms and looked around to make sure her voice had carried to all the onlookers. They weren't many, but they were all she had. "I come in not as a traitor, but as a true woman to the Queen's Majesty."

"Well, if it prove so, it will be the better for you," Gage said.

Sussex stepped forward, eyes blazing, and put a hand on Gage's arm. "Remember, Sir, that this is the daughter of the King, our old master, and therefore let us use such dealing that we may answer it hereafter…for just dealing is always answerable."

Her heart lifted slightly from its puddle.

Gage glanced back at her before answering Sussex. "I am always guided by the spirit of justice. But thank you for the reminder."

Winchester nodded. "We will be off for now. The Lord Chancellor will want his report."

Again Elizabeth was reminded that her enemies knew every tiny detail; she tightened her grip on her emotions.

Gage nodded. He lifted a finger and guards closed around her. "Follow me."

Turning to Kat, Elizabeth once more made sure her voice would carry. "My trial here is nothing compared to the trial of our Savior. Let us praise Him as we enter. He will watch over us and keep us safe." She took Kat's arm and began to sing psalms as loudly and confidently as any Catholic martyr. Gage almost had to leap to take his place ahead of her on the winding stone path that led to the center of the stronghold.

During a break in the tunes, Gage explained: "You come at a time when we are overfull. We ran out of space in the Beauchamp Tower, and had to house most of the rabble in the crypt below St. John's Chapel."

Elizabeth looked across Tower Green to the Beauchamp Tower, but her eye halted on a scaffold, its raw wood already turning grey. That would be where Jane Grey had met her end a month before. They had not dismantled it. Were they saving it for Elizabeth?

She forced her thoughts back to the present. "You cannot mean to put me in the crypt."

"Your pardon, Your Grace. I was just sharing news. No, you will be lodged in the palace complex adjacent to the White Tower. It is much more suited to your station."

Elizabeth's mouth went so dry that she tasted dust. "Is that where my mother was kept?"

"It is, Your Grace."

Elizabeth's knees buckled but she braced herself. *Display no fear*, she screamed at herself.

Fear was guilt. Only the guilty feared; the righteous trusted in the Lord.

She lowered her gaze. As they walked, she let her full attention center on her feet and the number of steps she took to each breath. The nightmare passed easier that way.

"Here we are," Gage announced.

She held her breath as she crossed through the great guard chamber to the stone threshold of her new lodgings. Her apartments boasted four rooms: a Presence Chamber, dining room, bedroom, and small oratory. The rooms were light and in no way mean. But it was still the Tower, and what Elizabeth noticed most of all was that since she had arrived all she'd heard was metal: swords that rattled with each step taken by the hundreds of guards, endless keys that clinked together on their rings, clangs when a lock turned.

It was enough to drive her mad.

"You will be comfortable here," Gage said. "Though you will not be allowed outside your rooms."

She looked around, aghast. "May I not walk on the grounds?"

"We dare not tempt fate. Your supporters are not to be trusted."

On the one hand, the thought that she had such support was encouraging. On the other hand, these hard stone walls were already closing in on her like a tomb.

"Shall I get no fresh air, then, for however long I am here? Locked away and treated as your worst prisoner when I have done nothing wrong?"

"No provision has been made, and my instructions are to maintain the highest security around you." He shifted his weight from one foot to the other. "There may be a way. I will speak with the Queen."

"Thank you."

She looked around again, and all she wanted to do was scream and wail. But she would not. Her mother had allowed herself to descend into madness when she first arrived, and they had used her words against her. Elizabeth needed to keep a tight grip.

And pray for Grace.

CHAPTER 9

March 23, 1554

It was Good Friday, the day Jesus had been stripped and whipped and made to carry the cross onto which he was then nailed. This was the day the Council had chosen to question Elizabeth.

They had already celebrated the morning office, already unveiled the cross and crept on their knees to adore it. From that state of ultimate reverence and humility, they would come to plague her.

Elizabeth was sitting by the fire telling her beads when Gage came to get her. She made him wait until she had finished a decade – partly to demonstrate her faith, partly to stress her status, and partly because she had come to enjoy the graceful fingering motion that accompanied the prayers.

Finally, she kissed the beads and crossed herself to begin this new test.

Six officers came to surround her chair, suffocating her with their brassy body odor. "The Council is ready for you," Gage said.

She nodded and rose, the look on her face as cool as if the intimidating phalanx were meant as an honor guard. "Lead the way."

The hallway was lined with guards, many of whom nodded to her discreetly. She appreciated the show of support, and it felt all too soon that Gage turned into one of the rooms.

She walked in and looked around the dreary room that smelled of damp stone. Eight men sat behind a long table. Gardiner was in the center; on his right, the Earl of Arundel. No one stood for her or removed his cap. The jarring departure from protocol reminded her that she was a suspected traitor and not the second person in the land.

Elizabeth nodded. She did not smile; there was nothing to smile about. "Gentlemen."

Gardiner pointed at the lone chair across from the table and motioned her to sit. Elizabeth considered whether she would prefer to stand, whether such a move would bolster her confidence, make her feel less vulnerable. But if the questioning dragged on, sitting later might suggest defeat. Better to leave herself the option of rising to make a point.

She had barely settled into her seat when Gardiner began. "You are here because you had a hand in the rebellion of that foul traitor Thomas Wyatt."

"Then I should not be here at all, for I never had knowledge of his practice or proceedings."

"You would do better to confess your sins," Gardiner said. "Your lies will worsen your plight."

She knew this game. "Only the guilty confess. I have done nothing wrong."

Gardiner shrugged, a small smile playing around the side of his mouth. "You have been sick, I understand."

The non sequitur to an obvious fact troubled her. "I have been."

"And you were sick in January, when the Queen invited you to court."

"The Queen's own doctors worried for my life," Elizabeth said.

"If you were ill, why did you consider removing to Donnington Castle?"

The question caught her by surprise, and the lie leaped from her lips. "Do I have such a house? I have many estates and I cannot recollect this one."

"I find your lack of memory hard to believe," Gardiner said with a malicious purr. "Especially given the care with which you have traded and husbanded your properties."

Before she could answer, Gardiner raised a hand to alert the page. "Bring in Sir James Croft."

Elizabeth blanched. She did her best to control her breathing as Croft was brought in, hands chained. There was no chair for him.

"Well? Have you no greeting for your accomplice?" Gardiner asked.

"Accomplice? What is this?" She tried desperately to make her words sound angry rather than panicked.

"He came to warn you at Ashridge, isn't that right, Sir James? Tell us what you told me."

Croft did not raise his eyes. "I warned that there would be danger in the area. I spoke to one of her servants."

"And what did this servant say?"

"He said they would move to Donnington to avoid the danger."

Gardiner turned to Elizabeth, an evil smile on his face. "Your servants know your properties but you do not? Or does the sight of this man help your memory?"

Elizabeth waved an arm. "Yes, yes, now I recollect the house. I rarely use the name – I speak of it as Berkshire, since that is where it is located."

"And with your memory restored, what have you to say?" Gardiner asked.

Elizabeth turned to anger. "You ask him what my servant said but nothing that would show my innocence. Have him testify – have all my household officers testify – whether they have ever heard any rash or unbeseeming words pass my lips."

Gardiner's face twisted but most of the other Councilors nodded. And Croft finally looked up. His eyes filled with tears and he kneeled to her. "I was heartily sorry to be brought in this day to be a witness against Your Grace, but I take God to record that I never knew anything of you worthy of the least suspicion."

More grimaces from Gardiner, more nods from the others.

"I thank you for your honesty," she said.

"We shall see if William Saintlow will say the same. He is the servant to whom Croft spoke," Gardiner said. "He is being fetched as we speak."

She froze at the name – and the fear of what he might say. She had firmly refused to bless the rebellion, but would he hold to the truth if they racked him? She could not think about that now. She had to do something, anything, to counteract the suspicions Gardiner had just raised.

She turned to the Councilors. "My Lords, methinks you do me wrong to examine every mean prisoner against me. If they have done evil, let them answer for it – but I pray you not to join me with such offenders."

"They offend in your name," Gardiner said. "And you did consider removing to Donnington."

"I was planning visits to several of my houses come spring, but what is that to your purpose?" Elizabeth again turned to the other Councilors: they hated her less. "Might I not, my Lords, go to mine own houses at all times? Do any of you doubt that it is a good thing to visit your homes?"

"It is not the visiting that troubles us," Gardiner said, "but rather the timing of the visit. It seems suspicious."

Elizabeth's face twisted. "You sift me narrowly, but you can do no more than God hath appointed. I pray He will forgive you all."

Gardiner looked like he was going to continue, but Arundel cut him off. "Her Grace speaks true. Not one of the prisoners questioned told us of any inappropriate behavior or words. Including Croft, whom we brought here now for I know not what reason. For myself, I am sorry to see her troubled about such vain matters."

Gratitude flooded Elizabeth for this unexpected defense from an unlikely quarter. "Thank you, my Lord," she said. "For your honesty and support."

"I agree with Arundel," said Sussex. "Let us take heed that we go not beyond our commission, for she is, we know, the prince next in blood. Wherefore let us so deal with her now, that we have not, if it so happen, to answer for our dealings hereafter."

"Not all traitors are lowborn," Gardiner said, wagging his finger at his peers. He turned to Elizabeth, eyes blazing. "The truth will out, my Lady," he said. "And when it does, you will burn."

The look on his face was pure evil, and she could almost smell the smoldering wood. She shuddered, wanting to scream. Tightening her grip on her emotions, she forced herself to breathe calmly. Good Friday was a potent reminder that no one escaped God's trials.

If it came to the worst, she would ask Mary for a French sword rather than the English axe. It was the ironic favor that her father had done for her mother, ensuring that her delicate neck would be severed with a single clean stroke.

Surely that would be enough for them.

April 17, 1554

Elizabeth sat by the window in the Presence Chamber, desperate for connection to the outside and the illusion of life. She poked a needle at her sewing, wishing it would occupy more of her thoughts. Danger had stagnated, but tedium still made it too easy to wallow in melancholy.

Unable to break Saintlow, who had proved not at all abashed at the charges, Gardiner was still reportedly questioning every ruffian brought into the Tower, hoping that one of them would implicate Elizabeth. At least so said the gossip Blanche heard the other day in the kitchens, where she had made as many friends as she could.

A muffled sound of cheering arose. Elizabeth lowered her work to stand. She opened the window and the sound grew louder. It was coming from across the green, from the Bell or Beauchamp Tower, where the more important rebels were held. Like the Dudleys, at least the ones left. Convicted but not yet dead.

She turned to her ladies, well, to Blanche and Kat. Her other women, like poor Isabella Markham whose husband was in this grim place, had been replaced for refusing to attend Mass; Elizabeth ignored the new arrivals. "What celebration is this?"

Blanche lowered her own needlework. "I'll go find out."

Kat sighed. "Maybe the Queen has decided not to gift England to Spain after all."

Elizabeth whirled around, eyes piercing as a hawk's: if a spy reported this, they would have to admit that Elizabeth had condemned the disparaging statement.

Kat rolled her eyes but accepted the chastising. "Sorry."

Elizabeth started to pace and was once again frustrated by being able to take only six or so strides before turning around. The walls were closing in on her, cutting her off even further from the outside world. Thank God for Blanche, who was able to sneak in occasional news. Without her, Elizabeth's only contact was her confessor, and he refused to speak of anything but Scripture.

Blanche burst in, eyes wide, and quickly closed the door behind her. "Nicholas Throckmorton was just acquitted of treason."

Acquitted? Elizabeth's heart leaped.

"And even more than that," Blanche added. "When Thomas Wyatt went to the scaffold the other day, he exonerated you."

Elizabeth's knees buckled and she staggered to a chair. *Praise God. Praise God. Praise God.*

Kat was immediately upon her. "My Lady, are you all right?"

Elizabeth waved her away. "Tell me again," she said to Blanche. "Sit. Tell me everything. Start with Wyatt."

Blanche sat and collected herself. "Apparently, Gardiner promised Wyatt he would go free for implicating you – so when he was instead brought to the scaffold, he recanted. Right before he knelt for the headsman, Wyatt swore that you were in no way privy to his rising."

Secrets spilled in a life's final minutes carried a crushing legal and moral weight; this was the ultimate testimony in Elizabeth's favor. She lost herself in contemplation but was brought radically back when Blanche continued.

"And then Nicholas Throckmorton was tried today at Guildhall for his part in the rebellion. They say he ran rings around his accusers."

"What rings?" Elizabeth asked. "How?"

"He ridiculed the prosecutors' attempts to find him guilty by association – apparently he even caught them out on points of law. The jury acquitted him completely and unanimously."

The sheer impossibility of such an occurrence stunned Elizabeth. No one was ever brave enough to defy the Crown. Even the nonsense claims against Anne Boleyn had been confirmed without dissent. "Acquitted?" Elizabeth repeated.

"The jurors have all been jailed for it," Blanche said. "Two were brought back here with Throckmorton, the rest were taken to the Fleet."

That sounded more like the royal justice system. "So, Throckmorton was not freed, despite the verdict?"

"No."

Elizabeth sighed. It was still good news. It had to help her. Didn't it?

May 3, 1554

Oblivious to the conflict and hostilities housed within the Tower battlements, nature had covered the grounds in the season's *muguets*. Elizabeth lifted her face, savoring their scent along with the warm sun that almost thawed the chill in her bones. "I am deeply grateful for this kindness," she said to John Gage.

"It is the Queen's kindness, not mine."

Elizabeth flashed him a serene smile. "As I said, I am deeply grateful."

The Lord had brought her from the pit of despair to calm hope: James Croft had been brought to trial the day after Throckmorton, and four jurors had defied the government's threats and voted to acquit him as well. Every day, evidence against Elizabeth slipped like sand through the Council's fingers, justifying small, incremental improvements in her treatment. First, she had been allowed to walk in the Queen's apartments so as to escape the rigid confinement of her own suite, though both Gage, Bridges, and half the Tower guards were required to accompany her, and all the windows had to be carefully shuttered to prevent anyone from gazing upon her. Gradually the windows were ignored, and finally supervision was relaxed to Bridges and only three guards.

Now the small army had returned because the Council had agreed she might walk in the Privy Garden, a quiet area surrounded by towers. Bridges had gone to them for this small liberty, God bless him.

She lifted her face again, and noticed that the windows overlooking the garden were all closed with their curtains drawn. Her first reaction was to sigh, but she forced hope into her heart. Surely this too would pass.

She turned to Kat and Blanche, whose faces were lifted as well. "Shall we?"

Without waiting for an answer, Elizabeth took off, basking in the quickened heartbeat and deepened breath of honest exercise.

May 9, 1554

The sun in the Privy Garden shone bright as Elizabeth took her third turn around the garden. The windows of the surrounding towers were no longer tightly shuttered; the guards were stationed by the corners instead of crowding her. Only Bridges accompanied her, and he walked with her ladies a step behind. She was glad to be spared his conversation – she had never suffered fools, and the man owed his position to his connections more than his wits.

A spot of orange to the side caught her eye, and she turned to the figure racing towards her: a ginger-haired boy of around five, flowers clutched in an outstretched hand. His clean woolen tunic suggested he was the son of someone who worked here.

He was quickly upon them, and he bowed fully but awkwardly. Elizabeth's lips twitched. He'd clearly not had a lot of practice with gallantry, though this was a prison, after all.

"These are for you, my Lady," he said between pants. "To brighten your rooms."

His shining eyes and tender earnestness touched her. She took the flowers and brought them to her nose. "I thank you, my good lad," she said. "I will treasure them." The boy beamed and ran off as quickly as he'd come.

Blanche laughed. "Quite the admirer."

"Would that the whole world was like that," Elizabeth said. She turned to hand the bouquet to Blanche, but Bridges grabbed it. "That should not have happened."

"You would begrudge me a few blooms from a child?"

Bridges scrutinized the random branches of the grubby bouquet and flushed. Without a word, he handed it to Blanche.

Her good mood restored, Elizabeth started off again. Partway down the lane, she noticed two men standing in the walkway waiting for her, and her hackles rose. They calmed when she recognized Sussex and Howard, but she still wondered what new vexation this was.

"Greetings, Cousins," she said, before noticing the silver cloth in Howard's doublet. No one lower than a baron was permitted such finery. "I see congratulations are in order." She bowed. "How shall I name you from now on?"

"First Baron Howard of Effingham," he said. "And Lord High Admiral of England."

Elizabeth's heart missed a beat – Thomas Seymour had been Lord High Admiral – but she kept the smile on her face. "May the honors continue."

"They say the Queen means to make him a Knight of the Garter," Sussex said. "It was all his bravery that prevented Wyatt from entering the City at Ludgate. The rebels surrendered a few hours after."

Elizabeth mentally replayed the conversation back at Ashridge, his description of how Mary's speech at Guildhall had stemmed the tide of the uprising. "When we spoke about that day, you were too modest to share your own exploits. I am glad my sister rewarded loyalty such as yours."

"Allow me to add my own greetings and congratulations," Bridges said.

"Ah, thank you," Effingham said. "In fact, it is you we have come to see. We need coins to be delivered to Westminster and

Windsor later this week. We gave the specifics to your guards, but they will do nothing further without your approval." The Tower's impregnable walls not only detained prisoners, they also guarded the Royal Mint. Of course, its operations were hidden from most of the fortress.

Bridges's chest swelled. "We keep a tight watch on the Mint staff, especially if treasure is to leave."

"Of course," Effingham said, then turned to Elizabeth. "And this gave us the chance to pay respects to your charge."

She smiled. "I am grateful to your duty for bringing you here." Hoping they had not noticed the boy with the flowers, she continued, "You and the Council are the only men I have spoken to besides my confessor, the only men I have seen except my guards. I am allowed only prayer and needlepoint to pass the time." She waved an arm around. "You have all these ramparts and soldiers – why have I been so straightly kept?"

"You are outside now," Sussex said with a wry smile.

A week ago, she had counted the fresh air as God's ultimate gift, but reflecting on her circumstances had dissipated that. "Would it be so terrible to allow me books?"

"The books will come," Effingham said.

Sussex leaned forward. "The accusations against you may be less damning than they first appeared. The Queen continues to grant you freedoms, but you must be patient."

Less damning? Instinctively, she pressed her point. "Patient? I have been wrongly accused, gentlemen. My righteousness has sustained me so far, but my good name is sullied just from being in this place. People will think I am a traitor because I am shut up with traitors."

"You are here because you are under terrible suspicion," Sussex said. "You had motive and opportunity, and some believe you took action."

"But I did not."

Effingham shrugged. "Gardiner still hopes to prove it, and Simon Renard thinks he can."

"Then bring me to trial," she challenged. With Throckmorton acquitted and Croft nearly so, it was time to call their bluff.

"It still would be better to avoid that."

The words hung in the air. Finally, she broke the silence. "Well, I will try to be patient but the calumny is hurtful. I thank you both for believing in me and interceding on my behalf."

She had perhaps given them more credit than they deserved, but she hoped it would make them try to live up to her regard. Sure enough, they both bowed. More awkward silence, then Effingham's eyes narrowed. "And you are attending Mass?"

Elizabeth smiled. "The Lord Chancellor causes it to be said and sung before me every day." She tactfully avoided mentioning that two of her ladies had been dismissed for refusing to attend her at those services. "And it brings me more comfort than I thought possible."

"Good," said the Earl of Sussex. "The Queen will be glad to hear it."

"Glad enough to allow me books?" She kept her tone deliberately playful as she repeated a request that had already been denied. "Right now, I am deprived even of psalms for comfort."

"Psalms?" Sussex rubbed his eyes. "I cannot see forbidding you books of prayer. Even Gardiner could not want that."

She thrilled to the support and curtsied to emphasize her gratitude.

"May I ask a question about protocol?" Bridges added. "It is customary for the Lieutenant of the Tower to occasionally invite prisoners of rank to his table, where they are sure to find foods suitable to their humors. I have not yet extended this courtesy to the Lady Elizabeth, though Jane Grey and her husband joined me every ten days or so."

Elizabeth leaped at the prospect. She said a silent apology to her dead cousin and turned to Effingham and Sussex. "Surely an innocent woman can expect a courtesy shown even to convicted traitors."

Sussex turned to Effingham, but Effingham shook his head. "All our efforts on your behalf have not even resulted in books. This is not the time to introduce another request."

"You would not long tolerate the fare that is served me," she said.

Bridges bristled. "That is entirely within your control." He gestured toward Blanche. "We allow your own lady to work with the cooks – you should speak with her if your specifications are not met."

"You see?" Effingham said. "You are shown courtesy."

She narrowed her eyes. "Another courtesy shown even to convicted traitors. Anyone with the means to pay can secure their own food."

Effingham's mouth twisted. Fearing she had gone too far, she put a hand on his forearm. "I know I vex you terribly. I just keep thinking that my innocence deserves better treatment, but I take out my frustration on people who are trying to help. I am sorry."

"I cannot fault you." Effingham's sigh turned to a chuckle. "Well, not completely."

"Good," Elizabeth said, relieved. "We are friends again."

"Always, dearest Cousin."

"We will leave you to your walk, then," Sussex said. "And tend to reports we must make and the requests we will pursue."

Elizabeth smiled. "Thank you."

May 15, 1554

William Cecil found St. James Palace a much sadder place than it had been the last time he had seen it, the last time he had been a part of things. Even then, England's ruler had been a pawn in someone else's game, but at least Northumberland had been

English. Cecil stopped himself. He was here. This was not the time to ruminate.

He had spent the last year at home, mourning the loss of his ideals and patiently awaiting the right time to return to court – or begin to try. Instead, prospects worsened as Mary handed more each day to Spain and the Pope. Cecil had finally come to see for himself – and discovered things were even worse than he'd heard.

He caught the eye of his sister-in-law, one of seven women huddled in the corner awaiting the Queen's attention and pleasure. Anne Bacon had been accepted as one of Mary's ladies, giving Cecil an excuse to visit court, if only for a quick greeting from a distance. *Is it always like this?* he wanted to ask.

The worst part was, he felt alone in his horror. Only the embroidered figures in the massive tapestries lining the Presence Chamber joined him in looking upset or perturbed: the hundreds of people watching the Queen on her dais maintained insipid half-smiles. Could they not hear the terrible conversation she was having with the lords arranged in a half-circle before her, a conversation that threatened England's very future?

Any attempts to secure fair treatment for Elizabeth were being met with escalating malice. William Paget's proposal to release Elizabeth from the Tower into strict house arrest had prompted the Spanish Ambassador, Simon Renard, to urge her death instead. "You know she is guilty. She deserves the block," he said, using foxlike charms to make his point. "Your Majesty's throne will never be safe while she lives."

William Howard, newly Baron Effingham, raised a warning index finger. "I remind you that, in England, only overt acts of treason merit the block. At best, you might show Elizabeth consented through silence, which entails only imprisonment – and now that Wyatt has exonerated her, even that is doubtful."

God bless Effingham. Cecil and he had never been close, but Cecil had always respected him. Even more now that he was willing to defend Elizabeth against another deadly plot to remove a threat. He wondered whether Renard and Gardiner would feel it necessary to confess their duplicity to gain entry to Heaven. Just as the scaffold had extracted the admission from Northumberland that Somerset had been innocent.

"She sent Wyatt an encouraging message, for sweet Jesu's sake," Gardiner said.

"We must strike now," Renard said.

"We will never prove the charges," said the Earl of Sussex. Another strong Catholic voice that could not be easily dismissed.

"Then attainder," demanded Renard.

"Attainder is for people so guilty they need no trial," Sussex retorted. "It is equally likely to fail."

Cecil bowed his head at Sussex's argument, glad there were people to champion Elizabeth when he could not. It hurt how little his opinion mattered to this new court. Though at least he had some modicum of access – most of his fellow members of Parliament were routinely turned away.

Stephen Gardiner grabbed Sussex's arm. "She has bewitched you, as her mother used to do. Her evil must be stopped." Religious zeal infused Gardiner's voice, or was it just vengeful anger? On his deathbed, Henry VIII had rejected the cleric, excluding him from any future government posts. Now Gardiner was working to destroy not just the political vestiges of Henry's legacy, but also the personal ones.

"Thank you, my Lord Chancellor." Renard's voice was silky. "I am glad someone places more importance on the Queen's safety than on the false trappings of justice."

Gardiner whirled around to Mary. "Your Majesty, your father never would have shied from making sure a traitor received her due."

Cecil balled his fists, his nails digging into his palms.

"Which should be done sooner rather than later," Renard

said. "For until Elizabeth is executed, it will be impossible for Prince Philip to approach England."

Bile rose in Cecil's throat from the evil blackmail, higher still when Mary blanched and her eyes widened.

"He signed the treaty." Her lower lip quivered. "I wear his betrothal ring. Does he love me so little as to stay away?"

Renard shook his head. "Do you love him so little as to risk his person?"

Mary wavered for a moment before shaking off the comment. "I cannot spill blood without a trial."

"Strict house arrest is the best course of action," Paget said, resurrecting the original source of the dispute. "Your Majesty will remember your decision to show mercy." He turned to Renard. "We discussed this, you and I, and you agreed that mercy would help put the incident behind us and increase support for the marriage."

"We were speaking of mercy for the masses, not for the Lady Elizabeth," Renard said.

"The principle is the same," Paget said. "If we are emptying the Tower, then we should send the Lady Elizabeth home as well."

"It is better that ten innocent men suffer than one guilty man escape," Gardiner said.

Cecil's eyes darted from one Councilor to the next. The Bible said the opposite, as had English law for the past hundred years. How could no one challenge the Lord Chancellor on this point?

"She would be too carefully watched to escape." Paget turned to Mary. "It would remove the last cloud over Your Majesty's marriage. Please consider it."

"Your Majesty, her very existence threatens Philip's safety. God forbid something should happen to him," Renard said.

"And Elizabeth is guilty, with or without a trial," Gardiner added.

A single tear escaped from Mary's eye. "I would rather never have been born than any outrage should happen to my beloved. But I will not have this death on my conscience. Or your master's."

The Councilors mulled around until Paget raised a finger, signaling an idea that might break the stalemate. "If we lack sufficient evidence to convict her, and you crave a more permanent solution than house arrest," he said, "then perhaps the best way to address the threat she represents would be to send her out of the kingdom, through a foreign marriage."

The possibility was an interesting one, and Cecil appreciated Paget's ingenuity even as it pained him to think that banishing Elizabeth might be the only way to save her. Part of him wondered whether these calls for death were all a negotiating ploy meant to make a foreign match acceptable.

Renard nodded. "Savoy. He could neutralize the danger she represents."

Cecil coughed to hide the snort that escaped him. Emmanuel Philibert, the Duke of Savoy, was an empty doublet: the French had seized control of his hereditary lands more than two decades ago; in the hope of recovering them, he fawned on his Spanish cousins.

Gardiner wagged a finger. "The only way to remove the danger she represents is to exclude her from the succession."

"And that as quickly as possible," Mary said.

"I can see no way by which she could, at present, be excluded or deprived of the right which Parliament gave her," Paget said, his voice firm.

Mary reached a hand to Gardiner's arm as if to calm his response. "She will be excluded when my son is born," she said. "That is the solution."

Paget stroked his chin. "And in case that does not happen, perhaps Elizabeth's rights in the succession could be secured to her consort."

Mary glared at him, clearly unwilling to consider any

scenario in which her sister would inherit. Paget seemed oblivious to his misstep, or at least indifferent. "And in the meantime, such a convenient union would obviate all the dangers and difficulties involved in the unpopular marriage between Your Majesty and the Prince of Spain."

Mary opened her mouth as if to object but closed it again and turned to Renard. "Do you see why your master must come? And quickly? The kingdom needs our heir for its tranquility." Her eyes narrowed. "I am sure that is Spain's priority as well."

Renard bowed, and Cecil was relieved that Mary had forced him to back down. But Gardiner resumed his own dangerous efforts. "All of us will rejoice when a noble imp is born to Your Majesty," Gardiner said. "But until then, we deserve to see the traitor Elizabeth brought to justice."

"This talk has made my head ache." Mary rubbed a temple and looked at her ladies. "I would rest now." Jane Dormer approached and helped Mary from the dais.

"I will consider your proposal later and pray on it," Mary said.

"Shall I wait on Your Majesty later?" Gardiner asked.

She turned back to him and rubbed her forehead. "The auras I am seeing tell me I will be several days abed. I will send for you when I am better."

Cecil mopped his forehead and said a quick prayer for his friend. Much as he hated the thought of Elizabeth married to a Spanish pawn, such a prospect had slowed Renard's calls for her death, and for that Cecil was grateful.

Out of the corner of his eye, he saw Renard and Gardiner exchanging glances, and Gardiner raising a hand as if giving a blessing. Or urging patience.

Cecil's bowels iced: what mischief were they planning now? He did not want to know. Not that he could help if he knew: he had no place in this court. Still, he would try to wait on Paget, bank the coals of that friendship.

Cecil would have to be patient.

May 16, 1554

The clanking from the hallway told Elizabeth guards were approaching. She put down the devotions she'd been reading – the Council had finally authorized religious texts – and stood to receive the men.

The jangling of the keys and the thuds of the tumblers grated more than usual. A constant reminder of her impotent captivity.

"They're probably still mad about the boy," Kat grumbled.

"What boy?" Blanche asked.

"The boy who brought me flowers," Elizabeth said. "The cook's son. They thought he carried secret messages from Edward Courtenay, and they whipped the poor lad."

"How terrible," Blanche said. "How did you know?"

"The poor thing waited in the stairway today for the Princess to pass by," Kat said. "He told her, 'My Lady, I can bring you no more flowers,' and ran off."

Elizabeth would never reveal there had been a message, once, though not from Courtenay. "*Superabo*," it had said, bringing tears to her eyes but steel to her resolve.

Finally the door opened. Two guards entered, their swords facing her. Bridges followed and came to kneel before her, shoulders drooping. "I am sorry to bring you this news," he said, his voice breaking. "But the case has gone against you and it is time to prepare yourself."

The words did not fully register immediately; she had to sift them to understand. When she did, her whole body folded in on itself in anguish. Loud weeping burst from her ladies. Kat grabbed her and hugged her hard until Elizabeth could not tell whose snot and tears smeared her face.

How could Mary have done this? How could Mary have condemned her without a trial, without any pretense of justice?

She limped to the chair and sank into it, raising her hand to a neck that could not be larger than her mother's. "When am I to… when is it to be?"

"The sentence is to be carried out immediately."

The weight of his words swung like an axe through her neck. But she found herself breathing after the blow and it propelled her to action. "Without notice? What honest witnesses have you assembled so quickly?"

"It is to be a quiet matter. My guards are honest men."

Elizabeth kept shaking her head, kept swaying back and forth. "Let me see the warrant," she said. "Let me see whether her hand was shaky or strong." Elizabeth needed to read the judgment in the writing, the final, horrible decision.

"It is not the Queen's hand," Bridges said. "It is Gardiner's."

"Gardiner's?" The name echoed in her brain and her voice rose. "Gardiner's?" She almost spat. "Only my sister can order my death."

"The Queen was too sick to sign. The Lord Chancellor signed for her."

Elizabeth tried to keep calm. She knew her eyes were wild; she didn't want to be dismissed. This was her life. "The warrant is not legal without the Queen's signature."

"Gardiner is the first man in the land."

"That is not enough. Only the sovereign may sign this."

Bridges's eyes flickered. "I dare not go back to ask Her Majesty. I accompanied Winchester and Sussex to deliver your letter, the one asking to be heard before you were taken to the Tower. The Queen raged mightily then. I dare not fail to obey another of her orders."

Elizabeth's heartbeat pounded in her ears. "This is different," she wailed. "This is not an order she ever gave."

Bridges's face didn't change from its resigned sympathy. Elizabeth wanted to shake him, penetrate his shell of stupidity and gullibility. Instead she marshalled her ultimate argument. It was treason in the saying, but what did that matter to a woman already condemned? "You say the Queen is sick – what if she dies? Will you execute the next heir with the Queen on her deathbed? The Spaniards will rule here, you know they will. England will be lost, and it will be your fault."

He swayed as the full import of her words hit him, but still he resisted. "I cannot refuse the Lord Chancellor."

"The Lord Chancellor will deny everything. Once I am dead, he will say he gave you the paper for safekeeping, that he never believed you would act upon it. You will lose your own head for this. You know that, right?"

Now Bridges's face took on the fear of a beaten dog. Elizabeth pressed on savagely. "The Chancellor will say you should have known not to implement a warrant that hadn't been signed by the Queen, a warrant you know is not based on a trial and probably is not based on an attainder either. He will insist on the full measure of death for you."

"He would not have given me this warrant if he had no right to do so."

"You will die – and not by the axe since you are not of gentle blood. You will be drawn and quartered." She took a step forward and lowered her voice. "You've seen that death; you know its horror. Don't kill both of us for fear of asking a righteous question."

He covered his eyes with his fists as if to shut out the vision she had painted. "Fine," he yelled. "I will check."

Only when he had left with his men did Elizabeth allow her knees to buckle. She fell to the floor and stayed there, silent, her heartbeat still hard against her ears. Her ladies did not even twitch as they watched her, hands clasped as if they were praying over her.

Elizabeth breathed slowly until the world returned to normal. Finally, she pushed herself to standing. She looked at Kat

Ashley's ashen face and nodded. "I'd like some wine, please." Her voice was barely a croak.

The room was silent as only stone can be. She fought off the desire to crawl into bed and pull the covers over her head. If she was to end her days, she would end them upright. If God demanded her martyrdom, so be it.

She grabbed a rosary and retired to her oratory to kneel and pray, her face hidden from the world. There were no tears, only ice. And iron.

Would this end like the last time, her sister infuriated over Elizabeth's attempt to delay? Would Jane Grey's scaffold get another use?

Or was this overreaching by a man who had made it clear he sought Elizabeth's death?

Would Mary don a killer's mantle? Even their father had given Anne Boleyn a chance to defend herself.

But Anne had still died. Eighteen years ago, almost to this same day. And she had said of Mary, *She is my death and I am hers.*

Elizabeth began to pray in earnest.

CHAPTER 10

May 18, 1554

Clanking sounded in the hall, the first in two days. For two days Bridges had left Elizabeth in suspense, two interminable days of waiting that had paradoxically calmed her. They had tried to kill her unlawfully. Surely their treachery had been brought to light during this delay.

She stood to meet her fate. Her ladies raced to crowd behind her. Everyone's fingers clenched beads – superstition, it turned out, was more reassuring than Elizabeth had once believed possible.

The heavy door swung open and Bridges stepped in. His face wore neither sorrow nor joy, only grim exhaustion. She swayed in spite of herself, her mind racing with desperate pleas to God. "What news do you bring me?"

"An apology." He dropped to one knee. "And freedom."

As his words sank into the parched ground of her soul, her heart soared. "Praise the Lord."

Bridges looked up. "There was a…misunderstanding. As you surmised, the warrant was merely to ensure I would be prepared.

The Lord Chancellor had no intention of issuing such an order on his own and is relieved that a terrible outcome was averted."

Elizabeth bit back the curses and insults she longed to hurl. Instead, she said a quick prayer and patted Bridges's head. "We have both been blessed with a narrow escape. Come, let us share some wine."

She led him to the table. They sat together in a silent daze as the precipice receded, leaving numbness in its wake. The trance dissolved when Kat handed her a filled cup. "Pour for yourself as well." Elizabeth waved her arm around the room. "Pour for everyone." Surely she was not the only one who desperately needed the drink.

She stood, surveying faces, while her ladies and Bridges's guards were served. Even Mary's spies seemed relieved. "To the Queen's justice," Elizabeth said, raising her glass.

She took a deep draught, savoring the earthy scent, and smiled at Blanche. "Best wine you have procured yet."

She sat and leaned forward toward Bridges. "Now tell me about this new freedom. Does this mean I am finally allowed paper and pen?"

"The Council has engaged in far greater soul-searching than that, my Lady." A gentle smile widened across his face. "You are to be released from the Tower."

She clenched her emotions, afraid to trust the words. "I am to go free?"

He squirmed. "You are still under suspicion. You will be closely confined, but not in a prison."

She raised a single eyebrow. "Who will 'closely confine' me? And where?"

"The Queen has chosen Henry Bedingfield for the task. And the Palace of Woodstock for the place."

"Woodstock?" Elizabeth wrinkled her nose. "The hunting lodge?"

"Your grandfather spent more on its renovations than he did anywhere but Richmond."

A hazy story played around the edges of her memory. "Was that before or after the murder there?"

"That is a vicious rumor."

Elizabeth rubbed her temple. Was this another trick of Gardiner's? How ironic that the Tower was feeling safer to her. "And who is this Bedingfield?"

"A Norfolk man. Knighted by your brother."

"What manner of man is he?"

"He's a good man." Bridges looked off to the side, nodding as he spoke. "Well intentioned. Loyal."

Gardiner, too, could be called loyal. "Is he one to kill me if told to do so?"

Bridges jerked back but recovered quickly. "He is the son of the Bedingfield that held the Queen's mother at Kimbolton."

Had Mary figured out another diabolical way of reminding Elizabeth how old tables had turned? Or was this just a coincidence given the favor Mary showed to anyone connected to Catherine of Aragon? Most important, had Bedingfield's father been an honest gaoler?

The thoughts swirling in her mind parted like birds before a predator. "You did not answer my question."

"I cannot believe you need to worry. He will come wait on you shortly. You will see for yourself."

Elizabeth drummed her fingers on the table, uneasy.

Bridges sighed and stood. "I expected this conversation to go differently. You are being allowed to leave despite the charges against you. You should be grateful."

Heat flooded her face and Elizabeth bit back her exasperation – how could this fool not understand the danger, especially after the malice he had just witnessed? "This episode exposed the full extent of the enmity that some of the Queen's counselors bear towards me despite my innocence. How do I know this is not another attempt to have me killed?"

His face turned grim. "I must caution you against accusing the Queen."

Now it was Elizabeth who jerked back. "No, no, I accuse only her advisors." She glanced around the room, conscious of all the people who could repeat her words. "My sister has been most merciful – but I continue to fear…mistakes."

"The distance will ensure that any mistakes will have less dangerous consequences." Bridges's voice was firm. "Now, have your ladies start packing."

The door slammed behind him. Elizabeth slumped back in her chair. There had been rumors that Catherine of Aragon had been poisoned – rumors Elizabeth had always rejected since the same stories accused Anne Boleyn of giving the orders. But what if the poison part was true?

Blanche stood. "Assemble my Lady's gowns," she said to the others. She came to refill Elizabeth's cup and leaned in to speak in a quiet voice. "They would not hesitate to murder you on these grounds, like the two York princes. You should not fear to take your chances elsewhere."

"Assuming Henry Bedingfield is an honest man."

"He surely is more honest than Gardiner or Renard. Console yourself with that – and with the fact that Her Majesty is now aware of their corruption. Their words will carry less weight from now on."

Elizabeth nodded and drank deeply. Blanche was right. But Elizabeth would be sure to have her food tasted.

Just then, more clanking echoed from the hallway. A guard knocked without waiting for an answer. "Sir Henry Bedingfield." He stepped to the side for Bedingfield to enter.

Elizabeth rose. Her new gaoler was about her height, and… doughy. Not far past fifty, his wide eyes were earnest, not evil, topped by a forehead wrinkled from concern, or perhaps fear.

He knelt before her to speak. "I wish we had met under better circumstances, but I am Henry Bedingfield, charged by the Queen your sister to bring you to Woodstock and there to keep you close confined."

"You may rise."

Determination entered his eyes, but his stubbornness bore no malice. "Nay, my Lady. I intend to respect as much of your dignity and station as is possible. I will have to strictly limit your activities while you are under my guard – but I will honor you properly."

Elizabeth kept her face carefully bland. Bridges was right: Bedingfield did not have the air of a killer. "I appreciate that, though I confess I still feel myself ill handled."

"I am sorry for that, my Lady, yet it will not stop me from doing as the Council orders. I have a detailed commission and I will adhere to every item."

Kat Ashley stepped forward. "You must show my Lady the document so that she knows what is allowed. As her servants, we need to know, too."

Bedingfield bit his lip and shifted on his knees. He looked as if he were considering rising to speak with her, but he stayed where he was. "You remain under suspicion as well, Mistress. You will be released to the custody of Roger Cholmley in Highgate."

Kat paled and took a step backward. "What is this news?"

Elizabeth raised her chin. "There has been no suggestion of charges against anyone but myself."

"Mistress Ashley's history of poor judgment warrants keeping you separate," Bedingfield said. "This is a precaution, nothing more."

History of poor judgment. Elizabeth flushed. "So who will serve me?"

"You may have three ladies."

"Only three?"

"Mistress Parry, Mistress Sandes, and Mistress Willoughby," he said firmly.

It could have been worse. They had left her Blanche, thank God. And Margaret Willoughby was the least offensive of Mary's spies – Elizabeth needed someone to taste her food, after all.

"These are my orders," he repeated. "Until they change."

His words reminded her of the many restrictions relaxed over the course of her captivity, and freedom beckoned stronger. How much longer until she could escape the deadly stone walls? How much longer did Renard and Gardiner have to change Mary's mind? "When do we leave?"

"My commission instructs us to leave tomorrow. May nineteenth."

Elizabeth took a step back to hide the slight buckling of her knees. She would leave the Tower on May nineteenth. She closed her eyes to embrace her mother's specter. This was a sign. Instead of dying on that day, Elizabeth would be released.

She clamped down on her emotions: the danger was not yet past. "What time?" she asked.

"We will take our leave of the Constable and Lieutenant right after dinner. No later than one."

"And when will we arrive at Woodstock?"

Still on his knees, Bedingfield took out a handkerchief and mopped his forehead. "The palace is a little more than sixty miles away. It will take us about four days."

She leaned forward. "Where will we stay each night?"

"We will only go as far as Richmond Palace the first day. That will give time for William Dormer in Buckinghamshire, and Lord Williams of Thame in Oxfordshire, to prepare to receive you."

Elizabeth turned over the names. Jane Dormer's father, and King Henry's former Treasurer of the Jewels. Rabid Catholics, obnoxious but not sinister. Indeed, Williams had always been kind to Elizabeth. She sat back again, struck by the visceral understanding that she might actually leave the Tower. It felt like the sun was starting to break through the cloud of suspicion that lingered over her.

"I will see you a little before one tomorrow, so that we are prompt with Gage and Bridges, who I assume will be waiting at the gate."

Elizabeth started to thank Bedingfield as a subtle dismissal, but three loud bangs overwhelmed her voice. She looked over at the window. "What are they doing out there?"

Kat looked out, surveying Tower Green. "They are dismantling Jane Grey's scaffold." Her voice quavered.

Elizabeth turned back to Bedingfield. Much as she knew it was too soon, she could not stop exulting at the promise of a new, free life.

Surely she could best this pudgy little man with his trembling hands.

"Thank you, Sir Henry," she said with a smile.

May 22, 1554

From her open litter, Elizabeth waved and smiled, drinking in the sight of the crowds that had come to watch her pass, and reveling in the clearing sky of freedom. Her cortege was necessarily long, between her hundred blue-coated guards and the train of wagons laden with her household goods. But instead of suggesting captivity, the huge retinue conveyed importance, and Elizabeth fed on the image.

Word had spread of her release, and people had thronged the banks of the Thames to see her barge leave London. Over and over, Bedingfield had fretted that such gatherings presented danger, threatening again and again to close the curtains of the barge.

"They celebrate my innocence – how is this dangerous?" Elizabeth would ask.

"You are not cleared of suspicion," he would answer.

"Ah, but I soon will be," she would say, which would prompt him to cite his "commission" and recite all its points until Elizabeth had to sit on her hands to stop from slapping him. But each time he relented.

Blessedly, he had allowed her litter to remain open when they began to travel overland, after Richmond. He had continued this courtesy even after the situation intensified with the ride through Buckinghamshire. Multitudes streamed from homes and shops, smiling and calling to her, lifting their children to see and bringing her flowers and sweet cakes. Even as the cortege moved on to the more Catholic Oxfordshire, the villagers risked arrest to ring church bells whose joyous peals warmed Elizabeth's soul.

"I cannot suffer their clamorous outcries," Bedingfield grumbled. "The babblings grate my ears and their presence goes against my commission."

"You have read me the instructions," Elizabeth said. "Not one of them applies."

"The very first item prohibits any man seeing you in your chambers save such servants as are appointed to attend upon you."

Elizabeth waved an arm. "I am not in my chambers. Surely seeing me from a distance can do no harm?"

"What of the flowers and cakes?" He sniffed. "Item six requires me to inspect any message, letter or token you receive. This bedlam prevents me from fulfilling my duty."

"When I dismount, I will leave everything behind so you may sift through to your heart's content."

Approaching the next town, Gosford, Elizabeth sat taller in her litter. As always, her cortege cut through the crowds of the main road, past shop after shop, their purposes advertised by the rough painted sign above each door: a large key for the locksmith, a glove for the milliner, a fish for the monger. Deep in the country like this, few people added any words to their banners. Elizabeth blamed the priests: for too long they had husbanded learning. Reform had helped, but not so much here. Still, as in Wheatley and Stanton St. John, entire village populations turned out to cheer her on and call out their blessings.

"They should all be at work," Bedingfield said. "Or at prayer."

Elizabeth rolled her eyes. "You are no better than a gaoler at the Tower," she said.

He recoiled from the term, wringing his hands like an old lady tasting something she did not like. "I beg of you not to name me such. It dishonors me."

She smiled at discovering a weakness and prodded it further. "It is no matter, Sir Henry," she said. "That name and your nature agree well together."

"I am no gaoler." He straightened his sagging shoulders. "I am a gentleman with a commission."

"Speak to me no more of your commission – for I will call you gaoler every time you do."

He pressed his lips together and spurred his horse to pull ahead. *Good.* She resumed her waves and smiles to the people, humming to herself until they left the crowded village and snaked down the quiet country road. With no people to greet, Elizabeth reclined in her litter and gazed at the fluffy clouds that dotted an endless sky. Such a difference from the sliver of grey that topped the Tower. Praying that Woodstock would maintain this expanse, she closed her eyes and dozed.

All too soon, Bedingfield was back beside her litter. "We are approaching the Town of Woodstock. The palace gates are just past it," he announced.

Elizabeth's pulse raced, and she sat up to show special favor to the townspeople who would be her neighbors until Mary relented. Their obvious pride to have her there provoked Bedingfield's harshest scowls, but Elizabeth did not care.

When they reached the curve, she could see the stone wall encircling Woodstock's grounds. Given the extent of crumbling, it was more property marker than barrier, more moss than rock. A faint haze above the waters of the River Glyme added a gloomy note to the composition that provided a sharp contrast to the joy left just behind.

The litter lurched and bounced down a path lacking half its cobblestones. As they approached the bridge that led to the dark brick building, the stench of mud marshes assaulted her nose. Her heart fell.

They passed through the gatehouse to the outer courtyard, where Bedingfield dismounted first so that he could help her descend from the litter. In a daze, she watched her foot land on the dirt that blanketed the ground, perhaps a layer of old manure. She grabbed her skirts to keep them off the carpet of filth and strode to the first of the inner courtyards, where she found more crumbling stone but at least a less offensive ground.

Feeling somewhat outside of her own body, she climbed the freestone steps to enter the manor's historic main hall. The brickwork was darkened with soot, making it look like an ancient mausoleum. She whirled around to Bedingfield and stomped a foot. "You cannot mean for me to live here," she said.

He, too, had been looking around, shaking his head. Now he met her gaze, horror written large on his own face.

A maid scampered in from the kitchens, wiping her hands on her apron before bobbing a curtsy. "Apologies, Your Grace. The Steward should have met you. He must be in the other hall. Or the Jewel House."

Bedingfield stepped forward. "Where is everyone?"

"Working, my Lord." The girl looked around nervously. "Still preparing for you. We've all been working hard since we heard you were coming."

"How long ago was that? This morning?" Bedingfield looked around the entrance, at the missing tiles in the walls and glass in the windows. "There are no locks on the doors. This is not fit to house the Lady Elizabeth."

"No, Sir," said the maid. "But you can work here and pray here, and Her Grace can be lodged in the gatehouse."

"The gatehouse?"

"It is much newer and grander than the palace, Sir. It has four rooms, which should be enough."

"Well, let us see it. Lead the way, girl."

Bedingfield's condescension irked Elizabeth. Putting kindness on her face, she looked at the maid and asked, "What is your name, my dear?"

The girl blushed and curtsied. "Agnes, my Lady."

"I shall be sure to remember that, if we stay."

Agnes straightened, clearly flattered, and led them out a side door leading back to the courtyard, where Blanche and the others were dismounting. Elizabeth shot her attendants a dismayed look before following Bedingfield, who had forged ahead, his gaze sweeping from side to side. Elizabeth gave the same perfunctory inspection of the premises until they came to the building that did indeed look in far better shape than any of its surroundings.

The entrance was in the middle of a stone archway between the two raised portcullises. Bedingfield paused to check the lock on the door, a large newer-looking brass contraption that made him grunt in satisfaction.

A cramped vestibule led to a small room on the left and a larger gothic chamber ahead. The chamber itself led to two more small rooms. All the doors sported large brass locks; Bedingfield tested each of them. "This will do," he said. "The guards will use the vestibule and you can have the rest. And you can take your dinner in state either in the gothic chamber or the main house."

Just then, Blanche and the others tumbled into the room, mouths open. They must have heard Bedingfield's words because Blanche immediately noted, "These won't hold all the furnishings we brought."

"We will be using rooms in the manor as well," Bedingfield said. "Or, rather, I will be. But this will allow me to keep Her Grace safe."

Although compared to the Tower the accommodations were luxurious, Elizabeth found herself a little resentful. Angry at herself for allowing her hopes to get ahead of her, she let her voice rise. "The place is cold and wet," she said. "I begged for dry accommodations; my doctors begged for dry accommodations. And now I can't even sit."

After four days of travel, she was tired and stiff and wanted only to stretch out – but there would be no place to rest until the wagons were unpacked. "We will get that sorted out first," Bedingfield said. "And everything will be fine."

"The tapestries my sister chose so carefully – scenes of the saints' lives – will soon reek from the noxious odors around us."

"Ah, that will improve," Bedingfield said. "You'll scarcely notice in a bit."

"Actually, the stench seems to be getting worse," Elizabeth said. "Is there nothing to be done?"

"This location was carefully chosen for you."

Only fortification and local Catholicism had been taken into account; comfort had clearly not factored into the decision. "I shall write to the Queen," Elizabeth said. "Surely she was not aware of the conditions."

"That is not permitted," Bedingfield said. "Her Majesty wishes to communicate with you only through me."

Elizabeth could no longer contain herself. "Tell me true, Sir Henry, is it your commission to murder me?" His eyes widened and filled with tears at the accusation. Which of course goaded her on. "Is this why I have been brought so far from London, to such an unhealthy place? For I do not see hope to live even to the morrow."

He trembled a bit before throwing himself to his knees. "God forbid that any such wickedness should be intended against Your Grace. If that were so, that God who hath thus favorably supported you hitherto will defend you still. He is God omnipotent, God all sufficient, God that hath relieved, God that can help, God that never will forsake all such as put their trust in Him. Be of good courage. Let not Your Grace be dejected. Though sorrow be here in the evening, yet joy will be in the morning."

His sincerity was somewhat comforting, but she was not about to show it. She thanked him with as little enthusiasm as she could, deciding to send a message to Mary in the only way open to her: Bedingfield's reports.

She dropped to her knees. "Be merciful unto me, O God, be merciful unto me, for my soul trusteth in Thee, yea, in the shadow of Thy wings will I make my refuge, until these calamities be over."

June 5, 1554

The gothic chamber of the Woodstock Gatehouse had been transformed into a passable Presence Chamber. Mary's tapestries had been hung strategically to hide the worst cracks in the wall, and well-placed lighting camouflaged other flaws. Elizabeth took her meals alone at the round table set in the corner, claiming what she could of her status despite the lack of visitors to witness it. To abandon privilege was to forfeit it. Besides, she needed the table for times like this.

Tom Parry sat to her right, leaning forward to point at the pages laid out before her, lists of her tenants and the rents due from each. Bedingfield sat to her left, eyes craned to make sure the documents contained no secret messages. Every so often, he sighed melodramatically, a nod to his frustration at being forced into this situation.

Originally, Mary had wanted Bedingfield to oversee the finances for Elizabeth's household, so as to keep Parry far away, but that was more than the gaoler was prepared to do. Bedingfield had begged off the task with the excuse that he had no head for figures. Elizabeth was not about to reveal that neither did Parry.

"Will you be done soon?" Bedingfield asked.

Parry laughed. "We are only beginning! The tenants stopped paying their rent once Her Grace was arrested. It will take huge effort to collect what is owed."

"Why would they stop?" Bedingfield looked genuinely confused.

"They assumed I must be guilty because I was shut up in the Tower with guilty men," she said.

"And?"

Was the man really so dull headed? "The Crown confiscates the property of a convicted traitor," Elizabeth explained. "They did not want to take the chance that the tax collectors would demand a payment they had already made."

"And likely they intended to claim they had paid and thus live freely for a time," Parry added. "But it's not just that rents need demanding – the locals have been hunting her deer."

Bedingfield nodded, and Elizabeth realized that he knew even less about business than he did about figures. She thought of William Cecil and stifled a sigh. Now *there* was a man who understood business.

"All of this must be attended to." She kept her voice sickeningly sweet. "So that I may provide food and drink to you and your men. A task the Council has disclaimed." She looked down at the papers, bitter over the losses that were no fault of her own and the draining of the cash reserves she had so carefully husbanded.

The sound of hooves accompanied by horns made them all

jump. Elizabeth caught a flash of green through the window. Crown livery.

The sight made Bedingfield jump up. "Come, Thomas. You must not stay while I am not here."

"We have a lot to get through, answers I need," Parry said.

"I am to monitor every conversation."

"So speak to the messenger in the doorway, as you did the last time. Don't make your men search me a second time."

Bedingfield contemplated Parry's pile, then picked up several of the pages, turning each over to glance at the verso.

The knock brought his jitters back. He slid the pile to Parry and sniffed before hurrying to open the door. As the keys clanked to unlock it, Parry pointed to the top page. "Richard Moody," he said loudly. "He was seen taking down a stag on your lands. His straits are too dire for him to pay the fine."

Bedingfield glanced back and stayed at the entrance, speaking with the messenger there.

"What is good Richard's trade?" Elizabeth asked.

"Farrier."

"Well, surely we have horses to be shod; let him pay with his sweat instead of a finger. As long as he knows how lucky he is."

Parry smiled. "He will bless your name." He leaned in, and whispered without moving his lips. "They all do. Everyone who leaves my office."

It was Elizabeth's turn to smile. Mary's original rejection of Parry meant that he was not among the three gentlemen allowed to her, so he was not crammed into the noxious quarters of the manor house. Instead, he provisioned her household from a room at Woodstock's Bull Inn, meeting as many as forty people each day to do so. For all Bedingfield's care for the details, for all that he searched every bolt of cloth delivered to her and every piece of laundry carried away, his fear of numbers had opened this door.

"The country supports you. They will not see you mistreated. And they all pray for the day when you inherit your proper role."

Elizabeth nodded, reassured.

Mary had kept her rights during Edward's reign because she had the might of Spain looking over England's shoulder, threatening to avenge misuse. The people were Elizabeth's Spain.

In a louder tone, she pointed to the next page. "What is this bill? Why am I being charged for ale when we can brew it ourselves?" It was time to return to thrift, especially with all the soldiers she had to feed. A home brewery was a place to economize.

"We should check to see whether that is allowed," Parry said as the clinking of the lock announced Bedingfield's return.

Clutching a letter, he approached the table but did not sit. Not a good sign. Elizabeth recognized Mary's cramped writing, so like their father's. Elizabeth kept her face from twisting as she imagined her sister hunched over the page dreaming up new tortures.

"Her Majesty has revisited the question of your ladies," Bedingfield said.

"Has she decided to allow Mistress Ashley to return?" Elizabeth asked, knowing that Bedingfield's standing meant she had not.

"No," Bedingfield said. "Her Majesty has asked that Elizabeth Sandes be replaced by someone more honest. She is sending Elizabeth Marbery."

Elizabeth's anger flared. "My ladies are honest."

Bedingfield sniffed. "Mistress Sandes does not attend Mass."

Another reminder that Mary's judgments were all filtered through the same lens. "Is that what you told the Queen?"

"I tell Her Majesty everything. As I should."

Elizabeth wanted to smack the self-righteous smirk off his face, but she set that aside. "Let me write to my sister."

"It is not permitted."

"The worst criminals may write to their sovereign, but I am not allowed? I am treated worse than anyone in the land."

Bedingfield mopped his forehead, as he tended to do whenever she pressed him. "It is not permitted."

"Ask again," she demanded.

"The Council has more important things to concern them. They are preparing to welcome Philip of Spain."

Elizabeth sat back in her chair, the breath knocked out of her. She wondered what Philip's arrival would mean. Would he add his voice to Renard's and Gardiner's? It was traditional for a consort to argue for mercy – but then, consorts were usually gentlewomen rather than warriors.

"She should still have a care for justice in her realm," Elizabeth said, knowing it would make no difference: Mary cared nothing for her sister's comfort. And Mary's advisors had shown themselves ready to commit murder.

Elizabeth resolved to be even more careful with her food.

July 25, 1554

Untouched by the furious storm that raged outside, Winchester Cathedral glowed magnificent. It was one of the largest and finest cathedrals in Europe, but that was not why it had been chosen to host the Queen's wedding to Philip of Spain; rather, it was the seat of the Bishop of Winchester, where Stephen Gardiner would officiate, rather than the disgraced Archbishop of Canterbury, Thomas Cranmer.

William Cecil was thankful to be there. He would have been more so if the invitation had resulted from his own efforts instead of stemming entirely from Mildred's sister, but he was pleased nonetheless. Anne had procured them prominent seats on the side of the raised causeway which had been constructed for Their Majesties to proceed to the two thrones in the choir, gifts from the Pope who had specially blessed them for the occasion.

"There he is." Mildred pointed, one of a hundred people to do so. "The Prince."

"King now," Cecil said. "Charles V ceded his kingdom of Naples so that the marriage would be one of equals."

"Well, that was one way to force us to name him such."

Cecil smiled at his wife's matter-of-fact tone over the shrewd trick. "It was the least he could do to overcome English resistance."

Parliament had not wanted to call him King Philip; they had barely given their blessing to the match. It had taken Stephen Gardiner distributing copies of the marriage treaty, and explaining how Spain's power and wealth would save the bankrupt English nation, to procure the endorsement. Cecil did not trust that, but he would keep his mouth shut.

He would also stop regretting the Queen's lack of religious tolerance. This was the reality, and it was time to learn to live with it. It was time to make a bigger effort to return more regularly to court.

"Philip doesn't have much of a chin," Mildred said. "And he looks short. Or perhaps is it just that his attendants are tall?"

Cecil stifled a chuckle. "I have heard he is indeed... compact."

"Well, I suppose he is handsome enough that it doesn't matter..." Mildred's voice trailed off for a moment, but her humor returned. "It looks like he brought all of Spain with him." Indeed, some sixty Spaniards attended him at the altar, all wearing funereal black. Philip at least had added some happy accents: white satin trunk hose, worked with silver, and a collar of beaten gold covered in diamonds. And of course, the Garter badge at his knee, studded with colored gems.

"See those?" Cecil pointed at the four men clad in magnificently decorated armor. "They are the Dukes of Alva, Medina, Egmont, and Pescara. The most formidable soldiers of Spain."

"Soldiers," Mildred said. "Just the thing for romance."

The organ began to boom and the Queen appeared in the doorway, the picture of wealth and majesty. Her robe, richly brocaded on a gold ground, was set atop a kirtle of white satin wrought with silver. Her sleeves were turned up with clusters of gold set with pearls and diamonds. Still more diamonds bordered her coif. She swayed a moment, as did the giant diamond that hung at her breast, a gift from the bridegroom, or, more accurately, the bridegroom's father.

"Why in the world did she choose to dress in the French style?" Mildred asked. "Is this some political statement I do not understand?"

The thought had not occurred to Cecil, but Mary had indeed chosen to clothe herself in the one country not represented in this union of England, Spain, the Netherlands, even Italy. The country with which her new husband was at war. "You are likely right," Cecil replied.

Mary started down the aisle, showing no sign of tiredness, though she had walked on foot from the episcopal palace. Her cousin, Margaret Douglas, carried the long train that was thickly bordered with more enormous diamonds and pearls. Then came her principal ladies, though the word *principal* implied she had others, and Cecil could not think of any of the realm's noble women who were not included.

Except for Elizabeth, of course. Cecil put the conspicuous omission out of his mind.

"There is Anne," Mildred said, pointing to her sister. "The French style suits her well. Be sure to tell her that when we greet her. Tell all the ladies."

Cecil had many chances to repeat that admonition to himself during the four hours that the ceremony consumed. For a Protestant like him, it was that much more torture, with everything said first in Latin, then repeated in English and Spanish – as if there might be someone in the congregation who might not understand what was transpiring. Even the stoic Mildred began to fidget.

Finally, the bride and groom walked back down the aisle together and led the rest of the company back to the episcopal palace, where the wedding banquet awaited.

Mildred clutched Cecil's arm and sucked in her breath with almost every step – far more excited about the feast than she had been about the ceremony. Of course, a church could not be decorated as impressively as the palace, whose entire hall was hung with arras striped with gold and silk. The upper end raised a stately dais for the King and Queen, built a fourth step high so that all the other tables in the room could have a clear view of the royal table and its solid-gold place settings.

Their own plate was less impressive, but if Mildred was disappointed she did not let it show. Instead, she did her best to grill Nicholas Bacon, Anne's husband, about the goings-on at court. But since her sister had never been a gossip, Mildred had to give up and turn her attention to Cecil. "I love the music," she whispered, pointing at the musicians playing in a gallery set up opposite the royal dais.

"I'm just glad they're playing quietly. Most musicians play too loudly for conversation." He sniffed. "Too impressed by their own skill."

Mildred swatted his knee and laughed. "You sound like an old man," she said.

"Perhaps I am," he admitted with a rueful smile.

"Oh, look," she said, pointing at the back of the room. "They are removing the tables. The dancing should begin soon."

Cecil looked at the dais, at the thirty-eight-year-old Queen and her twenty-seven-year-old groom. "I wonder if Their Majesties will stay for it."

As if he had heard the question, Prince Philip – King Philip – pushed himself slowly to standing. He looked as if he had tasted something bad, and Cecil had a sudden moment of fear that some rebel had stooped to poison. But instead of collapsing, the King held out a hand to his wife.

Her expression was the opposite of his. She was glowing, and her slight blush lent her face an almost youthful charm.

"He seems disgusted by something," Mildred whispered.

"Maybe he does not want to dance either," Cecil said.

Their chuckles were interrupted by hoots and whistles from the men and women closest to the dais, followed by applause and delighted laughter from the rest of the assembly. The bedlam continued until the royal couple had left the room.

"He looked like he was being led to his execution rather than his marriage bed," Mildred said. "I hope the Queen is not bothered by it."

Mildred was right, of course, but William Cecil was not prepared to consider the implications of that fact. Especially if there was a more innocent answer. "He wore the same curl to his lip as his portrait. Perhaps it is no more than his usual face."

Mildred nodded. "This is a political marriage, after all. If this was the face that led to the treaty, she will not find ill with it now." She sat back, apparently satisfied, though for Cecil her words lingered. How far did politics extend? Was a French gown simply the choice of a woman who wanted to look beautiful on her wedding day, or was it a nod to the fact that her husband hoped to capture the land for himself?

None of this boded well for England.

August 23, 1554

Elizabeth did not believe in boredom. There was always something to do, something necessary or productive. But these summer days were endless, and, try as she might, Elizabeth could find little to help pass the time.

Reading was limited, as Bedingfield was afraid that books might hide secret messages. He had already paged through every volume in her tiny library, and he burned any new tome sent to her, no matter how trusted the sender – even Matthew Parker's gift had been turned away with instructions to desist. Conversation was scant as all her ladies were cooped up with her: they had already dredged up every moment of their lives to-date; denied letters and further news, they had nothing more to discuss.

Writing was also impossible, as Bedingfield had taken away her ink and quills after she wrote a poem bemoaning how Fortune's wresting, wavering state had fraught with cares her troubled wit. Apparently, Bedingfield found the line "So God grant to my foes as they have thought" too vengeful, Now, all he would allow her was an embroidery needle and cloth, though he was reconsidering that luxury after she sewed a book cover with the motto *Vicit omnia pertinax virtus. Elisabetha Captiva*: Tenacious virtue overcomes all. Elizabeth the Captive.

But there had been one tiny step forward: she had been allowed to write one letter to Mary. Bedingfield had brought Elizabeth three sheets of paper – two fine, one coarse – three quills, and a small pot of ink. He stayed in the room while she wrote, and carried away all the equipment when he left. Still, she had rejoiced at the chance to reiterate her innocence and, confident now that they did not have the evidence to convict her, to challenge them to either try her or release her – or at least move her to new lodgings. Normally, a household would move regularly to allow for a thorough cleaning and airing, yet the women had been in these three small rooms for nigh on four months without even a fresh carpeting of rushes.

Elizabeth sighed. A move would add activity to days where only extended routines remained to preserve her sanity. She heard two Masses a day, a morning service and Vespers, and took a walk before each, regardless of the weather. She also had two meals a day, which she insisted on eating in state. While her original purpose had been to remind her captors of her rank, she had quickly realized the formalities also consumed time, relieving her of the burden of those extra minutes.

The sound of horses' hooves in the distance broke the monotony. It would not be Bedingfield: he had not left the grounds this morning. It would not be Tom Parry either: he had just come the day before. Deliveries from the market would use wagons, but she heard no wheels. That did not leave many possibilities.

She looked around to her ladies; their faces, too, wore quizzical looks. Blanche ran to the window and craned her neck out. "There is a messenger, and he wears the Queen's livery."

Elizabeth's heart leaped in spite of herself. "This must be the reply to my letter." Hopefully she would soon see relaxation in the rules that smothered her life.

She flounced over to the *prie-dieu* in the corner, so as to be "caught" at prayer when Bedingfield entered. It took longer than she expected, but she willed herself to remain until Bedingfield's timid knock came at the door. "I have a letter from Her Majesty," he said upon entering.

Elizabeth made a big show of crossing herself and kissing her rosary before answering. "What does my dear sister say?"

"She…I…" Bedingfield stopped. "You will not be pleased."

Elizabeth stiffened. "Why is that, gaoler?"

"I have asked you not to name me such," Bedingfield said.

Elizabeth crossed her arms and lifted her chin in response.

Hands shaking, Bedingfield began. "Her Majesty feels offended and ill-used. She says you have shown ingratitude for the clemency and favor you have received, clemency far greater than is customary under the circumstances."

The blood drained from Elizabeth's face, and she thought back to the letter she had written to her sister. At the time, she was proud of the righteous indignation she had summoned, but the choice had clearly backfired.

"She says that she does not need 'plain, direct proof' to be convinced of your guilt – that she already has 'probable conjectures and other suspicions and arguments enough'."

Blanche patted Elizabeth's arm but it gave her no comfort.

"She says that further letters would be futile until you have squared your conscience with God and ceased to entrench yourself further in defensive lies. 'Wherefore our pleasure is not to be hereafter any more molested with your disguised and colorable letters.'"

Elizabeth gasped. "She calls my letter colorable, yet I included only the truth. Even as I desire to be saved afore God almighty, I swear it is so."

"Well, Her Majesty will not hear of it," Bedingfield said.

Elizabeth looked at her hands, turning them over as if to find some answer there. "Take down my reply to the Council."

Bedingfield drew back sharply but quickly recovered. "No."

"No?"

"I cannot."

"How can you refuse me such a request? Even prisoners in the Tower are allowed to send word to the Council."

"I dare not."

Elizabeth rose and began to pace, grinding the rushes beneath her feet. The rancid odor they released fueled her rage. "I am treated worse than the most unfortunate prisoner in Newgate. I must have the chance to gainsay the false statements about me. If you will not help me, I will be utterly bereft."

"I dare not defy the Queen, no matter what you might say," Bedingfield said.

"So, I must continue this life without any worldly hope other than the truth of my cause."

"For now, yes."

Elizabeth saw her life stretching out endlessly. An empty existence with no relief in sight. "I don't know if I can."

"There is no other choice. The Queen wants you to submit," Bedingfield said. "She has promised to be merciful if only you would confess your fault."

Elizabeth set her jaw. She had not come this far to be tricked – and anyone who believed otherwise was a fool. Elizabeth had no doubt that the mercy Mary promised meant a sword instead of the axe. "I will never submit to anyone whom I never offended in all my life. If I am a delinquent and have offended, *curat lex*, let the law take its course."

"But the Queen will be merciful."

Bedingfield's whine grated on Elizabeth like metal scraping metal. "I crave no mercy at all. The law is just and will not condemn me," she said. "God in His good time will either mollify His heart or move some other to procure my further enlargement. And I must pray for patience to endure the trial that the Lord has set before me in the meantime."

Bedingfield bit his lip and bowed out, powerless as he always was when Elizabeth introduced God into her arguments. The frustration strengthened her. It was better than nothing.

When he had gone, she went over to the window and removed her diamond ring. Slowly, she carved into the glass the final lines of the poem that lost her writing privileges.

Much suspected by me, nothing proved can be, quoth Elizabeth, prisoner.

September 17, 1554

The chill to the days had worsened Woodstock's wet air. Now sadness was Elizabeth's only blanket, thin as the morning fog. She took a ring from her jewelry box, but her fingers were too swollen to get it past the first joint. She left it there, a mute reproach to anyone who might notice.

She attached a silver pomander to her belt, bringing the perforated case to her nose so the mixture of damask rose and ambergris could provide some relief. The foul odors surrounding her were worse than ever, with the musty smell of dead muck wed to the stale and sour smell of a manor lived in far too long.

Still no books, still no letters, still no hope of delivery. Mary was apparently too busy celebrating her wedded bliss by harassing Protestants to give a charitable thought for the sister she had imprisoned in this noxious place.

"I am ready to walk," Elizabeth said to Blanche. The twice-daily outings remained a lifeline. And since only Blanche felt the same need for exercise, they were also the only times when Elizabeth could feel any kind of safety.

"I cannot believe she means to leave me in this terrible limbo for months more," she said. "And here of all places."

Mary's latest letter to Bedingfield had detailed the repairs he was to make for winter and listed the provisions she would send. She clearly had no intention of setting Elizabeth free or even allowing her to move to somewhere more healthful.

The dogs barked eagerly as they passed the stone kennel built into the smaller inner courtyard. The structure was the legacy of a time when King Henry I housed his menagerie of wild beasts here rather than the Tower. The dogs needed better protection against the lions than mere wood.

"They think I can release them. Me, a prisoner myself," she said. "They do not realize they are better off than I am – they are allowed out periodically to run around."

She dragged her feet through the kitchen garden, whose ripe produce would fulfill the depressing plans to feed their army for months. An offkey tune drifted out to them through the open windows.

"I am worse off than the milkmaids – they are happy enough to sing each day while they work."

Blanche looked at her, a sad smile on her face. "You are safe here, and that is all that matters. Just to stay safe until…" Blanche looked around. "Until you need not fear anymore."

Elizabeth took her own look around for good measure. "But I am not safe. Every day Mary takes further steps towards Rome, further steps towards naming me bastard and excluding me from the throne."

"She has not been successful yet – and I cannot imagine

Parliament allowing that." Blanche chuckled. "Especially not with all the work that Tom Parry is doing to make your situation known."

"But what if she has a child? A son would unseat me."

Blanche rolled her eyes. "She is thirty-eight years old and sickly. Don't go searching for troubles."

Elizabeth knew the reality as well as anyone, but her fears still littered her thoughts like dead leaves covering a pond. "I just want some freedom, some progress. I want someone to listen to me."

"That may yet happen."

"But when? They will not let me plead my case."

The path's white pebbles crunched their sympathy but provided no answer.

"I need some gesture that will make my argument for me," Elizabeth said, half to herself. "Something more than mere words."

"Your most effective gestures have involved a show of religion."

"I already hear two or three Masses a day. I finger my beads whenever I gaze out a window. What more can I do?"

"Swear on the sacrament."

The idea was simple – and perfect. Better still, it was a gesture that Mary's own mother had used to prove her marriage to Arthur Tudor had not been consummated. It would resonate with Mary and amplify Elizabeth's message.

"I should have thought of that myself," Elizabeth said. "She would believe that."

Elizabeth pushed aside the impulse to cut short her walk. Instead, she used the rhythm to imagine the scene, and by the end had it all worked out.

As always, her chaplain was waiting in the chapel to hear her confession and say Mass for the household. She let him continue as he always did, but when he got to the offering, she raised a hand to stop him. "I wish to make a statement in the full holiness of the moment."

"What is this?" the priest asked.

Instead of answering, Elizabeth rose and went to kneel before Bedingfield. "You have seen me these many months; you well know that I make all Catholic observances. Father Young can tell you how much I love the Mass."

Bedingfield looked at the chaplain, who nodded. They both looked back at her.

"Now I call you both to witness my oath, that I have never taken part in any scheme dangerous to my sister's person. I seal this oath with the sacrament."

Bedingfield's eyes widened. "Do you know what you say? Will you risk your soul for this?"

His reaction told her just how effective this ploy would be. "It is no risk," Elizabeth said.

Without rising, as if leaving the spot would void the promise, she turned and waved to her chaplain, who brought her the wafer for the communion rite. "The body of Christ," he said as he held it out.

"I swear on it," she said, then took the wafer on her tongue. She closed her eyes and let it dissolve slowly. When she opened them, the world seemed brighter.

"If the Queen could see you now," Bedingfield said, "she could not help but be persuaded of your loyalty. I will tell the Council myself. It may prompt her to be merciful."

"Thank you."

CHAPTER 11

October 12, 1554

illiam Cecil licked his lips as he speared a slice of venison from the array of platters and set it on his plate. William Paget had invited Cecil to a private supper, and while Paget's apartments were not the largest lodgings, any place at court was a mark of favor. Paget liked to receive friends in them to show off, but he slept at his magnificent townhome on the Strand.

"You always did set a superb table," Cecil said to Paget. "I was honored that you shared it with me during the life of the late King, and I am even more honored that you do so now."

"The Queen graciously allows me to eat in my rooms on occasion. The hospitality is hers," Paget answered.

Attendance at court assured everyone of two meals each day in the Great Hall. Only the highest-ranking courtiers were allowed to take their meals in their own apartments, and while Paget was but a baron, he was Lord Privy Seal. Cecil counted himself lucky to have such a connection and said a silent prayer of thanks to Somerset's soul for creating it all those years earlier.

"Ah, my friend," Cecil said, "Her Majesty would not extend such grace to me, so my thanks remain with you."

Paget's laugh filled the modest chamber. "You have always been smart and honest." He wiped his mouth with an embroidered napkin. "Would you be interested in a position?"

Interested? This was Cecil's exact hope from this invitation. He needed more work, as much for his sanity as for his survival. "I would be honored to work for you," he said, bowing his head.

Paget drew back. "And I would be pleased to have you, but I was hoping to place you with a government that needs your skills as much as the last one did. Talent like yours should not be wasted."

Cecil sighed. "I agree fully, and yet I will always be connected to Northumberland in the Queen's mind."

Paget let out a noise between a snort and a guffaw. "You did what you had to do with Northumberland, and you supported Mary when it mattered. All the world knows that."

Cecil worried Paget was oversimplifying. "I wrote the letters demanding her compliance with King Edward's laws; Queen Mary has mistrusted me ever since." He raised his hands. "I do not mean to complain – I am grateful for the mercy shown me over the sin of sitting on the Council of the usurper Jane Grey."

"Many of us were forced to follow Northumberland," Paget said. "That is not an insurmountable obstacle. Especially not now."

"Then thank you." Cecil smiled. "I would be honored to serve."

"Not so fast." Paget brought a mouthful of boiled capon to his lips. "First, we need to convince the Queen you are a true Catholic. She has lost her tolerance for secret heretics."

There was the rub. Cecil pushed food around on his plate. "I attend Mass," he said. "You can ask any of my neighbors."

"That is a good start," Paget said. "But everyone does. You will need more than that to return to court."

Cecil tried his best to calm the resentment that heated his face. He swallowed his conscience every time he took the wafer. Was that not enough?

He unclenched his teeth to ask his question. "What else would you have me do?"

Paget took another bite of the capon. "Cardinal Reginald Pole will soon return to England."

The change in topic troubled Cecil, but he reminded himself that Paget surely had a point. Besides, information was good currency at court. Cecil could be patient.

"What took him so long? I would have thought he would come home right after the Queen's accession." Pole had fled England more than twenty years earlier to preach against Henry VIII's divorce from Catherine of Aragon. His family had paid for his bravery: Henry had taken his revenge on Pole's mother in a botched execution that took eleven strokes of the axe to complete.

"He is still attainted," Paget said.

"The Cardinal should have no fear of arrest now," Cecil said. "Parliament surely will reverse his conviction when the Queen asks them to. I am surprised they did not do so when last they sat."

Cecil could not help but feel he was missing a piece of the puzzle. Or perhaps that was just a reflection of how unsettling it was to watch Mary undo so many of her predecessors' actions. A reminder that power was absolute only while a ruler was alive… and that God sometimes had an unexpected way of manifesting His will.

"She was in no rush." Paget cackled and signaled to the page in the shadowy corner to bring more wine. "The story they tell is that Mary waited until he could arrive in state, but they were really only delaying until the marriage was celebrated."

Cecil smiled, wanting to share the joke but not quite understanding. "Why?"

"I keep forgetting you have been away from court," Paget said, refilling their cups. "Pole did not approve of the Spanish match. He thought Mary should wed Courtenay – some say himself. He was kept away until his advice no longer mattered."

Cecil brought his cup to his lips to hide their sudden curl. He had to stop resenting Queen Mary's poor judgment, her religion, her husband, her place in the world. She was the rightful Queen, much as he wished otherwise. Why else was he here?

Paget raised his glass. "When Parliament meets next month, he will be free to return in triumph. And the Queen has asked me to escort him home."

When he was sure his face would not give him away, Cecil responded. "That is quite an honor."

Paget drew back as if Cecil were a child who had given the wrong answer to a lesson. "I want you to come with me to escort him home," he said slowly and earnestly.

Cecil closed his eyes, acknowledging his lack of acumen and praying Paget would understand he was merely out of practice.

Paget's voice softened. "How better to convince the Queen that your conversion to Catholicism is genuine than to be an active participant in bringing papal supremacy back to the realm?"

A dramatic, concrete gesture weighed so much more than words alone. But the scale of this one was far greater than Cecil expected. And right now he didn't trust himself to think through the implications.

"Is…is it a good idea to seek government office by incurring the resentment of every man who holds former church property?" Henry VIII had gone far further than just breaking with Rome: he had "reformed" the monasteries to correct their abuses. In truth, he had merely closed them, distributing their assets to his courtiers in the largest transfer of wealth in history. That was behind much of the resistance to Catholicism – no one wanted to give back the spoils of Henry's destruction.

"Ah, no need to worry. The Pope has agreed to forego restitution."

"What?" Cecil was shocked. "He's not insisting on some compromise?"

"Forbearing now brings England back to his fold, with all our annates paid to him." Paget sighed. "The Queen has also promised to reopen some religious houses, though the Treasury can little afford such a luxury."

Melancholy flooded Cecil over the finality of all this. The religious changes had not felt fully real until just this moment when he realized that the Church of England would soon evaporate like fog on a summer morning. He raked a hand through his hair.

Paget nodded sympathetically. He knew Cecil was a reformist at heart. Hell, Paget had always been one too, until the world flipped.

"Here is another thing you will not have heard." Paget's voice was low. "The Queen is with child and intends to show her thanks to the Lord. Restoring the Church, prosecuting heretics… you need to be part of this."

The Queen is with child. That brought added urgency. It also signaled God's judgment. Who was Cecil to argue? "Th-thank you," he stammered, overcome.

Paget took a large sip of wine and sat back in his chair with a self-satisfied smirk.

Cecil should have been relieved over his political salvation but he found his heart heavy.

Paget patted Cecil's knee. "These changes will be made with or without you. With or without any of us. It is only by participating that we have a chance to shape the future. You need to get back to court."

It was the truth; Cecil knew it.

But it still hurt.

November 3, 1554

The Mass dragged on, a wearisome trawling for faith. Elizabeth shifted her weight to stay awake. She could not afford the luxury of disdain for the old religion; her safety depended on the appearance of belief.

But it was so difficult.

She mentally counted out the remaining minutes. Young had begun the intercessions; the Communion Rite would follow, then the close. Still, she wanted to groan.

She dug a fingernail into her palm and returned to silently translating the Latin so she would follow entirely in English. The secret protest comforted her.

"For the King and Queen and the heir to be born to them—"

Elizabeth sat bolt upright, transfixed by the words hanging in the air. "What did you say?" she called out.

Father Young froze, clearly shocked by the interruption, but a beatific smile spread across his face. "Have you not heard the glad tidings?"

Elizabeth felt a chill to her bones, the kind of numbing she thought she had left at the Tower. "Glad tidings?"

"The Queen is with child."

Elizabeth stifled a retch, hiding it by turning to Bedingfield. "When did we learn this?"

"It was in today's letter."

Elizabeth had noticed the messenger but assumed that Bedingfield's failure to mention the message meant her requests had been denied: Bedingfield always delayed giving her bad tidings. "How was I not told?"

He flushed. "I did not rush to share that Her Majesty again refused to move you closer to London, as I knew you would be upset. I myself am disappointed that I am not to receive more help in my charge." He shook his head, distracted by own thoughts. "I have barely left the manor for a few hours since this commission began, and I have been paying for the guards out of my own pocket since no money has arrived from the Crown. I have—"

"The Queen's child," Elizabeth said, to get him back to the issue at hand. "You shared the news with Young but not me."

The accusation returned Bedingfield to wide-eyed guilt. "There was a covering letter from the Council in the pouch, with instructions as to the prayers. I discharged that duty immediately, of course." His chest puffed and his tone changed. "Besides, the news found you quickly enough."

Afraid that further anger might be seen as disloyal, she bowed her head to hide her face while she summoned an explanation for her lack of excitement. "I have prayed for this day. And the thought that the news was delayed gives me pain."

"Of course," Bedingfield said. "These are tidings to warm every man's heart, and I should have been sure to share them immediately."

She arranged her face into a smiling mask and looked back up. "My cup runneth over."

"We are all praising God," Bedingfield said.

"And celebrating His blessings," said the priest.

Elizabeth turned to Blanche, needing some succor in a conversation involving her greatest nightmare. Her ladies' faces wore smiles, though she could see dismay beneath Blanche's.

"You should work something for the baby," Blanche said. "A tiny shirt."

"Or the cover for his first Psalter." Elizabeth knew only Blanche would hear the sarcasm.

Blanche clapped her hands, equally sarcastic.

"We can make our plans later," Elizabeth said. "After the joy of the Mass."

Elizabeth turned towards the altar, bowing her head in an

outward show of piety. Inside, rage and despair swarmed like bees around a new hive. She carefully breathed through the onslaught, hoping time would help her exhaust the sense of futility that gripped her.

For the first time, the Mass ended sooner than she wanted, before she was ready to face the world.

She forced a playful smile on her face and turned to her ladies. "While Blanche and I walk, you will go start a list of biblical verses we might work – or that I might translate."

The instructions might not be needed – Beth Marbury and Margaret Willoughby usually avoided the walks, not liking the exertion – but Elizabeth needed to make sure they did not join her today.

The lazy ladies nodded happily; Bedingfield and Young seemed taken in as well. Elizabeth stood and swept out of the chapel. "Come, Blanche."

The lilt to her steps would have charmed at a court dance, but her mind trod the future that stretched out before her, dark and endless. How much longer could she stand this? Once they reached the garden and could no longer be seen, Elizabeth let her shoulders sag. "Oh, Blanche, what shall I do?"

"The people love you." Blanche's words sounded strangled through her tightly set jaw. "Think on all Tom Parry's stories about the people arrested for praying for your freedom, the placards calling for God to deliver you from your captivity."

Elizabeth bit her lip. "The people may love me, but God has abandoned me."

"You don't know that."

"He has clearly spoken in this matter."

"Because your sister is with child?"

Elizabeth looked sharply at Blanche. "How many more miracles does He need to work for you to believe?"

"She still has to carry it to term. We have discussed this."

"It was different then. I never believed she could even get pregnant."

"She is thirty-eight years old. Older women often die in childbirth."

Katherine Parr was thirty-seven. Elizabeth's heart flooded with memory, but she pushed the distress away. "If Mary dies in childbirth, Spain will rule in the child's name."

"And if the child dies?" Blanche's voice was barely a whisper.

Elizabeth thought of Katherine's daughter, dead at two. Of countless children, dead before they turned six. Her resolve stiffened. "I will fight for my rights."

"Good."

"If they let me live."

"They've not proved anything against you," Blanche began. "And Parry is careful."

Elizabeth stopped. She grabbed Blanche's arm and looked deep into her eyes to drive the point. "I love my supporters; I wish them well. But he must give my sister no excuse to try me."

"He knows that," Blanche said.

As they walked, Elizabeth thought again of Catherine of Aragon's miscarriages and Anne Boleyn's unjust death. And prayed that only one destiny had been inherited.

March 23, 1555

After three days of rain, rare for this time of year, the dark grey clouds had stopped spitting. Elizabeth squinted as she took another quick step on the garden's pebbled path, determined to give her muscles the exercise they had missed. As usual, Blanche was the only one with her, the only one who shared Elizabeth's need to purge the energy that accumulated in her body.

Blanche put a hand on Elizabeth's arm to halt them. "Do you

hear that? Is that thunder or just a villager out hunting while he can?"

Elizabeth lifted an ear to the wind. "I think a horse." The torrential rain had kept the animals indoors as well; they would feel as caged as Elizabeth.

Blanche dropped her hand and they set back off.

The sound got louder, and jealousy mounted in Elizabeth's throat. "If only they'd let me ride."

Now, *there* was sweet exertion. But hunting was not on the list of approved activities. Silently she cursed her sister and Bedingfield for their fears, and Thomas Wyatt for losing his fight.

"You could ask again," Blanche said.

"My dear sister suggested I just dance in my rooms as I always used to." Elizabeth sniffed. "As if I could dance in a prison."

"If you just used the movement—"

"No." Elizabeth tried to soften the tone of her refusal by patting Blanche's shoulder. Elizabeth loved the athleticism of a galliard, reveled in the exertion from the leaps, jumps, hops, and figures it required. But she had tried briefly to dance in the Tower when she badly needed the release, and the disparity between the joy of her steps and the bleakness of her situation had tormented her into nausea. Blanche still pressured her to try again, but Elizabeth knew she could never dance as a captive.

The sound of dogs barking added to the thunder of the hooves, and a flash of green told them a rider came from the Queen. The sight brought a bitter sense of finality. "The bitch must have whelped."

Elizabeth flinched at her own crassness, but Blanche just laughed. "It's too early," she said. "Barely eight months since the wedding – surely no baby could survive."

"She would never hasten to spread bad tidings," Elizabeth

said. "She only contacts me to remind me how sharply the wheel of fortune has turned."

"Hmmm."

"More likely she wants to seize something of mine for the baby. Like my mother did to hers." Anne Boleyn had demanded the magnificent christening gown that Catherine of Aragon had brought from Spain. Or so the story was told. In truth, Henry had spurred the request, though that did not help Elizabeth now.

"She does love to taunt you."

Elizabeth sighed and resumed walking.

"Should we go see?" Blanche's voice was husky.

"Bedingfield will come running if he thinks it's good news. That's as quickly as I want to hear anything."

They paced the garden in silence for a time while the rider was welcomed in the courtyard. Elizabeth emptied her mind of its barrage of thoughts, matching her breaths to her steps to calm her foreboding.

Her throat tightened when she saw Bedingfield speeding towards them.

"Look at the grin on him," Elizabeth said. "It's a boy for sure. Another miracle God worked for her."

"Your Grace," he called to Elizabeth as he loped.

"What is it?"

He arrived before her and dropped to one knee. "I have long wished for this day," he said, breathless. "This glorious day."

Defeat chased the air from her lungs. "God be praised," she managed to croak. "Do we know the Prince's name?"

Bedingfield's eyebrows pinched in puzzlement, but then understanding spread across his face. "No, no. No prince yet – but Her Majesty wishes nothing but joy throughout the land while we wait. You are set free. *I* am set free."

The reprieve returned Elizabeth's breath. *Free.* Her heart soared. "I praise God for this blessing. Disappointed as I am that the Queen has not yet delivered, of course."

He laughed. "She will soon enough, and you will be there when she does. You are summoned for the birth."

Only years of training and practice kept her face impassive. *There it was.* Mary wanted Elizabeth there to deliver the ultimate slap in the face. To watch Elizabeth pretend to be delighted over being displaced in the succession. *Lord, why do you try Your servant so?*

"I shall be honored."

"The day cannot come soon enough for me," Bedingfield said. "I will be glad to end this duty."

"Ah, gaoler, you will miss me."

Bedingfield's mouth set in a thin line. "Will you never stop naming me that?"

Elizabeth laughed. "Quite soon, in fact, since your role is ending. Just be patient for another day or so."

"Well, more than that." Bedingfield scanned the letter. "The Queen said mid-April."

Elizabeth tried not to let her fingers twitch as she mentally counted on them. "Am I to attend in taking to her chamber?" Her voice came out higher than she'd planned, but the idea was nightmarish. A queen took to her chamber forty days before an expected birth, remaining cocooned inside with only her ladies. As if that would not be bad enough, Elizabeth's great-grandmother had added claustrophobia-inducing requirements: Margaret Beaufort, who pridefully titled herself The King's Mother rather than using her ducal rank, insisted that all the windows be covered in arras to create constant semi-darkness and thicken the air, and that all men be banished to a different palace. The experience would be more confinement than Elizabeth suffered here, or even in the Tower.

"No," Bedingfield said. "The babe is expected on the ninth of May, so Her Majesty will retire any day now."

Despite her relief, Elizabeth shivered. Mary's summons was

less about watching Elizabeth's reaction than making sure she could make no trouble.

"Do not be disappointed." Bedingfield clasped his hands together and gave her a pitying gaze, assuming she was sad to be excluded. "This is the first time in twenty years that the realm has awaited the birth of an heir. You would…your presence…" He shifted his weight again. "Your presence would command attention, take it away from the blessed event. You will be there when it matters. I'm sure you will assist at the baptism."

Another nightmare to endure.

But endure it she would, and with a smile on her face. If nothing else, her presence would remind everyone that she'd overcome the accusations, that she was still in the line of succession. Parliament's decision still held, despite everything, and the child might even distract them from further efforts to change it.

It was something.

April 18, 1555

Elizabeth's cavalcade turned the bend in the road, bringing Hampton Court Palace into view. While the nighttime dulled the red bricks and obscured the fanciful stone beasts hoisting royal heraldry, there was no mistaking the dark forms of the turrets against the silvery moonlight.

She was glad this journey was over. Mary had issued instructions to keep Elizabeth's litter closed, to minimize "disruptions". Though, truth be told, any discerning witness who saw such a strong force of royal "honor" guards would guess her identity. Not that this surfeit of "attendants" could compensate for Elizabeth being allowed only her same three ladies and four manservants to attend her.

"Halt," ordered the guard at the gate.

Elizabeth peered out the window to show her face, but he had already recognized the officers surrounding her. "The Lord

Chamberlain is waiting for her. You'll be taking her things to the Duke of Alva's apartments."

Alva, the most feared general in the world, was Philip's mentor. Hopefully this meant they were not segregating her like they had at Whitehall.

"Is the Duke away? Are all the men away?" Blanche asked quietly.

While it was customary for a queen to be surrounded only by women during this time, Mary was the blood sovereign. She needed men around her, at least her Council – unless she had given away the running of the country.

"They must be," Elizabeth said.

John Gage awaited her at the far side of the main courtyard. Elizabeth found it ironic that the same man could serve both as Lord Chamberlain and as Constable of the Tower, simultaneously responsible for both the realm's most luxurious household and its bleakest prison.

"Sir John," she called, "I am as happy to greet you now as I was to take my leave the last time."

He chuckled and raised a hand to steady her descent. Blanche followed, while Beth and Margaret and the others alit from the other carriage.

"Will I have the opportunity to thank the Duke of Alva for making room for me?" Elizabeth asked. "Is he here? Is the Council?"

"The King and Council are here, and the Cardinal of course. But we did not dare transgress too many of your great-grandmother's ordinances, so the Duke and the other lords lodge in London."

It relieved Elizabeth to know that the Council remained close to the Queen, and that at least some Spaniards were being kept away. She prayed Renard had been exiled with Alva as well.

"Right this way," Gage said, as he led Elizabeth off. Again, she could not help but contrast this reception with the one given her at Whitehall, and she prayed that the relief she was feeling was deserved.

Her gratitude flagged as they left the palace's central courtyard. Proximity to the monarch signaled status, after all, and rooms around the first quadrangle most honorable. But then Gage brought her to the corner of the Clock Courtyard: the Prince of Wales lodgings, her brother's childhood apartments. While Elizabeth appreciated the symbolism, she had to breathe deeply to overcome the melancholy of her memories.

The Presence Chamber was as large as the whole of the Woodstock gatehouse and far more sumptuously furnished. Sweetbriars in vases filled the room, and their scent almost made Elizabeth weep with joy. She was finally putting the stench of her captivity behind her.

"I hope you will be comfortable here," Gage said. "I shall leave you for now."

After he had bowed out, Elizabeth quickly started to survey the rest of the rooms. They were equally beautiful, though she could not see any personal touches. Was Alva spartan or had he taken all his things?

"Let's get you settled," Blanche said. "Shall I have them bring some hot mead?"

Elizabeth nodded. "I would welcome that."

Blanche walked off and Margaret interrupted the unpacking to begin removing Elizabeth's travel clothes.

The process calmed her, further proof she had left Woodstock far behind. But she was still agitated from the road. "I am not ready for bed yet," she said. "Just find me a loose gown I can leave open laced."

"I already anticipated that," Margaret said, brandishing the green velvet robe with yellow embroidery that was Elizabeth's favorite comfort attire.

Blanche reappeared as the transformation completed. Warm

posset in hand, Elizabeth resumed opening cupboard doors, searching for clues into Alva's psyche.

The main door thrust open and Stephen Gardiner entered, his cassock billowing. No warning, no announcement, he just strode into her rooms.

Ignoring the insult, she smiled. "Ah, my Lord, I am not dressed for this honor. You are so kind to come and wait on me," she said, stressing the word *wait*. She stared at him with a pleasant smile until he gave her the bow that was her due. It was brief, but it was a bow.

"How now, my Lady?" he said, the barest minimum of greetings.

She smiled, but she could not force the smile into her eyes. "I am most well, my Lord. How is it with you?"

"I am hopeful that the extraordinary favor being shown to you will finally persuade you to confess your crimes and cleanse your soul."

Elizabeth inhaled sharply. Was this how her days here would be filled? For a moment, she questioned whether she had the strength to deal with unending accusations, but calm descended with her exhale. She had not come so far to be caught now. An enemy's antagonism would only bolster her resolve.

She raised her chin. "Then we are at cross purposes, since I believed this extraordinary favor meant you had finally accepted that I am as loyal a subject to the Queen as has ever been."

"You were given Alva's rooms because you will be expected to keep to them as much as possible."

"Even in the Tower, I was allowed to walk in the gardens. Surely you will not deny me that."

"I would if I could." He snorted. "Rebellions sprout up in your path, like flowers around a nymph."

She looked him in the eye, allowing her exhaustion to show. "I have nothing to do with them."

Gardiner harrumphed. "I see through your lies, and Her

Majesty does as well. You have one final chance to save your-self: she will be most merciful when she first sees you. Honesty will earn her favor."

"I look for neither favor nor pardon at my sister's hands. I pray only that mercy will show her my innocence."

He shook his head. "Her Majesty will be the judge of that. Come along."

"Now?" Elizabeth looked around wildly. She was not prepared for this moment. She had planned to wear white for their first meeting, with a rosary hanging from her belt.

"Yes, now." His smile was smug. "Follow me."

As they walked in silence, he kept a half pace ahead of her. She decided to pretend the slight was courtesy, that he was showing her the way rather than pretending precedence. Besides, his neglect allowed her to consider how to address her sister in the opening moments of the audience. This would be the first time they had seen each other in more than a year; should Eliza-beth display regret over the cloud of suspicion that still plagued her, or joy over the coming heir?

When they reached the entrance to the Queen's apartments, Elizabeth made her decision. Much as she hoped that Mary had softened from her marriage and pregnancy, Elizabeth would take her cue from Gardiner's own behavior. He had tried to bully Elizabeth into confessing her guilt, so Mary likely would be stern as well.

"I will leave you here. May God put truth into your words." Gardiner then nodded to the page, who carefully looked away as he opened the door.

"He already has," she said, and turned all her attention to the upcoming audience.

The Presence Chamber's darkness disoriented her, and its stifling heat oppressed her. It was the arrases that were hung everywhere, sealing the windows against light and air. It seemed wrong, but there was no bucking Margaret Beaufort's rules. Instead, Elizabeth forced herself to take shallow breaths.

Two women opened the bedchamber door. Elizabeth could not make out their faces, but the jewels on their gowns showed them to be attendants, not female pages. When Elizabeth got closer, she realized the smile of the one on the right belonged to Frances Grey, here despite the execution of her husband and her daughter. Or perhaps because of it. The thought grieved Elizabeth, and she embraced it, wallowing in it to coax tears into her eyes.

"Dear Cousin," she said in the middle of her efforts. "You look well."

"As do you," Frances said. "It is good you are here."

From the doorway, Elizabeth could see Mary in a chair by the window. The low light of the sparse candles shone on her hands, one cradling her stomach and the other telling her beads.

When her sister finally looked over at her, Elizabeth took three paces forward and threw herself to her knees, letting loose the tears she had managed to raise. "I feel as blessed as a visitor to the Virgin Mother herself," she said. "It is an honor to kneel before you, dearest Sister, and swear that I have always been true and loyal to Your Sovereign Majesty, let whoever assert the contrary."

Only silence greeted her, and she ventured a glance at Mary. The downturned mouth was the most salient feature on her face, which seemed more haggard than was usual for a pregnant woman – other than one at the height of morning sickness.

Given her sister's appearance, Elizabeth was happy to be wearing a loose gown. It might less inflame Mary's jealousy.

Mary motioned to her ladies to help her rise. She shuffled to Elizabeth, glaring down at her. "You will not confess your offense, I see, but rather stand stoutly on your truth. I pray God the real truth may become manifest."

No greeting, just accusation. So be it. "My truth *is* the truth," Elizabeth answered.

The Queen grimaced. "Are you claiming to have been wrongfully punished?"

Elizabeth's heart skipped a beat at this new tack. While she had indeed called her punishment unfair, she had always been careful to blame Mary's Councilors and not Mary. Perhaps a gentle jest… "I must not say so to Your Majesty."

She knew it was the wrong choice when her sister's face twisted.

"But you will say so to others, it seems," Mary said, her gruff voice a full octave higher than Elizabeth had ever heard it.

"No, no," Elizabeth quickly replied. "I have borne the burden thereof. I humbly beseech your Majesty's good opinion of me, as I am, and ever have been, Your Majesty's true subject."

Mary turned to the tapestry and spoke aloud in Spanish. Elizabeth could only understand Mary's last words: "God knoweth."

For some strange reason, Elizabeth felt watched. The hair stood on the back of her neck and instinctively she glanced towards the ceiling. Hampton Court was famous for the carved heads, called watchers, peeking out of the hammerbeam ceiling of its Great Hall. But the theme had not been repeated here; only octagons and their heraldic cartouches adorned the plaster.

Mary threw up her hands and turned away from the tapestry. Her face had softened; now she merely looked tired, not angry. "Whether you be guilty or innocent, I forgive you."

Elizabeth had to repeat the words to herself, to make sure she had not misheard. Finally, she allowed them to shatter the nightmare of the past two years. She was forgiven, she was safe. She was almost afraid to trust it.

She pushed all that emotion onto her face. The proper attitude was not celebration, it was humble gratitude. With a touch of papism. She crossed herself, kissing her fingers after they finished the shape. "I have prayed for this moment."

She felt her sister's mood change, felt a wisp of the affection Mary had shown during Elizabeth's youth. Then, too, Mary had extended a magnanimous olive branch for the daughter of the disgraced Anne Boleyn. The kindness had been based in pity, but had been welcome nonetheless.

Mary removed a ring from the first joint of her index finger; because her hands had swollen, she wore her rings at her knuckles – all but her black enameled betrothal band, which she had not removed since Philip placed it on her finger. She weighed it almost absent-mindedly, then placed it into Elizabeth's hand.

Elizabeth took it and kissed it and looked up at her sister with more tears in her eyes. "I think I could not be happier than I am right now," she said. "No, wait, that is a lie."

Mary looked shocked. Elizabeth continued. "I will be even happier on the day I may kneel to the son you will soon deliver. I pray that you have an easy and safe time with him."

"Thank you." Mary glanced back at the tapestry. "You must be tired after your trip. We will speak more soon."

Elizabeth stood to curtsy deeply. She gave her own glance at the tapestry as she backed out. No telltale bulge or shoes peeked out.

But still …

April 19, 1555

The grey rain hit the ground hard enough to bounce. Elizabeth did not care if it moistened the hem of her gown, she was just grateful for the covered colonnade.

"Tell me again how it happened," Blanche said.

For the fifth time, Elizabeth repeated the sequence. "She turned to the tapestry and spoke in Spanish. Then she forgave me."

"But the tapestry lay flat?"

"Perfectly."

Blanche sighed. "I am convinced she was speaking to someone, but how could that be?"

Blanche lapsed into reverie, and Elizabeth returned to her own swirl of thoughts. Had Philip indeed been watching? Why? What would that portend?

Just ahead, a man stepped through an archway onto the path, his black jerkin sparkling from bands of gold-thread embroidery and gold brooches. Two steps behind him, another man in simpler clothes.

They all froze. Elizabeth took in the details of the living version of the Titian portrait she had seen in Mary's apartments. A strong, athletic build made him seem tall, but in truth most of the height came from the white plume on his black hat; uncovered, he would be about Elizabeth's height. His chin was more pronounced in person, his eyes darker and more piercing.

After looking her up and down, a sardonic smile spread across his face. He doffed his cap gracefully. "Greetings, my Lady. I am pleasured to finally meet you."

Aware that this encounter might affect the rest of her life, Elizabeth offered a reverent curtsy. "The honor is mine." Still, something inside prodded her and she donned her own crooked smile. "I see I am as easily recognized as you."

He laughed and waved at the air. "The *tiempo*…the weather…" His English was heavily accented; she couldn't yet tell if it was good. "I had not thought to see you – I never see anyone – outside. In such terrible weather," he continued.

"It is pleasant here, with the walkway covered. I had no such feature at Woodstock." She could not resist the gentle jab.

"We are lucky to have many in Spain. My father builds a castle in Granada now to make the greatest one of all. A circular inner patio *de*…of…two stories. Ionic pilasters for two hundred and more feet around. It will be magnificent and keep the court outdoors all year."

Show-off.

"Such a feat is harder here, since rain and snow come more often to England." She shrugged. "I do not let the weather bother me."

One side of his mouth lifted. "An admirable determination."

She cast about for a different topic, since he had given her nothing on which to build this one. "I hope I have not interrupted you on your way elsewhere."

"No, surely." He looked up for a moment as if searching for something. "We are both come with the same plan. Shall we walk together?"

"I would be honored," she said with another curtsy, this one smaller. "I must warn you, though, I walk fast."

His eyes narrowed in approval. "All the better."

"I will present my chief gentlewoman, Blanche Parry. Blanche has been with me all my life." Blanche curtsied.

"And I, my man, Luis de Requesens. Luis has been with me all of mine."

Loyal, Elizabeth noted.

Philip raised his hand for her without waiting for Luis to complete his bow. *Arrogant?*

She placed her hand atop Philip's and they started off. Luis and Blanche fell in behind them, close enough for propriety but far enough to allow for separate conversations.

Elizabeth tried to keep a smirk off her face. She had hoped to make friends at court; this could be her best possible conquest.

They walked in silence for a time, Elizabeth wanting to let him begin the conversation – and analyzing him in the meantime. As she had immediately noticed, he was small for a man, though proportioned…except for his chin. He was fair, pale even, with a countenance either sad or severe – perhaps both. And he wore a smug self-sufficiency that made her realize she would have to speak first.

"Your presence must be a great comfort to my sister. I would hate the utter isolation." Elizabeth laughed. "But, of course, I have only recently been released from my own confinement. It is not a way for a person of royal blood to live. It is not the way for an innocent person to live."

Her light tone balanced the heaviness of the words. A combination to signal she felt wounded but resigned.

Philip looked at her sideways. "Mistakes were made and, thankfully, corrected." The side of his mouth lifted again. "As for me, I am glad to be here, glad to lend…reasonableness to decisions."

Had he just taken credit for the gentling of her treatment?

"Well then, welcome."

He laughed and they walked on. *Now what?*

"I confess," she said, "this is the first time I have been this close to a royal birth, so I am unsure what is expected of me. How do you handle things in Spain?"

"I tell you my own secret," he said, bending his head close. "I have no idea. I was sent away when my first wife delivered my heir, so I never learned."

"Ah, so that custom is everywhere. Shielding men from women's trials."

His face darkened and she worried he had taken her words as insulting. "Trials that can kill them, as this one did. But we honor their sacrifices forever." His voice was tight.

"I am sorry for your loss," she said. "You are blessed that the Lord gave you a son to comfort you in your sorrow."

He nodded.

She tried to steer the subject to an easier place. "But He clearly had other plans for you. And my sister." She regretted the words once she'd said them, for God's plan must seem cruel: his first wife was his own age, a reputed beauty he was said to have adored.

"We bend the knee to His decisions," Philip said.

"Amen," Elizabeth said, crossing herself. A smile played around Philip's mouth at the gesture.

She moved on to a lighter topic. "May I say, you speak English marvelously well," she said.

"When it is not important," he said. "For matters of the Council, we must speak and write in Latin or Spanish."

Elizabeth kept her face impassive over the idea that England was being governed by a foreign prince, in a foreign language. "How did you learn to rule?" she asked instead.

"My father taught me statesmanship, and Alva taught me war," he said.

She couldn't help but tease. "Who taught you finance?"

"That is for clerks. Men for hire, not men of valor."

She digested that for a moment. "Were you a good student?"

"Studious and prudent beyond my years," he said with no irony. "And strong enough that, when I was sixteen, my father made me regent of his Spanish kingdoms so I could practice my lessons."

"You were fortunate to have such an experience," she managed to croak, for his words had cast her into an anguished wonder. This was the way to shape a ruler; this was not the legacy Henry VIII had left. The only lesson Elizabeth could remember her father imparting was how he summoned the strength to execute people he loved; he had terrified a six-year-old Edward with that one. Edward had sworn to her he could never do such a thing, but he had broken that oath twice in his short life.

She forced herself back to the present, though in truth Philip seemed not to mind the silence. Indeed, the small smile on his lips suggested he appreciated it, so she decided to let it continue until he chose to end it.

Behind them, Blanche was asking Luis about the Spanish court and its customs, about the men Philip had chosen to bring with him. The delicate melody of a faraway lute muffled their conversation, but Blanche would tell her later. *God bless her.*

Elizabeth hummed along with the tune, and Philip added a baritone harmony. They continued that way until the song's end, only then acknowledging their brief cooperation. "I always want music around me, a reminder of how things can move from background to foreground just from attention," she said.

"Can I make another confession?" he asked with a wink.

"As long as you do not expect absolution, of course."

"The music is my favorite part of the Mass. To hear the collective voice of the organ, the choir, and the congregation brings a serenity that eludes me elsewhere, and is all the more valuable because of it."

She nodded. "That and the incense smoothed my path back to the Catholic fold," she said. "I recognized them as vessels of the Holy Spirit to sanctify our receipt of the Host."

He stopped and looked at her, eyes piercing. "Well said."

She curtsied and smiled to hide the smugness she feared to display, casting about for another comment to further prove her religious orthodoxy.

"*Vuestra Majestad,*" called a voice behind them, and Elizabeth almost sighed with relief.

They stopped and turned. A man in dark Spanish attire was striding towards them. Tall, thin. More piercing eyes and thin lips, like an older version of Philip.

The man reached them and knelt, panting, but before he could speak, Philip turned to Elizabeth. "I present you my good friend and especial advisor, Don Fernando de Toledo, Duke of Alva." He turned back to the interloper. "Nando, you can have no doubt who this is."

Alva. Yes, his looks matched his reputation for both ruthlessness and practicality. "I am honored to meet you," said Elizabeth. "Quite unexpected, as I was told you lodge in London."

Alva took her hand and kissed it. "I am here just for the day.

I regret that I must interrupt your audience, but His Highness is needed urgently."

Elizabeth raised her arms towards Philip. "By all means."

Alva rose and quickly began. "*El Consejo se prepara para considerar aranceles sobre ciertos bienes.*"

Consejo was council, *aranceles* were tarrifs, and *bienes* were goods. Was the Council calling him for advice, or did Philip want to make sure any taxes would favor him?

As if to stop Alva from saying more, Philip raised a hand. He turned to Elizabeth, took her hand and brought it to his lips. "This was my pleasure, dear Sister, a welcome diversion while duty confines my wife. I hope we can walk together another time."

"I would enjoy that," Elizabeth said, curtsying.

Blanche and Luis made their own reverences to each other before Blanche made a deeper curtsy to Philip – one he missed as he had already set off.

Elizabeth watched him walk away, slightly stunned from the encounter.

"Well, he's a good-looking man with a fine calf," Blanche said. "Rich, powerful. Mary got lucky."

Again, Elizabeth thought back to her distant past, to the matches considered and abandoned. Still watching Philip, she wiped the kiss from her hand. "Never judge a man without weighing his flaws."

Blanche laughed. "And what are Philip's? His sour look? Coldness?"

"He thinks too much of himself – and only of himself. And he loves war."

"Like Mary. It's the Spaniard in him," Blanche said. "He's still good-looking."

"And he seems to like me."

Blanche swatted her arm. "Be careful."

"Are you warning me to not lose my head over him?" Elizabeth rolled her eyes. "Have no fear."

Blanche looked out at the curtain of rain. Are you ready to stop? You did not go as fast as you usually do."

"No, I did not. Nor as far."

"Then we can continue," Blanche said.

Elizabeth squinted at the sky, but the rain showed no sign of abating. She had told Philip nothing kept her from walking, but in truth she was cold and wet. "No," she said. "I think I shall return to my rooms and just dance a galliard there. That will get my heart pumping."

Blanche's eyebrows rose halfway to her hairline.

"We are at court now," Elizabeth explained. "I could use the practice."

CHAPTER 12

April 30, 1555

William Cecil grabbed the fire iron to poke the top log in the hearth, drawing out embers from the dying flames. "Shall I add another log before I go?" he asked Mildred.

"The day is warm enough; I would rather wait."

"I'll be off then." Standing, he clapped his hands to shed the dust. "I won't be long."

Although it was already late afternoon, he had time to check the records of the Royal Courts of Justice in the Palace of Westminster, just a short walk away from the family town home on Canon Row.

"This is work for a paying client," Mildred said. "Take as long as you need."

Bells pealed; the insistent ringing came from Westminster Abbey. He turned to Mildred. "It's not time for Mass – is it a feast day?"

Her eyebrows knit. "Maybe Catherine of Siena? Swithbert? I

have a vague recollection of celebrating both of them on this day, but why ring the bells outside of Mass?" Before Cecil could respond, the bells of St. Margaret joined in and Mildred's eyes widened. "Something has happened," she said. "Maybe the Pope's pardon arrived?"

The ringing spread to other churches, and the peals were joined by cannon fire.

Cecil raced to the window, his heart thudding in his ears, or perhaps that was just Mildred's footfall. Out on the river, boats scurried along with men waving their arms, their yells carrying faintly to the shore: "It's a prince! We have an heir!"

People filed out of their homes, looking around in wonder before adding their shouts to the rest: "God save the Queen!"

Mildred gripped his arm. "She did it."

The crowd stirred into an even greater frenzy. Cecil and Mildred watched, stunned, as the jugs of ale multiplied, cups were hoisted, and men and women began to clap and hug and dance. And, of course, chant. "A prince! A prince!"

"God save the Queen," Cecil called in case anyone was still watching. He stroked his beard as he turned to sit back heavily on the window seat. "An heir."

Mildred remained standing, gazing out at the celebrations which now included a bonfire. "The first in almost twenty years."

Cecil sighed and Mildred patted his shoulder. "This is a blessed thing," she said.

He sighed again. "I had such hopes that Elizabeth might rise like a phoenix from this morass."

"She is lucky to be alive," Mildred said. "This is not the time to think of her, nor to wish or plan for her future. We must accept that she has been displaced, or we will surely die."

He sighed again. "'Trust in the Lord with all your heart and lean not on your own understanding; in all your ways submit to

Him, and He will make your paths straight.'" The quote from Proverbs succored him, though it hurt that the straight path favored popish superstitions.

Mildred's lip trembled. "For now, the straight path leads to Hampton Court. You should be there; you should be seen to celebrate. To remove all doubt about your loyalty."

Cecil shuddered. Mary had started to burn heretics – sixteen so far this year – even John Hooper, Bishop of Gloucester. Sixteen good souls, who had asked nothing more than to worship the Lord with honesty.

"I have proven myself already," he said. "Mostly."

Mildred plucked at his sleeve. "The 'mostly' is why I worry. And I want you to regain the position you deserve – and that will only happen if your face is ever before them."

He patted her hand to comfort her. "There's time enough for me to get there tomorrow; nothing will happen before then. Besides, the Queen will want to rest after the exertion. I need tonight to exorcise regret over my lost hopes of religious freedom and justice."

"Fine. But let us drink wine and celebrate with the crowds. So you have happy stories to share of the people's joy."

He looked out the window. "I can see them from here."

May 1, 1555

Elizabeth rode slowly back to Hampton Court after the morning's hawking had lifted her soul. Flying a peregrine, you looked up to vast potential, not down to the world's limitations. She had sorely missed this reminder to bring grace into every effort and to see failures as only valleys between successes.

She turned to Blanche, who rose beside her. "Although we came to court for an unwelcome event, I am content. My world has turned around."

Blanche nodded. "Woodstock feels a lifetime away."

Elizabeth was gripped by a visceral memory of the place, its oppression and stench, and she shivered to shake it off. "Aye."

She turned her gaze to the palace. She had never loved it until this visit, when a small escutcheon high on the wooden screen at the end of the Great Hall happened to catch her eye. Among a sea of *HR*s for her father and *JS*s for Jane Seymour, one tiny clover that the craftsmen overlooked bore the initials *AB*. More searches, in earnest now, had uncovered two other remnants of Elizabeth's mother: another set of initials under the clock tower, and a falcon peeking out from the hammerbeam ceiling.

As they neared the palace, Elizabeth noticed a boat approaching the dock, its passenger standing ready to leap out. He turned his face, and she recognized William Cecil. "Blanche, look," she said, pointing to him.

"Oh! Cousin!" Blanche called.

Cecil's eyebrows raised as he looked toward them, then his arm waved. "Ahoy!"

They walked their horses to the dock, waiting while he debarked. "Your Grace," he said, then bowed. "And my dear Blanche," he added. "It is comforting to see you both."

"You look well, Master Cecil," Elizabeth said. "Does this mean you have been reinstated to your old post?"

"No," Cecil said. "Apparently Her Majesty considered doing so, until I opposed a bill that would allow her to confiscate the estates of Protestant refugees."

Many good Protestants had fled the country: not just Catherine Knollys who had joined a large community in Germany, but also Kat's husband who was in Padua, John Cheke in Basel, and so many others.

"I am glad to hear it," Elizabeth said. "I hate to think that friends might never be able to return to England. Though that must have made trouble for you."

"Indeed. I rely on my private clients now. Like yourself, thank you."

"But surely you also draw another salary? After all, if you opposed a bill, you must be in Parliament."

"For now. Lincolnshire. But I do not know whether they will send me up again."

Elizabeth shot a sidelong glance to check where the boatsman was. He had tethered his barge and set off to the palace. Far enough away that he could not hear, though she would keep her voice low. "You should take care. With the Inquisition come to England, protecting reformists could be a dangerous business."

He chuckled ruefully. "I am careful to prove my Catholic credentials. And Cardinal Pole likes me well enough that he has asked me to accompany him on his trip to Calais this month."

"We all make our shifts," she said.

The silence after that was awkward. Thankfully, Cecil filled it. "Did I catch you leaving or returning?"

"Returning," Elizabeth said. "Pray accompany us."

"Gladly," he said. He took hold of their horses' bridles, one in each hand, and walked them off.

"You seem in quite a rush," Elizabeth said. "I take it you have business?"

"Celebrating this event is business, yes, though not formally so."

"What event is this?" she asked.

He stopped and turned to her, brows knit tight together. "Is there more than one it could be?"

"I am obviously not as well informed as you," Elizabeth said.

He looked around, as if searching for something in the tops of the trees. His face wore surprise. "I don't hear bells."

Elizabeth glanced at Blanche, who looked equally puzzled over Cecil's strange behavior. "It is not time for Mass," she said.

He frowned. "Last night in London, the world celebrated the

Queen's safe delivery of a son. Many are still passed out on the street from too much drink."

For a moment, the news provoked fear, but its patent falseness quickly calmed Elizabeth, and the irony of the situation made her chuckle. "I see I am not the only target of false rumors."

Understanding spread across Cecil's face and he began to snicker. Letting go of the bridles, he leaned over, resting his hands on his knees while his body shook with laughter. When he stood again, a twinkle in his eye betrayed his remaining mirth. "Is she at least in labor? Is that how this started?"

"I have not even heard that," Elizabeth said.

"Nor have I," Blanche said. "And there would have been bustling in the kitchen or the stables had that been the case."

Cecil looked at Elizabeth. "Why would you look to hear the news from such places? Are you not attending on her in her chamber?"

"No," Elizabeth snorted. "They pretend I do not exist, just as they pretend there are no men in the palace, as if the Council did not count."

"In some ways it doesn't." Cecil sighed and reached again for her bridle.

"Tarry a moment, Master Cecil," she said. "I would speak to you away from eavesdroppers."

This was her chance to ask her burning question, in an opportunity too accidental to arouse suspicion.

His eyes narrowed. "Is the topic so dangerous?"

"Not dangerous, merely sensitive, and I would have your insights."

"Go on, then."

She smiled. "I have noticed that Philip seems to be making the choices for England, seems to be governing. Is that indeed the case? Has my sister ceded all her authority?"

He looked up as if to find the words in the sky. "She would if she could, but the Council will not let her. The Lords follow many…suggestions from Philip, but they continue to set limits that require the Queen's input."

"Well, God bless them for that," Elizabeth said.

Cecil jerked back as if struck by a sudden thought. "How did you know this? I thought you said they pretended you did not exist." He cocked his head towards Blanche. "Is this from the kitchens? Are the servants so well informed?"

Elizabeth laughed. "The servants are always well informed. You should know that. But no, the guess was my own. Based on things the King told me when I walked with him."

He raised an eyebrow. "He sought you out for a walk?"

"The first time was accidental, but he did invite me on a second. And that has apparently made us good enough friends that he is urging I be kept here instead of packed off to Flanders as Gardiner and Renard would have it, married to the Duke of Savoy."

Cecil snorted. "Philip is right to keep you here, though, at least until the Queen's child is born. The better to keep control of you," Cecil said. "No offense, my Lady. It is but fact."

Elizabeth bristled. "You don't need to tell me that; I have been a pawn all my life."

He had the grace to look a little embarrassed. "Of course. It is easy to forget how smart you are."

Flattery always mollified her, even when she knew it was meant to. "See that you never do again."

"So, Philip is now an admirer?"

"Hush," Blanche said, looking around. "Don't encourage her in this."

"He makes a good ally," Cecil said. "And she needs every one she can get. Indeed, she should charm every Spaniard she can."

Elizabeth snorted. "I already do, despite my limited opportunities. I have exchanged pleasant words with the Duke of Alva and the Count de Feria, both of whom I am told are highly trusted advisors."

"Excellent," Cecil said.

Elizabeth pointed at Blanche. "You see?" From the corner of her eye she noticed the boatman returning. "We should move on."

Following her lead, Cecil nodded. "Actually, I may simply return home. With the Queen still in her chamber, there will be no one for me to greet. And I certainly do not want to be the one to tell people of the mistaken celebrations."

"I will be delighted to do that," Blanche said. "It will be nice to share information for once, instead of always seeking it."

May 12, 1555

Elizabeth stepped into her courtyard and squinted from the bright sun, enjoying the sudden warmth on her cheeks. Her ladies followed, raising their hands to block the rays. "Will it be too hot in the gardens?" Blanche asked. "Perhaps we should remain under the colonnade."

"The sunken garden will have shade," Elizabeth said.

"*Mon Dieu*," said a voice behind her.

Elizabeth recognized the French Ambassador's heavily accented baritone and whirled around. "*Monsieur*," she said. "What in the world are you doing here?"

"I was hoping to meet with the Queen, but she will not see me right now." He donned a wicked smile. "Perhaps she is in labor? It is three days past the appointed hour."

As if summoned by his words, the royal chaplains appeared in the distance. They made a daily procession around the palace grounds, singing and begging God to release the Prince from the Queen's womb. Today some of the Councilors and other court officials were trailing behind, Henry Bedingfield among them. She smiled and waved to her former gaoler; he blushed and waved back.

"I wonder whether that really curries favor with their mistress, or whether she resents the world's impatience," Noailles said.

"They are praying Catholic prayers, *Monsieur*," Elizabeth said. "That makes her happy."

Margaret Willoughby's tittering behind her caused Elizabeth to cringe: she hadn't intended to be heard mocking her sister.

Noailles glanced at her ladies and raised his hand. "Perhaps we could discuss this over a walk in the garden? I understand it is your favorite pastime of late."

Elizabeth's body stiffened for an instant, but she forced herself to seem normal. Of course he would know she sometimes walked with Philip. More worrisome was whether she would look to be plotting if she accepted Noailles's invitation. "I worry that people may wonder why our conversation needs to be private," she said.

Noailles laughed. "I wish only to enjoy blooms as fine as the ones I am missing from home. And the company of a beautiful princess. Surely that should not arouse suspicion?"

He was right. It would be easy enough to explain their walk. Besides, half the Council had just seen them speaking, so any suspicions had already been raised. "*Honi soit qui mal y pense*," she said. Shame on him who thinks evil of it.

"Exactly," he said.

"My ladies and I were on our way to the sunken garden," she said. "Let us walk there."

He wasted no time guiding her down the path. "I rejoice to see you here, looking so well," he said. "Far better than your sister when I waited on her last month."

Elizabeth decided to be generous. "I am sure she was just tired. It is a difficult thing to carry a child, I am told."

"I'm not the only one who thinks so."

Elizabeth glanced back to confirm that Blanche was keeping the others discretely away. Noailles checked as well but still lowered his voice. "You remember the rumor weeks ago that the Queen had given birth to a son?"

"Ye-es."

"Well, last week your conspirators spread the rumor that the Queen was dead."

Elizabeth blanched. "My conspirators? Who names them such?"

"Is that the wrong word?"

His face exuded innocence, but Elizabeth knew his English was better than that. This was not a game she was prepared to play. "The term implies that I am somehow involved."

The French Ambassador waved his hand. "That was not my meaning at all. I referred only to the people who wish you were on the throne and seek a way to put you there."

"They do me no favors by such actions. They place my life in danger."

"You are under guard here. Surely that shields you from suspicion."

Such different advice from the last time they spoke, when he argued that distance would keep her safe. The thought made her bristle. "That reminds me. It was said that a letter of mine was found in your correspondence."

He gave a Gallic shrug. "I apologize for any discomfort that may have caused you. But anything you do is of interest to the world, so when someone brought me a copy, of course I sent it on. I told the Council as much. And that is all I told them."

Elizabeth bit back her pique. He had not betrayed their conversation and that was all that mattered.

"If you forgive me, I will share gossip."

The Ambassador's tone was playful, and Elizabeth had to laugh at his wheedling. This was the whole reason she had risked walking with him, and she responded in kind. "Go and sin no more. Now tell me."

"I hear that Philip has designs on you."

"That is your gossip?"

"I have heard that if your sister should die in childbirth, he will try to marry you."

"Preposterous," she said, knowing it was not.

"How else could he maintain his control of England?"

Noailles clearly did not understand that Philip's desire to control England was precisely why she would never marry him. Or perhaps he did, and this was a discreet warning.

"How could we marry? Leviticus prohibits it."

Noailles laughed. "The Pope could fix that. After all, England is a Catholic nation again."

"Dispensations are not always efficacious. Catherine of Aragon could tell you that."

"*Touché*," Noailles said. "I am glad to hear you say this. When it is time for you to marry, we have husbands for you. Charming Frenchmen, not dull Spaniards. Not to mention you'd save yourself from a rake."

She needed to change the subject before it sounded like plotting. "My brother-in-law," she said, stressing the word *brother*, "has never been anything but proper."

"To you, maybe. But he was caught spying on Lady Magdalene Dacre at her *toilette*."

Elizabeth's eyes widened. "Finally, you fulfill your promise. I had not heard this story."

"Her dressing room has a small window that gives onto a quiet corridor. He waited for her like he would wait for a deer in the woods. He is a patient man, our Spaniard, and he likes to watch women wash."

Noailles paused to let Elizabeth digest the words before continuing. "By the way, it is said that he knows every peephole in the palace. I would exercise caution when you undress."

Elizabeth felt herself transported to her initial audience with Mary; she was sure now that Philip had been behind the tapestries. But there had also been several times in her bedchamber when the hair on Elizabeth's neck had stood for no reason. Had he been watching then, too?

"I pray you are wrong. But I shall indeed use caution," she said. "Your warning has earned my forgiveness, even if it is not quite the gossip you promised."

"Your forgiveness I had before I began, so consider the warning a friendly gift. As for the story, there is more to it."

"In that case I am in your debt," she said lightly. "Pray continue."

"The sight enflamed him. He opened the window and reached through to touch her."

Elizabeth's mouth dropped open. "What did she do?"

"She seized a staff she had in the corner – I suspect Philip was not the first man to forget himself – and gave his arm a hard enough rap that he ran away."

Elizabeth fully believed Philip capable of acting like that. His eyes had always betrayed carefully controlled desire, just as she had always infused hers with regretful interest. The right combination to keep her safe and him bound.

"How does he treat her now, after the incident?" she asked.

Noailles laughed. "He is much more respectful."

"I am glad to hear he can accept rejection," she said.

"He satisfies his lusts with prostitutes."

"The perfect husband," she said.

"As I said, you should choose a Frenchman."

"I have no choice to make at the moment," she said. "Other than to remain a maiden. I would be happy in this state forever."

Noailles smiled, clearly convinced, as she intended, that she was amenable to his proposal. In truth, though, a husband represented only danger to her. She was being fully honest that she preferred to wait for a man who would be worth the risk.

If such a man even existed.

June 15, 1555

Elizabeth stood by the window where the light was best. She held up the hand mirror to check her face and coif, then lowered it to check the fit of her gown. It was almost time for her daily walk. As she wondered whether she and her ladies would be joined, she heard sounds in the hall of someone approaching, and it made her smile.

A page opened the door and took a step in. "A message from King Philip," he said.

"Send good Señor Requesens in," she said.

"Beg pardon, my Lady, but it is Robert Dudley who brings it."

She caught her breath and quickly put the mirror down on the window seat before turning to the door, where a smiling Robin stood in a russet-colored doublet that looked rich despite the lack of jewels adorning it. She felt her eyebrows rise but could do nothing to stop them.

He took three strides in, then stopped to doff his cap and drop to one knee. "Greetings, my Lady. I am sent by King Philip to inquire whether you would care to join him on his walk in the garden."

He was leaner, harder, but his eyes still twinkled. Elizabeth grinned. "I would be delighted to join King Philip," she said. "But first you must explain how you come to be delivering his message to me? Last I heard, you were in the Tower. I am glad we both escaped that dreadful place."

"Indeed." He rose and put his cap back on. "My mother died early this year, and—"

"I am sorry for your loss," Elizabeth said, not mentioning the others.

He put his hand to his heart and bowed his head briefly

before continuing. "She wrote a deathbed letter begging the Queen to pardon her sons, and Her Majesty graciously agreed. I came to court to thank her, and to enjoy the Masses of the Chapel Royal, so much more beautiful than those in my parish church." He glanced around the room briefly, as if checking reactions to the Catholic bent of his assessment, but no one was paying him any mind. "I chanced to speak with the King one day when he tarried. He was expanding his household just then, and somehow agreed to include me. And Ambrose."

"Somehow?" She arched a single eyebrow.

"Generals are always looking for commanders," he said. "Where better to find them than among noble scions, especially ones who have proven themselves on the field?"

In his face she saw the Robin of her youth, earnestly believing that war was the path to greatness. Of course that would endear him to Philip. "Smart man you are, she said.

"Usefulness is the truest path to safety," he said.

"I am glad your mother was able to die as your champion," she said.

"I hope you will allow me to live as yours."

She winced, unable to stop herself. "Says the man who supported Jane Grey against me."

He dropped to his knees, eyes piercing. "I have confessed my crime and my regret to the Queen, but I have never apologized to you. I am sorry for my part in a plan that removed you from the succession. I only beg you to accept that I had no choice in the matter. As God is my witness, I will spend my life making amends."

His face wore the same contrition that had helped to excuse so many of his transgressions in their youth, pushing a laugh from deep in Elizabeth's stomach. Their long past together stretched out before her, driving away any residual resentment. They had all made mistakes, all found themselves on the wrong side of things at times. And yet survived.

Besides, the perpetrators were dead, the incident over: she could be generous. "You already did. *Superabo*."

He grinned. "I told you it worked. May you only ever use it again to mean, 'I will transcend.' Does this mean I am forgiven?"

"For a time your father's betrayal made the Queen love me, since it united us against him," Elizabeth said. "It would have been worse for me if your father had sought the throne on my behalf, for I would be as dead as Jane Grey is now."

Robin's eyes filled with tears. "Thank you. I swear you will never have cause to doubt my loyalty again."

"In that case, I am happy to have a champion," she said.

Robin rose and held out his arm, a rueful smile on his face. "May I escort you now?"

She stepped forward and placed her hand on it. "Of course."

As they walked through the relatively crowded hallways, she began a conversation designed to be overheard. Favored as they might seem, neither Elizabeth nor Robin was truly trusted.

"Look how this surprise has driven the important things from my mind. What news have you of my dearest sister? Please tell me her pains have started."

This was always her first question to anyone. Both because the answer was critical, and because the question made her seem loving and caring.

He winked. "Not yet. The prayers continue."

And burnings, Elizabeth thought: Mary's heinous attempt to appease the Lord who withheld her joy. A week after the ninth of May due date, the doctors and astrologers recast their predictions and discovered their error: the child might arrive on the twenty-third of May or even wait until the full moon in June. Now it was already a day past that extended estimate, and spies were reporting that Mary seemed weak and upset. And that her belly was somehow sagging, as if the child was shrinking.

Not surprisingly, Elizabeth's sense of calm increased every day.

The small talk continued after that, until they arrived at the garden where Philip awaited her, smiling warmly. *"Buenos dias,"* she said, showing off her Spanish lessons.

"Greetings, my Lady. I hope you were happy to see Master Dudley," Philip said. "He claimed you were old friends."

"I was delighted. And the timing was perfect, as I received his advice on my favorite courser. Master Dudley is an expert horseman, you know."

"I shall keep that in mind," Philip said as he gave her his arm.

Out of the corner of her eye she saw Robin's smile of thanks, but kept her full attention on Philip. "I was hoping Master Dudley was bringing me happy news, that my dear sister's pains had begun. Not that I wish her a moment of discomfort, of course."

Philip laughed. "I share your hopes and your dilemma. But the Lord has still not blessed us."

Elizabeth smiled. "Perhaps it is just her age. I understand older women keep their babies longer."

"I had not heard that, but it makes good sense," Philip said.

Elizabeth had not really heard that either, but she never squandered an opportunity to goad Philip. "It must be terrifying for her. For all women, to give birth for the first time at such an age."

"At any age," Philip said.

She realized her mistake immediately. "Oh dear. Your first wife. I am so sorry."

"It was hard to see my son without a mother."

She crossed herself and kissed her fingers. "The Lord would not be so cruel as to do that to you a second time."

He took a few steps before continuing. "You know, some of your English Council have suggested that I marry you if my wife dies in childbirth. I thought that a bit presumptuous of them."

Mary must be sicker than they let on for him to broach the

topic that had been rumored for some time. Interesting that he had manipulated the Council to satisfy his desire – or had he? Perhaps Noailles had gotten the story backwards.

"I cannot entertain such a thought about my dearest sister, whom I love and honor above all others."

He raised his eyebrows and nodded. "As do I. It is just that sometimes the duties of state require consideration of things that most people can avoid."

She looked demurely to the ground to hide her scorn for his self-serving justification. "How difficult that must be."

"Men are built to shoulder such decisions. It is why women take husbands."

He was as oblivious as a terrier chasing a rat. But she had a refuge. "I cannot even imagine such a thing. My sister was lucky to find a man equal to her, pleasing in looks, strong in religion." She turned to look Philip full in the face, a smile teasing her lips. "And utterly devoted to her. I dare not hope for such a blessing."

He licked his lips.

"But let us not speak of this on such a beautiful day," she continued, leaving her answer to be whatever he imagined.

Usefulness, after all, was the truest path to safety.

July 14, 1555

The rich furnishings of Hampton Court Palace seemed tarnished by the stench of a court that had lingered too long – without even changing the urine-soaked rushes. Unusually wet weather intensified the rot and was starting to drive everyone mad. It made Elizabeth almost miss Woodstock.

Almost.

At least here she was free. She was still ordered to be discreet, but the expectations surrounding that discretion had evaporated. She had graduated from walking in the gardens to taking her meals in the Great Hall, and now she was playing cards in the Watching Chamber. The only thing still denied her was visiting the Queen, and Elizabeth was in no rush for that.

Elizabeth turned over the knave of clubs and smiled triumphantly at Effingham, who had become one of her staunchest supporters on Mary's Council. "I won," she said.

"I daresay you have," he said, and she could tell he was not referring to the card game: Blanche had heard in the kitchens that Mary's belly had fully deflated, leaving only fat. That was fine with Elizabeth, but she could not help prodding. At some point the situation had to be acknowledged.

"I am so glad we still have you with us, though for such a sad reason."

When Mary had first taken to her chamber, she had appointed important lords to personally deliver news of the birth to the international courts. Effingham as Lord High Admiral of England was deemed to be the most reliable; he had been chosen to inform Charles V. Less reliable representatives would do for France and the Pope, but Mary did not care. France was at war with her husband, and the newly elected Pope had hated Spain since he served as Papal Nuncio there.

Effingham looked around the room. "I don't expect to ever fulfill my mission."

Elizabeth leaned forward, eyes wide. "Really? Why not?"

"I understand that all signs of the Queen's pregnancy are gone. As if there was never a baby at all."

Elizabeth drew back, arranging shock on her face. "Really?"

"Her mother had almost a dozen miscarriages; the failure is likely in her blood. Or lack of it. They say she has always had menstrual troubles; we should have known she was unnatural."

Unnatural. Elizabeth had menstrual troubles and a mother who had miscarriages. Did that make her unnatural as well? She folded her outrage back into its quiet depths.

Effingham narrowed his eyes. "I also hear that she suffers terribly." He looked around before continuing. "She sits whole days on the ground, crouched with her knees higher than her head."

The kitchen gossips had not mentioned this. "How does the Council mean to help her?"

"I have not shared this with the Council," he said. "Not formally, anyway."

"My poor sister, to experience such grief."

"It is more than that. This is a malady."

Mary might die. The thought pounded in Elizabeth's ears, but she reined herself in. It was wrong to hope for ill to befall others. More important, Mary had always been sickly; this might be nothing more than another bout. And so much could happen before she died. Spain might fight harder than Northumberland before ceding power.

But possibilities were none of Elizabeth's concern, not yet.

"Have her doctors told you this?" she asked, pressing for information. "Or just her ladies?"

His face twisted as he gathered the spent cards. "The doctors are afraid to tell her she is sick. She will not even consider the possibility that there is no child."

Of course. No ruler ever accepted bad news with grace, and Mary had been so sure that God had favored her above women…

"That is terrible," Elizabeth said. "Surely someone will tell her, and soon. You cannot be the only one to know this."

He shrugged.

Such indifference made her sit back and narrow her eyes at him. "I don't understand. I would think you would want her to know. She must have ceded a great deal of authority to Philip – it is only when she leaves her chamber that she will be able to resume her control."

"Just the opposite." Effingham blinked as if he was choosing his words carefully. "While Philip acts for her, he cannot insist that England join him in the Empire's ridiculous war with France. Only the Queen can make such a decision."

Elizabeth tried to put the puzzle together, but the pieces did not fit. "I thought the marriage treaty specifically rejected such a possibility. I thought that was why it was approved so easily."

Effingham sighed and shuffled the cards. "The treaty only specifies what Spain can and cannot force England to do. It does not limit England's discretion to take whatever action we choose, and I believe the Queen might desire to support her husband in his military endeavors. The man can be quite persuasive."

Elizabeth shook her head in disbelief. "But she has the perfect excuse to deny him."

Effingham paused. "And I pray she uses it. Stephen Gardiner is dedicating every Mass he says to that same hope."

Elizabeth sat back, mulling over the information. One fact stood out starkly: "Stephen Gardiner and I are in agreement on something." She allowed sarcasm to rock her tone.

Effingham laughed. "You are in agreement on a lot more. You just need to charm him the way you have the rest of the Council. And the King."

"Stephen Gardiner is beyond charm," she said. "The man earnestly wishes me dead."

"Time and circumstances are overcoming that resolve," Howard said.

Elizabeth refused to allow herself the smug smile that threatened to break through. "So we wait," she said.

Patience was her greatest need right now. Thank goodness it was also her greatest strength.

August 2, 1555

Flashes of color appeared through the window, bright against the somber linenfold paneling of the surrounding walls. Elizabeth stopped to peer out and make sense of the flurry of activity. Red, russet, yellow, blue – rich gowns, Mary's ladies. Green – grooms running towards the stables.

"Something is happening," Elizabeth said to Blanche.

Blanche approached to survey the scene. "There was no gossip this morning," she said. "Perhaps I should go—"

An urgent rap at the door interrupted them; the page did not wait to enter. "The Duchess of Suffolk," he announced.

"She is welcome," Elizabeth quickly responded. Swallowing her trepidation, she wiped her hands on the front of her dark red gown to smooth any lines in the damask before turning to the door to receive her cousin's first-ever visit.

Frances lumbered in, her face lined and pale under her black hood, her eyes unfocused. Elizabeth reminded herself that the woman had spent the last three months in the semi-darkness surrounding Mary. It could be no more than that.

"Is my sister well?" Elizabeth asked as they kissed hello. "And you," she leaned forward, "are you well?"

Frances sighed. "As well as can be expected. Both of us."

"Praise God." The silence that greeted her words unnerved Elizabeth and she waved at the window. "I saw people running, and now you have come to me. You can understand my concern."

Frances nodded. "Of course." She sighed again, her eyes downcast, before continuing. "Her Majesty has decided to remove the court to Oatlands so that Hampton Court may be cleansed. She decided within the last hour."

That statement raised so many questions. *Has Mary admitted she was wrong about the pregnancy? Am I going with you?*

Elizabeth chose her words with caution. "How may I be of service?"

Frances smiled sadly. "There is nothing you or anyone can do. The Queen is in the grip of a deep melancholy over the recent events."

"Events?" Elizabeth asked, desperate to spur answers.

"The King prayed with her a long time, to help her accept

that there is no child. To help her understand that miracle has been denied her."

Elizabeth crossed herself. "May it be as in the Psalms, 'He heals the brokenhearted and binds up their wounds.'"

"Amen," Frances said reflexively before resuming her mournful tone. "She has spent the last month curled up in the corner of her room, weeping bitter tears. We ladies wept with her, even as we worried for her sanity."

Poor Mary. What a fall for the warrior Queen. Although their fates were at odds, no one deserved such pain. "Healing can only begin with truth. I am glad the King found the courage to help her see it."

Frances's face twisted. "He did it so he could resume the fight against France. He could not leave England while she still believed a babe was on the way…"

Her voice trailed off and Elizabeth clung to nonchalance. "King Philip is leaving?" she asked.

"At the end of the month. He thinks it secret, but enough people speak Spanish that we know."

Elizabeth made a sad *moue*, but inside she was furiously counting. Three weeks did not leave Mary enough time to be churched – the purification ritual that allowed a husband to lie with his wife was not performed until forty days after childbirth or miscarriage…but when would the counting begin? Would Mary even need to be churched when there was never a baby to begin with? Elizabeth could only pray that these three weeks would not allow a new seed, a real seed, to be planted in Mary's belly.

"But he will be going to Oatlands?" Elizabeth asked. "To help her through this?"

"Of course. So will you."

"I will be happy to give all the comfort I can, though I suggest my own efforts will pale next to his. And yours."

"I will not be going," Frances said.

Elizabeth looked at her quizzically. "Why?"

"I am remarried," Frances said. "You must not have heard."

Elizabeth furiously cast her mind over potential matches. There had been talk of marrying Frances to Edward Courtenay – there had been talk of marrying almost every Tudor woman to that fool – but after Wyatt's rebellion he had been exiled to Europe. No one else came to mind. "A Spaniard?"

"English. Adrian Stokes," Frances said, shaking her head. "My Master of Horse."

"Oh?" Elizabeth said, with as little condemnation as she could: men in that position were usually attractive and gallant, but a carnal marriage to a commoner did not befit a woman with royal blood in her veins.

Frances twisted her mouth in a rueful smile. "It is a relief to have a man with no ambition. Safer."

"But how…What if…"

Frances shook her head firmly. "With this marriage, I have forfeited my place in the succession, if I ever had one. You can rest easier."

Elizabeth immediately began to protest, but Frances waved her hand to hush her. "Now I can retire and live my final years in peace."

Elizabeth jolted. *Final years. From a woman a year younger than Mary.* "Are you ill?"

"I am tired. And seeing the Queen, so sad and frail…" Frances winced as she straightened her back. "I know what comes next, and I want to enjoy my remaining time."

A vision of Henry Grey filled Elizabeth's thoughts, and she shuddered. Henry Grey, who was so desperate for power he had used his oldest daughter in a bid for the Crown, not once but twice. It seemed folly for Frances to risk taking another husband after that experience, but some women never learned. At least she knew this one would never betray her like that – if only because he could not.

"I wish you every happiness," Elizabeth said, meaning it. "For many years."

August 29, 1555

Elizabeth raised her chin to survey the huge crowd in the Great Hall, swishing her new skirts to make them shimmer in the light from the double bank of windows.

Philip was leaving England, and the court had cut short its stay at Oatlands to see Philip off from Greenwich Palace. Since it overlooked the royal naval yard, the Queen and her Council would survey the departing convoy of ships in a scene reminiscent of old Rome.

The illusion of empire had begun with Mary and Philip's overland trip – with Mary in an open litter to show herself to the people and encourage them to offer blessings and throw flowers. Meanwhile Elizabeth had been sent in a small, rickety barge kept closed until it docked. Not that it mattered now: Mary had decided that this iconic moment deserved a new gown for Elizabeth, made from enough silver thread to fill a treasure chest.

Stifling a smile, Elizabeth saw movement near the door, the trumpeters raising their instruments to their lips. She gave another swish to her skirts as she composed herself for this final formality.

Philip entered the room to the sound of fanfare, his gold brooches gleaming against his black doublet. Renard and Feria entered immediately after but remained near the doorway along with the other gentlemen of Philip's household, their uniformly muted browns functioning like the background of a painting.

The crowd parted to open a path to the Queen on her raised throne at the head of the room. All eyes turned to the pitiful creature surrounded by dark gloom. Elizabeth sighed and turned back to the more pleasant *tableau* at the doorway.

Philip bowed formally to his wife before walking towards

her. He did not stop to offer goodbyes to anyone on his way; he had already taken his leave of anyone important. Well, he had taken leave of Elizabeth, and she assumed he had a list. Robin certainly did. She had helped him make it.

When Philip arrived before Mary's dais, he bowed again before opening his palms to her. "Madam, the final preparations are done and my men await me. I shall set off now. I pray God to keep you safe until my return."

Before he could continue, Mary lurched to her feet and descended the three stairs. The confusion on his face quickly ceded to cringing as she clutched him and stroked his cheeks. He permitted the inept caresses for only a short time before grabbing her hands and continuing his speech. "I must leave to remedy evil in this world. To help my father defeat the despicable French who have lied and provoked both our nations. To keep our realms safe, and to keep you safe."

Still clasping his wife's hands, he looked to the Councilors on Mary's right. "I pray you, good men of the Council, do not hesitate to write to me. Your cares are mine and the proper governance of England demands it."

Elizabeth used all her strength to keep her lip from curling. When she knew she was about to lose the fight, she set her mouth into a smile instead. It was not her place to condemn Mary's choices. It was only her place to mark this moment and make sure she never made such mistakes herself: never gave her love to a man who wore only the thinnest veneer of caring, never threw away her legacy with both hands.

"I wish I could come to Dover with you, to see you off properly." Mary's words were almost a whisper.

Philip narrowed his eyes; when he finally spoke, his voice bore a honeyed tone. "The trip would tax your strength. I would not needlessly risk your health."

She nodded. "I will have daily orison made at my chapel for your safety – and your speedy return."

"I pray the Lord is merciful to us both," he said as he pried her hands off. He backed away for ten paces then bowed, his hands over his heart. "I will look for you on the open gallery." Without waiting for an answer, he turned to the door and strode out of the room. His attendants made their reverences and quickly followed him.

Mary stared at the empty space even after the sound of footfalls had faded. Finally, she sighed and motioned to Margaret Douglas for an ornate pocket square to wipe her nose. "Let us move to the gallery, to watch our own Aeneas sailing forth to defend his empire."

"Well said," Elizabeth said in a loud whisper, then covered her mouth in fake apology. A spontaneous expression of admiration was much more flattering than a conversational compliment that inevitably sounded contrived.

Mary nodded at her briefly before squaring her shoulders. "You will of course join us, Sister. My husband wants to see you treated with all honors. He is convinced of your innocence, and thus I am as well. And we have all seen your piety."

Elizabeth wondered whether she had heard sarcasm. She was tempted to indulge her natural resentment, but Mary was in a state of pain, in desperate need of affection. This was Elizabeth's chance to restore their relationship, and she would be a fool to waste it over an imagined slight. "Thank you for being patient and providing me with teachers," she said. "For that example is what inspired me and opened my heart."

"Come with me now so we can give example to the world." Mary lifted her chin and led the court out, her majesty restored.

Taking her place at the center of the balustrade, Mary motioned Elizabeth to stand to her right, well ahead of Margaret. Below them, Philip's men were assembled in perfect formation.

Philip turned first to address the buzzing crowd around him. "Good people of England, duty requires me to leave you for a time. But you and this great land will be ever in my thoughts, your good will always guide my actions. Saint Paul urged us all to walk in a manner worthy of our calling, with all humility and gentleness, with patience, bearing with one another in love, eager to maintain the unity of the Spirit in the bond of peace. I promise you I will live by those words, and I expect the same from you."

He turned to Mary, pausing to allow the crowd to cheer. A hint of a smile raised one corner of his mouth, enough that he looked almost tender. "My dearest wife, I thank God for the portion He has given me. Together with the Proverbs, I say each day that a virtuous and capable wife is more precious than rubies. I shall count the days until I see you again."

He bowed his head, waiting for Mary's blessing, the final formality before he could escape.

Mary's chest rose. "As you invoked Saint Paul, so will I: 'I can endure all these things through the power of the One who gives me strength.' Go with God, husband."

He bowed, clearly impressed, and led his men onto the lead ship. If any of them were nervous about submitting to the unpredictable waters, they did not show it. Perhaps they assumed that drowning at sea, although common, was not a fate for someone anointed by God or doing His work. Elizabeth smiled to herself. *Not that Philip had yet been anointed by God. Or did His work.*

Mary remained immobile, staring out like a marble statue while sailors raised anchors, hauled cables, and clambered around unfurling sails. She was rewarded at the end, when all the preparations were final, and Philip went to stand next to the pilot on the quarterdeck. He faced the shore one final time to bow again at his wife as if he truly loved her.

Mary squinted as if to see him better, and finally sighed. "I am the luckiest of women."

Elizabeth swallowed. "If God ever puts it in my mind to marry, I hope I will find a husband I can esteem as much as you do yours."

"I know you and my husband walked sometimes while I was…indisposed," Mary said. "He enjoyed it immensely."

"I-I am honored," Elizabeth said, hoping this was not the precursor to jealousy.

"I would do the same. It would comfort me to continue his habit." Mary paused. "And it would be good for us to spend time together."

"I thank you from the bottom of my heart."

PART THREE: THE LORD'S DOING

CHAPTER 13

October 11, 1555

Out of the corner of her eye, Elizabeth watched Mary's lips move in silent prayer as they walked the garden path, trailed by twenty-five Franciscan Observant friars. Elizabeth also fingered her rosary beads, sometimes even quietly hummed a hymn, anything to slow her steps to the impossible crawl Mary preferred.

True to her word, Mary had made significant overtures of friendship since Philip's departure five weeks earlier. The sisters had moved back to London – Mary to St. James Palace and Elizabeth to Somerset House – but Mary had her sister visit every day. With monastics constantly in the background, the two women heard Mass together, ate together, and walked…usually in silence. Thankfully Woodstock had inured Elizabeth to tedium, otherwise frustration would have burst her skin like an overripe plum.

Mary crossed herself, and Elizabeth did likewise in case this meant her sister wished to speak with her. She was quickly rewarded.

"I prayed about you this morning," Mary said.

Elizabeth smiled. "Oh?"

"I was thanking the Lord for the station to which He called me, for rescuing me from my old life."

"Amen," Elizabeth said, not understanding what this had to do with her.

"But then I felt ungrateful, for in truth He has always provided for me." Mary raised her eyes from the path to the treetops. "Oh, He tested me, of course He did, but He gave me a life filled with quiet joy. A life that would content me even now."

Still not understanding, Elizabeth chose the safe path with a quote from Ecclesiastes. "'He hath made everything beautiful in its time.'"

Mary nodded approvingly and patted Elizabeth's arm. "I know you enjoyed a life of learning, and that it ceased. It is time I allow you to return to it, return to Hatfield, while I retreat further into prayer and healing." She smiled ruefully. "You tempt me into more activity than I like."

Elizabeth's heart soared. *Hatfield.* Then it crashed: was this a sneaky way of throwing her to the wolves? Realizing her emotions must have been written on her face, she hastened to explain. "The thought delighted me, until I realized I would no longer be close to you every day."

"You will join us for Christmas and other celebrations. And of course when the King returns. I suspect he might bring the Duke of Savoy with him, or some other husband for you."

Elizabeth's throat constricted. "Oh, Sister, I pray he does not." She swallowed. "I have never wanted to marry. You know that."

Mary's face twisted. "The King wants to see you settled."

Elizabeth's heart fell. She thought she had slayed that beast, but it had returned, even more terrifying. How far would they go to force her?

She did not have to pretend tears for her response. "I pray God you can dissuade him."

"I promise nothing."

Elizabeth put a hand on her stomach, a cryptic reminder of the stakes. Mary was desperate for a child. Her ladies whispered that she often snuck out at night to go minister to peasant women and hold their babies in her arms. For all her pretended friendship, Mary was jealous of Elizabeth – it would kill her to watch Elizabeth carry more than air in her womb.

"I do not wish to marry," Elizabeth repeated. "I never have."

"But it would define your position," Mary said.

Surprise almost made her stop walking. "Why does my position need defining?"

"The world considers you illegitimate. This would prove you are not."

Elizabeth forced herself not to roll her eyes at the accusation that had dogged her all her life, the stain of bastardy that Parliament, God bless them, had made irrelevant. Only if they removed her succession rights would she benefit from "defining her position".

Not that she could say such a thing to Mary.

"That is a philosophical question that may never need answering," Elizabeth said. "It weighs little against the slavery of marriage."

Mary blinked slowly. "Slavery," she breathed, clearly stunned anyone would use such a word to describe a biblical imperative.

The silence from the next steps gave Elizabeth the pause she needed to steer the conversation to a safer berth. "It does strike me as such," she said. "Though I wonder whether I would have conjured that word had we not been speaking of freedom right before."

Mary's eyes narrowed. "So my court is a prison."

"Nay, nay," Elizabeth said, stung at how awry this conversation had gone. "To me, spending time in study and prayer is the ultimate freedom. You yourself acknowledged you wish to do the same. That is all I meant."

"I would call such time a blessing, not freedom."

"Ah, such a wise correction," Elizabeth said, seizing the opportunity. "You are right: the contrast is better expressed as blessing and curse, rather than freedom and slavery. Thank you."

Mary hooted. "I don't know that I would see marriage as a curse any more than I see it as slavery." She thought a moment then laughed again, good nature restored. "But I do agree a contemplative life is a blessing."

"Thank you, dear Sister, for your understanding."

They walked on a few more steps, and Elizabeth prayed she would hear no more of this topic, prayed a stranger would not be forced upon her. *How could any woman do that to another? Even a queen?*

Mary nodded, as if she had convinced herself of something. "I am happy to give you this gift."

Elizabeth knew that was an understatement. It was quite clear Mary was delighted to be rid of her. Elizabeth just hoped she was better at hiding how desperate she was to get away from the despair that suffused the very air Mary breathed.

"It is so generous that I hesitate to ask for the one thing that would make it perfect."

"What is that?" Mary waved an arm. "You shall have it."

"I would ask that Kat Ashley be allowed to return to my household."

Mary's lip curled. "That woman always causes trouble. She offers only bad advice."

Elizabeth chuckled. "I do not love her for her advice, which I have not followed since...for a long time. No, I love her for the care she has shown me since my earliest days, a devotion that touches my heart. She is family to me."

"Simon Renard will take me to task for granting you this wish. He does not trust her."

More evidence of the Spanish Ambassador's outsized influence and another annoyance for Elizabeth to put aside. She put an impish smile on her face. "Ah, but he was also wrong about me. Besides, he is returning to Spain within days: he will not be able to quarrel with your mercy."

Mary laughed. "You speak true." She shrugged. "Very well."

Elizabeth dropped to her knees and bowed her head. "Thank you, Your Majesty. Thank you."

November 14, 1555

William Cecil sighed over the fragility of life. Only two weeks ago, Stephen Gardiner had given what might have been the greatest exhortation of his life, and now Edmond Bonner, Bishop of London, was singing a Requiem Mass over the small silver urn that held Gardiner's heart and entrails.

The Lord Chancellor had briefly risen from his deathbed to champion the Queen before the House of Commons. Hoping to move the members to grant her a large subsidy, his thundering voice had shamed them over the Queen's great need, itemizing her expenses and the debts she inherited from her father and brother. Gardiner had exhorted them to respond with the respect she had surely earned, reminding them of her clemency in allowing so many rebels to keep not only their lives but also their lands.

Cecil had led the opposition. This was not the time to increase taxes. The heavy summer rains had not only destroyed the harvest, putrefying any crops that managed to emerge from the ground, but also caused the sheep to sicken and die. Meanwhile, the Queen's needs would have been covered by the income and assets of the monastery properties she had chosen to return to the rich Roman Church.

The pews in front of Cecil emptied out, but he tarried in his seat. He was not in the mood to mingle outside with any members of Parliament who might try to waylay him. Cecil had only come because the man's death had carried the day: Cardinal Pole had beseeched Parliament in the name of the dying Gardiner to pass the requested subsidy, sharing the Queen's gracious promise to remit a third of whatever they granted her. The Commons had complied.

Cecil took a cautious glance around, but still people funneled through the doors at the rear of the church, so he sat back in his chair and continued his meditation.

He'd risked himself. For nothing. And now he was truly likely to lose his seat. Maybe it was time to just cede it, let someone else spit into the wind. Perhaps he should just surrender.

They were all surrendering now. After Mary's fires had reached all the way to Latimer and Ridley, even Thomas Cranmer had recanted. *Thomas Cranmer!* Another victory Stephen Gardiner had claimed before the end.

Cecil sighed again, and the echo told him that the church was almost empty. He took one last look around before standing to leave.

As he stepped out the heavy doors of St. Mary Overy, a sharp wind made him lower his head and pull his collar around his chin before setting briskly off for home.

With each step, he indulged the melancholy that flowed from the day's reminder of man's common end. He didn't even hear the surrounding wind, let alone the approaching steps, and startled at the rough voice right behind him. "I did not know you were such a friend to Gardiner."

Cecil whirled around. It took him a moment to place the ruddy face rising out of the grey woolen cloak as belonging to James Croft, pardoned after a hung jury trial and now freed, along with almost all of Wyatt's alleged conspirators. Croft had aged since Cecil last saw him – the Tower could do that to a man. But he still looked like the same foolhardy soldier that Cecil remembered from Somerset's glory days, the start of Edward VI's reign.

"I came to make sure he was dead," Cecil said. "And you?"

Croft laughed. "I owed thanks to the man who advised the Queen to pardon me."

Cecil marveled at how quickly fortunes changed. In only a year, Gardiner had transformed from the man urging Elizabeth's execution to the man urging clemency for rebels. "They say he also wanted to slow the burnings," Cecil said. "But Pole is the better man. One of the reasons I can work for him."

"Is that what made you so comfortable at a Catholic service?" Croft asked. "Not that I am surprised – you were never one to stick overmuch to principle."

Cecil laughed and lobbed back the insult. "What is your excuse?"

Croft chuckled. "I have learned how dangerous principles can be when you lose."

The lighthearted comment hid a terrible truth. "You are a lucky man to have fared as you did," Cecil said. "You barely escaped from supporting Jane Grey, then you joined Wyatt. And yet you stand here before me. This, truly, is a miracle."

Croft shook his head. "The real miracle is that you have remained in Parliament. To keep some reasonable voices in its debates."

"Losing voices, you mean."

"But you are there. Too many of us have been ejected, like me, like poor Henry Carey. And now they say Mary hopes to subvert the succession."

"The Members will never agree to that," Cecil said, trying to reassure himself as much as Croft. "Even Gardiner knew it was fruitless to try."

"Gardiner is gone. Things have changed. At the Queen's

insistence, only good Catholics are being called up, and their numbers could distort decisions. Who knows, the next Lord Chancellor might agree that a Spaniard is a good next heir and push for change as hard as for taxes."

Croft was far off the mark. Cecil shook his head. "The Queen has already appointed Archbishop Nicholas Heath. He hates the Spaniards as much as Pole does. Though he will send more money to Rome."

"And more men to the stake," Croft said.

Again, Cecil was able to dismiss Croft's fears as alarmist. "Churchmen would rather convert men than burn them. They were delighted to let Thomas Cranmer save himself."

"Cranmer is looking to a better future, like us." Croft eyes lidded. "You must keep your seat."

A gust of wind made Cecil grab his hat, and he noticed parishioners mounting the steps to the church for Vespers.

"God forgive you if you don't," Croft said, slipping away as quickly as he had arrived.

As Cecil watched Croft's figure recede, melancholy returned. Not for Gardiner, but for himself. And for Elizabeth.

Another gust of wind slapped his face, this time with an answer. Croft was right: Cecil could keep his seat if he were less vocal about his opposition. He would still mount it, but in truth he could be more effective doing so from the shadows. Elizabeth needed him, needed all of them.

He could also work harder for her. She was back at Hatfield, only seventeen miles away – and he was still in her service. He could claim to need her signature on some document and bring her news from time to time – heck, he could seek out news to bring her. Information was currency at the Tudor court, and he could share with her, offer discreet advice during these dangerous times.

He turned and set off for his home, more at peace than he had been in a long time.

March 23, 1556

The Hatfield library was awash in sunlight, bathing Elizabeth in warmth as she danced her fingers across the keys of her virginals. The haunting notes of the Gregorian *Dies Irae* were perfect for the day, expressing her own desolation beneath the piety that a choice of sacred music suggested.

Music had replaced translations as her favorite pastime: it offered her the same delicious suspension of time without being associated with the reform religion. Her ladies appreciated her new habit as well, swaying their heads in time to the music as they sat sewing in the corner.

The return to Hatfield had meant a return to her old life. Elizabeth was no longer limited to three ladies and four gentlemen: she was once again mistress of a real household – entitled to bring back more of her old friends. Not just Kat, but Missi Cheke and Isabella Markham. And Liza FitzGerald, now Lady Clinton from her marriage to Edward Fiennes, Baron Clinton. Life had not been this enjoyable in a long time.

Little George, the cook's son and her newest page, entered.

"You are supposed to knock," she said without rancor.

His eyes widened. "I did, Your Grace. You must not have heard over the music."

"I daresay you are right. So, what have you come to tell me?"

"William Cecil asks leave to wait on you."

Elizabeth jumped up. "More commotion I had not heard! Welcome! How do you come to be here?"

"I work for you. I have an excuse." Cecil entered with a slower stride than usual, but was quickly before Elizabeth and kissing her hand. "It is a comfort to see you fully free." He swept a hand towards Kat. "With Mistress Ashley returned to your service."

"My Spanish friend helped persuade the Queen of my innocence," Elizabeth said with a chuckle. "And I must thank you for finding a reason to come in person."

"I will come again, and more regularly too. But for now, I had to bring tidings. I only wish they were better."

A shadow fell across the room, or perhaps Elizabeth imagined it. "What happened?" she asked.

Cecil's eyes filled with tears. "Can we sit?"

Her stomach tightened. "Of course." She guided him to the window seat in the corner.

He dragged his feet following her, clearly loath to speak. He delayed again when they were seated, waving Kat and Blanche over. Finally, he spoke. "They have executed Thomas Cranmer."

Blanche and Kat gasped, but the statement made no sense to Elizabeth. Surely she had heard the wrong words. "But he recanted." Her stomach clenched, forcing a quiet wail into her voice. "I read the pamphlets."

In hopes of mercy, Thomas Cranmer had repudiated the beliefs he had held so dear, and the government extracted from him a series of six increasingly detailed essays that were quickly published and circulated widely. The first was little more than a submission to the King and Queen, and recognition of the Pope as head of the Catholic Church. Only in his fifth statement did Cranmer actually embrace the Mass, only in the last did he abjectly abandon reform. For his followers, each tract had been another torment, a mean-spirited attack by dogs on a baited bear. The government had not been satisfied with outward compliance, they wanted to compel men's hearts. Elizabeth had cried for her beloved godfather then, despite her relief that these declarations would keep him safe.

"They killed him anyway, right after the Pope ruled him a heretic and removed him from the See of Canterbury."

"But that violates canon law." Her chest swelled with fire. "They can remove his offices, but recanting apostates are to be reprieved." Elizabeth took a breath to calm the venom that threatened to spew forth, but it emerged anyway. "That was murder."

"Yes, and it signals great danger," Cecil said. "You must take no chances in matters of religion."

Elizabeth sighed. "I have long been careful."

"Be more so."

"There is no more I can do. Even the spies my sister placed in my household know me as an exemplar of proper worship." Elizabeth picked at a thread in her skirt. "Though I confess, I did not expect this latest travesty."

"The Queen thinks burning heretics will buy God's favor. And her husband's."

Elizabeth felt her lip curl. "Not that he will show her that favor any time soon. With his father retired to a monastery to live out his days, the King of England is now King of Spain, with a good excuse to stay away."

"But it is his duty to get her with child. And now he has signed a treaty with France at Cambrai."

"A treaty? That certainly was not his intention when he set out."

Cecil shrugged. "At least it ends the aggression. Hopefully he will confirm that when he returns."

Elizabeth shivered. She was happy to have Philip safely away during what were surely the waning days of Mary's fertility.

"My Lady?" Cecil had a gentle hand on her shoulder, and she realized her face had twisted from her thoughts.

She took a deep breath and looked at him, at the profound concern in his eyes. He was a good friend.

She nodded. "Thank you for the warning; I appreciate your counsel. Never shy from telling me what you think I need to hear."

Relief flooded his face. "I...I...There is more."

"Oh, Lord." She squeezed her eyes shut. "Please tell me you shared the worst news first."

"Of course," he said. "This is only more warning. Of rebellions throughout the land to raise you to the throne."

She drew back, an exaggerated gesture. "I have nothing to do with any of them."

"Even the smallest mistake could implicate you in this climate," he said. "Just last week, twenty men were arrested and sent to the Tower for a conspiracy headed by Henry Dudley. It was based out of Calais, but actively sought adherents here. Their handbills urging riot reached even to the Queen's chambers."

She could not help glancing at Kat, who joked with all the men and women who handed her their pamphlets on market days, handing back the calls to riot but accepting the ones merely insulting the government. As Elizabeth began her answer, she realized that Cecil had noticed but held his tongue. "Sir Henry is not someone I have ever met, despite his name," she said. "And thankfully he never wrote to me."

"Good," he said. "But there are others – even one that claims your brother is still alive."

"You warn me of a rebellion not even in my favor?"

"I warn you because there is danger out there. You should be limiting visitors."

Kat stepped forward. "We already do. We learned our lesson."

He frowned. "I entered easily."

"You are my cousin," Blanche said.

"Parry knows not to bring anyone dangerous here," Kat said. "And Blanche and I won't allow anyone into my Lady's presence."

Elizabeth patted Cecil's arm. "You see, Master Cecil, my people are careful."

Cecil nodded. "Good. That and outward shows of faith will keep you safe."

Cranmer's gentle face loomed before Elizabeth's eyes. "Not that they saved the Archbishop."

Cecil smiled. Or was it a smile? His look was both rueful and smug. "I never finished the story. Before they burned him, the Church authorities had him preach publicly before a large crowd, to warn them of the damning dangers of heresy. He had given them his text in advance, so they could prepare their final pamphlet."

This should not have prompted a smile; she must have misread the twist in Cecil's face. "Reveling in his final debasement," Elizabeth said. "And they call themselves righteous."

"He departed from his script."

She snapped to attention. "What?"

"He renounced his earlier recantations and specifically denounced the Pope, with all his false doctrine, as Christ's enemy and Antichrist."

That sounded more like the cleric Elizabeth had known all her life, and she closed her eyes in pride.

"They pulled him from the pulpit to silence him before he could say more and brought him directly to the stake. But once they lit the flames, they had to stand back, and Cranmer again recanted his recantations, even stretching out his right hand into the heart of the fire and explaining that it should be punished first for signing his name to such terrible falsehoods."

"Bless such courage," Elizabeth said, her voice a whisper.

"His dying words claimed he saw the heavens open and Jesus standing at the right hand of God."

A martyr's ultimate glory. Elizabeth prayed the story was true – stories often improved in the retelling. But no matter what, Cranmer had salvaged his soul and his legacy when the true test came.

Elizabeth bent her head and sobbed quietly for her godfather.

May 5, 1556

Elizabeth felt the thrumming through her embroidery hoop before she heard the horses' hooves. Seconds after she looked up, Mimi's face snapped towards the window, her own needle frozen midair. Elizabeth raced over, a commotion of ladies following her.

A display of might marched down Hatfield's parkway approach: a line four abreast of more than fifty guards in black and red uniforms. "That's the Queen's men," Liza said.

"So many of them," Blanche said. "Might she be with them?"

"There'd be triple the guards for the Queen," Kat said. "Not to mention courtiers."

Elizabeth forced herself to breathe calmly and put aside Cecil's warning. If this visit portended bad news – and the number of guards suggested it did – she'd learn soon enough. No need to borrow trouble.

The grim resolve on their faces as they entered the courtyard fueled Elizabeth's trepidations. "Have them brought to me immediately," she said. As if she would have a choice.

The first two to enter the room offered the briefest allowable bows. The men who followed were equally abrupt. *Not a good sign.* They spread out alternating sides of the door, until twenty of them lined the walls. Only then did the captain approach her with two more men.

"Greetings, gentlemen," she said, her mouth dry. "How may I be of service?"

A look that might have been sympathy flashed in his eyes, but the hardness returned. "We have warrants to arrest Mistress Katherine Ashley and three other servants of your household and convey them to the Fleet Prison."

Elizabeth's heart thudded at the recurrence of a nightmare.

Her eyes went to her ladies. Kat was ashen and the others wore terror as well.

Elizabeth summoned the righteous indignation that was her chief weapon, now and always. "What is this?"

"We found seditious materials in your apartments at Somerset House."

Elizabeth felt her throat constrict. "S-seditious materials? What do you mean, 'seditious materials'?"

"We have pamphlets, libels, and other writings against the King and Queen and the Pope."

Pamphlets. Had Kat not been smart enough to burn them? After all the care Elizabeth had shown, after all the horrors they had been through, how could Kat risk something like this?

Kat stepped forward, eyes downcast, and knelt before Elizabeth. "I am so sorry, my Lady, but they speak true. Every week, when I went to the market, people I didn't know would press papers into my hands."

"You could have refused them," the captain interrupted.

Kat looked at him, wide-eyed. "Sometimes they came from the government – like the Archbishop's recantations. I did not want anyone to think I insulted the Queen."

"We did not find any of those."

"Because I gave the honest ones to Her Grace. The rest I…I tossed in my rooms and paid no further mind."

The captain's eyes narrowed. "You could have burned them, to stop the spread of such filth."

"Since I shared them with no one, I saw no harm at the time."

Elizabeth closed her eyes, dizzy and nauseous as she had once been in front of Tyrwhitt, in front of Gardiner. Before she could speak, Kat stood and went to the captain, hands outstretched before her as if ready to be bound. "Take me away, gentlemen. I do not deserve to be in my Lady's worthy company."

Elizabeth breathed slowly to soothe her panic. Surely mere possession of writings could not prove treason – surely that was why they were to be taken to the Fleet and not the Tower.

"We will leave you now," said the captain as he led Kat away.

All Elizabeth wanted to do was cry. Surely this could not give Mary an opportunity to destroy her. Surely the people wouldn't let her. Elizabeth turned to her other ladies. "Who else knew of this?" she asked them, desperate to ascertain the extent of the danger.

"The pamphlets are everywhere on the street," Liza said. "They cannot fault us for taking them."

"Perhaps not," Missi said. "But they can fault us for keeping them. Even if they do not specifically reference rebellion, they contain scurrilous observations that might be said to inspire it."

Elizabeth crossed herself and staggered to her *prie-dieu.*

Lord, do not forsake me.

June 9, 1556

Sheltered by her green damask canopy and draperies, Elizabeth brought her heavy fur blanket closer around her neck.

Edward Hastings, Mary's Master of the Horse, and Francis Englefield, a lord of the Council, stood at the foot of her bed, looking uncomfortable. "We are sorry to hear of your illness," Hastings said.

Elizabeth had taken to her bed after Kat's arrest, waiting for them to come for her as well. But their respect and solicitude were at odds with her fear. "Prayer has sustained me," she said in a small voice.

"The Queen sent us to console and comfort you after the shock of having your servants arrested."

Mary was apologizing to her? What was this?

"My sister is the most gracious of sovereigns, to worry about me despite the many other cares that beset her," Elizabeth said.

"The Queen worries about the confusion this must have caused to the household. Your servants have been released, but they are not to return here. Instead, the Queen has sent you the rich and grave Thomas Pope to act as guardian of your establishment."

"Guardian?" Were they imposing another Bedingfield?

Hastings raised his hands. "To help govern your household."

She thought a moment, reassured by Kat's release and the fact that she was being left in her own home. In truth, Pope would be an added safety. A member of the Council who could bear witness to her innocence if more accusations arose. "I appreciate her concern and accept him completely."

"And provided that you continue to live becomingly, you shall retain the Queen's goodwill." Hastings walked around to the side of the bed and held out a large ring. "As a token of which, she sends you this."

Elizabeth took the magnificent piece of jewelry. It had to be worth at least four hundred ducats. This was quite the token. She kissed it and slid it onto her slim finger. "I cannot think how to express my joy over the love that my dearest sister shows me. I pray you, tell Her Majesty that her kind words are the balm I needed."

"Her Majesty wants you to know that you are neither neglected nor hated but loved and esteemed. King Philip, too, worries about you. He sent word that he would be quite angry if he heard that you were harshly handled."

Philip was protecting her and her place in the succession. With Courtenay dead from a sudden fever, Philip's alternatives had shrunk: Reginald Pole was too old to sire an heir, the Greys were Protestant, Margaret Douglas's husband was bound to uphold an alliance with France – and Mary Stuart was actually living in France and betrothed to their dauphin. Spain's nightmare.

Everything had flipped. Mary might still claim that Elizabeth was the daughter of Mark Smeaton instead of their father, but Spain needed Elizabeth.

"I am deeply grateful to both Their Majesties. Please convey my love and thanks to my sister, a more gentle prince there never was."

"We will indeed. Though surely once you recover, the Queen will invite you to court so that you may do so yourself."

"It is always a joy to see Her Majesty's countenance," Elizabeth said.

"Yes," Hastings said. "It will also be a good opportunity to discuss the issue of your marriage. For if you had a husband to guide you, this never would have happened."

A husband? Of course. She should not have expected to escape so easily. Now that they were looking to her for their future, they would be eager to tie her down. They would apply more pressure than ever to settle her fate. At least Gardiner was dead: one less official ready to cheat for success.

She prayed again for the strength to refuse, prayed that they would not be able to force her, emotionally or physically.

CHAPTER 14

December 7, 1556

*E*lizabeth smiled to everyone she passed as she made her way down the long hall at Richmond.

Mary had summoned her to spend Christmas at court, and of course Elizabeth had come. Still, she was relieved to be lodging at Somerset House, away from the tediousness of daily scrutiny by the world.

This summons had also called her to attend Cardinal Reginald Pole, a man who had studiously avoided her since his arrival in England some two years earlier. Not that Elizabeth was eager to meet him – he was said to blame Anne Boleyn for his mother's brutal execution.

The guards at the door to the Cardinal's apartments silently stepped aside at her approach. She entered the lavish chamber, its wood paneling as ornate as Mary's own. The fifty-six-year-old Cardinal sat in one of the two chairs before the fire, staring vacantly at the flames.

Elizabeth gave a quiet cough to draw his attention, and he immediately stood. He was tall and he moved well, but his skin had the translucence of extreme age. His red cassock seemed large on him, as if he had withered within it.

She curtsied. "Bless me, Father," she said. "I am glad to finally meet you."

"And I you." He sat and motioned to the other chair. "Join me, Cousin."

"Thank you."

"I called you here because there is a matter quite important to the Queen, and I hoped I might offer some gentle influence. And a warning."

She was taken aback when he dispensed with the niceties; she was even more upset by the inflammatory word. "Warning?"

"For a long time, the Queen was opposed to you succeeding her." He raised a hand as if Elizabeth had contested the statement. "Yes, yes, Her Majesty questioned your legitimacy, questioned whether you were even her sister."

Elizabeth's lip curled and she did not try to stop it. "That is a foul lie. I am as much the daughter of Henry VIII as my sister. Look in my face and tell me you do not see him in there."

Pole nodded. "Ah, but I do see him, in your looks as well as your gestures and speech." He sighed. "Even so, the Church considers you illegitimate, and your sister does not want you as her heir. *Did* not want you as her heir. King Philip has managed to change her mind."

She reined in her anger over the insults. She needed a cool head. "Oh?"

"His Majesty has persuaded the Queen that you should be married to a worthy ally. And she has agreed to recognize your rights to allow this to happen."

This was no more than the same prospect Mary had dangled, and just as unwelcome. "Marriage is not a state that calls to me. The Queen's Majesty has accepted this answer from me in the past."

"King Philip is insistent."

Without raising her voice, she put more force behind it. "I do not wish to marry."

"Even to secure your place in the succession?" His tone was taunting.

"My rights have been secured by Parliament."

"Your sister was preparing to alter that," Pole said. "You should rejoice that she has agreed to this important concession. I advise you to accept before she changes her mind."

Mary had always wanted to amend the Succession Act, but she never had the votes. Might she attempt Northumberland's trick of corrupting the King's Bench? Surely someone would warn Elizabeth if that threat was near.

Elizabeth raised her chin. "Marriage has never held any attraction for me," she said. "And since you entered the Church, it must not have held any for you, either. You press me to take a step you yourself reject."

"Women's natural frailties make marriage more important — especially when that woman is the heir to a kingdom."

She smiled. "I believe you began with a threat that I might not be the heir to the kingdom."

His eyes widened slightly, as if he was surprised by her quick wit. Nevertheless, he pressed on. "The security of the realm requires that you marry, and that you marry someone appropriate. If you chose unwisely, you could convulse the entire kingdom into confusion."

"What seems wise now may not remain so in the future," Elizabeth said. "Why sell me into slavery now?"

"S-slavery," Pole began to sputter.

"The Church agrees with me. They do not force women into marriage."

Pole's mouth twisted into a wry smile. "The Church is your problem, not your sanctuary. The Pope is too kind to France right now, and France will support the rights of Mary Stuart. You will need Spain's backing when the time comes."

When the time comes. Dangerously close to treason. Not a trap into which Elizabeth would fall. "My sister may yet be blessed with a son," she said.

Pole sighed. "I see you are resolute. But the Queen is determined to change your mind."

"I do not see how she could."

"You will," he said. "Go to her now."

He made no move to rise. "Will you not come with me?" Elizabeth asked.

"No," he said. "I will stay here and pray you see reason."

Elizabeth wondered whether this would signal her intransigence to Mary. Not that it mattered. "I am glad we finally met, Your Eminence."

"Go with God, child," he said.

She stood and left, her nerves taut.

Walking back down the long hall, she assumed quite a different posture than on her arrival. Then, she had smiled to one and all; now, she kept her eyes lowered to avoid being distracted by greetings as she considered her predicament. She needed to raise the stakes surrounding her refusal. During their brother's reign, Mary had confronted Edward with the phrase, *Mine is the true religion, I would gladly die for it.* Mary had dared Elizabeth to apply it to her own situation, and Elizabeth had wisely refused where religious details were involved. But this was different. Mary could not burn her for refusing to consent to marriage.

The guards were less welcoming at the doorway to Mary's apartments; they waited until Elizabeth was upon them to move aside. She paused and squared her shoulders to begin the ordeal.

Just inside, Susan Clarencieux stood to welcome her. "Her Majesty is almost done. She will join you soon."

Elizabeth glanced at the corner, where Mary was kneeling at her *prie-dieu.* Or what must be Mary, based on the cloth of gold and purple velvet, embroidered with fleurs-de-lis and Catherine of Aragon's pomegranate device.

Elizabeth clasped her hands and bent her head to wait for her sister. Finally, Mary crossed herself and pushed to standing. Her eyes looked behind Elizabeth, probably for Pole, and she swayed slightly.

"Welcome, Sister," Mary said, stretching out her hand.

Elizabeth walked to bow and kiss it, noticing how the smile on Mary's face could not conceal the latent anger signaled by the furrow in her brow.

"It is a joy to be here with you," Elizabeth said.

"I regret that my husband cannot join us for the season."

The niceties that Pole had dispensed with grated on Elizabeth now. She knew what was coming and she just wanted to get on with it.

"Too many impediments seem to rise daily to hinder his return," Mary continued. "He has been sick, did you know? I worry about him."

"Of course, a wife worries about her husband, though I am glad you have the comfort of knowing that the King has excellent physicians," Elizabeth said. "Surely they will strengthen him enough to return to you."

"It is the Pope," Mary said. "He sides with France in every dispute; it is infuriating."

Elizabeth had to work hard to keep her face completely impassive, to display no change, no smile, not even a twitch at the rich irony that Mary had chosen this unfair yoke.

"But my husband has his own methods, and the Pope will surely see reason," Mary continued. "One of those methods involves your marriage."

And so it begins…

"I do not wish to marry," Elizabeth said.

"Religion, piety, and the security of the realm require it."

"St. Basil tells us that only the single life enables the soul to devote itself to God. Marriage enmeshes us in the world and its cares."

"Ah, Sister," Mary said. "Your position is what enmeshes you in the world's cares. Marriage would shield you from them."

Elizabeth shook her head. "The state does not call to me."

Mary's jaw set. "My husband wishes to see you well married and has persuaded me to agree. His son is still too young yet, so it must be the Duke of Savoy."

"I beg you, Your Majesty, not to make me enter into such a match."

Mary waved her hand. "Surely you could do much worse. Emmanuel Philibert is a worthy general, and they say he has a pleasing presence and fine Italian manners."

"I beg you."

"This is a matter of import to my husband, and therefore to me. Will you really force me to disappoint my Lord?"

Who leads you by your nose, Elizabeth longed to say. "King Philip will see reason. Surely."

"You think you would persuade him where I could not?"

Elizabeth heard the jealousy in Mary's bitter tone. "Nay, Your Majesty, I never expected to plead my case to him. Only to you."

Mary snorted. "If you wish to be treated as a princess, you must do your duty. If you want me to consider you my heir, you must marry the Duke of Savoy."

Elizabeth knew this was the time to stress the personal nature of this refusal, to remove the taint of political expediency. She needed to open her heart and her soul, to make clear her genuine horror of marriage. She dropped slowly to her knees. "Your Majesty." Elizabeth swallowed. "I have suffered such afflictions as to remove any wish for a husband, afflictions that would make me prefer death."

"Afflictions?"

Mary's face remained stern; Elizabeth summoned hot tears. "Too many women close to me have suffered greatly at the hands of their spouse. I have no desire for any of their fates."

Elizabeth kept her eyes lowered so that Mary would not read challenge in them. For the list was not limited to Anne Boleyn and Catherine Howard; it included Katherine Parr and Frances Grey. It reached even to Mary, shamed and rejected by her husband as Catherine of Aragon had been before her.

"Since my earliest days," Elizabeth continued, "the thought of submitting to a man has made me ill."

Mary paused and softened. She put a comforting hand on Elizabeth's shoulder. "The first time can be fearsome, but then a husband brings comfort. Marriage is a sacrament."

"Only if it is entered into with a joyful heart."

"A pious heart is all that is needed. The joy will come."

"In religion, yes. In this, no."

"It is the same submission," Mary said, patting Elizabeth's shoulder as if the argument was already won.

Resentment and fear mingled until Elizabeth could not help herself. "You cannot force my consent. The Church is on my side."

The tears in Mary's eyes dried instantly. "I may not have the right to force you, this is true. But it is equally true that you cannot force me to make you my heir. If you thwart me in this, the Queen of Scots will rule here after my death."

Elizabeth kept her head bowed, refusing to be sucked into such a conversation.

"Leave me," Mary said. "Go back to Hatfield; I am done with you."

Shocked, Elizabeth was about to protest, but she quickly realized she was grateful for the dismissal. She was happy to put some distance between herself and Mary's anger, eliminate the public and private pressure that would otherwise be brought to bear on her throughout the season. And pray that Philip would be loath to see the Crown turned away from Elizabeth.

"Thank you, Your Majesty, for not forcing me into a state

that would kill me," she said with a bow, backing all the way to the door to add to the formality.

She did not bother to look behind her; she knew her ladies would follow. She just strode straight to the river to make her way to the royal barge. Put at her disposal during her visit, it had been festooned with rich garlands of flowers and covered with an awning of green silk embroidered with branches of eglantine and golden blossoms. Gifted when Mary thought she would get her way.

Elizabeth settled into the special chair designed to allow her to sit in state as the rowers brought her in all speed away from the court.

March 20, 1557

Rhythmic hoofbeats and the crunch of gravel drew Elizabeth to the window to peer out, her curiosity piqued by the rider approaching Hatfield Palace. He sat his steed gracefully, relaxed despite the speed, his jerkin revealing the muscles in his arms. A cap at a rakish angle covered his eyes, but there was no mistaking the chiseled jaw.

Robin.

The corners of Elizabeth's mouth lifted and she ran to the mirror. She pulled a small mesh of hair from her coif and added a bracelet before racing to the courtyard.

Robin came to a precision stop directly in front of her.

"What are you doing here?" She could not help laughing as she spoke. "Has Philip returned to England or has he dismissed you?"

Robin's chuckle was throaty. "Philip is on his way and sent me ahead to bring word. I am still a valued member of his entourage. The man appreciates my military skills."

She smiled at past echoes. "You always knew that as your power."

"And you always knew it for a waste. We have no business warring with France, though I still would rather be there than in Ireland with Ratcliffe – I mean Sussex."

Elizabeth crossed herself, sad to be missing friends and advocates. Her own beloved champion had died, and his heir had been sent to subdue the anarchy in Ireland.

"Is the Irish situation really so bad?" The Irish had initially been happier to bow to a Catholic queen than a Protestant king, though tempers flared when Mary dispossessed two old families of their properties in favor of English settlers.

"Ireland is a bog. I'm safer with Philip. And Sussex and I have never gotten along."

She smiled. There was a long list of people with whom Robin had never gotten along. A bit of a handicap in the Tudor court, where a man was defined by his friends.

"You are indeed better where you are," she said with a smile. "But how are you here? Does this mean I am allowed friends again? So far only Cecil has risked a visit."

Robin winked. "Who says I asked permission?" He dismounted in a single sure motion and handed his reins to the groom, who had come running to meet them. George. That lad did everything, and did it well.

Robin donned his doublet before stepping forward to kiss her in greeting. He may have lingered over it; she could not tell. "Will you walk with me?" he asked. "I rode straight here, and my legs could use the stretch."

"Of course," she said. She had taken the air that morning, but she was always happy for more.

Robin called to the lad who was leading his horse away. "Give her hay and a lot of water. And a brushing."

"Yessir," George said.

Elizabeth took the arm Robin offered and guided him towards the gardens. "The tips of the crocuses are emerging."

"A time of great promise."

"It does feel like that," she said, wondering whether she heard something beneath his words. "So am I summoned to court?"

Robin laughed. "No. And pray your luck holds. Philip is bringing Savoy, the better to force you to submit. Do not trust any dark corners."

She prayed he was exaggerating. "If I am summoned, I must go. But I will take care, and take ill quickly."

"That should be enough. They will not stay long – Philip is only here to get England to join his stupid war with France. So far, the Queen has refused, but he hopes his presence will persuade her."

"He values himself highly," Elizabeth said. "Especially after staying away for a year and a half. That is a long time to leave a wife."

Robin laughed. "It is a long time for a wife to be left. For Philip, his mistress more than satisfies him. And from what I hear, she will accompany him on the trip."

Elizabeth stopped. "Is he really so callous?"

Robin rolled his eyes.

"Heaven, help us." Elizabeth shook her head. "Though I am sure my poor sister will see nothing, like her mother before her."

Robin said nothing.

Elizabeth continued. "I wish she would notice – it might harden her heart against Philip's attempts to draw us into war."

"Unlikely. John Dee says the stars predict conflict."

"John Dee! He is still alive?" John Dee was the most accomplished astrologer in the land. He had been arrested two years earlier for casting horoscopes for Elizabeth and Mary, his treatment made worse because Elizabeth's future was so much brighter.

"Alive and thriving. Somehow he convinced Bishop Bonner that his actions were neither heretical nor treasonous."

"Bonner? The man who so delights in condemning apostates to the fire?"

"God worked a miracle, and now Dee is hard at work assembling his library. The Queen refused his proposal for a national repository of important volumes, so he decided simply to expand his own collection. He's already grown it larger than the Archbishop of Canterbury's."

"That library was the finest in the world."

"It was the finest when Cranmer was constantly adding volumes to it. Once Pole inherited it, he consigned shelves of them to the rubbish heap for containing heretical ideas."

"Such wanton destruction," she said.

"Well, we can't complain too terribly because Dee took so many of the discards." Robin chuckled. "Now his collection has made his home a center of learning for many scholars."

She sighed at the small mercy.

As they walked in silence, a thought came to her. "Why did you come to tell me of Philip's arrival if I am not being summoned? Or am I just a stop on a longer journey for you?"

"In fact, after tarrying two days at court, I must go to see my wife."

Elizabeth narrowed her eyes. "Is she close by? I had not realized."

"She is in the opposite direction," Robin said. "I wanted to see you first."

The thought made her happy, though she was not about to admit it. "I daresay Amy will scold you for that."

Robin shook his head. "I think Amy wishes to see me as little as I wish to see her. She disdains courtiers, thinks us shallow."

Pity filled Elizabeth for her old friend. He did not deserve this. "I am sorry."

"No need. If I valued her opinion, it would be different."

Elizabeth chuckled at his devilish smile. "It is an important skill, to know whom to heed."

"The real skill is to recognize good advice." His voice was smug.

"You need advice?"

"No, you do."

She drew back mockingly. In response, he dropped to one knee and kissed her hand. "Rather, I need to give it. As the champion I promised I would be."

She swatted his cap. "Get up."

He rose immediately and took her arm to continue their walk. "The conflict Dee saw may be more than war. We are entering a time of great storms, and your ship must hold a steady course."

Like Cecil before him, Robin seemed to think that Elizabeth was preparing to do something foolish. Of course, Cecil had been proven prescient given Kat's arrest. Elizabeth steeled herself to heed Robin's words. "Steady in what sense?"

"Philip is making giant plans to change the shape of the world. He sees himself conquering France and refashioning Europe to his vision. Which is why he wants you married to someone he can control, someone safe."

"I have long known that." Elizabeth shook her head. "And I have resisted such an imposition with every fiber of my being."

"His presence will make it harder for Mary to refuse him."

Elizabeth held on to serenity. "You said yourself his main purpose in coming here is to get money and men for his war. It will not be easy for him to win both fights."

"True," Robin said. "Especially thanks to the support you have, at court and in the realm."

"Support for which I thank God every day, even as I pray it is enough."

"You must cultivate it further. And brandish your future."

The words unnerved her. How could she flaunt something she had always been told she did not deserve? Only God's will would bring her that miracle. "It is not yet mine."

"It is less likely to be stolen from you if you show you can fight."

The thought made her clutch at her throat. "I have learned to be more careful than that. I will not take an action that could damn me," she said. "It is not yet time."

Robin raised an index finger. "I do not ask you to act, only to sharpen your sword."

"Ah, well, as a woman I am allowed only an archer's bow," she laughed, eager to deflect the conversation.

The raised finger wagged at her. "You are thinking too literally." He held out a bulging velvet purse.

"What is this?" she asked.

"Gold."

She put her fists on her hips. "You are giving me money?"

He took her hand and placed the purse in it, his eyes burning. "You have always been impressive, but now you must look like you already rule. Authority, like war, takes money. I know how much your father left you; it is not enough."

Under the terms of Henry's will, Elizabeth received three thousand pounds a year. A royal sum, to be sure, yet even her careful management was not always enough anymore. "Are you not impressed by how far I have stretched my funds?"

"I would have thought you had double. But now you need allies. Lots of them. And you must inspire awe in them."

She smiled, remembering Pythagoras. "'The engine of creativity, discovery, purpose, and health,'" she said.

"More than that. Awe will spin a web to catch the world. Most of the court supports you already. Hire some important gentlemen – or their wives. More than you need, just to bind them to you, to stop Mary and Philip from destroying your rightful future."

Elizabeth's thoughts hearkened back to her first household, how she had to send away servants she could not afford. "I would be foolish to use this up too quickly."

Robin shook his head. "Smart men will pay for themselves. You can expand your staff slowly, to prove that theory, but at least begin the process."

While she was mulling over his words, he grinned. "And see that visitors are treated to subtleties when they come to wait upon you. It will make you seem more powerful."

"Is that a hint?" She laughed. "That you expect some sugared treat?"

"A whole tray of them."

Robin was right. Lavishness drew allies; need pushed them away. She hefted the bag; its weight gave her pause. "How can you do this? You overspend – yes, I've always known it – and I suspect you went into debt to enter Philip's service."

Robin laughed. "You sound like my wife."

Elizabeth started to hand back the purse, but Robin refused. "Think of it as a loan, if that makes you feel better," he said. "But do not fight me on this point. You know as well as I do how important this is." He pointed at the bag. "For your army." At her grimace, he threw up his hands. "An army of friends."

She looked at him levelly. "Do you have reason to think I might need so many?"

"The waning of a rule is when a crown is most easily stolen, or at least when an attempt is most likely. I know whereof I speak." A flicker of a smile disappeared quickly from his face. "In a time when anything can happen, you must have the ability to react quickly. Action may be premature, but preparation is not."

She hooked the purse to her belt. Robin was right. She had ways to use it.

July 10, 1557

Twelve plates had been set on the heavy oaken table in Hatfield's Great Hall, and now Elizabeth's servants stood at the entrance with food for her visitors: four large platters – and a fifth tray of subtleties: a field of green marchpane bordered by a white candy fence and populated by tiny marzipan animals.

Silently she thanked Robin for his gift and the outsized impact it could have. Small instances of largesse conjured the specter of future rewards. And in the meantime, she could also afford now to share a whiff of showy luxury with friends.

Elizabeth smiled at Liza's husband Baron Clinton, who had become a more regular guest. He had just arrived with William Cecil to bring details about England's declaration of war on France. Elizabeth was eager to hear their insights.

"You must sit next to me, Master Cecil," Elizabeth said. "Across from Lord Clinton, so that the two of you will share all the details of the declaration."

Liza leaned forward. "We read the proclamation and found it rousing. Now we want the details."

And reactions, Elizabeth thought. Had Mary risen to the task? Her words were strong, but how were they received?

Swallowing her impatience, Elizabeth waited to begin the conversation until the men sat and the food was served. All to avoid interruptions and distractions that would inevitably come at inopportune moments.

The servants set the platters in the center of the table, before coming around with ewers for guests to wash their hands before grabbing food for their plates.

Finally, the bustle had passed, the dishes had been tasted and praised, and the time was right. "So, tell us of the Queen's momentous speech," Elizabeth said.

"She made it at Whitehall," Cecil began. "With as much pomp as a Garter Ceremony. The Queen sat in her chair of estate, under her finest arrases and—"

"What did she wear?" Blanche broke in, as she speared a morsel of venison.

"She and the King both chose highly ornamented dark purple

and black velvet. The Queen wore her state crown and held her scepter; Philip wore the Sword of State."

Although Elizabeth ate little during moments of stress, she brought a spoonful of pottage to her lips: she needed something to hide her grimace at the thought of Philip wearing a symbol of English sovereignty. Not that she was likely alone in this: even Thomas Pope's lips tightened in disapproval. Although dismissed from his duties – apparently Elizabeth no longer needed a guardian – Pope remained a frequent visitor, to her delight. His presence was a good reminder to tread carefully around certain topics.

"He won't take that with him to France, will he?" Blanche asked, speaking for all of them.

"I did not see him wear it again, so I believe not," Cecil said.

"Where was Cardinal Pole in this?" Elizabeth asked. "Or Archbishop Heath?" Heath, who had been named Lord Chancellor on Gardiner's death, disliked the Spaniards as much as Pole did. They could not be happy with this development.

"They both stood on the dais beside the Queen, dressed as they would for the highest holy day."

Cecil stretched out a hand to pluck off a subtlety from the marchpane field, the seagull that sat atop the candy fence. He didn't even seem to chew before he swallowed and continued. "The Queen began by detailing how her heralds would announce to London, and envoys would be sent to the French King and the Pope, to tell them what she was about to tell us. And much as we all knew what she was about to say, we were sobered by the reminder that this news would affect the entire world."

Clinton nodded. "There is a sense of responsibility that descends at such a time." He took a deep drink.

"The Queen acknowledged the solemnity. She paused as if to say a quick prayer before beginning to make her case, a recital of the treasonous acts that had convinced her and the Council that England had no other choice."

"Those were listed in the proclamation," Elizabeth said. "I had not realized the extent of the French King's interference, from Northumberland's attempted coup to Wyatt's rebellion."

Clinton shifted in his seat. "I can attest that we on her Council often urged her to more… aggressive responses to such insults. But such was her care for the peace of Christendom and the repose of her subjects, that she attributed these doings to the French King's ministers rather than to his own will, hoping thus to induce him to adopt a friendly attitude towards England."

"As Her Majesty put it, the acts were not only contrary to all honor but also to the peace treaties between our countries," Cecil said. He took another subtlety. "A tiger does not easily change its stripes."

And yet Mary had. She had gone from victim to war monger in a single step, ignoring all the possible responses in between these two extremes. "She did indeed show remarkable forbearance," Elizabeth said.

"It set my teeth on edge to hear all the crimes together." Clinton pushed his food around his plate as if uncovering the memories. "Henri receiving rebels at his court and financing their efforts – or collaborating with counterfeiters who put false coin into circulation in England. Worst, he encouraged French pirates to target English ships."

Liza patted her husband's hand. He had served as Lord High Admiral during Edward's reign, and still felt proprietary about the seas.

"The entire assembly hissed and booed louder with each provocation the Queen mentioned," Cecil said. "Crescendoing until the Queen ordered us to consider the King of France as a public enemy to the nation, to harm him and his vassals wherever possible, abstaining from trade or any other business with them. At that point, every man was happy to acknowledge England's obligation to defend Flanders against the invading French army."

Elizabeth had to admire the structure of the speech, more evidence of the warfare in Mary's blood.

"So no one sees this as a hardship?" Elizabeth asked, picking out a citrus sucket.

Cecil frowned. "Once we accept that we have no choice, the reckoning changes. All war is hardship, but Spain is our main trading partner because so much English wool is sold in Flanders. We can do without French goods."

"All the French people in town seem to have disappeared," Blanche said. "Have there been attacks on them in London?"

"Not yet," Cecil said. "They are still under the Queen's protection – she has given them forty days to leave this land."

"It's more than they deserve," Clinton said, drumming his fingers on the table. "Ten days would be more than enough."

"Ten days would be a bit short for several thousand Frenchmen to find passage on boats – and we would not want the French King to turn out our own citizens on such short notice," Cecil said. "I would have counseled twenty."

Elizabeth was impressed at how respectful Cecil could be in criticism. A valuable trait.

"And I would have limited the goods they can bring with them," Clinton said.

"Perhaps the Queen hopes that her generosity will make peace easier later," Blanche said. "If the French know we will be reasonable, they might be more ready to surrender when the time comes."

Clinton nodded thoughtfully. "That is consistent with her usual forbearance. Forbearance that has taught them bad habits."

"Is it possible such a delay is just a feint, to distract from the fact that we need more time ourselves to mobilize?" Elizabeth asked.

"I might agree with you," Cecil said, "except that the King has already left England to take the field."

"Already left?" Elizabeth asked. "He absented himself for a year and a half and returned only for four months?"

"He left to fight," Clinton said. "And many of us are planning to join him. If we are at war, we must win it."

"I had not thought to see you die in this cause," Liza said.

"I have no intention of dying but also no choice in the matter. It is my duty to serve."

They fell into contemplative silence for the rest of the meal, or rather what little was left of it. Elizabeth had questions, but she was not about to ask them publicly. Instead, she turned to Cecil. "May I interest you in a brisk walk through the gardens? Nothing better after a large meal."

"That is my own practice as well," Cecil said.

"We will come find you afterwards," Elizabeth said to Blanche, to keep her ladies from joining. Then she and Cecil were off.

Their talk was completely innocuous on the walk over. Cecil had a small garden plot at his home in Canon Row, so the discussion centered around plantings. But once they were through the garden gate and no longer worried about being overheard, the real conversation could begin. "So we are at war," she said.

"We are indeed," Cecil said.

"I must say, I could see how men were moved by that long list of insults. The French King's taunts seem intentionally provocative."

"There are many ways to stop a bully short of committing to war."

It was her own approach as well. God bless Cecil for not worshiping aggression. "What would you have advised?"

"I would have tried to hurt him without a massive commitment on our part." Cecil sniffed. "We will be bled dry of our own resources, when we have only begun to recover after years of trouble with the coinage, after droughts and rebellions over enclosures."

"Have we really promised that much?"

"Philip needed a huge sum, more than found in all of Spain. Though, in his defense, it is no more than he brought to England in the marriage."

"And no one on the Council resisted him?"

Cecil shook his head. "Gardiner would have stopped this. If only God had seen fit to leave him alive."

Gardiner's great legacy was in bringing spending and financing in line to save the realm from the bankrupt state it was in at Edward's death. Impressive skills, and yet…

"Rather than questioning God's decision in taking the good Bishop," Elizabeth said, "we should be asking Him to inspire another leader to intervene. Of course, Gardiner did try to have me murdered, so I am somewhat biased."

Cecil laughed. "Certainly that sort of thing can affect friendship."

They walked several paces before Elizabeth resumed her questions. "So let me ask you again: What should England have done here?"

"Sent our own pirates after their ships, put false coin into their currency – things where we would profit from the pain we inflict."

She put a teasing note into her voice. "So it is fairness that spurs you?"

"I weigh potential rewards against their risks, and here all the rewards inure to Spain, not us. We have no gain to counterbalance our losses. Except maybe another Boulogne." Cecil's voice dripped with sarcasm: Henry VIII had bankrupted the country to war with France, and in the end had won only a single city that his son then sold back at a loss.

"I agree. We need nothing beyond Calais," Elizabeth said.

Before she could pursue the matter, Cecil yawned. Elizabeth was immediately contrite. "In all the excitement, I completely forgot to ask after your wife and new daughter. I hope they are well?"

He rubbed the back of his neck. "Not so new anymore," he said with a rueful smile. "Seven months and she is already crawling everywhere."

Seven months. How quickly the time passed…

"I hope you are good to Mildred," Elizabeth said. "Please give her my love."

"She sends hers to you every day – every time she uses the spoon you sent for Anne's christening."

Elizabeth smiled. Gift giving was an important talent. A silver anything made an impressive gift, and the child-size saved half the cost.

Some might argue that she had no need to court Cecil's loyalty since she was already assured of it. Some would be fools. You showed more largesse to people you valued than anyone else.

Cecil was not the only one who weighed risks and rewards.

January 10, 1558

William Cecil staggered into the library of his Canon Row home, where Mildred sat in one of the two chairs in front of the fireplace, their daughter sleeping in the cradle beside her. Mildred looked up from her sewing, and her brows knit at the sight of him.

Breathing heavily, he walked to the chair next to hers and collapsed into it. A feeling of doom pressed his head towards his knees.

"Oh my," Mildred said, a trembling hand stroking his shoulder. "Did you run all the way home? What happened?"

Cecil had indeed raced away from court, as if to escape the news. Sharing it now would make it all the more real, yet he had no choice. "We've lost Calais," he said without raising his head.

For two hundred years, the port town on the French coast had been a bright jewel in the English Crown, the gateway to trade with the continent and a thriving center for wool production. Now the jewel had been stolen.

"But we sent reinforcements – did they not arrive in time?"

A week earlier, they had received a frantic message from Thomas Wentworth, the Deputy of Calais, reporting that the French had attacked like lightning, and begging for men and guns to help repel the forces. With so many English resources swallowed by Philip and Ireland, Mary had been able to provide only limited funds to the captains and soldiers ordered to assemble at Dover.

"Too little, too late," he mumbled.

Mildred sat back, disgust curling her lip. "They might have sailed sooner if the Queen had not insisted that the troops be garbed in white coats with red crosses."

"I tried to argue." Cecil felt the wail in his voice. "I went to Pole and Heath, begged them to try to persuade the Queen to just send the men. But they dismissed my urgency."

"What folly," Mildred said, "to sacrifice speed to such vanity."

"She wanted to claim that God was on our side, make rebuttal to the Pope." He snorted. "The man she believes to be God's representative on earth supports France."

Mildred arched an eyebrow. "Does she finally accept that nations must defy Rome when a pope's personal politics trumps his religious considerations?"

Cecil snickered. "She will never acknowledge the parallel."

He rose and went to pour himself a cup of wine. He brought one to Mildred as well. "We could both use some fortitude."

Little Anne sighed and turned over in her cradle. Cecil and Mildred froze until she settled.

"What does all this mean for us?" Mildred said quietly.

"Didn't you once tell me that the town's customs revenue amounted to a third of all government income some years?"

The question roused him out of his nationalistic melancholy: practical considerations had that effect on him. "We had already resolved to cease trading with France, so revenues would have decreased significantly anyway. And the goods from other countries…well, we collect import duties wherever goods enter the English economy, so we won't lose everything." He sighed again. "But we have lost a great deal."

"What does the Queen say to this tragedy?"

"Cardinal Pole says she is distraught, absolutely distraught," Cecil said. "And yet…"

"What?"

"She thinks herself with child. That softens the blow."

Mildred counted on her fingers. "Philip left six months ago, almost to the day. She should have a goodly belly. Does she?"

Cecil grimaced. "She is too unwell to don court clothes, so she spends most of her time behind her curtains. She only opens them when she wants to be seen, and then only for a short time."

"So no one has seen the belly?"

"She always has a belly. No one can see that it is much grown."

Mildred nodded. "Does she feel movement?"

"She says she waited until then to say anything."

"She felt movement last time too." Mildred's eyes darted.

Cecil's head lowered again at the thought of repeating such a nightmare.

"We may be blessed sooner than we hoped." Mildred's tone sounded pensive, almost calculating.

"Why?" he said, before understanding exploded and he raised his head. "You think the Queen might…?"

"You need to speak privately with my sister. She could tell you what is really happening."

"I have never been able to get her alone," Cecil said. "But I will seek out her husband. It will draw less attention."

And just like that, Cecil's spirits lifted.

CHAPTER 15

February 5, 1558

espite Richmond's magnificence, it always felt comforting. And comfort was what Elizabeth needed right now, as she prepared for her imminent audience with Mary.

With no one able to tell her for sure, Elizabeth had come to see for herself whether her sister was pregnant or delusional. And to place herself in the royal grasp before being summoned, more proof of loyalty.

"Mistress Dormer," the page announced as Jane Dormer stepped into the room.

"Ah, Jane," Elizabeth said with as much warmth as she could muster. "Always a pleasure."

"Yes," Jane said, equally dry.

Before Elizabeth could respond with more ironic pleasantries, Jane announced, "The Queen is ready for you."

"Oh?" Elizabeth asked, as if anything else would have gotten Jane to visit. "Thank you so much." She turned to Blanche. "Do you have all the gifts?"

"Right here," Blanche said, displaying the stack of baby

clothes that Elizabeth had made. A tiny cap, covered in pome-granates and frilled with fine, gauffered linen; silk swaddling bands embroidered with cloth of gold; and smocks with intricate blackwork. The garments were tiny enough that the work had gone quickly, giving Elizabeth and her ladies the time and the supplies to decorate a new set of sleeves. Another addition to the trunkful of outfits that could be assembled from the single gown that Mary had given her.

"Let us be on our way then."

Elizabeth forced herself to glide down the galleries with the hint of a serene smile on her face.

They paused at the door to the royal apartments, where heavy incense further darkened the already somber tapestries. It took only a single glance for Elizabeth to see Mary in her chair of estate surrounded on one side by the Count de Feria and on the other by sewing ladies. Elizabeth stifled a smile. Philip likely sent Feria to investigate this pregnancy as Elizabeth was now doing. Skepticism was inevitable after the last time.

Even from this distance, Elizabeth was careful to keep her gaze on Mary's face, which was pale and gaunt, not plump and glowing. "Your Majesty," she said, her curtsy low.

"Welcome," Mary answered, stroking her stomach.

Elizabeth swept into the room and bowed again when she reached the dais. "You look radiant, Sister. Thank you for allowing me to attend you at this joyous time."

Joyous. As if this figment of Mary's imagination made up for England's humiliating defeat at Calais, for the drought and hunger and resentment over the war.

"She speaks for us all, Your Majesty," Feria said loudly. "I know how jealous my master is that I am here for this glorious triumph."

"Ah, my dear Count, eloquent as ever," Elizabeth said by way of greeting.

Feria bowed his head but turned immediately to Mary. "I

confess to feeling guilty over my good fortune, ashamed to not be contributing directly to the war with France."

Mary wagged a finger. "You are helping me persuade my Council to approve the troops and money that keep England safe. I cannot do it without you." Her face turned forlorn. "And I confess it gives me comfort to have you here."

Feria bowed, and Mary turned to Elizabeth. "You came in time," she said. "I will be entering confinement soon."

Elizabeth kept her smile steady. That meant Mary thought she was almost eight months along. *Impossible.*

Mary cradled her belly. "Oh!" she exclaimed. "A kick."

Now Elizabeth could look safely at the bulge. She brought her hands to her heart, offering a picture of awe before slowly crossing herself.

She pushed aside her guilt over the deception: no one, especially Elizabeth, could tell the poor woman they did not believe her. Instead, Elizabeth vowed never to deceive herself so completely that people feared to tell her the truth.

"I have brought presents for him," she said, waving for Blanche to approach with the pile. One at a time, she handed the tiny garments to Mary, pointing out the details of her designs to simulate enthusiasm.

Mary looked at each with a tight smile, handing them quickly to Jane.

"When did you say the date was for Your Majesty to take to your chamber?" Elizabeth asked.

"Two weeks from tomorrow, to be safe," Mary said. "Though I may not be as far along as that. You do not need to stay."

Elizabeth kept her face bland. "I am Your Majesty's to command," she said. In truth, Elizabeth wanted to be here as little as Mary wanted her to. Especially since this "pregnancy" was so likely to end in the same shame as the last one.

God willing.

As she left Mary's presence, yearning filled Elizabeth's soul.

She was so close to the destiny that was never meant to be hers, and every footfall dislodged another plea for strength, for mercy, for grace.

If God gave this to her, she would do her best to deserve it. Mary had embodied all the perils of female reign that terrified their father – a woman who failed her sex, her country, and her god. Elizabeth would never repeat those mistakes. She would rule from her head, not her heart. She would never give the realm to a foreign power. She would be no fanatic to burn men for their beliefs. She would do right by the English people, His people, always. If only He would allow it…

She reined herself in, tamping emotions down to surrender.

Thy will, not mine, be done.

April 28, 1558

"Back so soon?" Elizabeth smiled at William Cecil. "Is it the subtleties I offer?"

Cecil laughed. "I cannot resist sugar," he said as he looked around Elizabeth's Presence Chamber at Hatfield.

The gesture struck Elizabeth, especially since she had seen his eyes sweep the empty room when he first entered. "If you have something private to share, this would be a good time, before anyone joins us."

Cecil nodded. "The Queen is having pains. She is once again curling up on the floor, weeping with distress. This pregnancy of hers is another chimera."

Although the room was empty, Elizabeth gave another glance around. "Does she understand it as such? Has she abandoned her chamber or is she burning more heretics?"

"Both," Cecil said. "She is feeding the fires but admits she does so from a sickbed. And it may get worse: there are whispers of cancer in her womb."

Elizabeth froze. "Whispers?"

"Mildred's sister, Anne Bacon, is one of Mary's ladies. She passed this on through her husband, Nicholas."

As Elizabeth turned over the news she had already guessed, gratitude mixed with pity. And fear. This changed nothing – yet everything.

She felt the same alarm she had all those years ago, staring at the pile of deeds to the properties her father bequeathed to her. Then, Cecil's touch had made all the difference. Now, she needed it more than ever.

Her memory shifted to Mary, staring at Philip's portrait in hopes of guidance. Elizabeth cringed but caught herself. This was different: Elizabeth had no intention of ceding power. She wanted advice and a first ally, and who better than the man she most trusted – and who could best handle the details? Much as the law required submission, fortune favored the brave. Surely she could take a tiny, careful step.

"I, too, suspected illness. And questioned how to respond," Elizabeth said, her voice creaking on a tentative note.

"It is coming time for that." Cecil rubbed the back of his neck. "Bacon is a lawyer, a good one, and while we were discussing the Queen's illness, I had him speculate on some hypothetical situations."

"Oh?"

"Whether you would be allowed greater latitude if the Queen were indeed dying, whether a country at war requires an heir who is prepared to lead."

Elizabeth stifled a smile at the gratitude that filled her. Once again, Cecil had completed a task before it had even been assigned, before he even knew it might be. He had an unerring instinct for what was important, what would be needed. Always had. And while her stomach fluttered at the danger of their discussion, she trusted his judgment to keep it within the law. "So, am I?"

"Yes and no." Cecil's eyes narrowed, his personal gesture of concentration. "Bacon believes you must take refuge in vagueness, cloak an undefined future in abstractions. He specifically recalled the waning days of your father's reign, when the then-Earl of Surrey was convicted of treason for promising appointments to a regency council. But Bacon noted that, as the undisputed next heir, you should be permitted to illustrate possibilities."

She sat back in her chair. "Vagueness has always promised a safe harbor, yet I was almost killed for thanking Wyatt for his concern."

"No amount of vagueness can protect you from traitors. I am speaking of necessary dealings with the people you need to secure your accession. Like Clinton."

She tilted her head, intrigued. After helping Philip win the Battle of St. Quentin, Clinton had returned to England and been restored to his old post of Lord High Admiral. He was loyal to Mary, but also loved Elizabeth. As did his wife.

"Interesting," she said. "Why him?"

"Upon the Queen's dea—upon your accession, you will want the ports closed immediately, to stop the news arriving in Spain or France before you are in firm possession of London: he is the one to do that. Bacon has confirmed that you may request this – vaguely – in advance, and that you may also ask about any standard practices upon the change of a rule. The problem comes up if Clinton asks whether you intend to continue him in the post."

"Why?"

"You are free to give hope to all, regardless of your actual plans. But you may not make promises."

Elizabeth thought for a moment. "His wife is one of my ladies. Am I permitted to tell her that I think the post of naval wife becomes her?"

Cecil laughed. "Yes, and that might be the best signal of all."

She picked at a spot on her skirt. This was not something she would have considered, despite its importance, and she wondered what else Cecil had on his list. Or would, if he knew she was depending on him. Her resolve hardened: perfect safety was as much a chimera as Mary's child. "This will be an important conversation, but right now my need is far simpler. There is only one discussion I need to have, and it regards your own role. You have always been my rock, and I need you more than ever now."

He bit his lip. "All you need to say is that you value me."

"Duly noted," she said. "But how then might I ask you to begin now to inhabit the role I may or may not have in mind for you when the time comes? That of my Secretary of State."

The Secretary of State was the monarch's most trusted advisor and most effective surrogate. The role was perfect for Cecil: no one would question the appointment as he had already served as one of several secretaries on her brother's Council. Elizabeth would have him serve alone now for greater glory – and responsibility.

His eyes lit up, but he calmed himself. "Naming the position is more specificity than I would counsel, but you made it clear that it was intended as guidance rather than promise, and it does convey what you are asking of me."

"I will be more careful with others, but I cannot do this without you. I need your lists, your discernment, more than ever."

"I am honored to serve. Thank you."

She saw the hint of a tear in his eye and nodded as the anxiety dropped from her shoulders. Before she could respond, Blanche knocked on the open door and entered without slowing. "A guest has arrived for you," Blanche said as she caught her breath. "The Swedish Ambassador."

Elizabeth narrowed her eyes, wary of this new development on top of Cecil's news.

"What is he doing here?" Cecil asked, his voice ringing with his new authority.

"We will find out soon enough," Elizabeth said. She positioned herself to receive her guest, and Cecil retreated to the corner.

They did not have long to wait before a bejeweled gentleman presented himself and stood before her. His blonde mustache was waxed into horizontal points, and he wore the oversized lace collar of a German lord. "I am Nils Gyllenstierna, sent to England by King Gustavas Vasa of Sweden," he announced in a thick accent.

"Welcome," Elizabeth said. "To what do I owe this pleasure?"

"I have been tasked with two purposes," the Ambassador said. "To expand commercial dealings between England and Sweden, and to negotiate a match between you and His Majesty's son, Eric. Here is the letter from my king accrediting me to your queen."

Elizabeth was rattled. Mary was sending an ambassador straight to her? And not even from a Spanish country? This was new. Did Mary think Elizabeth might be more amenable to a Swede?

"If you have accredited yourself with my sister, you need not show your letter to me, though I appreciate the courtesy."

"I have not yet met with Her Majesty. I have come here first to see if you might consider the marriage proposal. If you would, I will put both my proposals before the Queen."

Realizing that this was not a nefarious plot on Mary's part, Elizabeth relaxed – but quickly tensed back up as she grasped the lack of royal approval for this visit. This was another crime she had almost died for. "The Queen does not know you are here?"

"Not yet."

Elizabeth bowed her head to gather her thoughts. No one could blame her for the offer; she would invoke the Council immediately. This was a God-given opportunity to demonstrate loyalty, not just profess it – while reiterating her longstanding desire to remain single. "My dear Ambassador, you have put me in a terrible position. The heir to the throne may not consider a marriage that has not been sanctioned by the Council. This discussion would be treason."

Out of the corner of her eye she could see Cecil nod approvingly.

"I meant no offense, my Lady," the Ambassador said. "Nor would this proceed any further without the blessing of English laws. I merely thought it best to determine whether such an offer might be welcome, were it to be made."

An admittedly innocuous-sounding request, but Elizabeth had been through this before. "Even that is not permitted." She smiled widely. "Though I can tell you I have no desire for the married life, as I have often said. I hope you will not take this amiss in your discussions about more weighty affairs."

He gave a small bow.

There was a moment of awkward silence, and it occurred to Elizabeth that it would be fun to entertain this ambassador, interesting to learn about the Hanseatic League's dealings with the Holy Roman Empire. She knew what they once were, from Anne of Cleves, who had explained the politics of her own non-marriage. But things changed in a decade. Besides, this would make a good start to her education about England's strength, weaknesses, and opportunities.

"May I invite you to share supper with me before you return to court? A simple meal cannot offend, as long as we discuss only things of no consequence."

"I would take that as a great kindness," Gyllenstierna said.

"Excellent. Please join me in the Great Hall at eleven."

She looked around at her ladies, who now included Bess of Hardwick. Bess was not a strategic political appointment, far from it, as William Cavendish had recently died after being accused of embezzlement. No, Bess was an old friend who needed a place while she worked off her inherited debt. An honest worker who deserved to be known by her name of origin rather than the disgraced marital moniker. But she was not the right choice for the task.

"Lady Clinton," Elizabeth said, deciding that a lady of rank was better suited to an ambassador, "will you please show him to a room where he can rest until then?"

"You are too kind," he said, kissing her hand.

"That was perfect," Cecil said the moment Gyllenstierna was gone. "And I look forward to learning more about the Protestant states that dominate commercial trade."

Elizabeth kept her face steady, loving the praise but slightly bothered it was offered for such a small thing.

He went on. "You should write to your sister to tell her of this incident. Ideally, your report should arrive at court before Gyllenstierna does."

Elizabeth turned to Blanche. "Find a page to deliver my letter," she said, before whirling back around and striding to the desk. She pulled out a paper and quill as she sat, then started to scrawl. Well, as much of a scrawl as she would allow herself. She had always been vain about her writing, and this was no time to risk being misunderstood.

She was just finishing when Blanche entered with a page. "George here will deliver your message to the Queen."

"If you can't get in to see the Queen for some reason, you must deliver the message to Cardinal Pole," Cecil said.

That was important. With Mary curled up on her floor, the boy would likely be turned away.

"Thank you for pointing that out," Elizabeth said, then handed George the letter. "If you love me, you won't fail me."

His eyes widened and he swallowed before dropping to one knee and kissing her hand. "I will ride like the wind."

The promise was from his soul, and Elizabeth patted his cheek. He rose and ran off.

Elizabeth turned to Blanche. "I have seen the boy's skill. Excellent choice."

"He is the one to beat the Ambassador back to court."

"And I will help by delaying *Herr* Gyllenstierna here by at least two hours." Elizabeth winked, and Blanche and Cecil burst out laughing.

The muffled clanging from the clock tower sounded the hour. "Let us begin," she said, then led them to supper.

Elizabeth was happy with the sight in the Great Hall. In addition to the potage and meats, her table boasted comfits: spices, nuts, even sugarcoated seeds. Suckets, too, both candied fruit and marmalades. And wafers and hippocras with candied flowers. Usually, the cook rotated these treats to save money, but for this occasion they had all been pressed into use.

Gyllenstierna was already there with Liza, getting a tour of the tapestries that adorned the walls. Not the ones illustrating the City of Ladies that decorated Elizabeth's personal rooms; the ones on public display were those that Mary had sent to decorate Woodstock. Elizabeth had not wanted to part with the scenes of the saints' lives that made such a statement of Catholicism…a statement that might unnerve the representative of a Protestant nation.

"Greetings, my Lord," she said. "I hope you are not offended by the religious images."

"We are more reasonable in Sweden," he said. "After all, Luther himself said, 'If it is not a sin but good to have the image of Christ in my heart, why should it be a sin to have it in my eyes?' It would be different if we were worshipping the images, but I trust we will not go that far." His eye twinkled.

The man's wit gladdened Elizabeth. "Come sit by me."

He seemed gratified, though surely he must have expected good treatment. Regardless, this promised to be an interesting meal.

When they were all settled and served, she began with a

question to stimulate insights. "So how do you find our English court compared to your own?"

"Alas, I know nothing of it yet. Remember, I made the mistake of coming straight to see you."

"Ah yes." Elizabeth chuckled. "We had established that, indeed. So, tell me about Sweden. Is there much trade already between our two countries?"

"You send us wool, though the amount lags far behind what you export to Flanders, the Low Countries, and Italy. Same with lead and grain."

"What goods do you send us?"

"Bricks, wine, and food. A fair trade."

"I apologize that I am not serving you Swedish wine today," Elizabeth said.

"I should have brought you a bottle to try," Gyllenstierna said. "The better to convert you."

They all laughed over that, and the conversation turned from trade to religion, then back to trade again, before the topic centered around national pastimes and fashion. By the end of three hours, Elizabeth had learned all she might need to know about the Hanseatic League and what little support the Lutheran states could really provide England...even Cecil had run out of curiosity. Confident they had given George enough of a head start, she happily allowed the Ambassador to take his leave.

It had been a good day.

June 20, 1558

Elizabeth was finding it easier and easier to keep her expressions from revealing her emotions: ample practice had developed the talent. But today strained all her efforts. Feria had come to visit, and she did not know why.

"My dear Count," she said with her curtsy.

"Princess," he replied, the first Spaniard to give her that title.

He must want quite a favor. Everything had a price, and the bigger the gift, the higher its cost. "How is my dear sister, the Queen?"

Feria spread his hands. "Her Majesty is recovering well. As you know, she had been ill."

An answer which might or might not include a reference to the imaginary child. Elizabeth decided she would not broach the topic. "I am so glad to hear that. I have had Masses said for her good health."

"A commendable idea, which I will be sure to share with His Majesty," Feria said. "I am leaving England soon to join him, but I wanted to take my leave of you before I depart."

"You are too kind," she said.

"I also have a message which I would love to pass on. Is there a place we could sit?"

She led him to a window seat. Her women followed, sitting around her and picking up their sewing.

Feria looked at them pointedly. "Is there a more private place we could speak?"

Elizabeth stifled an insane desire to laugh at the idea that Feria could have something to say that he didn't want the Queen's spies to hear.

"I never thought about the matter," she said with a show of surprise. "I only ever have conversations that can be overheard."

His eyes narrowed and she relented: she had won that round, after all. "But of course, my conversations are of no importance. My sister's words carry much more weight, and I understand they should not be shared widely."

"The words are the King's, not the Queen's."

A message from Philip.

"His words, too, weigh more than mine," Elizabeth said, without missing a beat. She stood and moved to the window seat on the other side of the room.

Feria followed, wearing a conspiratorial smile. "The Queen's recent…er…condition…the mistaken taking to her chamber… prompted a discussion of the succession." He paused as if waiting for her to react, but she remained silent so he continued. "My master wanted to tell you of his support for your claim. To make sure you know how he has and will continue to try to persuade the Queen to recognize it as well."

Elizabeth's mouth went dry. "Your master is too kind to me."

"Of course, it would help to force the issue. Which would be easiest if you would agree to marry. The terms of the agreement would resolve the matter."

Reality settled around her. This was his game. She had given his story more credit than it deserved, but he was just putting more pressure on her. Was he so vain as to think that he might outfox her? "I have often said that I have no inclination to the married life."

Feria laughed. "The married state is the Godly state, my Lady, and you will come to it sooner or later."

"If I delay long enough, your 'later' may turn to my 'never' and I will be content."

He leaned forward and arched an eyebrow. "Perhaps it is that you have a secret hope?"

Elizabeth froze.

He looked around again. "Are you sure your ladies do not speak Spanish?"

"Quite sure," she said.

"I am speaking of a hope that is currently impossible. A man committed elsewhere…for now."

Her eyes narrowed. *Philip.* They had given up on their stupid notion of Savoy. Was her poor sister so close to death?

Elizabeth furrowed her brow, determined to make Feria work for it. "I do not understand."

"My dear Lady," Feria said, "if you ever come to the throne, you will need a great husband. As great a husband as your sister had, in order to save England from the damned French. There are not many such men in the world. Wise, brave, capable, devoted. It is a rare combination."

Feria was coming at her head-on, like a young buck crashing his antlers into a foe. She wanted to slap the smug confidence off his face – not that Mary would thank her for it. "Ah, my dear Count, I will consider such a need only if God so honors me."

"A wise woman considers all options."

This fool honestly believed he could get her to commit herself to treason. She took a deep breath to prepare herself for the intricate footwork of an answerless answer. "A wise woman considers only options actually before her," she said. "I learned this from my dear grandfather. I never met him, but some say I take after him in bearing, almost as much as I take after my father in looks."

"I never saw your father's face in yours," Feria said.

It took an effort to hold back a hiss, an effort she betrayed only with a smile. "Next time I am at court I will stand next to his portrait." She looked down at her trembling hands. "But what I was trying to say was that my grandfather delayed decisions until the time was ripe. For example, he did not consider marriage until he had defeated the unjust usurper, until he was crowned. Only then did he unite the red and white roses by choosing Elizabeth of York."

"Surely he knew this union was expected. Elizabeth of York had the better claim."

"Of course. But he climbed the ladder one step at a time."

Feria's eyes hardened, but he smiled knowingly. He had grasped her meaning, or rather what she wanted him to understand. "There is great wisdom in such an approach," he said. Unable to contain himself, he added, "But some risk as well."

She rose and turned back to him with a smile. "For me, risk comes from wanting something different than what the Lord wants for me. I have no mind for the future, only the present."

She held out a hand for him to slide his under it. "Come. Let us rejoin the others."

October 29, 1558

The autumn days might dim, but Elizabeth's star shone brighter. More people than ever were flocking to the woman who looked to soon inherit the throne. Elizabeth had received dozens of letters from old friends expressing longstanding love, and new ones pretending it.

She reined in her elation. She would not tempt the Devil now, so close to her impossible destiny. Better to focus on the lesson in the situation: the mutability of friendships where self-interest was involved.

William Cecil, newly arrived from London, reached for one of the suckets that sat in a silver bowl, a new permanent feature on Elizabeth's desk.

Elizabeth pointed at his black armband. "What *deuil* is this?" She moved her hand to her heart. "I hope it is not for someone close?"

"Charles V. Her Majesty ordered the court into full mourning. Black arrases cover her chairs of estate, black curtains frame all the windows. She even gave black cloth to ambassadors and other honored guests. Of course, lowly people like me got only ribbons."

"I am glad you told me," Elizabeth said. "I must write to Philip."

Blanche nodded. "I agree it is a sobering occasion, but it seems wrong to give a foreigner such honor. I can't help but remember when Somerset's mother died, and Northumberland insisted that the King's grandmother was sufficiently outside the 'immediate family' circle to eschew formal mourning."

"That was only to shame Somerset," Elizabeth said. "Honoring foreign royalty is good diplomacy."

"It is more than diplomacy," Cecil said. "The Queen said Charles was father to the King whether he was in England or not, and that she had always thought of him as a father as well."

"Not always," Liza said. "They were betrothed long ago."

Tom Parry hooted. Cecil coughed, but Elizabeth could swear she heard a snicker behind it. "I'm sure she worried that Philip might return and resent the lack of respect," she said, smiling but steering the conversation away from malice.

"If you ask me, it just reminds everyone that Philip is absent," Bess said.

"And not expected back," Cecil said, grabbing another sucket. "Even though they sent word his wife is dying."

Elizabeth froze. "Mary is dying? They admit it?"

"Her belly has swollen again, since she left confinement, with what seems to be a growth in her womb. Her ladies say she spent the last week curled up in the corner, begging the Lord for mercy." He shrugged. "And yet she can still rally at times: she went among the lords earlier this week. Not that she accomplished anything."

"What do you mean?"

"Pole may be dying as well, of a quartan fever. The poor people who came out of Calais brought the illness to the Isle of Wight, then to Dover. And somehow to Pole."

Elizabeth worked to summon compassion as she digested the news of her adversaries' weaknesses.

"In all, with the two of them so sick, there is almost no business being done," Cecil continued. "The courtiers are wandering about in limbo, not sure what to do, not sure whom to listen to or believe." He took another sucket from the silver bowl.

"You are here too often to count as a guest anymore," Blanche said, swatting his arm. "My Lady wastes her money trying to impress you."

Cecil laughed. "She does indeed – since she has always impressed me."

Tom Parry took his own sucket, almost as if challenging Blanche. "Does this change the chain of command? Do the Spaniards now control the military?"

Cecil looked puzzled. "What do you mean?"

Parry massaged the back of his neck. "Thomas Markham of the Berwick garrison wrote to say he is preparing to bring his troops southward for the maintenance of Elizabeth's royal state, title, and dignity. He only has three hundred men under arms right now, but he has written undertakings from northerners to produce ten thousand if necessary."

The Berwick garrison was the largest military force in the country outside of Dover and London. Elizabeth felt her stomach contract, and out of the corner of her eye she could see Cecil's brows knit.

"Troops?" she asked, working to avoid a stammer. "No men. No guns. Or I will pay too high a price."

Parry spread his arms. "He said he wants only to guard against foreign dangers. He worries that Spain will try to keep the throne, that France will invade. He made clear that these troops would serve none but the true monarch; they would be used only to assure a peaceful transfer of power. He merely wanted you to know that forces are ready."

"Well, this is the time." Cecil sighed. "God bless him."

Elizabeth allowed her shock to show on her face. "The most cautious man I know does not worry that the heir is gathering troops about her?"

Cecil rapped his knuckle on the table. "The whole country fears an invasion. The memory of Northumberland's attempted coup is a fresh wound."

Despite Cecil's words, Elizabeth still worried. She had sworn to herself that she would never take chances again – and this was the biggest chance of all. "I still do not understand how you can condone this."

"I actually discussed such a scenario with Bacon," Cecil said.

"And I well note that Markham specifically avoided putting his troops under your command. This is nothing more than is required for the lawful defense of the realm."

Elizabeth wiped her forehead, still nervous. "I would prefer this not be bruited loudly – I don't believe in testing these things."

"You don't need to announce it, but the remedy if you are worried is to tell someone you trust on the Council," Cecil said. "Remove the secrecy and you remove the danger."

She bristled. "The danger lies in the troops."

"Troops that serve the monarch, not you," Cecil said.

She shook her head. She had been at this crossroads before, where interpretation made the difference between life and death. "It still reeks of treason when Mary has not even named me heir."

"She has not named you such – but Parliament has," Cecil said. "And until they vote a different successor, she can change nothing."

"Parliament is still sitting. They could still take such a step," she said.

"I cannot imagine a single one of the members doing so," Parry said. "Especially not now."

"And remember, the Berwick garrison has merely informed you that they will assist a peaceful transfer of power," Cecil added.

She bit down her nausea. "Fine."

"I also will speak more openly with the Councilors, at least the ones I know to be your friends already, to suggest they may want to pressure Her Majesty to recognize your claim as a way of preventing foreign aggressions." Cecil smiled. "Even the Spaniards fear France's intentions."

She shuddered but Cecil and Parry were right. This was the time to welcome honest support, to keep usurpers at bay. Robin had said the same thing. "Please do so. But gently, and let it be known I pray for her recovery."

"Of course," Cecil said.

"If Markham's offer is not a problem," Parry said, "I also received another offer of troops from a rich man, John Thynne. Yours if anyone tries to divest you of a right that is legally yours."

She narrowed her eyes. "Do not dribble these out. How many offers have you received?"

"Just these," Parry said.

She looked at Cecil. "Does this change your legal analysis or your advice?"

Cecil shook his head. "You will receive many such offers, many pledges of future loyalty, since early support earns the highest rewards." He swallowed. "Use the opportunity to take their measure before the time comes."

She would not tell Cecil now, but she had taken people's measures for years. His was not the only reward she had already decided: she had a long list of people who would receive the thanks owed them. Robin, Saintlow, Effingham – she had particularly delighted in that toil, finding the perfect use of their talents.

"When you take my measure, I hope you will be generous," Parry said, banging a fist on the table, as if she had not already assured him that he would always be Comptroller of her Household – though admittedly she had not specified that the household in question would be royal.

She smiled. Oh, he would need someone to check his figures, but his real talent had proved to be collecting debts. Now he would do that on a much larger scale.

Yes, she had their measures.

"It is still dangerous," Elizabeth said.

"There is always danger when a throne passes," Cecil said. "You cannot avoid it."

He was right. This was nothing but another test to endure, as she had so many others. The throne would indeed soon pass, and if she did not reach for it, it might pass from her. It was time to step into her strength, to silence her father's voice, his conviction that she did not deserve this position.

The resolution settled her stomach and she reached for a sucket.

"So, what may I tell my rich friend?" Parry asked.

"Tell Sir John that I thank him for his readiness to do unto us all the pleasure he can. I will not forget him whensoever time and power might serve."

Cecil smiled. "Well said."

CHAPTER 16

November 12, 1558

*E*lizabeth peered out the Library window, her ladies crowding behind her. The closed litter, surrounded by forty heavily armed royal guards, had captivated all their attention after it had turned onto the road toward Hatfield.

Who would come here in a closed litter, especially a royal one?

As the carriage circled the fountain outside the entrance, Thomas Parry went out to receive it.

The figure that stepped out belonged to the Count de Feria.

"Feria?" Missi sounded surprised.

"Feria?" Elizabeth did not try to hide her indignance. "Does he think to try one last time to marry me off?"

After greeting Parry, Feria turned and held his hand back up to the carriage, where Jane Dormer's face appeared through the door. But instead of reaching for his hand to step down, Jane held out a large jeweled casket, which Feria accepted with a step back.

Next Jane said something to Parry, and he lifted a hand to

help her. When she was settled, she turned to receive her own casket from her maid. One much smaller but no less jeweled.

"What could you carry in such things?" Liza braced her arm against the sill so as to lean in for a better look.

A young page approached the couple and held out his hands for a coffer, but Feria shook his head and Jane gripped hers tighter.

Blanche let out a hoot. "Whatever they have, they don't trust that poor lad with it."

"We'll soon find out," Elizabeth said, leading her ladies to the window seat Feria had once rejected as not private enough for his purposes. They all arranged themselves prettily, brushing out their skirts and tucking in loose hair.

They did not have long to wait before the guards opened the doors and the envoys entered. Elizabeth took her time putting away her needle and setting aside her work, all to make sure Feria and Jane had completed their reverences before she rose.

"What a pleasure to see you both," she said, studiously ignoring the caskets. "Especially you, my dear Count. I did not realize you had returned to London." She hoped he would not notice the lie.

"I came to be with the Queen during her final illness. To bring messages from the King who sorrows that the delicate state of the negotiations with France would not let him come himself."

"I am sure my sister appreciates his deep concern."

"She was moved," Feria said. He shifted his weight. "And I hope you will be equally moved to learn that we have finally been successful at persuading the Queen to name you her heir."

It was not lost on Elizabeth that he claimed credit for this change. "Yes," she said with a deliberately bright smile. "The Comptroller and the Master of the Rolls came two days ago to give me the good news. I hope my sister has sent you to give me even better tidings of her improved health."

"The Queen continues to be…her infirmities are such that grave fears must be entertained on her score."

No one believed Mary could live out the week, though there was no way to know. "I pray for her every day," Elizabeth said sweetly.

Feria and Jane both shifted their weight, still not mentioning the coffers they carried.

"In fact," Feria said, "religion was one—"

Elizabeth raised her hand to interrupt. "Instead of jumping right into a lengthy discussion here, I hope you will join me for supper."

"We would be delighted," Jane Dormer said. "But before that, my mistress bade me give you her dying requests." She elbowed Feria, and he held out his casket. "Along with these, the Crown Jewels, at least the ones not stored in the Tower."

Aha. Elizabeth signaled to Blanche to take the chest, and Liza to open it. Inside were small leather boxes and embroidered velvet bags sitting atop trays lined with felted wool. Part of a rope of pearls peeked out of one of the bags, each bead as large as a grape. Elizabeth felt her chest constrict in covetousness. She loved jewels, especially pearls, and this whole box would soon be hers – indeed, it was being given to her now.

She bit back the anticipation that was inappropriate for this occasion.

"You will need an inventory of that," Tom Parry said from the corner. "And right away." He wagged a finger at Blanche. "Bring it here."

Elizabeth waited until Tom, Blanche, and Liza were settled at the desk before turning back to Jane. "What does my sister ask of me?"

Jane glanced at Feria before answering. "First, to be good to her servants. Second, to repay the sums of money lent on her privy seals."

"Of course I will do these things. Yea, without asking," Elizabeth said.

"Lastly, to continue the Church as Her Majesty has reestablished it."

Elizabeth bit her tongue. The Crown was not yet hers. This was not the time to antagonize anyone – far better for her that everyone see her as an ally, or at least not a foe.

"I am too honest to give a promise I cannot keep in its full measure," Elizabeth said. "I will never promise to persecute people for their beliefs, nor will I do to any loyal subject what was done to me." She softened. "You may reassure my dear sister that I do not intend any great changes, but every monarch follows his or her own conscience."

Jane and Feria exchanged glances, and Feria motioned with his chin for Jane to present her casket.

"Blanche," Elizabeth called.

Blanche held up a wood tray lined with felted wood, tilting it slightly to show the consort's pendant it held.

Elizabeth knew the piece immediately, remembered seeing it on the breasts of several stepmothers. And, of course, her sister. Elizabeth resolved to have the stones reset.

She pointed to the casket. "Will you please take that from Jane?"

Blanche was quick to comply, and Feria raised a finger to signal that she should not leave quite yet. "My master bade me add these colored gems that he had left at Whitehall. He knows you greatly admired them."

"I did indeed," Elizabeth said, curious how many of the stones were in the smaller casket. *Had he culled the most valuable ones?* "To show my gratitude, I will have his portrait hung in my apartments, to always remember such great friendship."

"The King has sent another token and has asked that I put it directly into your hands."

She smiled. "Well?"

Feria held out a beautiful emerald set in a gold pin. It would not be the largest stone in her collection, but its sparkling green bordered on blue, and the piece screamed royalty. This was the kind of gift sent to a monarch on their coronation, which made it as premature as the Crown Jewels. Still, this was a personal gift for which immediate enjoyment was appropriate and expected. She pinned it to her shoulder and whirled around to show it off.

"Ladies, how like you this?" she asked.

"Magnificent," Blanche said.

"It sets off your hair perfectly," Liza said.

Elizabeth curtsied to Feria. "Please tell your master that I will treasure his gift." Feria bowed back, a pompous smile on his face.

"Shall we to supper?" Elizabeth asked, then led the way to the Great Hall. As they reached the door, Feria stopped, confused by the high level of noise coming from beyond. It sounded like a crowd, like revelry, which it was.

Elizabeth signaled for the door to be opened and paused to allow Feria's and Jane's gapes to subside.

"What is that?" Feria asked.

"I have had many visitors lately. They congregate in the afternoons." That was a gentle way to put it. With Mary so close to death, the court had moved to Hatfield. Dozens of people crowded Elizabeth's tables, all eager to be early in their proclamations of loyalty, eager for the rewards that might bring. It was more proof of men's perfidy but Elizabeth welcomed them all. She knew who her real friends were.

As Elizabeth took her place at the head of the table, she swept her arm in invitation. "Mistress Dormer," she said, "your place is next to the Earl of Pembroke, with the Count next to Lady Clinton."

Elizabeth chose this pairing not only for protocol, but also to separate Feria and Clinton: she did not want to make it easy for Feria to inquire about ships and ports.

The feast before them was ample, ending with lavish subtleties. Today's masterpieces were marchpane chessboards with marzipan men. As it turned out, a perfect theme for this meeting.

"You were saying earlier that Philip hoped to make progress negotiating peace with France?" She sat back once she'd said this, knowing that someone would rush to be her champion in this conversation.

Clinton took the bait. "Where were negotiations when you left His Majesty?" he asked.

Feria's eyes narrowed for a conversation he clearly did not want to have. "We were still waiting for the Earl of Arundel, so that England could be separately represented during the negotiations."

For some reason Elizabeth wondered whether this was the real reason behind Philip's lavish gifts, to distract her from the fact that he was about to betray England's interests in settling his differences with France. Because, after all, there was no doubt that England's interests would be disregarded, even with Arundel there to promote them.

"Good, good," Clinton said. "We each will argue our own grievances. And both reiterate how peace requires the return of Calais."

"Of course," said Feria.

The smoothness of his words told Elizabeth they were meant as observation, not commitment. She had to admire how adroitly he had deflected the fundamental problem with the negotiations: Henri II's oath that he would never cede Calais.

"And also to the payments stipulated by the old treaties," Pembroke added. "We understand the French deny that they are bound to make them?"

Feria tried to hide a tightening jaw behind a gulp of wine, but it showed anyway. "Unfortunately, they maintain that the Queen waived any rights she might have claimed under them by declaring war on France."

Pembroke scoffed. "We declared war because the French gave us cause to do so. It was a justified response to their invading our territories, to their machinations against the Queen's person."

Feria pressed his lips so tightly that he could hardly begin his sentence. "The Earl of Arundel is fully aware of these legal points, as is the King. But it is in everyone's interests to make peace."

"We are told that King Philip has the French cornered," Pembroke said. "Certainly they understand they must make some concessions."

"We all must make some concessions," Feria said, pointing his knife like a weapon. "The French have promised that once Calais is disposed of, they will consent to whatever the King wishes. And the King, gentlemen, is determined to do nothing without the Queen's approval. I will be honest, I hope she sees the great advantage of making peace on reasonable terms."

Reasonable. That was a laugh. France and Spain's losses and gains cancelled each other out; all they had to do was revert their territories. Both would inevitably turn to England and ask her to bear her losses without compensation.

"But I repeat," Feria said, "my master is prepared to walk away from the negotiations if the French do not somehow satisfy the English claims."

Elizabeth knew that England was in no position to pursue war – her treasury was empty from funding Spain's vain pursuits instead of her own defenses. She sighed. This was not yet her problem: her current responsibilities were limited to hosting her guests. "Would you like more hippocras?" she asked Feria.

"No, I am quite done." He leaned in. "I was hoping to speak with you privately."

"Everything I do must be honest enough to be witnessed." She giggled. "But you shall have privacy since no one at this table speaks Spanish and no one who does is close enough to hear."

He looked puzzled at his failure to control the situation. She would delay teaching him the full extent of his impotence just a little while longer. After all, snakes struck when they were threatened. "*Por favor*," she said with a smile.

He flinched and looked around the table, but began in his native language. "Again, I offer my congratulations on your new estate as heir. You know, your sister was set against you, and her Councilors too, but my master prevailed in this difficult matter. You owe him a great debt."

His pompous tone grated on Elizabeth, and she permitted herself a small correction. "I am indeed grateful for his efforts." She gestured at the crowd in the room. "Though as you might guess there are many before you who have claimed the credit for my sister's change of heart. For myself, I give the greatest credit to my people: they were the ones who prevented any change in the estate that Parliament decreed for me more than a decade ago." She took a sip of wine as if toasting them. "I am of course relieved that my sister finally saw enough light to acknowledge it."

Feria looked a little chastened but set his jaw. "She could have taken other measures, but she was confident you would keep the religion as she has restored it, and not give in to the Protestant heretics."

Elizabeth donned a patient smile. "As I mentioned earlier, I was not well handled myself during the Queen's lifetime, and dear friends were persecuted when they ought not have been. I mean to change that."

She would say no more. Nothing that would raise anyone's

hackles. Until the throne was safely hers, she would imply with impunity, commit to nothing. Feria had played the same game earlier, but Elizabeth was more skilled at it.

It helped that men so often refused to see truths that were right in front of their faces, just because they had hopes for different outcomes. They would learn soon enough that Elizabeth would be ruled by no one. Except her people. She would always put them first, because she owed her greatest debt to them.

As for Philip, he was a shameful husband who was far less attractive than he thought himself. All these Spaniards were shameful men who were far less effective than they thought themselves.

She broadened the size of her smile. She needed to maintain every courtesy.

November 13, 1558

William Cecil closed his eyes and matched his breath to the slap of the oars. He opened them when the barge slowed to dock at the residence of Nicholas Heath, Archbishop of York and Lord Chancellor of England. Originally baptized Norwich Palace on the Strand, the newly renamed York House was one of the properties that Mary had returned to the Roman Church. Cecil could forgive her this one – the previous residence of the Archbishops of York had been forfeited to Henry by Thomas Wolsey; this was a poor substitute for the palace now called Whitehall.

Cecil handed his coin to the oarsman before stepping from the boat: it felt discourteous to toss it from the dock as so many men did.

He squinted against the late afternoon sun to look at the arched entrance, its heavy stones framing the visit the Chancellor had initiated. Straightening his cloak, Cecil entered air thick with incense and greeted the black-robed cleric who received him at the door.

With few words, the priest solemnly escorted Cecil to Heath's library, where the sixty-year-old awaited him.

Heath was telling his beads by the fire, but the second he saw Cecil, Heath kissed his crucifix to end the devotions. He rose, his arms extended. "Welcome, welcome. Thank you for coming so quickly."

"Of course," Cecil said.

"I wanted to discuss arrangements for surrendering the Great Seal. I think the time is quickly approaching when we will need to do so."

Cecil crossed himself, a safe response that acknowledged the religious side without conceding the legal.

The loud crackling of the fire and its dancing flames transported Cecil back to the days right before Henry VIII had died, the nervousness that something would go wrong with the transfer of power to the young Edward. A nervousness Cecil vastly preferred to the dread he had felt when Edward lay dying and Northumberland was roping them all into his treasonous plans.

"I do need to ask," he said. "Why approach me?"

Heath tut-tutted. "Everyone knows you are to be Secretary of State. Congratulations, I know you will excel."

Cecil raised his hands. "Neither the Lady Elizabeth nor myself has—"

"We are past all that." Heath put a hand on Cecil's shoulder. "The Queen has borne with patience all the Lord's tests, and she is ready to receive her heavenly reward. This is not treason but the orderly transfer of government: Elizabeth is the next rightful heir. If the Crown were to pass to anyone else, it would make a mockery of Parliament who gave her that station. I will not allow that to happen."

Cecil bowed his head. "In that spirit, I am delighted by your welcome and assistance. Thank you."

"The moment I hear of the Queen's death," Heath went on, "I

shall at once proclaim Elizabeth. And see to it that Mary's Council does the same."

As heartened as Cecil was that this churchman was placing England's interests first, as relieved as he was over this key legal step in the transition, he worried they might lack a quorum. "I suspect some of the Councilors may be at Hatfield when that time comes. Is there a consent they might give beforehand?"

"I counted carefully. There will be enough of us here to formally proclaim her to Parliament," Heath said. "Come."

He walked to the desk and caressed the white linen burse centered on it before taking out the double-sided metal matrix of the Great Seal of England. The matrix was used to make an impression in wax that would be attached by ribbon or cord to any official royal document. That Great Seal was the ultimate proof of the monarch's approval, and there was only ever a single matrix in existence at any time.

"I believe the Queen is beyond taking any earthly action," Heath said, "but she may yet have a deathbed request. The Seal will be safe here, and I swear on my soul that I will deliver it only to the Lady Elizabeth or her designee. She need never fear my loyalty when she comes into her rightful station."

Cecil nodded. "I will share your words with her," he said, knowing Heath wanted to hear that.

"Has she started to consider her own Great Seal?" The Seal carried the sovereign's image, and while Elizabeth could continue to use Mary's matrix for as long as she chose, she would of course want her own. Cecil smacked his head, shocked that he had forgotten this.

Heath laughed. "It is still quite early yet, but if you want an artist like Antonio Mor for the portrait you will want to begin the process soon. He is much in demand."

Cecil thought a moment. Mor was Netherlandish but his name sounded Spanish, and his portrait of Mary had been more realistic than flattering. No, Elizabeth was more likely to choose

Nicholas Hilliard, or even someone like Levina Teerlinc, one of the new denizens of Hatfield who had already made sketches of half the people there. Still, Cecil resolved to assemble a full list. He never liked presenting a problem without suggesting its solution – and he did not believe in stinting on his answers.

"May I borrow a quill?" he asked. "I need to add to my list."

Heath spread his arms to show the heavy brass quill holder and the ink pot next to it. "Be my guest."

As Cecil was writing, Heath laughed. "How about her motto? Has she chosen that?"

"She is currently considering either *Semper eadem* or *Video et taceo*," Cecil said.

"I will say, *Semper eadem* – 'Always the Same' – would be reassuring to the conservatives like me, a sign that she does not intend to change the current Queen's religious policies."

Indeed, Cecil knew that Elizabeth was actively courting the conservatives – she was smart enough to be actively courting everyone. But he also knew how tempting the phrase *Video et taceo* – "I see and say nothing" – was to the woman who had learned the power of silence. "I will definitely share your opinion," Cecil said. Heath would appreciate this reassurance as well.

Cecil finished and began to fold the paper when a heavily embroidered velvet pouch caught his eye. Redemption sprang to his mind: he would commission such a bag for Elizabeth's seal. The plain white linen burse that housed the current one, while admirable in its utilitarian simplicity, did not do justice to the state symbol. Cecil's bag would fulfill its powerful symbolic nature. Elizabeth would appreciate that.

"Thank you," Heath said, then looked around. "As for the rest of it, I stand ready to help."

Cecil gave what he hoped was an encouraging smile, though he had little real encouragement to give: Elizabeth did not like Heath, though she did not dare insult him.

"But that help will be necessarily limited," Heath continued.

"I have heard talk that the Lady Elizabeth wishes me to continue as Chancellor, but I pray you will understand my desire to be utterly disburdened of my office."

Cecil put a sad look on his face to counteract his amusement over such patently false rumors, and Elizabeth's skill in creating them. "Ah, my Lord, I will pass on your wishes. With the help you have promised today, she would be ungrateful to force your continuance in a post you do not want."

"Thank you," Heath said.

Cecil realized the meeting had ended. He chuckled to himself how nothing had really happened. The Seal had not been delivered, no arrangements made; they had only discussed procedures for an abstract future. As it should be.

Once again, Cecil pulled himself back, repeating the almost constant plea to the Lord to continue His will in the direction it seemed to be clearly headed.

November 17, 1558

Elizabeth sat by the window, leaning her embroidery towards the leaded glass. Her eyes strained to catch the morning light, and the rest of her strained to hear the thrumming of galloping hooves. She could sense the almost noiseless drizzling, but no amount of frustration would hurry the sound she sought.

The needle pricked her finger, and Elizabeth let out a small curse, hoping it was not an omen. Staring at her work, she undid her last three stitches. Sewing was not a good activity for hands that trembled from hopes and fears.

The nearby church bells tolled the hour, and again she jumped.

"I've never seen you so excited for suppertime." Liza giggled. "You must be ravenous."

"I am too nervous to be hungry," Elizabeth said.

Kat reached out and patted her knee. "You need never be nervous again."

Elizabeth put her hand on top of Kat's, glad that her old friend had returned to Hatfield. Although Mary had not rescinded the prohibition against Kat contacting Elizabeth, enforcing it would be the last thing on anyone's mind.

"I will still have cares," Elizabeth said. "Just different ones."

Bess waved an airy hand. "As long as you're well dressed for them."

Elizabeth laughed, the tension broken. For now, anyway.

"When the time comes, I most certainly will be," she said. "For now, this is more than enough for a quiet supper. Let us be off to it."

The hallways were quiet: the rain had kept away the crowds. Even the Great Hall looked empty with only about thirty people. At the head table, her closest friends leaned forward with their heads almost touching. Cecil and Parry, Effingham and Clinton. Robin had joined them too, claiming his well-deserved place at the table. He had proven himself, after all. She had to love him for that.

"What gossip is this?" she asked. They all startled and jumped to their feet to greet her.

Effingham laughed. "Clinton was lamenting his lack of robes and finery. Both for court and the ultimate pomp of a coronation."

"You are as bad as Blanche, thinking about clothes before they are needed," Elizabeth said, though she was glad he would be prepared.

"It is almost too late for him to buy silks," Clinton said. "There were shortages when Mary came to the throne – and you are much more popular."

Elizabeth breathed through a pinch of envy. "*Now* I am," she said. "But then, the people loved their warrior queen."

There was a moment of silence: no one wanted to praise the dying woman.

"Surely Antwerp will be only too happy to supply more," Parry said, to break the tension.

"They ran out too, then," Clinton said.

"Well, Mary had no trouble clothing her officers," Elizabeth said.

Effingham sighed. "She took first choice of all the shipments. That contributed to the shortages."

"Well, I too will take first choice, so we needn't worry."

She took her seat and waited for the others to settle back in around her before taking a small piece of venison and a tartlet from a platter. Not that she really wanted anything.

Parry raised a hand to his ear. "Did you hear something?" He sighed and lowered his hand.

Robin shook his head. "What in blazes is taking so long?"

Elizabeth raised a finger. "None of that. I wish no harm to my sister."

"Nor I," he said, and focused on his food.

"Good." She squared her chin and brought the tartlet to her mouth but then just put it back down. Despite her admonition to Robin, all she could think was that it had been more than a week since she'd gotten the news that her sister could not last more than a few hours. Had something happened? Had Spain or France intervened, seized the Crown? Were they lying in wait even at this moment?

She tried to sense inside her whether her sister still lived, whether Mary's last breath was nigh. Elizabeth could picture the deathbed scene vividly, as if she was there in the stuffy room, watching her sister's bloated face struggle to breathe, her fingers twitch around her rosary beads. She could also picture a fully recovered Mary plotting revenge against the sister so ready to take her place.

Still no horses, only the hum of expectation.

Elizabeth pushed food around her plate. Was this punishment for her making plans before it was time? That was hubris, no matter how inevitable the future might seem. And yet it was also prudent.

"We should feast now, before Advent begins," Blanche said, attempting a new topic. Unfortunately, no one engaged.

"I had hoped the rain would pass, but it may tarry longer," Liza said.

"Along with fierce wind," Cecil said. "Did you hear it last night?"

The inane conversation at least distracted from the torturous wait...but only for a short while. The walls of the room continued to close in on Elizabeth as those of the Tower once had, pushing her to stand. "I need to be outside," she said, backing away from the table.

"Are you sure?" Kat said. "It looks so wet."

"I'll be fine."

"Shall we go with you?" Kat asked, standing herself.

"No, no," Elizabeth said. "I need to be alone." Her ladies exchanged worried glances. "Thank you, but this is best," Elizabeth said as she left.

Reaching the outside, she lifted her face to the mist of the drizzle. The cold on her face spurred her past the garden and into the fields, the kind of expanse that had always been just beyond her reach at Woodstock. She trod grass and rocks and straw indiscriminately until she twisted her ankle.

The pain brought hot tears to her eyes, but it also brought her back to the present, to Hatfield. And somehow stopping the maniacal strides brought her back to calm again. As if she had been racing away from the reassurance she was pursuing.

She limped towards the house, but she knew she didn't want to return inside. It would be too stifling. She needed the crisp air. She walked to the bench under the old, majestic oak tree that dominated the park.

She wiped the seat to sit and looked out over the field. The clouds were thinning enough to allow an occasional ray of sunshine to escape, and the air around her gradually lost its grey tint as the mist evaporated. She breathed deeply and reveled in the peace surrounding her. There was nothing more promising than the end of a rainstorm.

She pulled out the small book in her pocket, an illustrated volume of Psalms. The thin ribbon placeholder brought her straight to the twenty-second verse of Psalm 118: *The stone which the builders refused is become the head stone of the corner.*

There was as much triumph in the verse as ever, and as much bitterness. This was no time to conjure past resentments. She turned the page to the twenty-third verse, and the words of praise unleashed the sound she had been waiting for.

The hooves were still far in the distance, but their thrumming was unmistakable.

She listened with all her senses, wondering whether this was just another guest arriving at Hatfield or the messenger that would change her life. She read the verse again, infusing it into her soul.

The rider arrived in the courtyard and disappeared into the house. Guest, she decided. She sighed and repeated her usual refrain: *Thy will, not mine, be done.*

Again she looked at her book, trying to wipe her soul of covetousness and just allow God's plan to unfold.

Out of the corner of her eye she saw the rider emerge from the kitchen door and walk towards her. It was Nicholas Throckmorton.

He approached with a sure foot. Behind him, a crowd had gathered to watch through the mullioned windows, with a few intrepid souls spilling out the door. She stood, holding her breath.

Arriving in front of her, Throckmorton threw himself to his

knees. Elizabeth extended her hand for the agreed-upon proof. Into her palm Throckmorton placed a black enameled band: Mary's betrothal ring.

Elizabeth stared at it, entering a strange trance in which she felt one with the very air around her. She closed her hand over the ring as if to brand it into her skin.

"Your Majesty," Throckmorton whispered.

Hearing her new title jolted her. Hot tears stung her eyes, for herself, for her sister, for her mother, for everything that had brought her to this day. All the emotion she had so long suppressed spluttered out in a jumble, and she raised her face to the sky. "'This is the Lord's doing, it is marvelous in our eyes.'"

She looked at Throckmorton and chuckled. She raised the tiny trophy to show her household, still frozen in anticipation. Cheers broke out, and they all started hugging each other, crying and laughing.

"You told them?" she asked Throckmorton.

"Before you? Of course not," he said. "Though they likely guessed."

She walked towards the group and they all dropped to their knees, careless of their clothes. As they kissed her hands, she felt their tears dampen her skin.

Elizabeth's eyes had dried.

Cecil was the first to stand and break the reverential silence. "Do you know if Heath has proclaimed her to Parliament as he promised?" he asked Throckmorton as he brushed mud off his breeches.

"I left before he had done so," Throckmorton said, "but I was there to hear the Council swear their loyalty."

"They should proclaim her to the City at Cheapside as well," Robin said, with an air of authority. "The Duke of Norfolk, as Earl Marshall, should go there with the Mayor, and distribute ale and wine for the people to celebrate."

Cecil bristled. "Norfolk has his instructions."

"Even the ale?"

"I will see that gets done."

Elizabeth stifled a smile over the unending irritation between her two oldest friends.

"We need to close the ports," Effingham said, "to make sure that Spaniards or Catholics do not send soldiers or remove valuables that should stay here."

"I left those instructions," Clinton said.

"You need to sign the announcements for the foreign rulers," Cecil said to Elizabeth, before turning to Clinton. "Those ships must be allowed to sail."

Elizabeth exulted over the demonstrations of forethought and efficiency, but her excitement quickly turned to nervousness. Was there a hidden mistake made somewhere that would put this all at risk? Could she really trust that this great gift was hers? And could she really trust herself to use it properly, despite all her father's old doubts?

This is the Lord's doing, she repeated to herself, relaxing into awe.

As if reading her mind, Blanche held out an enormous topaz pin, its orange stone a promise of invincibility. "This has been in my pocket for days."

Elizabeth recognized the piece as one of her father's, from the casket. She nodded and allowed Blanche to pin it on her shoulder, the first time Elizabeth had donned one of the Crown Jewels.

Its weight was comforting, and Elizabeth sighed.

Kat curtsied. "I told the servants to prepare a celebration. It should be ready for us now."

"Thank you, Kat," Elizabeth said. "I will say a few words, but then I will retire to pray, to meditate, to praise. I feel the need to prepare for the great responsibility before me."

Elizabeth looked back at the house with a sigh, and Robin was by her side immediately, his hand out. She placed hers on top of his, and let him lead her into this new life.

She prayed for the strength to fulfill this great, impossible destiny, the grace to do right by her people and be good for England. Better than Mary, better than Edward. To redeem her mother's name and prove her father wrong. From this day forward, she would dedicate herself to deserving this great blessing.

She took a deep breath.

Superabo.

～

AUTHORS NOTE

Elizabeth's story is also the story of her friendships, people who surrounded her all her life – along with their children and grand-children (you met William Cecil in the Prologue, and his son Robert will voice the Epilogue to Book Three).

Yes, I put Cecil in the Prologue, along with Robert Dudley. While we cannot prove such a scene happened, surely it must have. And while I was at it, I tucked in other people who might well have been there, like Jane Grey, Liza Fitzgerald, and Mimi Dudley .

[Side note: Apologies for "Mimi Dudley" and "Liza Fitzgerald" but to avoid confusion, only Elizabeth and Mary Tudor kept their names: everyone else got a variant: So you will see Mimi Dudley and Missi Cheke, Liza Fitzgerald, Bess of Hardwick (who came with hers!), Lissa the tradeswoman and Beth Marbury. For Katherine Parr and Catherine Carey, I was able to just vary the spelling, and make Henry Carey's daughter Cathy.]

I also took advantage of other opportunities (especially the big Dudley/Seymour wedding and Elizabeth's visit to court one

Christmas) to bring together some surprising combinations (but again, the logic works). As for *Superabo*, it is based on a legend I thought I heard decades ago of a one-word message delivered to Elizabeth at the Tower – a legend I have not been able to find or confirm since and might have made up.

I hope you appreciate the choices I made — and I hope you love the book! Please consider leaving a short review (even just a star rating) wherever you purchased the book (or on your library's website if you borrowed it!) to help other readers discover it. It really does make a difference and it would mean the world to me!

Janet Wertman
Palm Desert, 2025

MORE TUDOR BY JANET WERTMAN

WITH EXCERPT FROM JANE THE QUENE

*E*lizabeth's story will continue in *What Love E'er Meant* (and after that in *Forever Gloriana*) – but if you want more Tudor fiction in the meantime, go check out my Seymour Saga, the tale of the unlikely dynasty that shaped the Tudor era. The series begins in *Jane the Quene* with a 27-year-old Jane Seymour increasingly desperate for the marriage that will provide her a real place in the world. It continues in *The Path to Somerset*, taking us through Henry's crazy years to show Edward Seymour's rise to become Lord Protector of England and Duke of Somerset. Finally, in *The Boy King*, Jane's nine-year-old son must grow up enough (and still before his sixteenth birthday) to execute both his uncles for treason before the story ends.

I've included the Prologue from *Jane the Quene* to get you started!

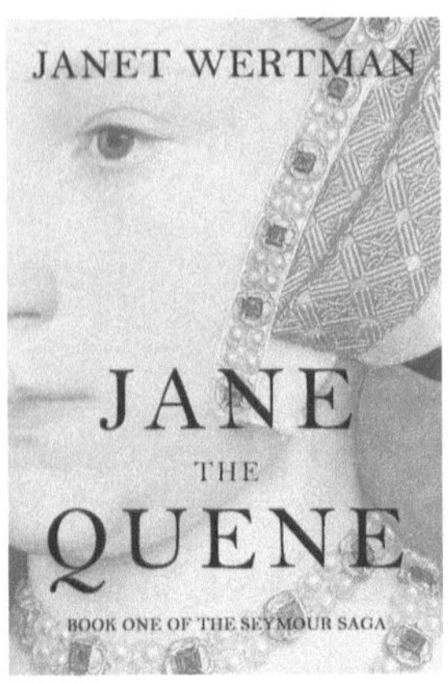

PROLOGUE

June 9, 1525 … 10:30 p.m.

Eighteen-year-old Jane Seymour paused at the entrance to the Queen's Presence Chamber, the formal public room in the royal suite of apartments. She breathed a quick prayer and smoothed the kirtle that peeked out from the red damask gown onto which she had painstakingly sewn two-dozen seed pearls. It was the most opulent dress she'd known, and its beauty soothed her nerves. Finally she nodded to her brother Edward, who signaled the page to open the double doors so Jane could be formally presented to her new mistress and begin the charmed life of a woman of the court.

The quiet dark of the hallway gave way to bustling light. The scene before Jane was grander than anything she had ever seen. She had arrived at court too late in the night before to get any kind of tour, something that would have prepared her for this moment. Now, the sights, sounds, and smells assailed her. Soaring leaded windows, carved wood paneling, and gilt edging surrounded her; incense and a heavy medley of perfumes stung her nostrils; and two musicians plucked at her nerves with each note of the soft hymn they strummed on their lutes.

Catherine of Aragon, saintly wife of Henry VIII of England, was in the center of the room, glowing on a raised chair of estate upholstered in rich arras. Seeing her there in quiet command calmed Jane, reassured her of order amid the madness. Like an oak among mushrooms, the Queen was surrounded by women on footstools who sat in small groups chatting among themselves. *That will be me soon,* Jane told herself. Her family had secured her a place in the Queen's household, as one of several companions who attended to Her Majesty's every need and saw to her every diversion. For now, Jane would be a simple maid of honor, happily living at the mercy of the Queen. Once Jane found a husband, which hopefully would happen soon, she would rise to the level of lady-in-waiting with far greater status and freedom.

The page rapped his stave and announced them. "Edward Seymour and Jane Seymour."

The Queen turned her attention to the door and inclined her head for them to proceed. She looked to be covered entirely in gold, from the cloth of her elaborately embroidered gown to the thick strands of her heavy rope necklace, to the solid frame of her tall gable hood. She was magnificent, and Jane was filled with a sense of inadequacy over her own gown that suddenly seemed far too simple.

Jane forced her legs to move forward despite their trembling. As she walked with Edward, she fixed her gaze on the Queen, whose own eyes were kind but lined and tired. Jane immediately thought of the cilice, the punishing haircloth shirt which the Queen, like Carthusian monks, was known to wear under her rich clothes; pain would certainly explain such a look. Edward, unkindly, had gossiped that it was to atone for whatever sin had caused God to withhold a son from her. Jane preferred to think it was a noble antidote to the ostentation of the Queen's life.

Three paces before the dais, Edward stopped and Jane did likewise. "My sister Jane, Your Majesty," Edward said as he bowed.

The Queen smiled. "You may greet us, Mistress Jane," she said in a voice tinged with her heritage as a proud princess of Spain.

Jane sank to the ground with a reverence she had practiced more than a thousand times. "Thank you for accepting me," she said. "I am honored."

"Rise, my child," said the Queen. "You are welcome."

"Thank you."

The Queen settled back and resumed her needlework. It was an altar cloth, and Jane could see even from her distance that the stitching was exquisite. Jane had always been proud of her own skill at embroidery, but again she felt inadequate against this unexpected new standard.

"You will join your cousins, I believe." Catherine waved her needle in the direction of Anne and Mary Boleyn, who bobbed a quick curtsy to Jane.

Jane looked over at the familiar faces of her second cousins, so different from each other – one slim and dark and exotic, the other soft and blonde and voluptuous. She was not thrilled to see them. The Boleyn girls had always been flighty things who thought themselves so much better than Jane. Now they were both in disgrace and Jane did not want to be too closely associated with them.

Jane turned back to the Queen, and was about to voice additional thanks when she saw the Queen's face light up. Jane turned to see what had caused that reaction.

A girl of around ten had just entered the Presence Chamber. She had flowing auburn tresses and was dressed almost as richly as the Queen. Jane knew immediately this was the Princess Mary, the royal couple's only surviving child. Mary would be heir to the throne unless she were supplanted by a brother, an unlikely event since the Queen was over forty and seven years past her last pregnancy. Indeed, Mary had been named Princess of Wales to reflect her status, and before the end of the year would leave for Wales to practice the art of governing.

Edward grabbed Jane's arm and pulled her to the side so Mary could approach her mother. The girl flashed them a sweet smile of thanks as she advanced with confidence. With impeccable decorum she paused before the Queen, curtsied, then spoke. "His Majesty has sent me to request your presence in his library. He is meeting with the Spanish Ambassador, who begs to greet you."

"I should be glad to attend."

Catherine rose and placed her needlework on her chair, descended the three steps of her dais, and gave her hand to Jane to kiss. "You will take your oath of office when I return. For now, your cousins will acquaint you with my apartments, and your brother will escort me to the King."

Edward bowed and Jane followed his lead with a curtsy. She stood in her spot as the rest of the room emptied out, then turned to the two sisters, who did not look happy with the turn of events. "I thank you both for your kindness," said Jane.

"The Queen ordered it," Anne replied.

"And truthfully, it was more a punishment for us than a kindness for you," said Mary. "She doesn't want to let me anywhere near the King. Not that she can stop me."

Jane said nothing, though of course she knew of the affair. And tried not to revel overmuch in Mary's disgrace.

All Jane's life, her mother had measured Jane against her similarly-aged Boleyn cousins. And found Jane wanting. Jane's resentment had reached its peak when Sir Thomas Boleyn managed to place both his daughters in the household of the French Queen, but jealousy faded as Mary developed the reputation of *una grandissima ribalda, infame sopra tutte,* "a great whore, infamous above all others." Then Anne had returned to England, and had tried to marry above her station by seducing Henry Percy, heir to the Earldom of Northumberland. She had been cut down and shamed for that by Cardinal Wolsey himself. Which had turned a vindicated Jane into the cousin to emulate. Finally.

Jane tried to imagine Lady Boleyn saying "Be more like Jane" to her own daughters. It strained Jane's imagination, but it was a lovely scene.

"Would that someone could," said Anne, and her voice was sharp.

"Stop pretending that I have a choice. You cannot refuse a king, and why would you want to?"

"It's about time you refused someone," said Anne.

Jane kept her face impassive. Mary and Anne had a long history of jealous rivalry and Jane did not want to get in the middle of their argument. She just wanted to get along with them as best as she could. And largely ignore them.

Jane had big plans for herself, after all.

She had been brought up to be just like Queen Catherine: sober and discreet, pious and pure. The ideal woman. It should be everything Jane needed to shine at this court.

She took a deep breath. Life was wonderful. She might be starting late, but that would just make her reward all the more sweet.

She was sure of it.

End Excerpt